STILL STANDING

WILD WEST MC SERIES

KRISTEN ASHLEY

ROCK CHICK
P R E S S

STILL STANDING

By Kristen Ashley

1

EARTHQUAKE

I pulled into the back lot next to the huge warehouse beside the super-hip home improvement store, Ace in the Hole, and as instructed, kept driving around the back of the warehouse to get to the long, squat building next to it.

I did this practicing deep breathing.

I'd done my research at the library the day before and I'd lived in Phoenix all my life.

I'd heard about Ace in the Hole, but I'd never been there.

Rogan took care of the house, or at least he took care of calling the people who took care of our house.

That was, he did that before he was incarcerated.

There was a large area between the warehouse and the building next to it.

At the end, there was a line of four vans facing the chain link fence that protected the area from the street (a fence with razor wire on top—it wasn't a great neighborhood in north Phoenix, it also wasn't the worst neighborhood in town—I knew this because I lived in the worst neighborhood in town, and that was on the south side).

The back doors of the vans had a decal of a playing card—the ace of spades, with the curves of the symbol being the eyes of a skull, flames coming out the top, black rivulets (meant to denote blood? eek!) dripping from the bottom, spatter around it (again, blood?)—and next to it, it said ACE IN THE HOLE CONTRACTING.

That area between buildings also held a variety of Harleys parked in a line. This in front of the long, squat structure. Under the overhang that ran the front of that space were three (three!) barrel grills. Two picnic tables. A scattering of mismatched outdoor chairs with equally mismatched tables, almost all of which had empty beer bottles or cans or overflowing ashtrays or all three on top. And I could see there was a misting system built into the overhang to cool it down during hot Phoenix days, of which, that day was one, it was just that the mist wasn't on right then.

The Aces High Motorcycle Club hangout.

Where I was heading because I was stupid.

Stupid and desperate.

"You've done this before, Clara, you've done it twice," I told myself under my breath as I parked outside the building, next to the bikes. "You did it and you walked away. You're fine. You'll be fine. You'll say what you have to say and then go. They're not going to kill the messenger. Right?"

I said these words to convince myself I was going to be perfectly okay.

And, truth be told, this was actually one of the less dangerous messages Esposito had sent me out to deliver.

The Aces High Motorcycle Club owned this long stretch of property on which they had a large home improvement store, a larger warehouse, and this building.

They were well-known.

This was because it was Phoenix. A haven for bikers. A haven for badasses. And perhaps the last bastion of the Wild West.

I'd heard others who did not grow up there say they'd lived their whole lives going into places of business and not seeing a No FIREARMS ALLOWED sign on the door.

To me, that was shocking.

To them, seeing that sign was more shocking.

During my research at the library the day before, I'd pulled up a variety of stuff that included a couple of articles about the opening of a home improvement store run by a gang of bikers and how that was instantly popular.

How Aces High MC were "changing the face of the MC culture" by running two successful businesses (the store and the contracting) as a club.

How people, especially Phoenicians, found it cool to turn away from a chain store like Lowe's or Home Depot and "shop local," when that local shop was owned by bikers.

I'd also seen pictures of the members of the club, all rough-looking guys. But they were bikers, they were bound to look rough. It wasn't like they were the kind to gussy up to have their picture taken for an article in a newspaper.

Or maybe they did gussy up and in real life, they were *really* rough.

Bottom line, I didn't know much about bikers (at all), but I figured they were who they were and part of who they were was rough-looking.

But whatever they did behind the scenes, they had a very visible face. A woman couldn't drive in broad daylight to their hangout and then disappear.

Unfortunately, no one but Esposito and Tia knew I was there.

If something happened to me, I doubted Esposito would care.

Tia would, but she wasn't in a place to do anything about it.

This part was bad.

And try as I might, I couldn't find good.

But I hadn't had much good in a long time (say, since the moment I was born), so at least I was used to it.

I switched off the ignition, grabbed my purse and slung it over my shoulder. Then I exited my car hoping that the repo man wasn't following me.

I suspected, however, that my car was safer outside the Aces High Motorcycle Club's hangout than it was anywhere.

Repo men undoubtedly had a variety of ways and means, but I didn't figure one of their ways was to repossess a car right outside a possibly dangerous motorcycle club's clubhouse. I figured members of the club might frown on that simply for territorial reasons alone.

I slammed the door to my car and walked to the hangout still sucking in deep breaths.

My message was short.

They were going to be angry, but that was Esposito's problem. Not mine.

I was just the messenger.

Simply the messenger.

That was it.

The front door to their lair was off to one side, close to the end, away from the street.

I pulled it open and stepped through into the dark, my eyes taking a moment to adjust as it was a shock after being out in the bright Phoenix sunshine.

This was unfortunate because I immediately heard the low, angry growl of a man.

"You've gotta be fuckin' shittin' me."

I turned my head toward the sound and my eyes adjusted.

It looked like a bar. A comfortable one like you'd have in your house if you owned a very big house, you'd lived in it a long time, you had a great number of friends, and you partied frequently.

Two pool tables. Some couches and armchairs. Some tables and chairs (most of these poker tables). A massive wide-screen TV hanging on the side wall close to the door. A long bar at the wall across the wide room opposite the TV. A bar with shelves behind it, liquor on the shelves, some glasses, stools in front, but no cash register. Things on the wall: pictures, plaques, flags, stickers, *carvings*.

Yes.

Carvings in the wood paneling on the walls.

Jagged ones.

Although I was surprised at this choice of decoration, and what it said about the easy and prolific access to knives the people who used that space had, I was on a mission, and thus, didn't pay much attention.

I took in what I could of the environment just to understand where I was, because I felt it prudent to focus on the humans and not the décor.

This was due to the fact that the room was also filled with about ten big, rough-looking, *angry*-looking men.

I focused on the one I was guessing spoke and said, "I'm here to see a Mr. West Hardy."

"Fuck you," the man replied, and I squared my shoulders automatically as a thrill of fear raced down my spine.

I wasn't one of those people who liked fear, who fed off it.

I didn't like fear.

In fact, I hated it.

And in all this time, the eighteen months since Rogan was arrested, feeling it nearly every day, I still wasn't used to it.

But I was desperate. I had no choice.

"Get your ass outta here," another man ordered, and I looked at him.

"Are you Mr. Hardy?" I asked.

"Get your ass outta here," he replied.

I ignored him because I had a job to do and I needed to do it. Desperation, obviously, made you do desperate things.

And, like I said, I was desperate.

My eyes scanned through the men.

I had to take this. If I didn't take this and say what I had to say, I didn't get paid and Tia got into trouble.

And I needed to get paid, and I needed that badly.

But more, I couldn't get Tia into trouble.

All the men were standing, save one.

One was sitting at a stool at the bar, slightly twisted to the side, but his head was bowed to it, looking at a bottle of beer in his hands.

I only saw his profile and not much of it since he had a very full beard.

He had a lot of tattoos on his arms which were exposed by a short-sleeved T-shirt. He had very muscular arms. And from what I could see from the tight T-shirt he was wearing that stretched along his broad back, a very muscular everything.

He had dark hair that was too long. Not *long*, long, as in, he could put it in a ponytail like some of the men had, but it curled around his neck and swept back from his face and looked kind of greasy-wet, but in a cool way, and I wondered inanely if he used product.

Then again, you couldn't blame him if he did. I suspected even bikers used product. Since it was so long in the front, if he didn't do something to keep it back, it would fall over his forehead into his eyes and that would be annoying.

If he wasn't so rough-looking, I could tell, even in profile, he'd be immensely attractive.

He just wasn't my type.

Not that anyone was.

Not anymore.

I also knew he was West Hardy, president of the Aces High Motorcycle Club.

I knew this only because, though he was sitting, staring at his beer, he had something about him—a charisma, a magnetism. He exuded the gravitas of a chief.

He was not one of the boys.

He was the leader of the pack.

I started toward him and a big man with long, dirty-blond hair not pulled into a ponytail (but it could have been) stepped in front of me.

I stopped, sucked in a breath and looked up at him.

"Get...your ass...outta here," he growled.

"I have a message to deliver to Mr. Hardy," I replied.

"Bitch, get..." He leaned into me and it took everything I had, but I stood firm because, it must be said, this man was big, but he was also seriously scary. "*Outta here*," he finished.

"Ink," a deep, rough voice said quietly, and the man in front of me glared at me, straightened, then twisted his neck to look over his shoulder.

"*What?*" he barked.

"Tequila," the deep, rough voice replied strangely.

The entire room changed then.

It was odd.

The atmosphere was heavy and dangerous one second, but the minute that voice said "tequila," a lightness flowed through, the tenseness immediately evaporated, and chancing a glance around, I saw some of the men actually smiling.

What on earth?

The man in front of me, who I suspected was called "Ink," stepped aside, his mouth moving like he was fighting back a smile, and the way was cleared to the man at the bar.

He was still cradling his beer with both hands and his head was still bowed, but now his neck was twisted, and his eyes were on me.

Okay.

Um.

Wow.

I had no type, but when I did have a type, he was *not* my type.

That said, if he was charismatic, magnetic and attractive in profile, those dark eyes with the laugh lines emanating from the sides, his thick beard with hints of gray in it, his strong bone structure (specifically his cheekbones, they were magnificent) and his intensity aimed at me, I had to admit, was beyond charismatic, magnetic and attractive straight to downright electrifying.

"Have a seat, Toots," he ordered, his head tipping to the stool beside him as the men around me moved away.

I pulled in a short, calming breath, thrilled beyond belief the scary portion of my task was over, and I walked up to the bar but didn't take a seat.

"This shouldn't take long," I told him.

"Have a seat," he repeated in his gravelly voice.

"I just came to say—"

"Babe," he cut me off, his voice going lower. He hadn't lifted his head, but his dark brown eyes changed in a way that both scared me and enthralled me, but not in a way I could describe, they just did. "I said, have... a... seat."

I decided it was judicious to have a seat.

So I pulled my purse off my shoulder and slid as best I could in my tight skirt up onto the barstool. Once situated, I put my purse on the bar and turned to him to see he'd lifted his head and was also lifting his chin.

A young man, as rough as the rest, but definitely younger (early twenties at most), came forward with two shot glasses and a bottle. I watched as he filled both shot glasses then stepped away.

The man seated beside me straightened and reached out to the glasses. He picked one up and extended it to me.

"Um...I haven't had lunch," I demurred, my gaze going from the shot glass to his eyes.

"Take it," he ordered. "Drink."

"I drove here. It would be irresponsible to drink straight alcohol on an empty stomach and then—"

He cut me off.

"Toots, I said, take it."

Oh dear.

I took it, and the instant I did, he reached out and nabbed the other one, put it to his lips and threw his head and the shot back. I watched his throat work and was vaguely intrigued through my what-on-earth-is-happening-now feelings to see his neck was as well-muscled as the rest of him.

He slammed the glass down, his head turned to me and then tipped to my glass.

"Shoot it," he demanded.

"Are you Mr. Hardy?" I asked.

"Buck," he replied.

I felt my brows knit. "You're Mr. Buck?"

"No, darlin', I'm called Buck."

"Oh," I muttered then asked, "Is the name on your birth certificate West Hardy?"

He grinned at me, all strong white teeth in a dark beard, and for some reason that made my heart skip a beat.

"Affirmative," he stated.

There it was.

Good.

I scooted my bottom on the chair, ready to get down to business, and stated, "Okay, then, Esposito says—"

He interrupted me again. "Shoot it."

"Pardon?" I asked.

"Babe, shoot the tequila."

"What I have to say won't take long," I told him. "And I appreciate your offer of refreshments, but—"

He grinned again, looking like something was immensely entertaining, and I stopped speaking because West "Buck" Hardy's entertained look went so far beyond attractive it was not funny.

"You appreciate my offer of refreshments?" he asked.

"Um, yes, it's very nice, but it's just past noon and—"

"Toots, quit jackin' around and drink the shot."

I stared into his eyes.

Then I decided to drink the shot.

One shot of tequila wasn't going to incapacitate me enough where I couldn't drive my car.

And perhaps, if I took it, he'd let me say what I had to say, and I could get out of there. I needed to go back to Esposito, get my money and pay my rent before they kicked me out of my apartment.

My apartment was a dump, but it *was* an apartment, and without it I'd have nowhere to sleep but my car.

That was, if I managed to avoid my car getting repossessed.

So I put the glass to my lips and took the shot.

I liked tequila, if it was cut with margarita mix, but I wasn't a shot kind of girl.

Therefore, even though I wanted to be ballsy and put myself out there as a cool customer, I couldn't help but flinch then make a face when I took the glass from my lips.

I looked back at West Hardy and saw he was tipping his chin up at the young biker again. Then I turned my head and saw the young biker move forward quickly and refill both Hardy's glass and mine.

Oh no.

"Mr. Hardy—" I started, and he turned his head to me.

"Buck," he declared.

"Okay, Buck, um—"

"You play pool?" he asked.

My head jerked.

I then looked over my shoulder at the pool tables and back at him.

"Pool?"

"Cues, balls, felt table, babe. Pool," he stated. "You play?"

"No," I replied.

"Shoot that." He dipped his head to my glass then went on, "And I'll teach you."

I was getting the distinct impression this wasn't good.

"Mr. Hardy—" I began, and something happened to his body. It tensed in a way that made me quickly say, "Buck, sorry, um...I have nothing against pool, but I really don't have occasion to play it very often and—"

"Toots, shoot the tequila and slide your ass off that stool. You're gonna learn to play pool."

I stared at him.

I then decided to try to bargain.

"If I let you teach me how to play pool, will you let me deliver my message and go?"

"Depends," he answered.

"On what?" I asked.

"On how you do with twenty questions," he replied, and my head jerked again.

"Pardon?"

"We're gonna drink, you're gonna learn how to play pool, and I'm gonna ask you twenty questions. Depending on your answers, I'll let you deliver your message." Once he'd stated this, he turned his head back to the young biker and ordered, "Give me the bottle and get Toots a Miller."

"Oh no," I stated quickly. "Beer is highly caloric, and I shouldn't mix alcoholic beverages. That isn't smart while driving."

Or, say, *ever*.

Buck shifted his focus again to me, and his eyes moved down my torso then back to the young biker who was placing the bottle of tequila on the bar. "Miller Lite," he amended his order.

"Buck," I started again, and regained his attention.

"Shoot it," he replied.

"But—"

"Darlin', not gonna say it again."

I stared at him.

I did this before I started to get angry.

"Maybe I should leave," I said to him.

"You leave, what do you tell Esposito?"

I had to admit, he had a point there.

Enrique Esposito wouldn't like that I didn't deliver his message.

"Toots, listen to me," Buck said softly, and my eyes focused on him to see he'd leaned toward me. "My guess is, you're new to this so I'm gonna give you a free lesson. You entered this game, you gotta play it."

"I'm trying to," I pointed out.

"Right, so, right now, the game is tequila, beer, pool and twenty questions. Now be smart, drink that shot and slide your ass off that stool because we're gonna play pool."

I studied him a moment.

Right before I tried bargaining again.

"Just so I have this straight, I drink with you, let you teach me how to play pool and answer your questions?"

"Easy," he replied.

"Do I get twenty questions?" I returned, and his brows shot up.

"You want 'em?"

"You ask me something then I should get something in return, so I ask you something. You like my answers, I get to deliver my message and go. That's the deal."

"Why do you want twenty questions?" he inquired.

I didn't know the answer to that, so I said, "I just do."

"All right, Toots," he stated then lifted his shot glass toward me. "Let's do this."

I nodded my head, lifted my own shot glass, and keeping my eyes on him while he downed his, I downed mine. I repeated my flinch and making a face, and when I focused on him, he was looking at me and again grinning.

He twisted his neck and ordered over his shoulder, "Rack 'em up."

The young biker had put a bottle of Miller Lite in front of me and Buck got off his stool.

I followed him, getting off mine.

He grabbed the bottle of beer and handed it to me.

I took it, he nabbed the tequila and shot glasses in one hand, his bottle of beer in the other, and he moved to the pool table.

I moved behind him, sipping at my beer and trying to ignore the gazes I felt following me.

I found this was easier than expected since I did this by watching

Buck's behind in his jeans, and the visual was so good, it automatically assumed control of all my concentration.

This concentration was broken only when a man shifted away from the pool table and I saw the balls in their triangle at the end.

Buck left the shot glasses, tequila and beer on the side of the table and went to the wall where he selected a cue.

I stopped by the table and wished I was wearing something else. Jeans, maybe. Gym shoes. Not a tight, buff-colored pencil skirt, a fitted white blouse with cap sleeves and ballet-pink, stiletto-heeled pumps.

I'd wanted to look professional and feminine.

Professional, so that the men I delivered the messages to would take me seriously.

Feminine, so they would think twice before hurting me.

Now, I was thinking this might have been a mistake.

Buck moved back to me, handed me the cue and looked at me.

"You wanna start or you want me to start?" he asked.

"Start?"

"Twenty questions."

I tried to decide which was the best strategy.

"You start," I told him because I wanted a sense of where this was going.

He didn't delay and he didn't shield his hand.

"You work since they fired your ass after your man went down?"

As I stared up at him, I felt my lips part and my stomach clench, and it didn't feel good.

He knew me. He knew all about me.

Oh God.

"Pardon?" I whispered as my legs started to shake.

He again didn't delay. "Your man was found guilty and handed a ten-year sentence. One month later, you were fired from the Hunter Institute. You work since then?"

Yes, he knew.

He knew all about me.

He knew more than just what he could read in the articles about all that Rogan did.

He'd looked into me. He knew I was coming. He knew Esposito was going to send me, slap him in the face by not coming himself or sending one of his lieutenants. He knew Esposito was the kind of man who had no respect, not for anyone, not even for the charismatic, magnetic leader of a biker gang.

He knew.

He knew and he'd prepared.

Oh God.

"He wasn't my man," I said softly.

"You were married to him, Toots," he replied.

I shook my head. "No, the divorce was final before then."

Something about him changed and it was almost like the very air around him gentled before he spoke again quietly.

"I know, darlin', but you aren't answering my question."

"No," I answered just as quietly.

He nodded, moved closer to me, and I was too out of it to step away.

"Your turn," he whispered.

I stared up at him.

"Have you investigated me?" I asked, and he shook his head.

"I'll let that one slide, babe, not smart," he said softly.

My heart skipped.

"Pardon?"

"Don't ask a question you already know the answer to," he advised.

"But you are," I pointed out.

"Yeah, but I have my reasons, you don't," he replied.

"Okay," I whispered.

"Go again," he prompted.

I didn't know what to ask.

Something was happening here. Something that had nothing to do with Esposito.

Or maybe it did. Maybe it was a power play and I was stuck in the middle.

Or maybe it was all about me.

Either way, I was on dangerous ground.

Far more dangerous than the ground I'd walked on when I entered this building and that ground was already pretty darned shaky.

My attention shifted, and for some reason, focused on one of the plethora of tattoos on his arm. Before I could stop myself, I lifted my gaze and asked my question.

"What's the snake mean?"

He tilted his head to the side as his brows knit. "Come again?"

I pointed at the snake slithering up his arm, starting low, curling around, the design opening larger at his biceps.

The snake was not thin, it was beefy.

It was also curled around a skull at the bulge of his biceps, head flared, eyes focused, mouth open, fangs exposed, ready to strike.

"The snake tattoo, what's it mean?"

I dropped my hand as he dropped his head and looked at the tattoo. Then he looked at me.

His expression was blank, but his eyes were alert, assessing, intense, drilling deep into mine, and if it could be believed I was even more uncomfortable than I was before.

"Kristy," he stated.

"Pardon?" I asked.

"Kristy, my ex-wife. She had occasion in our marriage to piss me off and do it a lot. She said, when I got pissed, I was not all bark and no bite. I wasn't even just bite. I was a strike. Like a snake."

"Oh," I whispered, my gaze slid away, and I took another sip of my beer thinking he didn't seem the kind of man to get angry enough to strike. He seemed totally in control.

Therefore, I found this fascinating.

"Line it up," he ordered.

I looked back to him.

"Sorry?"

"We're gonna break," he told me, tipping his head toward the table. "Line up your cue."

I looked at the table then to him. I did as he asked, set my beer aside, bent over the table, acutely aware that he was close, we were being watched, and my skirt was very tight, and I lined my cue up to the ball.

My body froze as his warmth curved around me, his hand on mine on the cue, his other arm stretching out so his hand could cover mine resting on the table with the cue over it. His back was pressed to mine, his hips pressed to my bottom.

Oh God.

"What are you doing?" I whispered.

"Only way to learn," his deep, rough voice said in my ear, but somehow I felt it on every inch of my skin, "is by feel."

Then he drew both our hands back on the cue and struck it forward. The cue hit the white ball and it accelerated, cracking soundly against the triangle at the other end, sending the balls scattering as his hand went flat to my midriff and he pulled us both up.

I watched the balls.

Two went into pockets, both solid colors, and Buck moved from me to the tequila.

He poured our shots and handed me a glass.

This time, I didn't hesitate.

I was not one for liquid courage, but at that moment, I was going to take anything I could get. Therefore, I threw it back and then watched as Buck threw his back.

He took the glass from me, set both on the side of the table, grabbed my bottle of beer, handed it to me, caught my free hand and moved me down the table.

He stopped, upended the cue he was carrying so its nub was to the floor and got in my space.

Again, I didn't retreat. The tequila was hitting me, I could feel it. I didn't remember the last time I'd had a drink and now I'd had three shots of tequila and sipped at a beer.

Drunk was going to come fast.

He knew this too.

I was definitely on dangerous ground.

"He leave you with anything?" Buck asked.

I blinked up at him.

"Who?"

"Your ex," he answered, my heart skipped again then he went on, "They didn't find all the money. They seized your house, the contents, your cars, your accounts. Did he leave you with anything? Cover your ass at all?"

"No," I told him and took another sip of beer. And it was at that moment I decided to fight fire with fire. "Why did you and Kristy get divorced?"

He looked down at me and answered without hesitation, "She didn't share my vision of what our lives would be. That being copasetic most of the time, not up in each other's shit nearly all the time. She married me with expectations of where our lives would lead, but she didn't share those expectations with me. If she did, I'd never have married the bitch in the first place."

"What were her expectations?" I asked.

"My turn, Toots," he didn't answer.

"Sorry," I whispered and took another sip of my beer because I had nothing better to do.

"You didn't know?" he asked

I studied at him, off balance again.

He asked questions I kind of understood, but they were questions that forced me to clarify in a way that I suspected he was trying to make me off balance.

"I didn't know what?" I asked back to clarify.

"About the whores," he clarified.

My middle moved back like he punched me, and I twisted my neck, looking away to hide the pain his words caused.

In doing this, I had no idea I missed the gentling of the air around him again, but even if I was looking at him, I wouldn't have caught it.

I wasn't numb to this.

Even after eighteen months.

Even after having my husband arrested in a middle-of-the-night raid of our house.

Even after having my photo, his photo, all those women's photos (okay, there were only three, but three was a lot) on the covers of newspapers, and even some magazines, for months on end.

Even after the hideous questions the journalists would shout at me whenever they had their chance.

Even after having everything I owned taken from me.

Even after losing my job.

Even after walking into multitudes of stores and restaurants and seeing people's faces change when they recognized me.

And even after hearing some of the things they said, either straight to my face or under their breath.

Truthfully, it wasn't that big of a story. We were just another in a never-ending cycle of greed, ugliness and negativity the public at large consumed with wild abandon like the news was a daily Bacchanal.

But Rogan was young, handsome, a fallen golden boy, and some of the details were salacious, and those kinds of descents from grace lived a life much longer than anyone's fifteen minutes.

As for me, I was forced into the role of the chump. The putz. I was so stupid I didn't know that my husband was living large from stealing people's pensions. Sleeping with high-class call girls in New York City, Chicago, Las Vegas. Squiring them around, drinking champagne, eating at the finest restaurants, giving them presents as well as paying them for sex.

I didn't know, but some people believed I couldn't be that stupid. Some people thought I put up with it for my fancy house and my fancy car and my fancy clothes (and I did have all that, but it wasn't *that* fancy). Some people thought I enjoyed my beautiful life living off other people's misfortune as handed to them by my thieving, cheating husband, and I'd turned a blind eye so I could keep that life.

Either way, everyone—and that was pretty much everyone nation-wide, but definitely in Phoenix—felt I got what I deserved.

I got what I deserved for being stupid enough to fall in love.

I squared my shoulders and buried the pain before I looked back at Buck, locked eyes and replied, "No. I didn't know about the whores."

"Toots—" he whispered.

I cut him off. "What did she expect?"

"Darlin'—"

I turned away and walked back to the tequila.

It was me who poured two new shots, grabbed both in one hand and walked back to him. I lifted the shots and watched his hand take one, but I didn't watch him shoot it. I just shot mine, flinched, belted back a gulp of beer and put the shot glass on the side of the table.

I looked at him again.

"What did she expect?" I repeated.

Buck studied my face a moment before answering, "She expected me to keep our lives as they were and not make any waves."

"And those waves you apparently were making?" I prompted.

"Sorry, Toots," he said gently. "That's another question."

"Right," I stated. "Fine, then ask one of me."

"I'm thinkin' we should focus on pool for a while," he told me.

I nodded instantly and turned to the table.

"Great. Perfect," I declared, examining the table. "What do I do now?"

"You're solids, babe. You see your shot?" he asked.

I stared at the table, focusing on what would possibly be my shot. I found it, set my beer aside and pointed.

"Good girl," he murmured, and I felt his body move into me. Forcing mine down, he situated the cue on the table. "Hands on mine," he instructed.

I did as I was told.

He moved my hands to where he wanted them and said in my ear, "See how this is lined up?"

I didn't. I wasn't paying attention to much except his heat at my back, his power surrounding me, the fact that I was careening toward drunk and the hollow feeling of despair that had a permanent hold of my stomach but was now sharpened to the point I wondered why I was still standing.

"Yes," I lied.

He again drew the cue back and then jabbed it forward in a controlled way, hitting the ball. The white ball cracked into the other ball at an angle and it shot straight into the side pocket.

"Finesse," he whispered into my ear.

"Right," I replied, pushing back against his body to straighten.

He allowed this and I walked away from him and grabbed my beer.

I sucked some back as I heard Buck call out, "Driver, another Lite and another Bud."

"Gotcha," the young biker called back.

I dropped my hand, looked at Buck and informed him honestly, "You should know, I'm already drunk, and if I have much more, I'll be very drunk and unable to operate my vehicle legally. You should also know I have exactly twelve cents in my purse and one dollar and fifty-seven cents in my bank account, and therefore I will be unable not only to order a taxi, but also to buy a bus ticket. And lastly you should know that, even if I wasn't wearing four-inch heels, I live too far away to walk home."

Buck studied me another long moment before he got close.

So close I could feel his warmth and his hand came up and curled around the side of my neck, sliding to the back.

I was shocked by this even after the pool lesson touching. He was so close I had to tip my head far back to catch his eyes and find he was actually so close that, if I lifted half an inch up on my toes, my mouth would be on his.

Oh dear.

"And you should know, Clara," he murmured, using my real name for the first time in his gravelly, deep voice, making it sound like another name altogether. Another name that belonged to another woman, that woman not me, but that woman being a woman I wished I could be. "That I know exactly what's in your account and I know you haven't had lunch and I know you haven't had breakfast, and I know it's because you can't afford either. I know you've got a master's in library science and I know no one will hire you because his mud stuck to you. I know Tia Esposito is the only thing you got, which means that put you in the path of her husband. And I know Enrique Esposito is the kind of cockroach that's able to sniff out vulnerability and manipulate it purely for shits and grins. And last, I know that you're tryin' to do your best with the hand you got dealt, but even so, babe, you are totally fuckin' this shit up by makin' all the wrong plays."

Something about that angered me, and with that, my heightened emotion and the tequila in my system, I didn't guard my reply.

"Okay, West," I stated. "You may know all that, and I suspect you know more. What you do not know is what it means to be me. There are a fair few people, thank God, who know what it means to be me. So, what *I* know is *you* don't know that first thing about how to play the hand I've been dealt. No one can know that unless they spend time in my shoes. So don't you stand there and make judgments about me. You have no clue, no *clue*, what it is to be me. And I not only know that because you're *not* me, but because, earlier, you said I entered this game. You were wrong. I didn't enter it. I was shoved into it. So you don't know everything, West Hardy. You know a lot, but you don't know anything that's important. So you cannot tell me I'm making the wrong plays because you don't get what it means when every breath is an effort at survival. I'm breathing so my take on this is, I'm doing all right."

He stared down at me and I held his stare.

Then, apropos of absolutely nothing, he asked, "Are you a vegetarian?"

I felt my head jolt and my brows shoot together before I answered, "No, why?"

Without taking his eyes or hand from me he shouted, "Driver! Order Toots and me the works!"

And it was then when I realized I'd read the situation very wrong.

I wasn't on shaky ground.

I was in the middle of an earthquake.

2

CLEAN

"Toots, have you paid attention to anything I've taught you?"

I looked up, leaned in, put a hand on the wall of a very muscled chest and grinned up at West "Buck" Hardy.

"You asked me if I knew how to play pool," I reminded him. "You didn't ask me if I was capable of *learning* how to play pool."

I was drunk.

Way drunk.

Unbelievably drunk.

In fact, I'd never been this drunk before in my life.

We'd had huge burgers, cheesy curly fries, and we'd chased them with beers, and that was more food than I'd had to eat in a long time. So I kind of sobered up a little when the food hit my stomach.

But then I shot more pool (sort of) while I shot more tequila and drank more beer, and I passed the drunk I was before like a *rocket*.

Now, I was *smashed*.

His hand hit my waist and slid around to the small of my back as he grinned down at me.

"All right, darlin', are you capable of *learnin'* how to play pool?"

I shook my head and gave him more of my weight.

"Nope," I replied. "I'm not very dexterous. Never have been.

Always picked last for teams in gym, and when I dissected my frog in biology class..." I trailed off and scrunched my nose before I finished, "It was seriously icky."

His hand at the small of my back put on pressure and he fitted my body to his.

"Then maybe we should give up," he suggested.

"This would be wise," I told him, nodding, and suggested back, "We could go back to twenty questions."

His face changed, and I liked the change, whatever it was. I was just too drunk to figure out what it was.

"Clara, honey, you didn't find that fun," he reminded me softly.

"Well, if you don't ask mean questions, West, maybe it'll be fun," I replied.

His eyes moved over my face as he murmured, "Mean questions."

I pulled away, grabbed his hand and dragged him to a couch. I moved in front of him, put both my hands on his chest, put pressure on my hands, and he went down. I collapsed beside him, curled my feet up under me so my bent legs were resting against his thigh, but I twisted my neck toward the bar.

"Driver!" I called. "Would you be a love and get us more beer?"

I heard Buck chuckle, and I turned to see his eyes were aimed beyond me and he was tipping up his chin which meant Driver was going to bring us more beer.

Excellent!

His gaze came to me, upon which I declared, "I'm smashed."

Buck smiled and asked, "No shit?"

"I've never been this drunk," I added.

His smile didn't leave his face as his brows went up. "Really?"

I shook my head and answered, "Nope."

"Babe, you gotta live more," he advised.

I smiled at him and noticed when I did, his attention dropped to my mouth, which made my belly feel warm, but I ignored this and drunkenly blathered.

"No way." I shook my head, then bragged outrageously, "I learned early to make all the right moves."

His gaze left my mouth, caught mine, and I realized in a vague way he looked kind of surprised.

"Come again?"

"Well," I started, felt Driver's presence, turned, gave him a huge smile as I took a beer from him and turned back as Buck took the other one and then Driver moved away. "You learn that in foster care."

Buck had started to lift the bottle to his mouth, but he stopped when his head jerked around, and his narrowed, lovely, rich, dark-brown eyes hit me.

"What?" he asked so quietly, I barely heard him.

But I heard him.

I was sucking back beer, staring at him and nodding all at the same time. I dropped my chin and my beer hand and looked at him.

"I mean, I messed up with Rogan, but I didn't know that. He was handsome and he wore suits and he drove a nice car and he acted from the beginning like he really liked me. Not to mention he had a seriously *cool* name. I mean Rogan Kirk. *Great* name," I stated.

I took another pull on my beer, swallowed it, and kept right on blathering.

"My birth mother gave me up for adoption then my adoptive father took off on my new mom when I was five, and she handled it for a while then, when I was seven, she killed herself, so I went to her sister. But she had four kids already, her husband had left her too, and things were tough. I wasn't blood anyway, so she called social services and they put me into foster care. That's how I met Tia. We were in a home together. I met her when I was twelve. We were thick as thieves. She was great. Like having a sister. She liked Rogan too. Neither of us expected to get something like *that*. We both expected to get something like...something like..." I trailed off and then stated, "Well, obviously, something like Esposito."

When I shut up, I saw he was staring at me.

He kept doing this for a bit, before he said, "Jesus, Clara."

"I know." I threw out my hand with the bottle in it. "No one knows *that*, right? No one knows *why* I believed in Rogan. Or why I *wanted* to believe." I sucked back more beer and went on, "In those articles, they didn't talk about how I worked my ass off at school to get academic scholarships to go to college. Which didn't cover it all, by the way. I had to get student loans and *I* paid those off. No one knows *that*."

I threw back more beer.

And kept blabbing.

"They also didn't talk about the student loans I took out to get my masters which I also paid off with *my* money. Money *I* earned. Rogan offered, but I said no. I didn't think it was fair. They didn't ask me questions about *that*. They didn't try to investigate *why* I was blind to what Rogan was doing. He treated me great. He traveled a lot, but when he was home, our marriage was *awesome*."

I leaned into Buck on the last word then leaned back and slugged more beer before continuing.

"I'd worked hard to get what I had. I thought Rogan was my reward. I thought, finally, *finally*," I leaned in again and stayed there, "it was *my* turn to have a taste of the good life."

"Baby," he whispered.

"But I was wrong," I went on like he said not a word and sat back. "And that's what I learned. You make all the right moves. You don't get into trouble, and Buck," I aimed a look at him, though not entirely successfully, "drinking until you're smashed is the *wrong* move. That'll piss off foster parents, get you kicked to a new place, or worse. So you be good. You do what you're told. You study and get good grades and be where they tell you to be or where you say you're going to be. You don't make trouble. You don't ask questions. You don't have expectations. You just wake up and get through each day doing the best you can and putting every foot right."

I threw back another swallow of beer.

And again kept talking.

"So I did all that, and I have to tell you, I've thought about it, like, *loads*, how I put my foot wrong with Rogan. But I swear, I *swear*, he gave me no clue. We had a great marriage, great sex, *shoo!*" I threw my hand out again. "I mean, seriously, he's a jerk of the jerkiest order, but you have to hand it to him, he has stamina if he was sleeping with all those women and still able to do the things he did to me." I leaned in again. "And how *often* and with such *energy*."

"Are you saying you're not pissed at him?" Buck asked, and I tried to focus more fully on him.

"Oh no. If it wasn't illegal and if prison didn't scare the bejeezus out of me, I would have killed him," I stated breezily. "I'm just saying he was *great* in *bed.*"

"So he ruined you for other men," Buck deduced, and if I wasn't so drunk, I would have noticed his tone was teasing, but I was drunk.

So drunk.

"Totally, and not because of the bed business," I answered in all seriousness. "Never going to go there *again*. No more men, *ever.*"

I felt something funny and it was so funny my drunken focus became a far more focused focus and I saw Buck was again staring at me with a expression on his face I couldn't decipher, but it made tingles slide across my skin.

"No more men, ever?" he asked quietly.

"Ever," I answered firmly, then turned my head and sucked back more beer.

"Baby, that's a waste," I heard Buck say.

I dropped my beer hand and looked at him.

"What? Why?" I asked.

"Because, Clara, you're fuckin' gorgeous," he answered, and I felt my eyes get big at the same time I felt my mouth drop open. "Great ass, babe, fuckin' unbelievable legs, fantastic tits, beautiful hair, gorgeous eyes, and shit, darlin', when you smile, fuck, your smile goes right to a man's dick."

I blinked again then I whispered, "I'm not gorgeous."

His hand slid around my thighs making his arm curl around both and he leaned into me to reply, "Don't know what you see in the mirror and it also doesn't matter. I feel your smile in my dick means I got a dick which means I'm a man and I'm tellin' you, Toots, top-to-toe, you're gorgeous. You weren't, babe, your ass woulda been thrown outta this building two seconds after you entered it. Since you are, you're drunk, and in about five minutes, you're gonna be in my room and I'm gonna convince you to forget about your vow of no men, ever."

Oh wow.

"You are?" I whispered.

"Damn straight," he answered.

"Oh my." I was still whispering.

"You want, you can bring the bottle with you." He tipped his head to the bottle of tequila still sitting on the pool table and kept talking. "But the only thing I'm gonna be tasting for the rest of the night is you."

Oh.

Wow.

"Oh my," I repeated on a breath.

"You want the bottle?" he asked.

"Buck—"

"Answer me, babe."

"No, but—"

I didn't finish.

He stood, yanked my beer out of my hand and set it aside with his. He grabbed my hand, pulled me off the couch and dragged me through the room to a doorway on the side wall by the bar. Through that doorway, he turned us left, we went down a short hall, then left again, and we went down a long hall where he opened the door to the second to the last room.

There, he pulled me in.

He closed the door.

I stared at the unmade, queen-sized bed.

Oh dear.

I turned to Buck.

"Um..."

I stopped speaking (not that I knew what to say) when he advanced.

I was drunk but not drunk enough to retreat toward the bed.

Instead, I shifted and moved away from it.

Buck shifted too and kept advancing.

"Um...Buck?" I called as I kept moving backward.

"Yeah, babe," he answered as he kept moving forward.

I hit wall and was forced to stop.

Buck's body hit mine and simply stopped.

I tipped my head back, feeling my scalp scrape the wall as I did so, and I stated, "I'm pretty...um, dedicated to that vow."

Buck spanned my hips with his hands and pulled them into his. He dropped his head so his lips were not even an inch away, but his eyes kept hold of mine.

It was then, I smelled him.

He did not smell of cologne.

He smelled of Buck Hardy.

Dark and decadent.

Um.

I was in trouble.

"Like I said, baby, you gotta live more," he whispered.

"But—" I started.

His head slanted, and he kissed me.

His beard felt scratchy. It also felt sexy because it came with his lips and his tongue.

And he tasted great, like beer, tequila and *man*.

Oh God.

My hands lifted, my fingers curled around his neck, and when his lips released mine and slid down my jaw to my ear, I felt it starting.

I had a strong libido, according to Rogan.

Rogan had loved that about me.

I thought it was Rogan.

Apparently, it was me.

Or, in this case, perhaps tequila, beer and all things *Buck*.

Specifically, the fact he smelled good, tasted good and was a really great kisser.

"Buck," I whispered, and he moved his hands from my hips to glide in and cup both cheeks of my behind.

Oh *God*.

"Buck," I repeated on a breath.

"Fuck, baby, you got a great ass," he muttered against the skin under my ear.

Oh...*God*.

"Buck," I said again, so low, even I could hardly hear it.

He lifted his head, but he also pressed his hips against mine. There was something lovely and hard there, and I felt my knees buckle so my fingers dug into his neck.

"I'm right here, Toots," he replied, slanted his head again and kissed me.

He was.

He was right there.

And I was right there.

And he tasted great and he felt great and his hands at my bottom felt even better and his tongue in my mouth felt *the best*.

Oh God, God, *God*.

I couldn't help it. I was too drunk, and he was too everything and all of it was good. I slid the fingers of one of my hands into his thick, over-long hair and the other hand moved around his shoulders to hold on. I tilted my head to the opposite side, pressed my body in and kissed him back.

That was it and what would happen next would make Rogan and all the fabulous things he could do to me be forever erased from memory.

I was all over Buck, and he was all over me.

I couldn't get enough of him, pulling his T-shirt from his jeans, my hands sliding in, over his hot, sleek, muscled skin, my movements fevered, hungry, my mouth more so.

And Buck felt the same, I knew it because he didn't hide it. He drank it from my mouth, he pulled it from my skin, he nipped it with his teeth.

Unbelievable.

I couldn't even keep track of it all. I could only feel, his hands at my bottom, my sides, my breasts. His mouth on my nipple over my blouse. My fingers yanking up his tee. His arms going up, pulling the shirt off then immediately my mouth went to his chest, his nipples, my hand gliding over his hard crotch then his hand fisting in my hair and positioning my head for him to take my mouth again.

He yanked up my skirt so it was around my waist, pushed down my panties. I stepped out of them and kicked them free and Buck's hands went to my behind again. I hopped up and wrapped my legs around him, but my hand went to his jeans. I undid the zipper, reached in, pulled his thick, rock-hard cock free and guided him to me.

He surged in.

My head flew back.

"Yes," I breathed.

Buck pounded into me, pounding me into the wall.

It felt *super* good.

My mouth found his. "Harder, baby."

He pounded into me harder.

"God," I whispered against his lips and he slid his tongue inside my mouth.

I took his thrusts, tilting my hips to deepen them, our tongues tangling, his hands at my bottom, my arms around his shoulders, holding on.

Then I couldn't kiss him because I couldn't breathe anymore.

"God," I moaned.

It was going to hit me, and when it did, it was going to be hard.

"Clara, baby, let go," he growled against my lips.

I let go even though I didn't know I was hanging on. My head flew back, slamming into the wall, and I cried out.

Ah.

May.

Zing.

Buck kept thrusting through my orgasm, grunting with his thrusts and I kept tilting my hips, offering myself to him, seeking the connection, loving the feel of it.

I curved my fingers around either side of his head.

"Baby," I whispered against his lips, "you feel beautiful."

At my words, he drove deep, stayed planted and groaned into my mouth.

Yes.

I moved my lips to his jaw, his neck, his ear, touching my tongue to his earlobe, tasting Buck, tasting *man*, smelling it, loving it as I felt his fingers tighten on my behind.

On my mouth's journey back to his, he pulled me from the wall, turned and walked us to the bed.

My lips hit his midway, his mouth opened, and I slid my tongue inside.

He fell back to the bed, me on top of him, and through it all, I never stopped kissing him.

I finally lifted up and looked down at him, my hands still framing his head.

"Okay," I whispered. "Maybe this once, I'll live more."

He looked up at me and smiled that fabulous smile, white teeth, thick, dark beard.

Then he rolled me to my back.

"Buck!" I cried.

"Let go."

"Oh God."

"Baby, fuckin'...let...go," he growled.

I let go, crying out loudly, my back and neck arching, my heels digging into his thighs. He slid his finger from between my legs so both of his hands could go to my hips, lifting them as he drove deep, deep and fast, his breathing labored, his grunts so powerful, they rumbled against the skin of my neck.

Amazing.

I came down and helped him out, whispering in his ear, and I felt the power of his thrusts intensify, telling me he liked what he heard. Then he lifted his head, his mouth slammed down on mine, and I slid my tongue inside so I could feel his groan against it.

Yes.

Amazing.

He stayed buried inside me as I kissed him then he took over the kiss, both were hungry. His kiss gentled to soft, sweet, then he stopped kissing my mouth in order to kiss my nose. Finally, he rolled off, pulling out, falling to his back, tucking me to his side.

I rested my head on his shoulder, my arm around his tight stomach, and I bent my leg so my thigh fell on his.

I was still drunk, but not so drunk I didn't feel his soft, sweet kiss or the softer, sweeter one he planted on my nose.

West "Buck" Hardy, president of a motorcycle club, kissed my nose.

I smiled against his shoulder.

He started sifting his fingers through my hair.

West "Buck" Hardy, president of a motorcycle club, was sifting his fingers through my hair.

My arm around his stomach tightened.

"Tell me about Tia," he said into the now dark room.

"What about her?" I asked.

"She all you got?" he asked back.

"Yes," I answered.

His hand in my hair stilled.

"Babe," he whispered.

"It's okay." I gave his stomach a squeeze. "She's enough."

"Fuck me," he muttered into the semi-dark (night had fallen, we'd been busy, Buck had only turned on one lamp, and it didn't cast a very wide glow).

I raised my head to look at his shadowed face.

"No, really, she is," I told him. "She's sweet and she's kind and she's generous."

"Darlin'," he moved his hand to cup the back of my head and bring it closer to him, "I can tell you're tight with her, but you gotta know, a woman who puts you in the path of a man like Esposito and lets him use you like he does is not sweet, kind and generous."

"That's not how it happened," I replied softly.

"Then explain how it happened," he demanded.

"He's done with her," I informed him.

"Come again?" he asked.

"He's done with her, Buck," I repeated. "But Enrique Esposito doesn't throw anything away. He keeps everything just in case it proves useful. And Tia is useful to him."

"How?"

Okay.

How did I allow us to get here?

I closed my eyes and looked away, wishing I was smashed again and not just drunk.

Smashed, I could forget.

Just drunk, it came tumbling back.

And just drunk, I didn't guard myself, and Tia, from me needing to relay this information.

But something was happening between Buck and me.

It might just last this day and that was probably precisely how long it would last.

That said, I liked him.

I liked having sex with him.

I liked talking to him.

I liked not-quite learning pool from him.

I just liked him.

And I wanted him to understand what made me.

In other words, since I did not guard myself, or Tia, from this, I needed to relay this information.

"Toots," he called on a prompt.

I opened my eyes and aimed them at his face.

"He loans her out," I whispered and felt his body go solid against mine.

Solid in the sense of *stone*.

Then he said in a way that I could tell his words were coming from between his teeth, "He does what?"

"She's very pretty," I told him.

"I've seen her."

"So you know."

"She's not hard to look at," he agreed.

"Well, if the price is right, he loans her out."

"Fuckin' hell," he muttered.

"That's about it," I replied. "So, Tia told me this and I talked to Esposito. Made a deal. He stops doing that and I work for him."

Buck's body went solid against mine again.

This before he asked, "You did what?"

"I made a deal. It wasn't a bad deal. Not only does he stop doing that to Tia, every message I deliver, I get a thousand dollars. It's actually, if you think about it, a really good deal."

Both his arms went around me, and he pulled me mostly on top of him and up so we were face to face.

"Toots, he's sent you with messages to Breaker Walinski and Imran Babić. Break's a biker who sells safe passage for drugs, guns and anything else illegal. Babić is a Bosnian lunatic who sells drugs, guns, pimps women, strongarms protection money, floats loans at a one hundred percent interest rate, makes book and is into anything else that's illegal. These are not guys you fuck with. Enrique Esposito is a sociopath and he's ambitious, *not* a good combination. Break's got a sense of justice. The disrespect Esposito dished out by sendin' you to the meet he'll take out on Esposito. Babić, babe, you gotta know, him lettin' you go in, deliver Esposito's message and walk out in one piece is a fuckin' miracle. I see you wantin' to look after your girl, but the deal you made is *not* a good deal."

"You're wrong, West," I whispered.

"I'm right, Clara," he replied not in a whisper.

"She's all I've got, and he was *loaning her out*," I reminded him. "Not to mention, I need the money."

"It worth that to her, to you, to get dead?" he asked.

"You do what you have to do," I told him on a shrug.

"Yeah, and what you shoulda done is put her in your car and got the fuck outta town, found yourselves jobs doin' whatever the fuck you could do under names that are not your own and prayed he never found you."

"He'd find us," I returned. "Therefore, that really wasn't an option."

"Clara, a man like Esposito burns fast, he burns bright and then someone snuffs him out. He's makin' enemies everywhere. He is not long for this world. All you had to do was wait him out."

His point held merit.

"Your point holds merit," I told him.

He was silent a moment before he burst out laughing, his arms tightening around me, and he rolled me to my back, him on top.

"Though," I continued, "I didn't have a biker advisor when I was making this decision."

"Bad luck, baby," he said softly.

"Mm," I mumbled in reply, before I asked, "Are you ever going to let me deliver his message?"

"His message is, no, he's not gonna pull his shit off our patch. He's gonna keep sendin' his dealers in, he's gonna keep movin' his product through, and he's gonna do this too fuckin' close to our shop. I knew that was his reply to my request the minute you walked in."

"So what are you going to do?" I asked.

"I'm gonna hafta expend the effort of pullin' his shit off my patch."

Oh dear.

That didn't sound good.

"Buck—"

He cut me off.

"No. Me and my brothers got mortgages and mouths to feed. We cannot have customers not show to buy ceiling fans and mix paint because some dealer is makin' a sale on the corner where they can see. We got a situation where people think it's cool to buy a paint roller from a bunch of bikers. We don't need them to think we got seedy shit happening on our turf. That would fuck everything."

It would, indeed, fuck everything.

Though, I had to admit, his commitment to this seemed pretty intense, considering, as mentioned, he and his boys were pretty rough-looking.

Not to mention, it seemed he knew a whole lot about men like Esposito, Breaker Walinski, and Imran Babić.

I shouldn't judge.

However...

"So you guys are totally clean?" I asked.

"We are."

Wow, I thought.

"Wow," I whispered out loud. Then, "Cool," I finished.

He was quiet.

I felt his hand rest against my face before he said softly, "And I take clean to my bed, baby."

Oh dear.

"Buck—"

"You're cute, Toots, you got courage and you got heart. Now, you gotta use both a' those to fight for clean."

Oh God.

"You think I'm dirty?" I whispered, horrified.

"Babe, point of fact is, you take drug and pimp money to deliver messages."

Oh *God*.

He did.

He thought I was dirty.

And that felt...

It felt...

Somehow, it felt *worse* than having everyone in Phoenix think I was insanely greedy or a chump.

A lot worse.

"Please get off me." I was still whispering.

"Toots—"

"No," I said, pushing at his shoulders. "Please get off me."

"Clara, listen to me."

"No," I repeated, still pushing at his shoulders and also bucking against his body.

"Cool it, Toots, and listen to me."

"Get off me."

He pressed me into the bed with his long frame and his hand slid from my face to my neck and curled around, the pads of his fingers digging in gently to make a point.

"I said, listen to me."

"No, Buck, you're judging me again," I retorted.

"You cannot say what I said isn't true."

I stilled. "You're right. Absolutely right. Now, before I sully your safeguarded cleanliness any further, you should release me from your bed."

"Babe, don't piss me off," he warned. "You're not lettin' me finish my point."

I stared at his face in the semi-dark.

There I was, drunk, naked, stupid, desperate, and in bed with a man I barely knew.

What was wrong with me?

When did it happen?

I'd kept myself safe for years.

When did I start making all the wrong moves?

"You know," I started conversationally, "I have to say, I don't care to let you finish your point. You've said enough. Now, I'd like to go."

"Yeah? And where are you gonna go?"

"What do you care?"

"Toots—"

"I get it. I understand fighting to be clean. I get that. Because the only person who ever loved me was pimped out *by her husband*. So I did what I had to do to help her stay as clean as she could get. Which, by the way, is never, *ever* going to be clean. Not in her mind. So yes, I took drug money to do it. If that makes me dirty, so be it. For me, my company is Tia, and I'll take that. So, I've asked you, *repeatedly*, to get...off...*me*."

I shoved his shoulders on my last word and lifted him off me enough to scoot out from under him. I almost made it to the end of the bed. But then he hooked my waist with his arm and pulled me back under him.

Thus started a tussle. Which, a few seconds in, I knew I wasn't going to win because, firstly, he was bigger than me, secondly, he was stronger than me, and thirdly, he wasn't (kind of) drunk like me. So I gave up and glared at his face in the semi-dark.

"You gonna listen to me now?" he bit off.

"I will hear you, but I can't guarantee I'll listen to you," I returned.

"Fuckin' hell, babe, you need to get smart real fuckin' fast."

"Oh, so now I'm dirty *and* stupid."

"You're the last if you don't learn to make the right allies, and the right allies are not sociopaths who'll send you to deliver messages hopin' you won't come out alive or, one way or another, no longer intact."

"So, what you're saying...your advice is I should sleep with you to keep you sweet so *you'll* take care of me?"

"Actually, yeah."

I stared at him through the dark.

I was being facetious.

He was not.

Then I asked, my voice pitched higher, "Is that clean?"

He lifted a hand and glided his fingers through my hair, down, pulling it over my shoulder and his voice was gentle when he replied, "Yeah, Clara. It's honest. We both know what it is. We both get somethin' out of it. So it's clean."

Oh God.

I was going to cry.

I thought my life couldn't possibly get worse, and here it was, *worse*.

This really cool, handsome man who listened well and was great at sex wanted me to *prostitute myself* to him so he would take care of me and I could "make a good ally."

"Please...*please* get off me," I whispered.

"You bring Tia with you, I'll keep her safe too."

Oh *God*.

"You can't, he won't let her go," I replied.

"Babe, he'll have to get through me and all of my boys to get to you or her."

"And all I have to do is sleep with you?" I asked.

"Well, no," he answered.

"Does Tia have to sleep with you too?" I pushed, and his body went stone solid again.

Except maybe *more* stone solid, something I wouldn't think was possible.

But it was.

"Babe," he growled.

A warning.

Definitely.

I'd gone too far.

I also didn't care.

"Okay, so then does Tia have to sleep with one, or, say, all of your boys?"

"Don't do that shit. You know that's not what I'm talkin' about."

"So maybe you'll explain what you're talking about."

"I would, you shut your trap."

I shut my trap and stared at his shadowed head.

He stared at mine.

Then he muttered, "Christ, need my head examined."

"You *could* get off me," I reminded him.

"Is this shuttin' your trap?"

I shut my trap again.

"You take of care my house and my business as well as me."

"What does that mean?"

"That means you move outta your apartment before they kick your ass out. You move into my house. You keep it clean. You keep me fed, that is, when I'm not feedin' you, and I like to cook, so mostly, I'll be feedin' you. You come to work with me and take care of the office, and you go home with me."

Wow.

Was he serious?

That sounded like...it sounded like...

My God, it didn't sound like a sex-for-safety arrangement.

It sounded like a *relationship*.

"What?" I whispered.

"The office work, I pay you for," he went on.

He'd pay me for it?

As in, *a job*?

"What?" I repeated.

"And give you a car since the repo men, babe, just gotta say, they'll get yours before you get a chance to sort that shit out."

Good God.

He knew everything about me.

"Do you know everything about me?"

"Everything from your master's degree up. That foster care shit, no. We didn't have the chance to dig that deep."

"Why did you dig at all?"

"Toots, I knew he was gonna send you and you don't go up against an enemy you don't know. Word about you was all over the street. Anything on radar that may touch my Club, I find out about it."

That made sense and it was thorough and protective. It kind of made me wish I had a club. Then again, I'd always kind of wished I'd had a club.

Buck kept talking.

"Clara, listen to me, I'm offerin' you a home, a car, a job, protection for you and your girl and the opportunity to stay clean. Are you seriously gonna turn that down?"

Something occurred to me.

"Did you know that you'd...that you'd try...that we'd—?"

"Saw pictures of you, babe, lots of 'em. Can't say they didn't catch my interest but in the flesh..." He tugged my hair, let that finalize his point and moved on. "So no. I didn't know you'd be where you are right now and I didn't know I'd make that offer because I didn't know the offer needed to be made. Though, considered *an* offer after our abbreviated twenty questions and definitely was movin' toward it after you got smashed, chatty and seriously fuckin' cute."

I missed the last part, which was too bad, but it was because I was stuck on what he said earlier.

"So this is pity?" I asked, my voice rising again, and I watched him arch his neck back and listened to him sigh.

Once he'd done that, I listened to him mutter, "Fuckin' hell."

"Well?" I demanded.

It was then I watched him tip his head down and felt his eyes burning into me.

"Let me sum up," he stated with unhidden, barely restrained patience. "You...are...fucked. You haven't worked in nearly a year. You've come to the end of the money you had in your own account, as well as the end of the money you got when you hocked anything they left you with that had value. You haven't paid on your car in six months. You're three months out on rent. You were six, but the money you earned from Esposito caught you up, just not enough. You were served an eviction notice a week ago. Your three credit cards are maxed. You haven't paid on them in six months either. They're with collection agencies who are at your door so much, they could move in."

Okay.

One could say he'd *really, really* looked into me.

And he wasn't done.

"Your girl is unsafe and the only way to keep her safe is to accept death-defying errands for a sociopath. That is, until he gets tired of watchin' you charm your way through badass bikers and psychopathic filth by wearin' tight skirts, high heels and bein' cute, and he decides to loan you out too."

This, I had to admit, was a concern I'd had as well.

And...

Buck still wasn't finished.

"Client one, my guess, Imran Babić, who hasn't made public his reasons for lettin' you strut away from him unharmed, but who I know likes blondes, tight asses and long legs. Client two, Breaker Walinksi's boy, Bug, who was there when you strutted in and strutted out and *has* made public his interest in Esposito's new piece of tail."

Fabulous.

Buck kept talking

"Like I said, you need to start makin' the right allies. Now, this is just my guess, but you walk outta Ace's Dive without my protection, three things can happen. Esposito keeps usin' you until he uses you up one way or another. Babić picks you up and has his fun with you. And babe, you're cute, you may be able to get him to be your shield, but Babić does not like brown skin and Tia won't be along for that ride. Or last, Breaker pulls you in for his boy, and Walinskis, they know and appreciate a fine woman. So they pull you in, babe, they like you, and they will, you ain't *ever* gettin' out."

At long last, he finally stopped talking.

But I didn't know what to say.

There was a lot there and none of it was good.

And regrettably, I had a feeling with all of it, he was right.

When I didn't speak, Buck did.

"Or you pick smart. You pick me. You make the right ally. You work an honest job, you get honest pay. You get a ride you don't have to hide from the repo man. You get your girl safe. And you and me, we enjoy what we gave each other four times before we had this chat and we keep enjoyin' it until it isn't so much fun anymore."

It had to be said, I *did* enjoy what he gave me four times before we had this chat. I enjoyed it *a lot*. What made it more enjoyable was that he could give it to me four times. He wasn't exactly sixteen. In fact, even Rogan, who was legendary, could only manage twice.

Definitely a point to ponder.

Just one to ponder when I wasn't still inebriated.

"Can I delay my decision until I don't have so much tequila and beer in my system?" I requested.

"I'm thinkin', Toots, you didn't get me when I told you that you should live more," he replied.

"So your advice is to make a major life decision naked, in bed with a man I barely know, after having four orgasms, our first fight and while somewhat intoxicated?" I asked.

"Definitely," he answered without hesitation.

I stared at his shadowed head.

Then I burst out laughing.

"Toots," he called over my laughter.

But I kept laughing.

So hard I had to lift my head up and shove my face against his neck at the same time wrapping my arms around him to hold on.

There was no reason to do this since I was horizontal, I just did.

"Clara," he called again when I kept laughing, so I struggled to control it, dropped my head to the bed and looked at him again.

"Give me until morning," I said through residual giggles.

"Gorgeous, just pointing out, you're holdin' on to me tight," he said quietly, my residual giggles died, and I started to slide my arms away until he ordered, "Don't," and I stopped.

"Buck," I whispered.

"You got until morning," he acquiesced. My body relaxed under his, his head dipped, and I felt his lips at my ear. "And so do I," he finished.

His mouth moved to mine, and he kissed me.

Then he went about giving me orgasm five and he took his time doing it.

Shortly after, he took more time and gave me orgasm six.

After that, I passed out, and my last thought was I could enjoy West "Buck" Hardy for a long, long time.

Especially if he could keep all that up.

And I meant *all of it.*

But mostly, if he kept kissing my nose.

3

REDHOT

I opened my eyes to see sun shining into Buck's room at the clubhouse.

I also saw Buck's (impressive) chest.

I saw this because my cheek was to his shoulder.

I'd been right and I had a variety of sensory proof.

Buck was muscled everywhere.

He also had tattoos on more than his arms. They slid up his shoulders and there were two on his torso. One, in black ink on his lower left abs over a nasty-looking scar that said, NEVER AGAIN and another one over his heart that said GEAR.

I looked beyond his beautiful chest, sensing my hangover, which I suspected would hit full swing the minute I moved any body part. So I tried only to shift my eyes because I didn't want my hangover to hit and because I didn't want to wake a sleeping Buck.

I'd been occupied last night so I hadn't taken in the room, which was not only messy, it appeared filthy. It definitely needed dusting and a pick-up. So much so, the chores might take a week.

Clothes everywhere. Bits of paper. Discarded disposable coffee cups. Beer and liquor bottles. Dirty glasses, dishes and take out cartons. And...my gaze narrowed...*bullets*.

Um...ack!

I closed my eyes again to shut out the filth (but mostly the bullets) and snuggled deeper into Buck's warm, hard side which made his arm tense around my back, the pads of his fingers digging briefly into the flesh at my hip before he settled again.

I waited and he didn't move any more.

Still asleep.

I could see that.

Last night had to exhaust him considering he did the vast majority of the work.

Then I remembered I had a decision to make and I opened my eyes, but didn't focus.

I liked this man against me in bed and not just because he had more stamina and skill than five Rogan Kirks.

No.

It was because he kissed my nose. Because he listened to me. And because he made me laugh really hard. He didn't mean to, but he did it, and I hadn't laughed in a really, *really* long time.

It felt good.

He protected his Club and he wanted to protect me.

That felt nice.

The part that didn't feel nice was that he wanted to do it until it wasn't so much fun anymore.

This wasn't surprising, of course. We'd not known each other even twenty-four hours. I knew he enjoyed me, it was impossible to miss. Not to mention he told me straight out after orgasm three (mine) and again after orgasm five (his). But I knew we were nowhere near avowals of love and shopping for wedding bands.

Still.

How long would it take for a man like West "Buck" Hardy to find me not so fun anymore?

Probably not very long.

And he'd kissed my nose.

Kissed my *nose*.

I'd probably find him fun a lot longer.

Hells bells.

I'd learned this lesson before, very publicly.

I thought Rogan was the key to a beautiful life and the reason I thought that was not because he was a beautiful man who gave beautiful orgasms who made me feel beautiful with the way he looked at me and all the things he was able to give me.

But instead, with the way he treated me.

I'd loved him.

And then...

Enough said on that.

Now I was offered Buck as the key to safety and security.

But I'd also learned a long time ago, and stupidly forgot along the way, that I needed to look out for myself.

And Tia.

Buck was right. We should just go.

I didn't have any money, but Tia could lay her hands on some. My car was being shopped out for repo and Esposito probably put tracking devices on his to keep tabs on Tia, but it would make it harder for the repo man if my car was five states away.

I was thinking Seattle. I'd always wanted to go there. And I liked coffee and they had a lot of coffee places in Seattle. Maybe I could get a job in one.

So, we'd go.

And then, when someone snuffed Esposito out, we'd come back.

When we did, I'd find Buck, and if he wasn't nailed down by some gorgeous woman who he enjoyed more than me, maybe he'd give me another shot without this hanging over my head.

Not for pity. Not for protection.

For me.

And I'd come to him clean.

I cautiously raised my head and studied his face.

I would never have imagined he'd be my type.

Way too rough, way too rugged.

But he was my type.

He was gorgeous.

In more than just one way that word could define a person.

I sighed quietly, slid up carefully and kissed the hinge of his whisker-covered jaw. Then I gave myself another moment with his face, memorizing it gentle in sleep like that but still masculine and magnetic.

After I gave myself that, I slid away.

I hurried through the room, grabbing my clothes as I headed to an open door where I saw a sink. I went through, found the bathroom was definitely way ickier than the bedroom, and I tried not to think what the soles of my feet were encountering as I dressed.

I used the facilities, washed my hands and splashed water on my face.

Mistake.

I knew this when I looked at the crusty towel.

Big time ick.

Bigger time ick with a hangover.

My stomach roiled as I used the edges of the towel that were less crusty and wiped my hands and face as best I could.

I walked out of the bathroom carrying my shoes.

Buck was still asleep in bed, and seeing him there, the sheet down at his waist, his tattoos, skin and muscles on display, it was hard not to disrobe and join him again.

Instead, I quietly searched for a piece of paper (this was not hard to find) and a pen (also not hard to find), and I wrote him a note.

WEST,

Thank you for the offer, but I need to start making the right moves.

You're a fantastic man and I'm glad I met you.

~Clara

PS: Thank you, too, for making me laugh. I haven't done that in a long time.

I STUDIED the paper and considered thanking him for kissing my nose then I reconsidered thanking him for making me laugh then he moved on the bed. I froze, and my eyes shot to him.

He rolled to his side and shoved a hand under the pillow.

I stayed still, but he made no more movements.

Not wanting to take any more chances, I didn't touch him, and I laid the note on his nightstand.

But I did clear some of the bits away so he'd see it.

I walked out of the room, closed the door and put my shoes on in the hall.

I was walking to my purse that was still on the bar (these boys definitely were clean, it was a nice purse, one of the few I didn't hock due to its size and versatility, and there it was, safe on their bar) when I heard, "Yo."

I jumped and turned to see the big, dirty-blond, long-haired man standing several feet behind me, smirking.

He had a ponytail today.

"Hi," I greeted.

"Babe," he replied.

Something about the way he was smirking made my cheeks turn hot. It wasn't ugly, it seemed almost teasing.

It was also knowing.

"You gettin' Buck breakfast?" he asked, coming toward me.

Oh dear.

Was this what a biker expected from a woman the morning after?

"Um..." I replied.

He made it to me, stopped to tower over me and advised, "You should hold out, woman, the brother is serious as shit with a fryin' pan."

I tilted my head back to look at him and asked, "What?"

"Buck can cook. We don't got a kitchen here, but it's worth the wait to get to his place."

"His place?" I queried.

"Yeah, babe, he doesn't live here."

"Oh," I whispered.

Of course he didn't.

And, wow.

I wondered where he lived.

I also wondered what he cooked.

No, no, no, I didn't.

Well, I actually did, but I couldn't focus on that.

I had to focus on Tia, coffee and Seattle.

When the big blond guy didn't speak, I said, "We didn't meet." I extended my hand. "My name is Clara."

His big mitt engulfed my hand and squeezed a hint too hard before he let it go while saying, "Ink."

"Right," I muttered.

Ink. Buck. Where did they get these names?

I should have asked during twenty questions.

"Anyway—" I started but stopped when I saw him smirking again, so I asked, "What?"

"Just a heads-up, now you got another name," he told me.

"I do?" I asked.

His smirk became a grin and it made him kind of cute, even though he was about four days away from a clean shave and a lot more than four months away from a decent haircut.

"Yeah, Redhot."

"Sorry?"

"Your nickname, babe. Redhot. Jesus, woman, listenin' to you all night, a man don't need porn."

Oh...*God!*

My face had been warm, but I knew instantly now it was pale.

Ink kept talking.

"Thought you were ice, but you ain't. You're fire. Buck can always pick 'em."

He grinned through that sock to the gut (*Buck can always pick 'em?*) as I stared up at him, and then he continued, leaning in.

"But breakfast?" He shook his head and finished on a meaningful, "Babe."

I should point out this "babe" was meaningful to him. It was confusing to me.

He shoved my shoulder playfully like he hadn't told me not too long ago to get out, gave me another big grin and sauntered away.

I stared after him, not knowing what on earth he meant, and I did this for a while trying to figure it out.

Then I thought about Buck always picking them and I felt that hollowness in my stomach again. The despair I forgot through tequila, beer, pool, hamburgers and Buck slid right into its place alongside the nausea of my hangover.

On that thought, I remembered Seattle, ran to my purse, grabbed it, and dashed to my car.

I LIFTED my fist to knock on Mrs. Jimenez's door, but it opened before my knuckles hit the panel.

Her bony hand came out, grabbed hold of my forearm, and she yanked me into her apartment. She swiftly closed the door behind us.

I turned to look at her.

Mrs. Jimenez was my next-door neighbor and she liked me.

She was a Mexican American woman who said she was seventy-eight, but she looked ninety-eight. She had pictures of herself, her husband, her kids and grandkids all over her apartment and I knew from those she'd shrunk about a foot. Her entire face was lined, and her hair was coarse, gray and always twisted into a bun at the back of her head.

She also had the brightest, sweetest smile I'd ever seen in my life, beautiful, warm brown eyes, and she made great homemade tamales. Her cooking, and Tia's, was the only food I'd eaten in the last two months. Without the two of them looking out for me, I'd be in more of a mess than I already was.

"Tell me you hid your car," she said.

"Of course," I replied then deduced, "The repo men have been here."

"Nosin' around," she said on a nod then her eyes got sharp. "The Jackal's been here too."

"The Jackal" was what Mrs. Jimenez called our landlord, Dallas Hill.

Mrs. Jimenez had been living there for years, and Dallas Hill had owned the apartments since she moved in. He raised the rent on a regular basis but didn't raise the level of service provided. Which meant, if a toilet flooded, a roof leaked, the hot water went out or a refrigerator stopped working, he'd take his time coming to fix it and the time he'd take could be weeks. In apartments with one bathroom, waiting even a day to have your toilet fixed was seriously not fun.

However, if you were a day late paying rent, he'd come around to call.

This meant I drove him batty, and Mrs. Jimenez was loving every minute of it.

So much so, she had her son, Raymundo, come in and change my locks so Dallas couldn't get into my apartment.

This was probably illegal, but when Dallas made an issue of it while standing outside my door shouting (while I was standing inside my apartment hiding) Mrs. Jimenez had come out to the open-to-the-elements walkway that the doors to the apartments faced.

I saw her out my kitchen window with her phone to her ear and heard her say loudly, "Hello? Can I speak to a building inspector?"

At that, Dallas had scowled at her and stormed away.

Still, rent was cheap, and my apartment came furnished.

Mrs. Jimenez had her own stuff in hers and her place was far homier than mine. This was because Dallas decorated in castoffs from Goodwill and Mrs. Jimenez decorated in history, love, memories and family.

"Are they gone?" I asked.

"They're never gone, but they're out of sight," Mrs. Jimenez answered. "Where'd you hide your car?"

"Two alleys over, by the dumpster that homeless guy sleeps next to. He let me use his tarp to throw over the trunk."

If I chose that location of the many I'd found the last few months to hide my car, that homeless guy always did that for me. I didn't know why. I didn't ever give him money, though I had brought him some of Mrs. Jimenez's tamales. Maybe that was it. Or maybe he saw in me what he'd seen in himself prior to his current situation.

Either way, I was grateful.

"*Bien, querida*," Mrs. Jimenez approved then her eyes moved to my feet. "You walk back in those shoes?"

"Yes, but I can't feel my feet considering I'm hungover," I replied.

Her eyes came to mine and lit with interest, considering I'd never said that to her before and a hangover would indicate having a good time and she hadn't heard of me having any of those before either (unless I was at her place eating tamales or chilaquiles and gabbing with her).

Thus, she grabbed my hand and pulled me to her velour, old-lady couch.

"Hungover?" she prompted.

"I did a job for Esposito yesterday," I explained as we both sat.

"*Dios mio*," she muttered, the light dying out of her eyes and concern washing in, knowing me, knowing Tia and knowing and not liking what she knew about Esposito.

"No, actually, it was good," I told her. "The man I had to deliver Esposito's message to...he was nice. He was..." I looked away then back at her. "He was kind. He gave me a hamburger, a pool lesson, a lot of booze and good advice."

She studied me astutely, and considering the time of day and the obvious fact I'd just returned home in yesterday's clothes, more than likely knowing I left out the fact he gave me multiple orgasms, and remarked, "You could use some good advice."

It couldn't be denied, she was not wrong about that.

"I need to use your phone," I said words she'd heard dozens of times.

I always used her phone. This was because I didn't have the money to have one in my apartment or to carry a cell.

I promised myself, one day, when I was out of my mess, I'd return the many favors she'd done for me and take care of Mrs. Jimenez. I just hoped she stayed of this world long enough for me to do that because it seemed this mission of mine might take a while.

"Of course, *cariña*," she replied as she always did.

"And I need to talk to you," I continued.

Her beautiful, warm brown eyes focused even more sharply on me.

"I'm packing all my stuff, getting Tia and leaving town," I announced.

She closed those beautiful, warm brown eyes as relief flooded her face.

She opened them and whispered, "I'm so glad, Clara."

"It's what Buck told me to do," I continued.

"Buck?" she asked, her head tilting to the side.

"The man I met yesterday. The one who gave me advice."

"Well then, this Buck is a smart man," she declared.

"You think it's the right thing to do?" I asked.

"*Querida, yes*," she answered, coming close and taking my hand. "Fresh start away from here. I can't say I won't miss you and your *linda sonrisa*, but I can say I'll sleep easier knowing you and *tu amiga* are somewhere safe."

I'd miss her too. She wasn't only about good tamales. She was funny. She was sweet. I loved her family. And she was the closest thing I'd ever had to a grandma.

I'd been wrong when I told Buck all I had was Tia.

I had Mrs. Jimenez too.

And, maybe, that homeless man.

I smiled at her and leaned in, putting my hand on hers. "Thanks, Mrs. Jimenez."

Her free hand covered mine and gave it a squeeze. Then she let me go, got up and walked to the wooden chest where she kept her sewing and cross stitch paraphernalia. She opened it, pulled out the top partition then dug in. She got something out, put the partition back, closed the box and came to me.

She extended a wad of cash in my direction.

I stared at it as my heart stopped.

"I've been wanting to give this to you for a long time. Now I *need* to give it to you." When I kept staring at it and not moving, she said, "Take it," then shook her hand at me.

My eyes went to hers.

"Mrs. Jimenez, I can't."

"You can. Take it."

I kept hold of her gaze and didn't move.

She had four kids, they loved her and took care of her, but neither Mrs. Jimenez nor her kids were rolling in it.

That wad of cash had to be her nest egg.

"I can't," I repeated.

She leaned down so her face was in mine.

"*Cariña*, you *can*. Not only *can* you, you *have to*."

"But—"

"This world," she cut me off, "is full of bad. Full of it, Clara, It's everywhere. But even so, *you've* had more than your fair share. We must, all of us, do what we can for each other to give this world some good. I'm giving you some good."

That despair in my belly shifted.

It didn't evaporate, but it shifted as I lifted my hand and placed it on her wrinkled cheek and whispered, "Thank you, I appreciate that. But I can't take it. I don't know when I can pay you back and someday you might need it."

"You being away from Esposito, away from Dallas Hill, taking Tia, that's all the payback I need, *querida*. I have my children to take care of me and you...you, Clarita, you have me."

I felt the tears hit my eyes.

Yes, she was the only grandma I ever had.

"Take it," she said again, shaking her hand at me.

"One day I'll take care of you," I whispered, and she smiled.

"Take it, *cariña*."

I took it.

She nodded, smiled, straightened, reached out and grabbed the phone. She handed it to me and bustled to the door.

"I'll go to your place, start packing," she announced, hand on the door.

"Mrs. Jimenez," I called. She turned, caught my wet eyes and I whispered, "Thank you...so much."

"*Fue mi placer*," she whispered back words I had no idea their meaning, except I knew they were nice.

Then she opened the door a smidge, stuck her head out and looked side to side like she was a spy casing for bad guys. The coast apparently was clear, because she grabbed my extra key from the decorative keyholder hanging on the wall, stepped out and shut the door.

I shoved the money in my purse, wiped the wet from under my eyes and called Tia.

She answered on the second ring.

"Where are you?" was her greeting.

"Um...honey, you have caller ID. You know I'm at Mrs. Jimenez's."

She didn't reply to my reply, she cried, "Enrique has been *freaking out*."

"He has?"

"Yes!"

"Why?"

"Because you didn't come back."

This was a surprise.

"He cared that I didn't come back?"

"I don't know what he cares about. I just know something is up."

Oh dear.

Something up with Esposito was never a good thing.

"Well then, perfect timing because something else is about to be up."

"Oh God," she whispered.

"Is Esposito there?" I asked.

"No, he's gone."

"How long?"

"I don't know. He didn't share his schedule for the day."

He wouldn't.

He'd left all husbandly duties behind when he started pimping out his wife.

Except one.

Not that he'd ever been good at husbandly duties.

Even, according to Tia, that one.

"Then we don't have much time," I announced.

"For what?"

"Tia, we're leaving."

She was silent a moment before she asked, "What?"

"Leaving. Leaving town. You and me. You need to pack a couple of bags and get your hands on some money or valuables we can sell that are easy to carry, like jewelry. We'll meet at the 7 Eleven on Thomas and 16th in an hour, ditch your car and we're going to Seattle."

"Seattle?" she whispered.

"Yes, Seattle," I replied.

More silence, then...

"Are you *crazy*?" she hissed into the phone, and I could tell she was moving, probably to make sure she had privacy.

Esposito might be gone, but that didn't mean his bevy of bad guys weren't around.

"No, I'm not crazy."

"Um, Clara, I think you were around when I asked Enrique for a divorce. I think you remember his response. So I think you're *crazy*."

His response was Tia getting an eye that was swollen shut and not being unable to walk without holding her ribs for a while.

And this fact made me even less crazy.

"Buck says he's making enemies. Buck says he's the kind of guy who burns bright then gets snuffed out. And Buck is the kind of man who knows what he's talking about. We just have to stay gone and lay low until someone snuffs him out."

"Who's Buck?"

"West Hardy."

"Oh God."

This was an indication she didn't think the president of a motorcycle club was the top choice for a life decisions advisor.

Then again, Tia had been in foster care with me, so she knew all about doing your utmost to make the right moves.

However, she, just like me, screwed up big time along the way.

"He's nice," I explained. "And he's smart."

"Clara—" Her voice had started trembling.

She was scared.

I hated to hear Tia scared and it happened a lot.

And I was done hearing it.

Yes.

Buck was *so right*. We had to get out of here.

We weren't safe, no matter what we did.

Not in Phoenix.

And it was me who had to make us that.

"Tia," I cut in, "I know how this is going to play out. Either Buck's right and Esposito's enemies move in for the kill or Esposito messes up and the police move in for the kill. Either way, you do *not* want to be around. Trust me, I *know*. You want to leave. You want to be far away from here. You want to be with me, in Seattle, making coffee drinks."

"Yes, Clara, but I have fifty dollars in my purse, can only take out two hundred from the ATM, and Enrique hasn't exactly showered me with jewels," Tia returned.

"We'll be okay."

"How?"

"We just will."

"And what if he comes after me? Which we both know he will."

"We'll figure something out."

"Clara, honey—"

"Pack clothes and some food. If we don't have to spend money on food, then we can just spend it on gas to get to Seattle."

"I can't," she stated.

"You can. I can. Mrs. Jimenez just gave me her nest egg. I don't know how much is there, but we'll sell your wedding rings, which should be good for something, and go as far as we can go until we can't go anymore. Then we'll figure something out."

"If he finds me," she whispered, "he'll hurt me."

"Tia, baby," I whispered back. "He's hurting you now."

Tia had no response and this was because she knew I was right.

When she didn't speak for a while, I didn't want to do it, but I had to.

So I pulled out the big guns.

"And he's hurting me." Tia still didn't respond so I continued, "We both know he's playing with me in ways I could get hurt. We both know he's doing it because he *likes* the idea I might get hurt. And we both know that when that doesn't happen, he'll make things more dangerous for me so I *will* get hurt. And, last, we both know my deal with him to keep you safe won't last forever. He'll get bored with that too. We have to go. We *both* have to go. *Now.*"

"I don't think—"

"Whatever happens to us out there cannot be worse than what's happening and is going to happen here."

Tia again fell silent.

"Honey—" I started.

"An hour," she whispered, and relief swept through me. "The 7 Eleven. He gave me a string of pearls and a pair of ruby earrings when we were dating. And I put all my change in that bowl in the kitchen. There has to be at least seventy dollars in there. I'll grab that too."

God, we were reduced to change in a bowl.

I used to live in a four-bedroom house with a pool in the backyard in a neighborhood where all the women wore Lululemon clothes and carried Louis Vuitton bags (both, I never did, because enough with the Lululemon already, it should be called Lululemming—even the LV, those stuck-up, entitled women who I hadn't liked even *before* my life turned to garbage (because they were stuck-up and entitled) were such they actually ruined the brilliance of LV for me).

And four months ago, Tia and Esposito moved into an ostentatious mini-mansion.

Then again, Tia had tried to talk me into taking that change for the last six months since it was the only thing she figured Esposito wouldn't notice was gone as he wasn't a fan of Tia helping me out, so he put a stop to it months ago.

Therefore, I'd essentially been reduced to change in a bowl for a while.

And seventy dollars was a couple tanks of gas.

"Perfect," I said.

"7 Eleven," she said.

"An hour," I replied.

"You and me," she whispered.

"Coffee drinks and Seattle," I whispered back.

We'd dreamed, Tia and I. We'd dreamed in whispers at night while in our twin beds in our foster carer's home.

We hadn't dreamed big. But we'd dreamed.

None of those dreams were about coffee drinks and Seattle.

But, for now, that would do.

I heard her take in a shaky breath.

Then I heard her say a shaky, "Yes."

"See you soon, honey."

"'Bye, babe."

I hit the button for off, and you couldn't say I wasn't scared. I was scared. Definitely scared. And I still didn't like the feeling.

But that despair in my belly shifted again.

It didn't evaporate, but it shifted and there was a tiny little niggle of hope.

I hadn't felt that in a long time either.

I'd have to send Buck a postcard from the road and thank him for that too.

I put the phone on its base, walked to the door, did the spy thing just like Mrs. Jimenez did, and then rushed one door over to my apartment.

I turned the knob, walked in and saw Mrs. Jimenez tied to my crappy chair, duct tape over her mouth.

Then I saw nothing more because a fist connected with my face so hard, it knocked me right to the floor.

Or at least I assumed it did.

I didn't know.

Because before I hit the floor, I was knocked right out.

4

VENOM

They slowed the car, but didn't stop, when he reached across me, threw open the door and shoved me out.

I hit the pavement on a roll and the pain made me miss just having a hangover.

I stopped rolling when I hit the curb, and I settled, breathing heavy, waiting, automatically categorizing what hurt the most.

Right now, it was my hip, which was what hit the pavement.

And my hip hurt *bad*.

I heard running feet. Fast, heavy footfalls. Whoever was running was wearing something like boots.

I opened my eyes and pushed up on a hand.

I might need to flee. I didn't know how I'd do that. I'd lost both shoes and there were a variety of places on my body that were burning and there were a variety of other places on my body that were stinging.

But if I had to run, I would.

I shoved up farther to sitting and saw jeans-clad legs in front of me, feet in black motorcycle boots. I looked up to see Driver, the young biker bartender, standing over me.

"Jesus, shit," he muttered, his eyes locked to my face.

I could just imagine what it looked like.

That said, I didn't *want* to imagine what it looked like.

But I could.

He crouched down beside me at the same time he pulled a phone out of his back pocket.

I scooted away from him.

"You're okay, darlin'," he muttered as he scooted in his hunker right along with me.

I looked up to the apartments, whispering, "My neighbor, Mrs. Jimenez."

"She's good," he said, and I saw he had the phone to his ear. When he spoke next, he spoke into it. "Buck, Driver. She's home, brother, but beat to shit. You want me to take her to Lefty?" He paused as my heart skidded on the word "Buck" and then he went on, "Right. I'm on it."

He touched his phone and shoved it back in his pocket.

"You think you could hold on to me on the back of my bike?"

"Mrs. Jimenez," I repeated.

"We found her in your apartment, babe. She told us what went down. Buck called her boy who came to get her. They tied her up but didn't hurt her. She's shaken up, but like I said, she's good. Now, do you think you can hold on to me on the back of my bike?"

I closed my eyes.

Mrs. Jimenez.

On this thought, visions of her tied to a chair with duct tape on her mouth flooded my head so I opened my eyes again.

"I need to go get cleaned up," I told him, trying to push up to my feet. His hands went to my armpits and he straightened, hauling me carefully up with him.

Fire shot through my ribcage and I winced.

"Fuck," he muttered, releasing my armpits, but both his hands slid lightly to my waist.

"I need to go get cleaned up," I repeated.

"Girl, you need to see a doctor."

I shook my head, and that hurt too, so I stopped doing it.

"I don't have any insurance."

"That's okay, Aces does."

I blinked up at him.

That hurt too.

"Aces does?" I asked.

"Babe," he said impatiently. "Can you hold on to me on the back of my bike?"

"I—"

"You can," he decided for me, grabbed my hand and pulled me to his bike.

That hurt too.

———————

THE DOOR to the exam room opened and Driver walked in.

I focused on him.

"Lefty" I found was actually Dr. Lefkowitz and he wasn't a lefty.

Dr. Lefkowitz wore a lab coat, he had a stethoscope and gentle hands, but he also had long, thick, curly hair pulled back in a ponytail, a beard which needed a trim, and I saw a hint of a tattoo on his neck.

So, I decided, Dr. Lefkowitz was either a member of the Club or a supporter.

He'd also examined me, gave me an ice pack for my face, cleaned me up, X-rayed my head and chest and gave me some pain pills.

Now, I was semi-reclining on an exam table wearing a hospital gown and covered with a thin blanket, and my torn, bloody clothes had disappeared since coming back from the X-ray area.

"Can I have my clothes back?" I asked Driver as he walked to me.

"How're you feelin'?" Driver asked back as a reply.

"Like I'd like my clothes."

Driver smiled then stated, "Let's see what Lefty has to say. He's lookin' at your pictures now."

I turned my head away.

As I did, I thought for perhaps the seven thousandth time that I needed to call Tia, as in *really* needed to call her.

Because I obviously wasn't going to make our rendezvous and I wasn't going to do it because her husband just beat the heck out of me and was so angry that I'd spent the night with West "Buck" Hardy at the

Aces High Dive (this, apparently, how everyone referred to their club-house), it could be described as being on a rampage.

And Tia needed to know when Enrique Esposito was on a rampage.

I looked back at Driver and asked, "Can I use your phone?"

He started to answer when the door opened.

His eyes went to it and so did mine.

At what I saw, I pulled in a deep breath that, incidentally, hurt.

Buck stood there wearing a tight, black T-shirt, faded blue jeans and black motorcycle boots.

He was also wearing a scowl.

Lastly, I realized that his ex-wife Kristy had it right.

Yesterday, I did not meet a man who I thought could strike in anger.

But the man standing in the doorway staring at me now definitely could. *Hard.*

To the point he shouldn't be called Buck.

He should be called Striker.

He walked to me while I watched, and braced (which also kind of hurt), and Dr. Lefkowitz followed him.

"West, I—"

"Quiet," he whispered in a way that I closed my mouth.

Oh dear.

Yes.

I totally saw it.

Restrained.

Coiled to strike.

Restrained or not, his fury still held immense heat to the point I figured his fangs didn't shoot poison.

They shot fire.

"The good news, Ms. Delaney, is that, miraculously, you've got no fractures," Dr. Lefkowitz spoke.

Since I was Ms. Delaney, I tore my eyes from Buck to look at Dr. Lefkowitz who'd come to stand where Driver was on the opposite side of the exam table. I also saw that Driver had stepped back.

"Ribs are just bruised, no breaks and no facial fractures," he carried on. "The bad news is that you're gonna hurt like a mother for a while, and that swelling in your face means no beauty pageants in your near future."

He smiled down at me in a kind albeit badass way.

I didn't return his smile, but I did say, "Thanks."

"Those pills kickin' in?" he asked.

I nodded.

They were. The pain was dulling, and I was beginning to feel drowsy.

The pain dulling was very good.

Feeling drowsy when my situation was uncertain with a clearly furious Buck on my hands and the fact that I needed to talk to Tia was very bad.

"I have to call my friend," I told him.

"You gotta get to a bed," Dr. Lefkowitz told me. "Rest as much as you can and go gentle with yourself. In a coupla days, you'll feel better. In a week, you'll be near as good as new." He looked across me to Buck. "I'll give you some pills. She needs 'em, she can take 'em for two, most, three days. Then move her to aspirin, Tylenol or ibuprofen."

"Right," Buck replied, and I looked to him to see he was leaning toward me.

"I need to call Tia," I told him as one of his arms went under my knees and his other slid around my waist.

"Later," he replied, lifting me.

I flinched, the pain dull but not gone, and then I fought the flinch when I saw him staring down at me, his face so hard it looked carved from granite.

"No, Buck, really, I need to call her," I braved saying.

"Later," he repeated, turned, but glanced over his shoulder at Dr. Lefkowitz and stated, "On our tab."

He said this while walking, and when I looked where we were going, I saw Driver had the door open.

I turned at Buck as he carried me through.

"You don't understand." I said urgently, "We were—"

"Clara, shut your trap."

"But Tia is—"

"Babe," he bit off, looking down at me and still walking but not to the waiting area, toward a back door. "God's honest truth, I'm hangin' on by a thread here."

This confused me so I asked, "Sorry?"

He bent a bit to use one of his hands to push the bar on the door and it opened. Blazing Phoenix heat hit us, and he walked through.

"I'm pissed, Toots," he explained, looked down at me. Still walking, he clarified, "At you."

The drowsy was getting drowsier but still my eyebrows shot up.

"At me?"

"You're not hearing my warnings and I'm speakin' English," he muttered.

"Why are you pissed at me?"

We stopped.

He dropped my legs carefully so my toes just skimmed the ground and the blanket fell away, the rest of me held close to him. His hand went into his pocket. I heard the sound of locks beeping on a car then he moved to open a door. Once opened, he lifted me and sat me in the seat of a very big, shiny black SUV.

Pain definitely dulled. Drowsy definitely drowsier. That barely hurt at all.

I turned my head when the blanket was thrown over my lap to see he was planted in the open door close to me.

Very close to me.

In fact, the second I turned my head, my face was an inch from his.

And he still looked ready to spit fire.

"Because," he answered, "I told you, you walk out of the Dive without my protection, bad shit would happen. And you slid outta my bed, left me a *stupid* fuckin' note and walked out of the Dive without protection. And, babe, you're sittin' here with a swollen eye, a busted lip and bruised ribs, so I don't have to tell you, in less than one fuckin' hour, bad shit happened."

I stared up at him, stung.

My note wasn't stupid.

I thought it was nice.

"I thought my note was nice," I whispered.

"Do not be cute now, Clara," he warned in a low, angry voice that was definitely tinged with heat.

And venom.

I didn't think I was being cute, so I didn't know how to stop.

Thus, I decided just not to speak.

His eyes dropped to my mouth and he muttered, "Smart," then stepped back and slammed the door.

Gingerly, since I was in no shape to make a break for it, I buckled in as he rounded the hood and got in beside me. He switched on the ignition, put the SUV in gear, hooked his arm around the back of my seat and twisted to look behind us as he backed out.

I fought the lethargy at the same time I screwed up my courage to murmur, "I know you're angry at me, but seriously, I need to call Tia. I also need to talk to Mrs. Jimenez and see if she's all right. And," I finished, "we left my clothes behind."

The SUV moved forward, and he replied, "Your neighbor is fine, I'll see to your girl and you can kiss those clothes good-bye."

Oh dear.

"Now, do yourself a favor, babe, and shut your trap," he concluded.

I didn't want to shut my trap.

I wanted, at least, to talk to Tia.

And I would have explained why.

The problem was, the minute the SUV hit the road and found cruising speed, my eyes drifted closed.

I then found I didn't have the strength to open them, and about a second later I was unconscious.

5

CRACKERS

I woke up in a big bed.

The sun was still shining, and this shine came from behind the bed.

And the pain pills had definitely worn off.

I gingerly lifted up on a hand and looked around.

Big bed, two nightstands, mismatched lamps, but both were pretty cool.

A dresser across the room, low, seven drawers. Picture frames on the dresser, a lot of them.

Two big windows behind the bed, the shades pulled up, and they were Roman shades and looked custom made.

A club chair in the corner by the dresser, leather the color of a penny, matching ottoman in front, both pieces of furniture covered in castoff clothes. A side table next to it that had two coffee cups and a spent beer bottle on it as well as some books. A standing lamp beside the chair, also pretty cool.

The headboard of the bed was covered in a plaid that had grays, blues, creams with some rust, the edges tacked with exposed nailheads.

A riot of clothes, belts and boots on the floor.

And tangled with them was a hospital gown.

I looked down at myself to see I was wearing a big, faded black T-shirt.

I guessed I was at Buck's place.

There was an opened door to a closet on the wall by a door to what looked like a hall, and on the opposite wall there were double doors, both now open, leading into a bathroom.

Which was where I needed to go.

Treating my body gently, I threw the covers back and slowly swung my legs over the side of the bed.

My face felt tight, my ribs ached, and my hip was killing me.

Therefore, I got out of the bed like a granny and took my time as I wended my way through the clothes on the floor to the bathroom.

I closed both doors behind me, turned, and was pleased to see it was far cleaner than the one at the Dive. Even the towels looked clean-ish. If not freshly laundered, they didn't look like lab experiments.

I went to the toilet, and lifting the shirt in preparation for my next activity, caught sight of my hip and stopped dead.

Already angry purple and maroon bruising covered my hip and upper thigh, dark scrapes scoring through it.

I moved to the mirror over the vanity and looked at my face.

I then closed my eyes.

But I could see what I saw in the mirror on the backs of my eyelids.

Swollen eye, swollen cheekbone, cut lip.

Not nice.

It started coming back to me and I opened my eyes to shut it out.

I couldn't relive it. I couldn't go back there. I needed to use the bathroom and then get to a phone.

So I focused on that, did my thing, washed my hands, walked out of the bathroom and through the bedroom, and I did this holding myself delicately.

The pain was constant, and I felt lightheaded.

I needed food.

But I needed to phone Tia first.

I walked through the door and was assaulted by sunlight. Big, wide windows which showed a stunning, if surprising, view of pine trees, a slope covered in pine needles, at the bottom of which was a meandering creek.

Amazing.

But...this was not Phoenix.

Where the heck was I?

I also noticed there was a big square deck jutting from the front of the house.

I further noticed I was standing on a landing that was four steps up from a large living space that was partially hidden due to the two side rooms of the landing jutting out to it, but I could see it included a living area and a kitchen.

The landing had several doors leading off it.

Buck's room was at the end beyond the wall to the kitchen.

The landing also had a set of open-backed stairs up to what looked like an attic space.

I saw the steps down to the open space and headed that way.

When I hit the bottom, the full big kitchen came into view to my right, living room to the left.

Ink was sitting on the couch, but his gaze was aimed at me.

There was a woman sitting at a stool at the counter that delineated the kitchen from the living room.

She wore a thin, tight, gray thermal, a jeans miniskirt and biker boots, and had long, gleaming, dark brown hair.

Her head was bent as she texted on her phone but suddenly her neck twisted to look at me, and I saw she also had on a lot of jewelry, a lot of makeup, and she was very pretty.

Maybe I wasn't at Buck's.

Maybe he'd dropped me off at Ink's.

"Hi," I said softly.

The girl swiveled around on her stool and dropped the phone to the counter, but my attention swiftly shifted to Ink.

This was because he got up and came at me, his long legs eating the distance. He was there so quickly, not to mention he had a face like thunder, I was taken aback enough at all that was him coming at me that I did not retreat or even move.

I tipped my head back and bit my lip (but stopped doing that immediately when the pain spiked through the cut there) when his big hand came up to cup my jaw lightly.

"Jesus, babe," he whispered, his eyes on the left side of my face, "they did a fuckin' number on you."

If you told me Ink's touch could be light, I would have called you a liar.

If you told me Ink's expression could be kind, I would have called you a liar about that too, and maybe even burst out laughing.

But both were true.

I felt tears sting my eyes.

"Don't be nice to me," I whispered back.

"Babe," he murmured.

"Hi, Clara, I'm Lorie," the girl said, thankfully breaking the moment. Ink's hand dropped and I looked to see her standing by him. "Buck said, if you wake up, we need to get some food in your belly. Do you want some soup?"

Wow.

Bikers and their women could be nice.

Really nice.

Who knew?

Well, I guessed I did, since, except for my chilly initial reception, that was all I'd experienced from them.

"I need to use the phone," I told her.

"I'll get it for you, but maybe you should sit down," she replied.

"Thanks," I whispered.

She moved into the kitchen and I moved to a stool.

Ink moved too, to the fridge, saying, "Buck's got loads of grub, Clary, you can name what you want. So what do you want?"

Clary?

No one had ever called me Clary.

Why did I find the sound of that so lovely?

"Um..." I mumbled as Lorie came to me with the phone. "That offer of soup sounded good."

"Get her some soup, beautiful," Ink ordered gently, closing the fridge.

"No probs," Lorie answered, handing me the phone. She then went to a cupboard, opened both doors, and recited, "You want chicken noodle, tomato or mushroom?"

"Mushroom," I answered.

"Drink?" she asked. "Buck's got Coke and water and pretty much anything with an alcohol content."

"Water, if you don't mind," I told her.

"You got it," she stated, whirling around so fast her shiny hair spun over her shoulder.

I looked down at the phone.

I punched in numbers, put it to my ear and listened to it ring while Ink got me a glass of water.

"Thanks," I said quietly when he set it on the counter in front of me.

"Whatever you need, babe," he muttered then reached across and slid the hair off my neck before turning back to the kitchen.

Yes, definitely nice.

And affectionate.

Bikers were touchy.

And sweet.

Tia's voicemail picked up and I closed my eyes.

Hells bells.

I waited for the beep and said, "Tia, honey, I..." I didn't know what to say, "I...well, Esposito got to me. Baby, I need to know you're okay. I'll call you back as soon as I can, and if this number comes up on your phone, pick it up." I pulled in breath and whispered, "Love you."

I beeped the phone off.

I beeped it back on and called Mrs. Jimenez, leaving somewhat the same message when her answering machine picked up.

I beeped it off again, put the phone on the counter, picked up my water and sipped at it knowing Mrs. Jimenez was probably freaked out and with her son Raymundo.

Tia not picking up...well, that was a bad sign.

I looked and saw Ink was at the counter spreading butter on saltine crackers. Lorie was at the stove dumping condensed mushroom soup into a saucepan.

"Is this your place?" I asked.

"No," Lorie answered, smiling at me over her shoulder. "I wish. It's Buck's."

I nodded then asked, "Um...where *is* Buck?"

Not that I wanted him to be there. He was pretty angry with me as I recalled. Him not being there was probably good.

"He's seein' to business," Ink stated, turning and moving to me to set a plate of buttered crackers in front of me.

I took one and nipped at it. It tasted awesome so I shoved it into my mouth.

Then, with mouth full, I looked up at Ink and said, "Thanks," while reaching for another cracker.

"Don't mention it," he replied while grinning at me.

"Can I ask...uh, what business Buck's seeing to?" I queried.

Lorie looked at Ink. Ink looked at Lorie. And then Lorie went back to the saucepan and Ink turned his attention to me.

"Clary, you woke up in his bed at the Dive," he told me like that was an answer to my question.

"Um...yes?" I replied as a question, since I didn't have an answer.

"In the morning," he stated.

I'd shoved another cracker into my mouth, so I chewed, swallowed and then prompted on a repeated, "Yes?"

"Baby, she doesn't get it. Look at her," Lorie said softly from the stove, pouring the milk she'd put in the empty soup can into the saucepan.

"Look at me?" I asked.

"It's not like you've been to a lot of cookouts at the Dive," she said on a smile pointed my way.

This was true. In fact, I'd been to none.

Thus, I was still confused.

"Sorry?"

"This is the deal," Ink cut in, having brought the sleeve of crackers and the tub of butter to the counter where I was. He started to slather more butter on crackers as I kept eating my way through them. "You woke up in Buck's bed, in the morning. Women don't do that."

This was surprising considering Ink himself indicated to me that Buck had a goodly number of women.

"They don't?"

"No, they don't," Ink stated.

"Um...okay," I muttered, now sounding as confused as I was.

Lorie approached the counter and looked at me. "Hon, he's a man and he likes to have fun, but once he's done havin' fun, his girls go. They don't spend the night. He doesn't wake up with them. And none of 'em ever made her way up here."

Oh.

Wow.

"Really?" I whispered, and Lorie smiled big and happy at me.

"Really," she replied and walked back to the soup.

"But," I started, "have any of them been beat up by a sociopathic drug kingpin?"

"Nope," Ink answered, dropping a cracker onto the plate, which I immediately snatched up. "But some a' them have been worked over. He might take his time to clean 'em up, but he never sent them to Lefty."

"Or brought them here," Lorie reiterated from the stove, stirring but facing me. "We figure this means you're his old lady."

"Moves fast," Ink muttered.

"His old lady?" I asked.

"His woman, babe," Ink answered. "That's why your ass is here. That's why he tore outta his room this mornin' pissed as all hell. That's why he made the callout to the boys and we rode to your apartment only to find that old woman tied up in it, which made him lose his fuckin' mind. And that's why he's out right now, takin' care of business."

Buck tore out of his bedroom pissed as hell, and when he found Mrs. Jimenez, this meaning he'd come after me, he lost his mind?

"He lost his mind?" I asked.

"You don't wanna know," Ink muttered.

"I kinda do," I told him.

His blue eyes locked on mine. "Babe, it was me who let you walk out of there this morning."

"Oh," I mumbled.

"Yeah," he agreed.

"Sorry, it seems I got you in trouble," I said.

"It's all right, darlin'," he replied quietly. "Buck wasn't really pissed at me. If he was, I'd probably look like you."

Oh my.

Moving on.

"And this business you were talking about, that would be?"

"Clary, someone took their fists to you," Ink said by way of an answer.

"But—"

"A woman wakes up in Buck's bed, she doesn't drive away from Aces and get beat to shit, hon," Lorie put in. "No way. No fuckin' way. That shit happens, a message needs to be sent."

Oh God.

"So he's sending a message to Esposito?" I whispered.

"Yeah, babe, and *that* message, he'll deliver himself," Ink told me, his voice rumbling in a scary way.

I didn't know what to make of this.

Any of it.

Then I thought of Esposito and blurted, "Will Buck get hurt?"

Ink grinned again and this one was different.

A lot different.

"Don't you worry 'bout, Buck, Clary," he stated firmly.

As firm as he stated that, I knew Esposito pretty well.

Therefore, I suggested, "Perhaps we should call him."

Lorie giggled, and Ink grinned again, back to good old boy biker.

He took a cracker, popped it into his mouth and replied around it, "Thinkin' he should stay focused, babe."

I watched him chew, thinking maybe he was right.

6

I GOT YOUR BACK

I woke up to voices.

"...she doin'?"

This was Buck talking quietly.

"Had some crackers, soup, called her girl about five dozen times. We could tell she wasn't feelin' good, so Lorie got her some pills and we got her to lie down in front of the TV. She was out in half an hour."

This was Ink, also talking quietly.

"She's cute, Buck. And sweet."

This was Lorie being nice, as I'd learned Lorie was.

I turned under the blanket Lorie had thrown over me on the couch and pushed up. Putting my forearm on the backrest, setting my chin on my arm, I saw they were all standing by the front door. And they all had their eyes on me.

I also saw that Buck looked to be in one piece, no visible marks, no blood, no bullet holes.

He further didn't look ready to release venom anymore.

And lastly, it was dark.

Night had fallen.

"Hi," I said softly.

"Hey, Clary," Ink replied.

"Hey there, hon," Lorie said.

Buck didn't respond to me, he turned to them and stated, "Thanks, later."

This obviously was a verbal hint to get out that both of them caught instantly. Lorie walked to her purse on the counter, Ink waited for her and I watched as Ink slapped Buck's upper shoulder stoutly and Lorie waved to me.

I waved back.

Then they were out the door.

Buck turned to me and I sat motionless as he walked up to the back of the couch and crouched so we were eye to eye.

"Hey," he said gently.

"Are you still mad at me?" I asked.

He didn't answer at first. His hand came up to cup my cheek and, feather-light, he slid his thumb along the swelling on my cheekbone then down to the cut on my lip where it came to rest.

His brown eyes watched his thumb's movements, then they came to mine.

"No," he finally answered.

Well, at least that was good.

"I'm starved, Toots. You feelin' up to keepin' me company in the kitchen while I make a sandwich, or you wanna lie here?"

Before I could control it, my mouth replied, "I'll keep you company in the kitchen."

I heard the roar of a Harley indicting Ink and Lorie were on their way home as Buck straightened and started to round the couch. I carefully rolled to the other side and threw the blanket off. But before I could swing my legs over the side, Buck had an arm around my waist and one under my knees. He lifted me and started toward the kitchen.

"I can walk," I informed him, sliding an arm around his shoulders.

"Tomorrow you'll need to move around so you don't get stiff. Tonight, you need to let your body rest."

His body had probably weathered more fists hitting it than mine, though I couldn't imagine anyone getting the better of him like they did me. Still, I figured he'd know, so I gave in.

He set me gently on my behind on the counter then he put a hand on either side of me and leaned in.

"You want a sandwich?" he asked.

"Sure," I answered.

He pulled away, which I didn't like all that much, considering I liked seeing his face that close, since it was a very handsome face.

He moved to the fridge, and I watched while saying, "Tia isn't answering her phone."

"That would be because it's in her bedroom," Buck replied, and my watching became staring as he turned from the fridge with bags of deli items and a jar of mayo.

"It's in her bedroom?"

"Yeah," Buck answered, dumping the stuff on the counter and reaching for a loaf of bread.

"You were in her bedroom?"

His hands—hands, incidentally, that had skin torn and angry-looking at his knuckles—worked the plastic wrap on the bread.

"You wanted her, we looked for her. But, babe..." He hesitated as he looked at me. "We didn't find her."

Oh no.

My heart clutched.

"Did you find Esposito?" I asked.

He nodded, looking down at the bread. "Oh yeah, found him."

Oh dear.

That explained the torn and angry-looking skin on his knuckles.

"What happened?"

"Thinkin' Esposito is not gonna fuck with you anymore, Toots," he muttered, lining up four slices of bread in a square.

This was good news that didn't hold a lot of detail for which I was grateful.

So I got to the important stuff. "And Tia?"

"Tia is in the wind," he replied, reaching to open a drawer and get a knife.

"In the wind?"

He looked at me. "Packed in a hurry, car's gone, found a tracking device thrown in a corner of the garage, 'spect it's from her car." He stared at me for two long seconds then finished cautiously, "She left you to him, Clara."

I closed my eyes and bit my lip, which hurt (again) so I stopped doing that, made a mental note not to do it again, then opened my eyes and whispered, "No. We made plans to make a break for it."

His brows drew together, and I kept talking.

"I'd talked her into it. We were supposed to meet at a 7 Eleven. I didn't show. She's probably out there somewhere and scared out of her mind."

"You were gonna make a break for it?" he asked.

"You said that was what we should do. I thought that was good advice. So that's what I decided to do, and I talked Tia into going with me. Now she's out there and—"

He put the knife down and moved to me, standing in front of me and leaning into his hands on the counter on either side of my hips again.

"Babe, I told you that was what you should have done, not what you should do. That was an option *before* you got tied up in Esposito's mess. It isn't an option *now*. Until I explained it otherwise, Esposito thought he owned you. He thinks that, you bolt, he goes to the end of the Earth to haul you right back."

"He thinks he owns Tia," I told him.

"No, his shit is centered on you."

"What?"

"Clara, honey, you're his toy. He plays with you. He gets off on it. She's nothin' to him. She was, but he played with her and broke her and now his interest has shifted. Unless she walks into a room and reminds him she exists, he forgets. He's got dozens of girls. He just made her into one of them. So now, sensin' your vulnerability, homin' in on it, usin' it and puttin' Clara Kirk out to work for him, *that* gets his rocks off."

I stared into his eyes as my heart slid up into my throat.

"My name is Clara Delaney," I whispered around the lump, though it wasn't, not really.

Delaney was my adoptive parents' name and I barely remembered them.

The fact was, I didn't know what my name was.

"Not to him," he whispered back.

I pressed my lips together (that didn't feel good either, but I kept doing it) and looked to the side.

He was right and Mrs. Jimenez was right. There was a lot of bad in the world and I attracted more than my fair share of it.

I felt Buck's presence leave me and I saw him go back to his bread. I watched him slather an alarming amount of mayonnaise on all four pieces before I spoke again.

"Maybe we should talk about Esposito," I suggested, even if I didn't want to.

"You're clear. That statement was made."

"And what about the Club?"

He glanced at me. "Come again?"

"You've made an enemy of Esposito today, Buck."

He went back to his sandwich making and did it talking.

"While I was sharin' how I felt about what he did to you, Chap was with the guys who pull Esposito's strings, sharing with them whose bed you were in last night. They understood the situation. Might be luck, since we hear word they haven't been happy with Esposito's games for a while. Might be they just get it. Probably both mixed with the fact these guys are guys who like focus, not dealin' with problems that shouldn't be problems in the first place. Esposito is a liability and proved that further today, seein' as you don't touch the woman of a biker, ever, and absolutely not like that."

Okay, well then, that seemed all good.

Though, "the woman of a biker" comment was perplexing.

I decided to sidestep that, because...

Priorities.

"I'm worried about Tia."

"I'll eat. I'll make a few calls, get the word out Aces High wants her. We'll find her."

This made me feel relief.

"Thanks," I murmured.

Buck turned his head and grinned at me.

No teeth, but still, his full lips framed by that beard tipped up was also pretty terrific.

Who was I kidding?

It was fabulous.

He then piled an alarming amount of shaved roast beef on the sandwiches.

"It's weird," I remarked while he was doing this, "that she didn't take her phone."

"You can track someone through their phone. She knew enough to find and dump the device on her car, she knew to leave her phone behind. Smart."

This was partly good, partly bad.

I didn't want Esposito to find her (once he, um...recovered), but that also meant we couldn't.

Further, it meant I couldn't communicate with her and she had no idea where I was.

I watched him put two slices of muenster cheese on the beef, then topped the cheese with the other slices of bread, pressed in, picked one up and handed it to me. Then he went back to the fridge, returning the mayo and deli products and coming back with a beer and a Coke. He popped the top of the Coke for me, twisted off the cap of the beer and flicked it into the garbage.

I stared at my humungous sandwich.

"This is a big sandwich, Buck," I noted.

"Yep," he agreed, downing a gulp of beer then putting it on the counter and picking up his own sandwich.

I stared at a big splodge of mayo coming out the side.

"With a lot of mayo," I went on.

He took a huge bite, his eyes on me. I watched as he chewed and swallowed.

Then he said, "Babe, like I told you, you gotta live more."

"I tried that," I reminded him quietly. "It didn't work very well for me."

His eyes grew dark and intense in an instant and it was fascinating as well as a bit scary.

"Don't do that, Toots," he said softly.

"What?"

"Twist yesterday to bad in your head. Don't do it."

"He knew I spent the night with you," I explained. "He heard about it. It made him angry. He said it was disrespect. He said..."

I stopped because the memories were coming back in a flood. Esposito's rage. His bad guy holding me while Esposito took that rage out on me physically.

And all this was a lot, so I couldn't go on speaking.

"You laughed last night," Buck broke into my thoughts. "You smiled. You opened up. You told me straight out you hadn't laughed in a long time, darlin'. What we had was good. What he did with it is whacked. That's on him. Don't let him twist that. You do that, he beats you a different way."

He was right.

He was right and I liked it that he thought what we had was good.

I liked that a lot.

So I turned to my sandwich and took a bite. It hurt to open my mouth that wide, but it couldn't be denied it tasted great.

As I was chewing, I looked back at Buck to see he was grinning down at the counter before he took his own bite.

He looked handsome grinning. He also looked handsome eating.

God, I was such a dork!

Time to put my mind to other things.

"Did you see my purse at my apartment?" I asked and his attention returned to me.

"Wasn't lookin' for your purse, babe, was lookin' for you."

"So you didn't see it?"

"No, why?"

"Because Mrs. Jimenez gave me her nest egg so Tia and I could go on the lam. I need to give it back to her."

He took a slug of beer and set it on the counter. "When the boys go get your shit tomorrow, I'll tell them to look for it."

After he said that, he took another huge bite of his sandwich.

But I was blinking at him.

And this blinking was repeated and rapid.

"When the boys go to get my shit?"

He swallowed and said, "Yeah," then took another big bite.

"Why are they getting my shit?"

He replied through a full mouth, "Bringin' it up here, Toots."

What? My brain screamed.

"What?" I whispered, but I'd lost his attention.

He'd turned his head and was scowling out of the plethora of windows that, by day, showed a magnificent landscape, and by night, showed moonlight-shrouded pine trees which was no less magnificent.

They also showed the headlights of a car coming up the lane.

"Fuck, what now?" he muttered, putting his sandwich on the counter and grabbing his beer. "Stay there," he ordered as he walked away while taking a pull on his beer.

I didn't have any choice but to stay there.

Sitting on the counter didn't feel great on my hip but nothing felt great on my hip.

The rest of me felt okay, muted pain in my ribs and face, but this was because I wasn't moving much.

I didn't want to face the consequences if I tried to jump down.

Buck exited the front door and closed it behind him.

I sat on the counter, ate my sandwich, sipped at my Coke and resisted the urge to get a plate to put his sandwich on.

I needed to live more and not worry about stupid stuff like sandwiches on counters. My life was such that I knew, in enumerable ways (of which that day I was reminded of a few), that a plate for a sandwich was not the least bit important.

I told myself this, but I still found it hard not to find a plate.

I was finished with my sandwich by the time Buck returned and I felt my belly get tight when I saw the man who walked in with him.

Detective Rayne Scott.

Darn.

What was he doing here?

I didn't really want to know.

I just wished he wasn't here.

I'd never forget him. Tall, dark-haired, interesting light-brown eyes, athletic build and incredibly good-looking.

He was also the detective who'd worked with the FBI locally in investigating and eventually arresting my ex-husband.

And me (without the arresting part).

I gazed at him remembering that I never wanted to see him again. Never.

He wasn't mean to me.

He was professional, all business, but not mean. Even the three times he was in the room with the men who interrogated me.

That said, although he was only doing what he was paid to do, he'd rocked my world so immensely, it came crumbling out from under my feet.

He had a job to do, I understood this logically, and I was just caught in the fallout.

It was Rogan who did the deed. I understood this logically too.

But that didn't change the fact that Detective Rayne Scott was a major player in the events that ruined my life and led me to the dire predicament I currently found myself in.

Now he was there, looking no less handsome, wearing a chambray shirt and jeans, and I was sitting on a counter in a faded black T-shirt with a busted lip, a swollen face, and I didn't even want to think of what my hair looked like.

Hells *bells*.

I continued to gaze at him, immobile.

He returned my look, something working behind those interesting brown eyes, something deep and meaningful and maybe even painful, before he clipped, "Jesus."

"You'll give us a minute," Buck stated.

This wasn't a request, it was statement, and it was clear he was displeased.

Rayne Scott didn't take his eyes off me as he nodded.

Buck came at me, put the beer bottle down by my hip then lifted me carefully off the counter to set me equally carefully on my feet. He took my hand and guided me out of the kitchen, up to the landing and into the bedroom. He flipped on the overhead light and closed the door.

Then he turned to me and dropped my hand but only so his hands could come to rest on my waist.

"That man is a cop," he told me.

"I know, he was one of the team that arrested Rogan," I told him.

This news did not make Buck happy. I knew this because his eyes flashed, and his mouth got tight as he studied me.

Then he went on, "No fuckin' clue how, but he heard about what Esposito did to you."

Fabulous.

I looked away.

"Toots, eyes to me," Buck ordered gently.

I looked back at him.

"He wants Esposito. He knows Esposito caught you in his net and he's here to convince you to press charges about what happened today. What he's not sayin' is he's also here to convince you to inform on Esposito and his crew."

Oh no.

I couldn't do this.

With all that had happened, neither Tia nor I had ever considered going to the police. We'd lived the kind of lives that you knew you never, but never, snitched.

Never.

"I'll never snitch," I whispered and saw Buck's eyes flash again, this time not with irritation but something else, something that looked an awful lot like approval.

"Then don't."

I felt my eyebrows go up. "You don't think I should talk to the police?"

He slid his hands at my waist around to the small of my back and pressed in so my body was almost touching his and my head had to go back farther so I could look up at him.

"Bikers, babe, we take care of our own business," he said quietly but firmly, and I felt a thrill race up my back at vague thoughts of whatever other "business" they might have. "You've had it shit and you've had it shit for a while, today worse than others. But you got another decision to make. You can walk out there and trust Scott or you can stand right here and tell me you trust me."

I didn't speak, and he pulled me closer so our bodies were brushing and his hand came up to thread into my hair as he dipped his head closer to mine.

"To help you with that, I'll tell you I got your back. And when I say I got your back, that means I got your back *and* all the boys in my MC got your back. You don't do us wrong, we will *never* do you wrong. Never, Toots."

I kept staring up at him as I thought of Ink teasing me that morning. Buck coming after me. Driver waiting for me and taking me to Lefty. Dr. Lefkowitz caring for me. Lorie making soup and throwing a blanket over me. Ink buttering crackers for me. And Buck sending a message to Esposito and looking for Tia and definitely looking out for me.

People wouldn't believe it of Rogan, considering what he did, but he took care of me.

If I was sick, he practically babied me. He often bought me flowers, just because. I'd come home from work and he'd be there, having come home early to make a special meal for me. He made me feel loved, he made me feel precious.

I'd had decent foster carers. It was what it was, and it wasn't great, but it wasn't a nightmare.

It also wasn't loving kindness, which Rogan showed to me, something I missed even though I hated him, what he'd done to the people he'd stolen from and what he'd done to me.

Tia and I looked out for each other as best we could, and Mrs. Jimenez did everything she could with the little she had.

But I'd never known the kind of protection and kindness Buck and his people had shown me in less than a day.

"I trust you," I whispered, his eyes flashed again, and his head dipped even further so he could brush his lips against mine.

He lifted away and whispered back, "Then let's take care of this shit so I can make some calls about your girl."

There it was again, and I couldn't help it. I closed my eyes and pressed carefully into him, the uninjured side of my face to his chest, my arms going around him to give him a hug. He gave me a gentle squeeze and stepped back.

"Do you have any sweats I can borrow?" I asked when he took my hand and headed to the door.

He turned and looked down at me, "This is your place, Toots, your space. He doesn't get to make you feel uncomfortable in it."

I was reeling from this pronouncement. So much, I didn't resist when he tugged me to and through the door.

We made it to the bottom of the steps to the landing and Buck dropped my hand but slid his arm around my shoulders and carefully turned me so my front was pressed into his side.

Scott watched this and I could tell he didn't like it before he wiped his expression blank and focused on me.

"Mrs. Kirk—" he started.

"Delaney," Buck growled, and Scott's eyes sliced to him. "She divorced his ass. Her name is Delaney," Buck continued.

Scott stared at Buck a beat then his attention came back to me.

"Sorry. Ms. Delaney," he murmured. "We need to talk about what happened to you today."

"No," I said softly, "I don't think we do."

I saw his jaw clench and he took a step forward. Buck curled me closer and Scott's eyes went to Buck's arm, his jaw clenched tighter and he stopped.

Then he looked back at me.

"I'm thinkin' you know Enrique Esposito is not a good guy," Scott noted.

"Yes, I know that," I stated the obvious.

"So, I'm here to tell you that what happened to you happens to others, sometimes it's worse. I think you know that too," Scott continued.

I knew that too.

Boy, did I know that.

I didn't answer.

I just held his gaze.

He carried on.

"That means, what happened to you, what you and your friend Tia Esposito know, what your friend's husband has done to her, you can help us make certain that what the both of you have been through won't happen to anyone else."

"You know she grew up in foster care," Buck remarked suddenly, and I felt my body go still as I looked up at his profile.

Why did he say that?

"I know," Scott replied, his voice tight and my eyes went to him.

"Figure you investigated her just as deep as you investigated her ex," Buck carried on, and Scott didn't speak, but he also didn't take his eyes from Buck. "You think of offerin' her this kinda deal two years ago before you turned her life to shit?"

Oh God.

I hadn't thought of that.

"That wasn't a possibility," Scott ground out.

"Yeah?" Buck asked. "Why? You investigated her. You knew she wasn't involved in his mess. You knew you took him down, she'd also pay. You think, maybe you explained that shit to her, she woulda helped you out and that woulda helped *her* out instead of gettin' her face on the front of every newspaper in the country as the dupe?"

Scott looked at me when he answered.

"You know we were surveilling you. You and Kirk were tight. We didn't know the extent of your knowledge. We couldn't approach you in case you knew what he was doing and disregarded it, or you could have told him we were onto him. It was discussed, but in the end, what he was doing had to be stopped and we couldn't endanger that by showing our hand to you."

"Just so you know," I said quietly, holding his eyes, "I wouldn't have helped you."

Scott's lips thinned.

I kept talking.

"But I would have left him. If you told me what he was doing, just knowing he was stealing from those people, I would have left him. It wasn't about him cheating on me. That just made it worse. But I would have left him, and if you'd told me, it would have saved me from what happened after. And I would never have told him about you."

"We couldn't know that," he replied, just as quietly.

"Now you do," Buck put in.

Scott didn't tear his focus from me when he said, "You got a chance to turn that around. To do good for people. To change your reputation. And you're sayin' you're not gonna take that chance?"

I felt Buck's body get tighter and tighter as Scott spoke, and when Scott was done, Buck growled, "You're fuckin' shittin' me."

"Man, she does," Scott clipped at him.

"Yes, you're right, I do." I butted in. "And I choose me. One thing I learned from all this is to keep my eyes open and put myself first."

Scott looked at me, clearly incredulous. "And you got your eyes open, hookin' your star to the Aces High MC?"

"No one else was there to pick me up and take me to the doctor when Esposito's boys tossed me, bleeding and beaten, from a moving vehicle," I replied.

I saw immediately that he took my point.

Then I said what I felt, for some reason, I had to say.

"I know you were just doing your job and I know your job is a good one, what you do is important. But you should know that I loved him. You may think it makes me a fool, but he treated me great. He acted like I was precious. When he was with me, I felt like I was the most important person in the world. And I'd never felt that before. If you investigated me, you know why. So maybe I was blind and maybe that made me stupid, but when someone loves you like that, why on earth would you question it?"

He closed his eyes.

But I kept speaking, so he opened them again and focused on me.

"He had to pay for what he did to those people, but what I want to know is, why did I have to pay such a harsh punishment when I didn't do a darn thing wrong? It's not your job to look out for people like me, but that doesn't change the fact that you left me to the wolves. You exposed him, which meant you turned me out, and they chewed me up. And you all knew, you *knew* what that was doing to me, and not one of you made even the remotest effort."

I'd been talking a lot, and I stopped to take in a breath.

Scott didn't fill the silence.

So I did.

"There are a lot of different kinds of victims to crime and I was one of them. You serve and protect, but no one was there to protect *me*. Now you want me to do something for you that puts me out there *again*. But you have not shown even an ounce of compassion for me. So yes, I'm hooking my star to the Aces High MC because, quite frankly, from experience, Detective Scott, I don't trust you to look out for me."

"Clara, if you had—" he started.

"What?" I cut him off. "Asked?"

"Yes," he gritted out.

"Did Nora Finnegan ask you for the escort to the courthouse? I remember, Detective Scott, struggling through the reporters closing in and shouting questions at me. I remember seeing you personally pushing your way through them, helping her get inside. She got *paid* to sleep with my husband. She also got *paid* to give all those interviews and write that book afterward. Did she ask for your protection? Is that why she got it?"

Scott didn't answer.

"I didn't think so," I whispered.

"We arrived at the same time," he told me.

"Obviously, so did I," I returned.

He stared into my eyes then he said quietly, "I lost sleep over you."

"I did too."

"I'm still losin' sleep over you," he went on.

"I am too."

His eyes didn't leave mine, but he leaned forward a bit when he stated, "You don't get me, Clara, you are not makin' the right choices."

Buck's tight body got tighter.

I spoke.

"Another thing I've learned, Detective Scott, is that if I make a mistake, I'll pay for it. I've also learned, even if I don't or I'm not the one who made the mistake, there's a good chance I'll pay for that too."

Scott flinched.

"I think we're done," Buck put in.

Scott leaned back, his attention cutting to Buck.

"You had a busy afternoon," he noted, clearly not agreeing with Buck that we were done.

"Yeah," Buck agreed.

"You know who pulls Esposito's strings," Scott continued, and that was when *my* body got tight and it didn't feel all that good.

Was Buck wrong that there would be no blowback?

"I know," Buck stated.

"Then you know that not only you, but now Clara is on his radar."

"I'm thinkin', Scott, that Clara made clear where she stands on this so maybe you can let me worry about that," Buck clipped.

Wait.

There was something to worry about?

Scott looked at me then back at Buck. "Look at her, Hardy, she doesn't know it all. How can she be clear where she stands if she doesn't know it all?"

"*You* look at her, Scott, she's had a bad fuckin' day," Buck returned. "And another thing, you showin' here after doin' what you did, knowin' what her day brought, knowin' what seein' your ass again would make her feel, that takes balls, brother. And not the good kind."

They glowered at each other with such intensity, I could feel the heat from their glares.

Luckily, Scott broke the angry-hot-guy scowling contest and moved to the door.

He stopped with his hand on the handle, turned and his eyes hit me.

"Cops don't fraternize with people involved in investigations, not during. It's not frowned on, it's somethin' that could lose me my badge. But I could have helped you after. I could have helped you get through those reporters. I didn't because if I did, I knew I'd want to help you more for reasons that go beyond protecting and serving. I didn't need that shit, but more importantly, you didn't need it either. So I kept my distance. Nora Finnegan is a piece of trash whore, she latched on to me. What you saw was not what you think."

I stared at him in shock and Buck's body coiled so tight, if it exploded, it wouldn't surprise me.

But the detective wasn't done.

"I lost sleep because I know precisely what I did to you, Clara, and still lose it because I've kept my eye on you and I know that I'm responsible for where you are and how you look right now. And I'm here because I finally have an excuse to do something about it." He paused then concluded, "You change your mind, I'll always be here."

With that, he opened the door and walked out of it.

Buck gave my shoulders a squeeze and went back to his sandwich and beer.

I stayed at the counter and stared at the door until I saw Detective Scott's car start down the lane.

Then I turned my head to Buck. "What was that?"

Buck swallowed a bite of sandwich and chased it with a tug on his beer.

He slid his eyes to me and replied, "Wants a piece of your ass, babe."

I walked to stand in front of him saying, "I'm not talking about that. I'm blocking that out. That didn't happen. I'm talking about the someone who's pulling Esposito's strings and how I don't know the whole story."

Buck transferred his sandwich from one hand to the other so he could put his hand to my waist, slide it around to my back and pull me closer.

"Scott knows about Esposito. But he clearly doesn't know Chap took care a' things."

Oh.

Right.

Onward.

"Is that the whole story?" I queried.

"Later," he said.

And I could take from that it wasn't the whole story.

"Later? When later?" I asked.

"Later," he repeated then shoved the last of his sandwich in his mouth.

"Is Tia in more danger? Am I? Are *you*?"

He pulled me closer, finished chewing, swallowed and bent his neck so his face was in mine.

"Baby, in my bedroom, you made a decision. Now you gotta trust me. You've had enough for today. But I'm tellin' you, I got your back, and soon's I find your girl, I got hers. So, let it go for now, and when I think you're ready, I'll tell you, but that's gonna be *later*."

I stared in his rich brown eyes that were so very close to mine. The brown was deep, intense. His lashes were thick and spiky.

His eyes really were beautiful.

"Okay," I whispered.

I watched those eyes smile. Then I felt his lips touch mine.

He pulled away and asked, "You doin' okay? You need pills?"

I shook my head.

He nodded, grabbed his beer, then let me go but took my hand.

He led me to the couch and put his beer on the coffee table, picked up a remote and arranged us so he was sitting, feet up on a coffee table, and I was lying on the couch, my cheek to his thigh.

He turned on the TV, the sound low, and handed me the remote.

I gazed blankly at the TV, switching programs randomly as I listened to him send out the call for Tia to someone named Gash. Then he talked to Breaker, who I figured was Breaker Walinski, the man Esposito had sent me to visit, and I figured this because it was unlikely there were a lot of men called Breaker.

After that, he talked to one other, and he called him Tucker.

Clearly finished with his rounds, he tossed his phone to the side table, grabbed his beer, took the remote from my hand, found a program and slid deeper into the couch.

We watched TV together for a while.

And doing it, I fell asleep.

7

IS THAT ENOUGH FOR YOU?

I felt the sun on my eyelids but didn't open my eyes.

I was on my back, the only position that was comfortable since my ribs were bruised, thus I couldn't sleep on my stomach, my right hip was scraped and battered, and the left side of my face was swollen and aching.

I felt something heavy on my belly and I knew it was Buck's arm. I could feel him close to my side and he was somehow managing to be close and hold me without causing pain.

Even when he was asleep.

This said a lot about him (especially the fact he could do this...even in sleep) and I hoped what it said was true.

I opened my eyes to see bright sunlight coming unhindered through the windows.

But without a view to the angle of the sun, I couldn't tell the time.

In August in Arizona, the sun shone bright from early to late.

It could be seven in the morning.

It could be noon.

I turned my head and saw Buck partially on his side, partially on his stomach next to me.

He looked good in his sleep, his face relaxed, those thick, dark eyelashes resting against his cheeks, his hair falling on his forehead.

He'd carried me to bed the night before, setting me in it gently.

I'd woken on the couch the minute his thigh slid out from under my cheek and stayed awake the twenty seconds it took for him to walk up to the landing and into the bedroom.

I was out when my head hit the pillow.

I hadn't slept this much in ages.

Usually I tossed and turned, wondering how I was going to manage to eat the next day, how I would escape the repo men, if Dallas would come around to give me grief.

Then my mind would move to remembering the night the police came knocking on the door or when I'd call a friend and the phone would ring and ring and I'd leave a voicemail that would never be returned.

I hadn't slept well in over a year.

Until last night where I slept the whole night through.

The night after the day I got beaten by a psychopath.

And that wasn't about the pain pills because I didn't take any before I went to bed.

It said something, and I was thinking about that something as my gaze moved over Buck's sleeping face and I felt an almost overwhelming urge to touch him.

But touching him might wake him and I needed a shower, *badly*. I hadn't had one in two days. I felt like walking, talking, breathing *ick*.

Carefully, for my body's sake and not to wake Buck, I slid out from under his arm.

I noticed with movement that I felt no better than yesterday, but also no worse.

I decided to treat this as good.

I picked my way through the clothes on Buck's floor to the dresser.

Top drawer, underwear and socks. I closed it quietly and opened the next drawer down and found his T-shirts, not folded but shoved in.

I grabbed a clean one off the top and headed to the bathroom, closing the door behind me.

I went to the medicine cabinet in hopes that he'd have an extra toothbrush.

He didn't.

He had a razor, shave cream, a beard trimmer, toothpaste, a comb and deodorant.

Even with this dearth of toiletries, his medicine cabinet was jammed full. The shelves taken up with gauze, bandages, medical tape, antibiotic cream and bottles of alcohol, hydrogen peroxide, ibuprofen, acetaminophen and aspirin.

If the contents of a medicine cabinet defined a person, Buck's said scary things.

Though I found no product for his hair.

That was interesting.

I closed the medicine cabinet, looked in the mirror and surveyed my injuries.

The swelling in my face had gone down.

This was good.

Unfortunately, that was all that was good.

The purple bruising around my eye had intensified. I lifted my T-shirt and saw the same amplification of color on my ribs and hip.

I dropped my T-shirt with a sigh.

Then I went about my business.

The water of the shower felt good—the stream strong and hot.

Again, if the toiletry stock of Buck's shower defined him, it would say he was not a man who wasted his life primping (more mystery behind why his hair always looked so good).

He had a bottle of drugstore shampoo and a bar of soap.

That was it.

The shower was a place to get clean, the end.

In fact, it was clear the bathroom only had utilitarian purposes on the whole and perhaps served as a mini-emergency medical ward.

Not that this was a surprise. Buck was definitely not the kind of man who took bubble baths.

Drugstore products were in my shower at my apartment too, except with the addition of conditioner.

But this lack of pamper paraphernalia was only due to necessity.

Back in the day, I had more bottles, tubes and tubs than a small but exclusive salon. My bathroom was not utilitarian. It was an oasis.

A soaking-tub, Swarovski-crystal-knobs-on-the-cabinetry, mirrored-trays-covered-in-masks-exfoliants-oils-and-lotions,   walk-in-closet-complete-with-massive-jewelry-island-leading-off-it oasis.

I was definitely the kind of person who wasted life primping.

Or I used to be.

Rogan teased me about it. Rogan used to say that I didn't need all that stuff. Rogan would tell me I looked beautiful, felt beautiful, smelled beautiful no matter what products I put in my hair, on my body and on my face.

And he said it like he meant it.

Then again, Rogan Kirk was a consummate liar.

There were a lot of things I missed about my old life, such as waking up and facing a day which consisted of making decisions on what to wear to work and what to make for dinner, not how to escape reporters or wonder if I'd get thrown into debtor's jail.

These things constantly nagged at me, but I pushed them down and focused on missing things like salon-quality shampoo and facial masks.

Since those weren't really important, I could handle that.

I shampooed and washed and then let the hot water run over me in an effort to work out the aches if not the pains. I got out, toweled off, and with difficulty, due to the tangles caused by no conditioner, pulled Buck's comb through my hair.

After I did that, using my hand to scoop water into my mouth, I downed two ibuprofens and two acetaminophens.

To end my toilette, I put on my undies and the clean T-shirt.

I needed clothes, specifically underwear, but really everything.

I had to talk to Buck about that and what he said last night about my stuff being brought here and this being my place, my space.

I ignored the fact that I liked this place, this space and that it was Buck's, who I also liked.

I further ignored the fact I liked to be somewhere that I wasn't imminently going to get tossed out of.

I didn't like Dallas Hill, but that didn't change the fact that I genuinely owed him money and was living on his dime.

Sure, his apartments were crappy, his rent was inflated, and he treated his tenants like nuisances, even though their rent allowed him to drive a brand-spanking-new Jaguar.

Still, I didn't like the guilt that not paying rent made me feel or the person that it made me be.

I ignored all that and thought about the fact that I didn't know what to make of what Buck had said or what it meant. Everything seemed to be going very fast. Too fast. Too much happening. Some of it dangerous, some of it scary for other reasons.

But I needed to prioritize.

And clean panties were always top priority.

Panties and making sure Tia was safe. Then making sure Mrs. Jimenez and her children didn't hate me after what knowing me had put her through the day before.

With these things heavy on my mind, I walked out of the bathroom being quiet so Buck could sleep, intending to go to the kitchen and make coffee.

I was two steps into the room when I heard Buck's deep, gruff voice calling my name.

"Clara."

His voice saying my name felt like a touch, a nice one that glided across every inch of my skin.

I stopped and turned my head to the bed.

He was on his back, sitting partially up, head and shoulders to the headboard. Covers around his waist, chest, muscles and tattoos on display, hair a sexy mess, eyes lazy, the Arizona sun shining into the room behind him.

He looked like an advertisement for the biker way of life.

Any man seeing him would want to be him.

Any woman seeing him would want to hook her star to the nearest MC if it meant she could be me, standing in his room, wearing his T-shirt after having taken a shower in his bathroom and spending the night in his bed.

And there I was, that woman.

My belly got warm.

"Morning," I said quietly.

"Come here, baby," he replied just as quietly.

I went there. I didn't hesitate and I didn't think. My feet just moved me to him, such was the power of his pull.

When I got close, he curled up slightly, grabbed my wrist and gently tugged so I was sitting on the bed by his hip. He released my wrist, settled back, and his fingers curled around the skin on my thigh, warm and strong.

"How you feelin'?" he asked.

"I've been better," I answered honestly.

His eyes moved over my face.

"Swelling's gone down," he observed, and I nodded. "Bruising's come up," he carried on, and I nodded again.

He curled to sitting, his hand moving to my belly and around to rest on my waist as his torso got close.

"We need to get you some breakfast and pills," he told me.

"I took a cocktail of ibuprofen and acetaminophen," I replied. "We'll see if that helps. Those pills knock me out."

"However you wanna play it, Toots," he muttered, his eyes dropping to my mouth.

I felt my belly warm again when they did, and it got warmer when he leaned in to brush his lips against mine.

I liked him doing that and how he did it, light, this rough man touching me gently, his beard tickling.

I liked it so much, my hand lifted to rest on his chest, and when it did, he brushed his mouth against mine again.

I slid my hand up his chest to curl around the base of his neck and he did another lip brush. My body leaned in closer and he did a lip touch, no brush this time, and I felt the tip of his tongue against my lips.

I liked *that* so much, my body leaned even closer, my lips parted, and my head tilted. His slanted the other way and then his tongue was in my mouth.

God, I'd forgotten how good he tasted. Even in the morning.

Amazing.

I slid my hand around and up, fingers in his hair. I wrapped my other arm around him, pressed my soft chest to his hard one and my tongue tangled with his as a low moan glided up my throat and into his mouth.

The minute it left my throat and moved down his, Buck's arms locked around me and pulled me closer as he took the kiss deeper. My arms tightened, the kiss deepened further, and his arms tightened too, powerfully as he growled.

I liked that growl, the taste of him, his arms around me.

I liked it so much the pain seemed to come from nowhere, not only in my ribs but also from the cut on my mouth.

I whimpered involuntarily, pulling a hint away.

"Fuck," I heard him mutter.

I opened my eyes as he loosened his arms, but he didn't let me go.

"Sorry," I whispered.

"Don't be, baby," he whispered back, the fingers of one of his hands stroking the small of my back over the T-shirt. "I didn't intend it to get heated."

He released me with his other arm so he could cup my jaw then his thumb glided along my lower lip.

I liked that too.

"You just taste good," he finished on a murmur, his gaze going back to my mouth.

It must be said, I liked that too, his thumb at my lip, what he said, the way he said it and his eyes on my mouth.

"Thanks," I said softly.

His gaze came back to mine, and when it did, his eyes were smiling.

His arm around me loosened more, his hand at my jaw moving back around me, and he pulled away a bit but didn't let me go. I left one arm around him but took my hand from his hair and trailed it down his chest.

My heart was still beating fast from his kiss, my breathing slightly escalated, and my belly still felt warm, so I took that moment in Buck's arms to recover before leaving him and making coffee. I was bruised and beaten, I didn't need to get up and topple over because my knees were weak.

Even so, I felt awkward, busted up and sitting on the side of his bed, barely knowing him and not only depending on him but also easily slipping into a make out session with him.

This wasn't me, none of it.

Not that I knew who me was. I just knew that wasn't it.

Or it didn't used to be.

I dropped my eyes to where my hand was on his chest and saw through my fingers the tattooed GEAR over his heart.

Without me telling it to do so, my forefinger traced the curved edge of the *G* in "Gear."

"Locke," I heard him mutter, and I stopped tracing and lifted my head again.

"Sorry?" I asked.

"My boy, Locke," he answered, and I blinked at him.

"Your boy?"

"Yeah, Toots, my boy," he replied, his gaze holding mine. "Gear is his nickname. Because he's a gearhead. From the time he could even minimally cogitate, he was takin' shit apart and tryin' to piece it together. Swear to fuck, I had Big Wheel parts and Tonka toy pieces all over my house for years. Even when he started to get it, and be able to put shit back together, I still had bits and parts, screws and spokes and anything you can think of all over, because the more he figured out, the more he wanted to learn."

"You have a son?" I asked, this surprising me.

I hadn't done an inventory of his home, but it seemed like a bachelor pad, a nice one, but a bachelor pad all the same.

"Yep, and a daughter," Buck answered.

Oh wow.

"A daughter?"

"Tatiana."

"Pretty name," I whispered, and he grinned.

"She's a pretty girl, which fuckin' sucks."

I blinked again. "It does?"

"Babe, a man does not want his daughter to be gorgeous. He wants her to be plain. Gorgeous attracts attention. Plain, not so much."

I smiled at him because he was being funny and sweet, and his attention dropped to my mouth again just as his fingers tensed on my back.

"They don't live with you," I remarked,

His eyes came back to mine, and they were no longer warm with sleep, necking and chatting while sitting in bed.

They were unhappy.

"They live in Flagstaff."

I felt my eyes get wide. "That's not very close."

"It sure the fuck isn't."

My belly got warm again at his tone.

He missed his kids. Not a little.

A lot.

This defined him too, in a good way.

"How old are they?" I asked quietly.

"Gear is seventeen, almost eighteen. Tatie just turned sixteen."

My wide eyes got wider. "Did you start early?"

"I was twenty-one when Locke was born."

Yes, early.

Though I was surprised.

Doing the mental math that made him thirty-eight (almost thirty-nine) years old.

He didn't look thirty-eight years old.

And he definitely didn't have sex like he was thirty-eight years old.

I'd have pegged him around thirty-two.

Thirty-three at most.

Though I'd never had sex with a thirty-eight-year-old man, so I wouldn't know.

But Rogan was thirty-six, and he didn't come close to Buck.

"Um..." I hesitated then braved, "Is Kristy their mom?"

"Unfortunately, yeah," he answered without hesitation.

"She isn't a good mom?"

"She's a bitch, babe," he replied and moved back, his arm coming from around me so he could indicate the scar on his lower, left abs with the other tattoo of NEVER AGAIN over it. "She gave me that."

I felt my body get tight at this news.

"Pardon?" I whispered.

"Bitch stuck me with a blade," he said.

My tight body froze, and Buck put his arm back around me but at my upper back. He did this at the same time he laid back against the pillows, carefully taking me with him so I was bent over, my chest resting lightly on his.

This wasn't painful, but it was uncomfortable, so I shifted my legs as he pulled me up over his body which meant I was lying full-body on him and not on my injured hip.

Now, *this* was comfortable.

Hmm.

Lovely.

When he got me in this position, I rested on my bent arms with hands flat on his chest and he carried on.

"Judge was fucked. Not a fan of bikers. Can't say I lived a clean life, have a rap sheet, nothin' big, nothin' like stickin' my wife with a blade. Still, the asshole gave my kids to her. She got 'em and took off. Like a shot, just to fuck with me. Went to Flagstaff. Fought that, lost it too. It took about a week before she got herself hooked to an asshole. She thinks his shit don't stink. My kids hate him, mainly because he's a dick. The minute Gear got his license, I gave him a car and they come down as often as they can to get away from that shit."

"That doesn't sound good," I noted.

"It isn't," Buck agreed.

I lifted a hand and rested it on his cheek. "I'm sorry, Buck."

His hand drifted up my back and into my wet hair. "Thanks, Toots, but it ain't as bad as it was before. I was supposed to have them every other weekend. She jacked me around, found ways to keep them from me. Sometimes I'd show and they'd be gone. I'd wait for hours, I'd search, no sign, no warning, no explanation. I'd drive two hours and come back without my kids. It was a pain in my ass and the kids suffered. They like bein' with their old man. Now, they can get in a car and come when they want. They're here nearly every weekend. They've been with me all summer, just went back for school, but they'll be back Friday night."

I found this both heartening and concerning.

I didn't want to meet his kids, not looking like I did, and Friday was only two days away, so I didn't figure I would look a lot better when they got to their dad's.

But I also didn't want to meet the children he obviously loved while living the life I was living. And I was getting the hint that he intended to be a part of that life which came with meeting his kids.

Still, I was glad he got to spend time with his children.

"That must be hard for them, being here every weekend when their friends at school are at home," I noted.

"Sometimes they bring their friends with them. Sometimes they miss a weekend because they're hangin' all weekend with their friends at their houses. One way or another, they escape home. Both of them are funny, make friends easy. They got as many friends here as they do at home." He gave me a gentle squeeze. "They're survivors, darlin'. Gear is nearly free, and he'll break for it. It won't be long before Tatie can too."

"Well, that's good," I mumbled.

He grinned up at me as he said, "Yeah."

Then, frighteningly, he kept talking.

"Gear'll like you, babe. My boy's been a flirt since he could focus his eyes. The prettier the target, the more effort he gives it, which means he'll put a fair amount of effort into it with you. Tatie'll be harder to win over. She's her dad's girl. She doesn't warm up quick to women around me."

Oh dear.

This did not sound good.

"Um...Buck, we should talk about that," I told him.

In response to this pronouncement, he twisted his hand around my hair and lifted his head to give me another lip brush.

Once he was done doing this, he curled up, taking me with him, moving me in his arms while he threw his legs over the side of the bed. He stood and put me on my feet.

When I was looking up at him, he stated, "Yeah, Toots, we got a lot to talk about. But we'll do it over coffee and breakfast."

Okay.

That sounded like a plan,

I nodded.

He grinned, lifted a hand to tug a lock of my damp hair and then he moved away, going toward the bathroom.

I stood still, watching him.

This was because he was naked, and my life might be uncertain and a little scary, but what wasn't uncertain was the fact that West "Buck" Hardy looked really, *really* good naked.

It was also because I saw that his back was tattooed too, from shoulder blade to shoulder blade, spanning his ribs and down his spine. It looked like an emblem and included snakes, flames, chains, motorcycle wheels and a poker hand.

And across his upper back, with flourishes (masculine ones, and those existed, trust me), in a kick-butt font, it said, simply, ACES HIGH.

I had never been cool, never in my whole life.

Growing up, I tried to be invisible and I'd always been thought of by my peers as a quiet, dorky, geeky brain, even as an adult.

But that didn't mean I didn't know cool.

And that tattoo on Buck's back was not cool, it was *super* cool.

It was the coolest thing I'd ever seen in my life, not just the tattoo but the smooth skin and muscled back it decorated.

That tattoo was so cool, and Buck's body was so hot, even in the state I was in, I felt it starting. My breasts swelled, my knees went weak and my feet really, *really* wanted to follow him to the bathroom.

I forced them to take me to the kitchen.

Ink had been right. Buck's cupboards were far from bare. I had the feeling this was partially because he liked his food. It was also probably because he loved his kids and any good parent kept the kitchen stocked.

This, too, defined him and it, too, said good things.

Therefore, I smiled to myself as I made coffee and found some frosted cinnamon Pop-Tarts, my favorite kind. A definite treat.

Thus, I was sitting at a stool in the kitchen facing a window with a cup of coffee and a plate of Pop-Tarts, nibbling and staring at the scenery, when Buck strode in wearing nothing but a pair of faded jeans, his hair wet from his shower, his cell at his ear.

That took no time at all.

Confirmation: West Hardy was not a man who primped.

His eyes came to me then dropped to my plate and the lines radiating from their sides deepened. I watched as he walked into the kitchen, and I twisted in my seat so my gaze could follow him.

He talked as he walked.

"You got a number?" he asked, pulling open a drawer and yanking a pad of paper out of it then going back to the drawer to dig around until he came out with a pen. He wrote something down and then said, "Right. Just go in, clear it all out. Yeah?" He paused then finished, "Later."

He disconnected, but was immediately clearly reengaging, his eyes on the paper, his thumb moving on the screen of his phone. When he put it to his ear, he moved to get himself a mug.

He was pouring coffee when he spoke again.

"This Dallas Hill?"

I felt my lips part at the same time I felt my eyes get wide.

Why was he talking to my landlord?

Buck shoved the coffeepot into the coffeemaker and kept talking.

"This is a friend of Clara Delaney. You padlock her apartment yesterday?"

Oh God.

I closed my eyes.

I opened them again when Buck went on talking.

"Right, asshole, that padlock is getting clipped in about five seconds, and seein' as we don't have her keys, we'll need to be creative gettin' into the apartment. Now, take this as friendly advice, as of today, you don't know Clara Delaney. She's no longer a tenant. Her stuff'll be gone in an hour and she ceases to exist for you in any way. That clear?"

I stared at him as he turned with his mug and walked to me.

He stopped across from me, listening at the same time leaning a hip against the counter and sipping at his mug, casual, calm, at ease while my heart was beating so hard I could feel it.

He put the mug down by mine, reached out, picked up one of my Pop-Tarts and was lifting it toward his mouth when he stopped lifting to speak again.

"You don't get me, Hill. I don't care how much she owes you. What you need to know is, she got herself some good friends. These friends had a look at you, and we know more than you want us to know. You don't want us usin' that information, you move on with your life and Clara doesn't hear from you again. Now, are we clear?"

That was when he took a huge bite of my Pop-Tart (*huge*), and even though what he was saying was freaking me out, I contemplated toasting another duo of tarts because it had been so long since I had one, and I liked them so much, I didn't want to miss out on a bite.

He chewed, swallowed and stated, "Man, that is not a threat. Test me and see."

On that, he disconnected the call, dropped his phone on the counter and took another huge bite of my tart.

There was a lot to talk about and a lot to say, but, as ever...priorities.

"Do you want me to toast you some Pop-Tarts?"

He looked down at me for a brief second before he threw his head back and laughed.

Golly, he had a great laugh.

I'd forgotten that too.

When he was chuckling, just like Ink (except better), he reached out and swept my quickly drying hair off my shoulder, his fingers curled around the side of my neck and his thumb pressed up on my jaw. He then leaned over the counter, bent in, touched his mouth to mine and moved back a couple of inches.

"I'm sensin' my girl likes her food," he muttered, his eyes, still smiling, looking into mine.

My lungs started burning and not because my ribs were bruised.

His girl?

Was I his girl?

When did that happen?

And why did his saying that feel like I felt the first time Ink called me "Clary," except loads better.

Loads.

He let me go, dropped the tart to my plate, moved to the cupboard and I watched mutely as he got out the box of Pop-Tarts and set another packet to toasting.

He came back and grabbed his tart (or the one he'd made his which was actually mine).

"Buck—" I started as he took a bite.

"This is the gig," he cut me off, his mouth full.

He swallowed and spoke again.

"I know your life has been shit and it bein' that way, normally, I'd take it slow with you. We don't have that luxury. Until I'm one hundred percent certain Esposito took my meaning yesterday, you need protection. I'm not farmin' that out, I'm doin' it myself. Which means you're here with me and you got me or one of my boys with you until I know you can breathe easy. When that happens, we'll talk about what's to come. Until then, you're in this house, and when you heal, you're on my bike and in the office at Ace. The girl who managed the office served only one purpose, eye candy for the boys. She said she knew what she was doin', but she took the job to land herself an old man. I fired her ass two weeks ago and I haven't found anyone to fill the position. I need someone takin' care of business. You want that job, it's yours. You don't, that's cool. You just hang and find some way to entertain yourself. Now, is that cool with you?"

In a perfect world, that would be cool with me.

Beyond cool.

Even dreamy.

I'd never lived in a perfect world.

"I..." I started, for some reason beginning to breathe heavily, "I don't want to offend you but..." My voice dropped to a whisper. "I don't know if it's cool."

He knew what I was saying.

"With that assclown ex of yours, you got taught a lesson, Toots," he said softly. "But don't let caution make you stupid."

"I—" I began.

"You're into me," he proclaimed, and my head ticked.

It couldn't be denied I was.

However.

I tried again, "I—"

"Don't deny it, babe. It's in your eyes. It's in your voice. It's in the way you touch me and it's definitely in the way you light up when I touch you."

Again, I couldn't deny that.

"But—" I started.

Buck interrupted me again. "I give you reason not to trust me?"

"No," I whispered.

"My boys?"

I didn't answer, just shook my head.

"I told you last night, you don't do us wrong, you don't do *me* wrong, you got nothin' to worry about." He bent so his face was closer to mine. "No promises. I don't know where we're goin', darlin'. What I do know is I want to find out. But if it doesn't work, the break'll be good." His gaze grew intense when he promised, "I'll see to that, baby. You have my word."

I had Rogan's word and I trusted Rogan. I trusted him with my love and with my happiness.

But Rogan had never beaten up anyone for me, putting himself out there.

And Rogan may have babied me when I was sick, but he also put me in a position where I was eventually thrown from a moving vehicle. And when that happened, Buck had planted one of his boys to watch out for me.

I was thirty-two years old.

Was I prepared to cocoon myself for the rest of my days, existing through a terrible life?

Or was I willing to live more?

I thought I'd been making all the right moves.

But had I?

"Okay," my mouth said before my brain processed it was going to say it.

Buck dropped his head so his forehead rested against mine a second as his fingers gave me another squeeze. Then he lifted his head.

The whole time he kept hold of my eyes.

"You get safe, you need space, I'll give it to you. But now, I want you close."

"Okay," I repeated, but before I could stop myself, I asked, "Why?"

"Why?" he asked back, straightening to his side of the counter.

"Why are you doing this? Why do you want to find out where we're going? You barely know me."

He grinned and took another huge bite of his, well, again, *my* Pop-Tart.

After he swallowed, he laid it out.

"Because you forget to be uptight when I got my hands and mouth on you. You totally lose control when I got my dick in you, going so far as to hang on so you don't come and lose my cock. Then, when you let yourself come, you come harder than any woman I ever had. You don't mind me knowin' it and you give as good as you get."

Hmm.

Well, it was nice he enjoyed me in bed as much as I enjoyed him.

That said...

He continued.

"You don't have any fuckin' clue how to play games, because when you do, you're really fuckin' bad at it which means you won't play me. You're not hard to look at, even with a shiner and a busted lip. I like to make you smile. And it does somethin' for me, knowin', even with your life as fucked up as it's been, that I can make you laugh."

He paused a beat and finished it with a question.

"Is that enough for you?"

With all he'd just said, it took me not a second to understand that was enough for me.

I had nothing so even a little bit seemed like a lot.

But that seemed like more than a lot.

It seemed like a gift, especially the fact that he liked to make me smile.

And laugh.

In fact, it made me breathe a little heavy again, but this time for good reason.

So he wouldn't notice me semi-panting, I didn't answer verbally.

I nodded.

His grin turned into a smile, deepening those lines by his eyes.

Then the Pop-Tarts popped up.

8

I TOOK YOU ON

"**B**abe, get your ass in gear. They're here," Buck shouted from the front of the house.

I was in his bedroom getting ready to go out shopping with the old ladies.

Buck had some business to attend to and he'd decided it was time for me to enter the real world again.

This meant he arranged for one of the MC's "prospects," or boys who had not yet been accepted into the Club and were now proving their salt to the members, to take Lorie, some of her girlfriends and me out shopping.

I wasn't certain how this would help the prospects prove their salt as rough and tumble members of a motorcycle club. But I was getting the impression that the recruits did whatever a member told them to do (no matter what it was) to demonstrate their dedication, loyalty and commitment to the Club.

And this included taking a bunch of the members' old ladies shopping.

The prospect selected for this task was Driver, who I already decided I liked and who had been my bodyguard the last couple of days.

I'd also already decided I liked Lorie.

So that was good.

The rest of it was bad.

I didn't make friends easily.

When I was young, it was because insularity was key to survival. You didn't want to form attachments when life was uncertain.

I'd learned that the hard way.

When I was older, it was out of habit.

After Rogan got arrested, it was because no one wanted anything to do with me.

It was Friday. Buck's kids would be there that evening. Buck had talked to them and they'd told him they were leaving right after school. He told them he had company.

What he didn't do was tell me how they reacted to this.

Thus, I decided it was probably bad, or if not bad, then not met with exuberant curiosity that their dad was all of a sudden shacked up with a virtual stranger.

I had been in Buck's house for three days, including the one where I slept most of the day.

This time was taken up with me inspecting Buck's place, unpacking my stuff that his boys delivered, picking up Buck's bedroom, doing some laundry and watching daytime television with Driver.

It was enough.

Moving around to keep my body from getting tight was one thing, but overdoing it was bad. I learned that clearing Buck's floor space. I was still tender, but after succeeding in that feat, I felt pain.

So when I was done, Driver and I fired up the television and watched soaps and reruns of *Dynasty*.

Most of the soaps we watched were Mexican because Driver thought all the screaming, dramatic music and narrowed looks were hilarious (and I agreed). Neither of us spoke a word of Spanish, but still, they were funny.

We watched *Dynasty* because it was even funnier.

Buck was not around this whole time. He left me with Driver to get work done at Ace and to do Scary President of an MC Things.

I learned to spot the difference quickly.

If he was going to Ace, he'd share this with me.

If he was doing Scary President of an MC Things, he didn't share.

The first night of my first full day in his house, Buck came home early with a pizza.

Driver was not invited to stay.

We ate it in front of the TV. Buck drank beer, I drank Coke, and Buck talked, mostly updates about my issues.

These included that Esposito was laying low...

"But darlin', he has no choice. I was pretty thorough."

Yikes!

Also no word from anywhere about Tia.

Which I was trying not to think about, planting visions firmly in my head each leg of her imaginary journey on her road trip to freedom in Seattle (I decided she'd gone to Seattle, just because that was where we'd planned to go).

When we were done eating, I cleared the box away (Buck didn't do plates with pizza either, something I found difficult—eating pizza with nothing but my hands and a paper towel—but I mastered it on my third and final slice), and I brought him another beer.

I fell asleep again with my head on his thigh, and as such, there was a repeat of him carrying me to bed where I woke up just long enough to feel my head hit the pillow.

The second night, he came home late, had a beer and gave me another update on my issues (brief, since nothing was happening, which included no sign of Tia). He then told me he'd talked to his kids, he'd spent the day at Ace and that was the extent of our conversation.

I was learning Buck needed to unwind at night and unwinding didn't mean deep, soul-bearing conversations.

It meant greasy food, beer and zoning out in front of the television.

This was okay since he liked doing the last with my cheek on his thigh and his fingers playing with my hair.

And anyway, I wasn't up for soul-bearing conversations. I had enough of that for a while.

I needed a rest.

Although all of this was uneventful, the state of play of my life had shifted substantially.

I had my stuff, such as it was, but at least I had conditioner and clean underwear. And I didn't have my unpaid rent hanging over my head.

I also didn't have my car. I'd left it sitting too long, and in one of his updates, Buck informed me the repo men got it before his boys could get it.

This stunk.

Buck told me to kiss it good-bye and stop thinking about it, and since I really didn't have any choice, I did that.

Though, I did worry that they took the homeless man's tarp when they took my car. He needed it. It didn't rain much in Arizona, but when it did, I suspected a tarp came in handy.

And not incidentally, when I shared this fear with Buck, he told me, "The boys'll handle that too."

Later, after he got a phone call, he confirmed that they did handle it.

I mean...

This guy.

And "his boys."

Seriously.

On Mrs. Jimenez front: she was back at home. Buck's men had located my purse and returned her nest egg. She reported to me she was fine—though Raymundo was looking for new accommodations for her.

She promised me this was not about me except for the fact she liked me next door and whoever might replace me might not be a quiet neighbor.

Unsurprisingly, Dallas didn't expend a great deal of effort vetting his renters. Except for me, Mrs. Jimenez and Mrs. Ramirez, who lived on the first floor, all of our neighbors were loud due to screaming matches or being rowdy or both.

"Sometimes, life gives you signs," Mrs. Jimenez told me over the phone. "You get tied to a chair, that's a big sign."

Well, at least she could be philosophical about it.

My bruises got angrier on Thursday, but now they'd begun to fade, as had the aches and pains. I was days away from being back to myself, but the healing was kicking in.

And last, but very much not least, it bore repeating, Tia remained unfound.

When I allowed myself to think about it, I came up with the good part about this being the fact that Esposito didn't have her. And word on the street (according to Buck), neither did any other bad guy.

The bad part about this was she was smoke (Buck's vernacular).

So I was all in for visualization.

Thus, after the time had come when she would have made it to Seattle, I tried to visualize her applying for jobs in coffeehouses.

But, if I was honest, my visualization wasn't working.

I was scared for her.

She knew Mrs. Jimenez's phone number, though, and I just hoped she'd give Mrs. Jimenez a call. And Buck told me the word was still out, they were still looking for her and he still seemed confident she'd be found.

I tried to suck confidence out of his confidence, but this wasn't working either.

I was worried about my friend.

"Clara! They're waitin' and I gotta go!" Buck shouted, and I jumped.

"Coming!" I shouted back, finishing putting in an earring, and my eyes dropped to the framed photos on his dresser.

I'd had time to explore his house the last couple of days and I'd spent a goodly amount of time studying those photos.

I did this because I was curious about Buck, I was curious about the pictures and I was curious about the people in them.

Some of them, I could guess.

His kids, both of whom were gorgeous, not just Tatiana. They looked like him. Dark hair, dark brown eyes, the boy tall and filling out, the girl was short though, and in some of the photos, getting curves. None of the pictures were recent but they weren't older than a couple of years.

The others I could guess.

Parents, definitely.

And a brother and two sisters, one of which was married (there was a wedding photo, and although she wore a pretty, albeit skimpy white dress, her other half was definitely a biker if the leather jacket he wore over a nice dress shirt to his wedding was anything to go by).

There were a lot of photos, something I thought strange for a man like Buck to have on display in frames spread across his dresser in his bedroom.

The frames weren't designer chic, they were no-frills, but he made the effort to buy them and put the pictures in them.

The photos ranged a lifetime, from when he and his brother and sisters were kids, to when they were young adults. None of these were recent either and they were a whole lot less recent than the ones with his kids.

But all of them, his kids, his folks, his siblings, were close. There were smiles, even laughter. Arms thrown around each other.

Hugging.

Good times.

Happy times.

I liked this for him.

I liked that he was a man who would display something like this, showing openly the people in them, and the times they shared, meant a great deal to him.

I wanted to ask Buck about them.

But I didn't.

He seemed very comfortable with our arrangement, but I was not.

It didn't escape me that I still barely knew him, I hadn't even known him a week.

Sure, asking him about those photos, his family, would be getting to know him, but I was hesitant.

I was this because I didn't want to pry. I didn't want to seem pushy. Buck was definitely capable of sharing, but I figured he was the kind of man who did it when he was ready, and he wouldn't welcome nosy questions.

So I didn't ask those questions.

I walked to the bed, sat down and slipped on one of my high-heeled, strappy sandals, bending cautiously, as had become my habit to treat my body the last few days, to buckle it.

I did this thinking that I'd also had time to explore the rest of his house.

Along the landing, there was his room and master bath, another full bath and two more rooms.

The one next to Buck's was an office—desk, battered couch, computer and full-on mess.

At the other end was another big bedroom, just without the master bath, and I guessed Tatiana slept there.

This was a guess because there was abandoned makeup scattered on a low dresser, some underwear and T-shirts in the drawers, some jeans and a very cool leather jacket in the closet, and a vampire novel on the nightstand by the bed. I'd also found tampons and hair straighteners in the hall bathroom.

But there was nothing else there that hinted at the personality of Buck's daughter.

Girls, I thought, claimed their space, made it theirs with posters and pictures of friends and boys they liked, jewelry dangling from mirrors, Christmas lights with flowers on the bulbs, stuff like that.

But it looked like a guest bedroom where the guest left in a hurry.

Not so the loft at the top of the stairs on the landing.

Buck's house was bigger than just what was on the landing and in the great room.

Off the great room was a kind of den, slouchy furniture, another TV, what appeared to be a communal PC on an old-fashioned roll-top desk, a free-standing cast iron fireplace.

Off the den was a large utility room with a deep, four-legged sink, washer and dryer, counterspace, not a small amount of cupboards for storage and an extra full-size freezer and fridge.

The freezer was filled with meat. So much meat, it looked like an entire cow was in there alongside an entire pig.

That was the extent of the bottom floors.

But the loft was full-on Gear's space.

Unlike Tatiana, Gear had claimed his room.

There were some deeply slanted ceilings and a skylight. There were also throw rugs on the floors and posters on the wall, mostly scantily clad, extremely buxom women, the majority of them wet with what little clothing they had on plastered to their bodies.

Unmade bed, the sheets of which seriously needed cleaning (and I made a note to do that, after I met Gear, of course, I didn't want him to think I was invading his space). Clothes tangled all over the floor with the rugs (just like his dad's room had been, though not as bad). A stereo with so many CDs, Gear could stock his own music store (and it was weird, but kinda cool to see CDs—I didn't know people did CDs anymore, I thought it was all about streaming). All of the music was hard rock or rap.

There also seemed to be car parts or other pieces of mechanical equipment lying around.

I could get a read on Gear from his room.

He liked girls with large breasts. He liked music. And as his father had mentioned, he liked to tinker with stuff.

I finished buckling my other shoe and walked quickly to the bathroom, not wanting to be rude, but at the same time stalling.

I looked at myself in the mirror.

Faded jeans but only faded because I'd owned them for a long time (I hadn't bought any new clothes in over a year). A delicate salmon-colored blouse which I'd managed to keep in decent condition even though it, too, had been hanging in my closet for a while. Strappy matte bronze sandals which had been very expensive when I bought them three years ago and I painstakingly took care of them too.

Luckily, when they seized Rogan's and my possessions, they'd left me with my clothes.

Unluckily, this was about all they left me with.

Further to that misfortune, a good deal of these things I'd had to commission for the money (mostly handbags and shoes, but also designer clothing).

I'd made careful selections of what to keep.

Clothes that might help me find a job and some things that I could live in and not be reminded every day that my life was in the toilet.

I hadn't been able to camouflage much of the bruising around my eye, so it shone in high relief and my scabbed-over cut lip was impossible to hide.

I wondered what Lorie's friends would think of me. I wondered if they'd like me. Lorie thought I was sweet, and I got the impression Driver liked me. I just hoped the others would too.

I wasn't looking forward to this on a variety of levels, including the fact I had no money in my purse, and I couldn't use my credit cards. If I tried, they'd probably be shredded by shop assistants at the register.

I couldn't even afford a cup of coffee.

I felt my anxiety rising as I stared at myself in the mirror, and I was intent on doing that when I heard Buck.

I jumped and whirled to face the bathroom door.

"Babe, what the fuck?" he asked.

"Do I look okay?" I blurted, and his chin listed back.

"Come again?"

"Do I...?"

Oh God, was I really asking Buck if I looked okay?

Did you ask a badass biker if you looked okay?

No.

No, you didn't.

From what I was experiencing, they seemed confident in every detail of their lives.

Then again, the mystery of why Buck's hair was always so fantastically cool had not yet been solved.

And it was always fantastically cool.

If my hair always looked fantastically cool, I'd be confident too.

I shook my head and my ridiculous thoughts away and muttered, "Nothing."

I walked to him, head bowed, spiked heels clicking on the tiles, but I had to stop because he didn't move out of the doorway. I looked up at him just in time to see his hand come up and then I lost sight of it when it curled around the side of my neck.

"Baby, you look fine," he said quietly.

Golly, I liked it when he was nice.

And it had to be said, he was nice a lot.

As in, all the time.

"You sure?" I whispered.

His fingers gave me a squeeze. "Yeah, I'm sure."

"Okay." I was still whispering.

"They're gonna love you, Clara," he told me.

I nodded, ready to believe him that I looked okay, not so sure I believed *that*.

I got another squeeze of his fingers. "Darlin', they will."

"Okay," I repeated.

He stared into my eyes a second before he bent his neck so he could kiss my nose.

All right, now I felt better.

He lifted his head, and I smiled at him. His focus dropped to my mouth, his fingers tensed on my neck, pulling me slightly up as he bent his neck again then his mouth touched mine.

Two days and I hadn't had that. Outside of the mini make out session on his bed that first morning, he'd not even brushed his lips against mine.

I missed it.

So much, I leaned in, and when his mouth started moving away, mine followed it.

Suddenly, his arms were around me and his tongue was in my mouth.

Oh, yes.

I missed this even more.

I wound my arms around him and kissed him back.

It was wet, it was heated, and it was effective. I knew this because I felt it starting, my knees got weak and my nipples got hard.

As ever...

Amazing.

He tore his mouth from mine, and with just one kiss, I was breathing heavy and holding on to him for dear life.

"You're feelin' better," he growled, his voice rougher than normal, which was saying something.

"Yes," I panted, and his arms squeezed gently, like he was testing me, his eyes studying my face.

"Good to know I can take your mouth without you whimpering in pain," he muttered, his gaze locking on mine.

It was then it hit me that he hadn't kissed me in two days because he didn't want it to get heated because getting heated might cause me pain.

Oh yes, I definitely liked it when he was nice.

He carried on, "Tonight, we'll see what else I can take."

Oh.

Wow.

"Buck—" I whispered, and I didn't know why because I had nothing to say except, maybe, "Yippee!"

He let me go, stepped back, and I watched him pull his wallet out of the back pocket of his jeans. I then watched him open it. After that, I watched him sift through a bunch of bills, all of them hundreds. One, two, three, four, five, six, seven, eight, nine, ten...

And onward.

Yes, *onward*.

And there were several more in there.

He pulled those bills out, flipped his wallet closed and shoved it into his back pocket. Then he grabbed my wrist, lifted it, and planted the wad of hundred-dollar bills in my palm.

I stared at it.

"Have fun, Toots, but I want you to use some a' that to get yourself a phone. Get a decent one with a good plan. They give you problems with the contract because of your credit history, you get Lorie to call me, and I'll sort it out. Yeah?"

My head tilted back slowly, and I stared at him.

Okay, so there was a lot of money there because phones cost as much as some cars these days (slight exaggeration).

However.

"I can't take this," I said.

His brows shot together. "Why not?"

"It's hundreds of dollars."

"So?"

"It's hundreds of dollars."

"Yeah," Buck said slowly, then repeated, "So?"

"That's a lot of money."

"Yeah," Buck said again, leaning slightly into me. "So?"

"I—"

He cut me off. "Babe, shut your trap and go have fun."

"I—"

"They're waitin', Toots, and I got shit to do."

"Buck—"

"Clara, go...have...fun."

He was losing patience, I could tell.

"Do you carry that much money on you all the time?" I asked.

"No," he answered. "I carry that much money on me when my girl's goin' shoppin' and she needs some cake to have fun."

Oh my.

Yes, I very much liked it when he was nice.

"I'll pay you back," I whispered, my fingers curling around the money.

"Don't piss me off," he replied, and this time, my chin listed back.

"What?"

He took in a deep, impatient breath.

Upon letting it go, he explained.

"I don't got time for this shit, but I'll make things clear considerin' I didn't before, though I thought I did," he said as preamble.

When he didn't continue, I nodded to indicate I'd heard and digested his preamble.

So he continued.

"I took you on. You're in my house, you're in my bed, and eventually you're at my shop. Tonight, you're meetin' my kids. This all means you're in my life. I let somethin' in my life, I take care of it. Down the line, you get on your feet, you wanna do somethin' nice for me in return, knock yourself out. But right now, the somethin' nice for me you could do is get your ass in the SUV with Lorie, Driver and the girls so I can get on the road and take care of business. Now, are you gonna stop bein' stupid and go have some fun or do we gotta talk about this for the next hour?"

I wanted to talk about it for the next hour, starting with a wee bit more discussion about taking so much money without paying it back and ending with him calling me stupid.

Considering his impatience, I decided to pick the part that might take the least time.

"It isn't nice, calling someone stupid," I noted quietly.

His expression changed to soft and sweet and warm, and his voice did the same thing when he replied, "I didn't say you were stupid, baby.

I said you were *bein'* stupid. I know you're not stupid. But you are gorgeous, so you don't gotta worry that you look all right. And you gotta learn to let people who wanna do nice shit for you, do it."

Okay then.

"Right. Now I'm going to go have some fun," I told him.

"Right," he murmured, his lips twitching, and he lifted a hand to curl it around the back of my neck as he bent his head and touched his mouth to mine.

His hand went from my neck to my wrist, he pulled me out of the bathroom, let me go but propelled me with fingers at the small of my back through the bedroom, out the door, onto the landing, and down the stairs to the kitchen where the girls and Driver were waiting to take me out to have fun.

I pinned a smile to my face when I saw them and hoped the day would be fun.

But I feared it would be torture.

And with things like this, I was almost always right.

9

PROFESSOR HIGGINS

I was right.
   The day was torture.

It was torture for a variety of reasons.

Firstly, we went to Scottsdale Fashion Square, an old haunt of mine I hadn't been to in ages.

This was because I had no money to spend.

This was also because I'd applied, interviewed and been turned down for so many jobs in shops there that I avoided it like the plague.

Secondly, Buck had given me hundreds of dollars, but I didn't feel comfortable spending them. I would buy a cell because he told me to, but I wanted to do that just with Lorie in case they gave me grief over the contract. And I didn't know how to get Lorie away from Minnie and Pinky.

Thirdly, Minnie didn't like me, and she made no bones about it.

Minnie was petite, had large breasts, abundant hips and hard, assessing eyes.

Minnie was one of the MC's member's old lady. His name was Gash.

I could see Minnie with a man named Gash. A man named Gash seemed perfect for Minnie.

The other woman was named Pinky and she was tall, lean and had fake breasts that were pert, round and perfect, and I knew this because, in the tight tank top she was wearing, it was hard to miss. She had shining, straight black hair, was the woman of a man called Cruise and she was quiet.

Then again, with Lorie gabbing a mile a minute and Minnie throwing attitude, making it clear she wasn't big on me being there and further didn't like Fashion Square too much, Pinky kind of faded into the background.

And lastly, it was torture because I was out in public.

I tried to avoid this too.

People still recognized me. It came rarer, but it happened, and that day was no different. But this time, they were recognizing me with a shiner and therefore staring.

It was never comfortable and that day it was worse because I was with Minnie who made it clear she didn't want to be with me.

Therefore, I retreated, became silent and tried to be invisible.

Also, as the slog through the stores wore on with no one really into shopping, I gave up on the cell. I'd ask Driver to take me to some phone store some other day. I hardly needed a phone when most of my time was spent at Buck's house. He had a landline there. I'd need one when I entered the real world for good, whenever that would be, so now, I decided, it was not a priority.

We were in Victoria's Secret.

I'd separated from the girls, and as I was noticing was usual, Pinky went her own way. Lorie and Minnie were inspecting black lace sets of underwear complete with garter belts when I accidentally wandered close, but I did this silently and they didn't know I was there.

Therefore, I heard Minnie hiss, "... shit don't stink."

To this, Lorie said, "I think she's sweet."

And this was when I knew they were talking about me.

Before I could escape or make my presence known so they didn't feel badly about talking about me, Minnie carried on.

"She thinks she's better than us, fancy-ass shoes, fancy-ass top, lookin' down her nose. Jesus, makes me sick. *Her*, lettin' that asshole play her for *years*, thinkin' she's better than *us*. What the fuck is that all about?"

Those comments hurt for a variety of reasons, but mostly that she thought I was looking down my nose at her.

I'd had that in my old life, though it was the other way around. The women in my neighborhood with their yoga pants and expensive water bottles and three-thousand-dollar designer bags, the messy topknots in their hair that looked thrown up, but I knew (because I'd YouTubed a video on how to do it) took twenty minutes to accomplish. They thought they were better than everybody.

And I'd had that in my older life. The kids at school with their real parents and real homes and real lives.

It didn't feel nice.

Pinky was wearing a tank top, jeans and high-heeled sandals. Lorie was in a mini-jeans-skirt and also was wearing a tank top and high-heeled sandals. Minnie wore a scrap of black fabric in a halter-top style that covered her breasts but completely exposed her back and stomach, tight jeans and high-heeled sandals.

I looked like the librarian I was (in better shoes) compared to them, this was true.

But they all looked nice, in a biker babe kind of way.

Just different than me, or really, anyone else at the mall.

I wasn't looking down my nose at them.

I turned to escape when I heard, "Minnie, shut your mouth."

This was Driver, who was right behind me.

I peered up at him to see he looked angry and sort of ridiculous being all biker and standing in Victoria's Secret, but he didn't seem uncomfortable. He didn't seem anything but angry and his eyes were locked on Minnie.

I turned again to see Lorie and Minnie were looking at Driver and me. Not only that, but Pinky had also gotten close.

Fantastic.

Lorie's cheeks were pink.

Minnie's face got hard.

"Um...you know, why don't you guys, you know, do your thing? I'm going to go get a coffee," I mumbled.

"Right," Minnie snapped, and I knew at once she took this as me trying to get away from them and not for the reasons I was actually trying to get away from them.

"I can..." I started, my mind whirling, "buy some for you guys. I'll take orders. What do you want?"

"I want lunch," Lorie stated, coming to me and hooking her arm in mine. "Forget coffee, let's get some food."

I didn't want food. My stomach was churning.

I also didn't want to protest.

So I didn't.

We hit the Yard House, and as we were led to our booth, all eyes came to us.

It struck me then that when I lived my life prior to it disintegrating, I hadn't really noticed bikers or biker babes hanging in the places I frequented. This was probably because bikers and biker babes had their own places to hang. And Fashion Square and the Yard House likely weren't on the list of those places.

We sat in a curved booth, me between Lorie and Driver, Minnie and Pinky across from us.

Minnie's mood hadn't changed.

Neither had Driver's.

Pinky and Lorie exchanged several glances, and I felt badly that they were clearly uncomfortable with the tense atmosphere.

I felt badly, but I didn't know what to do about it. So I studied my menu like I would be tested on it.

We ordered, and my menu was swept away, leaving me with nothing to hide behind. So my eyes wandered the restaurant.

They did this for a nanosecond, mainly because I'd caught three people staring at me and my black eye.

I suddenly felt like crying.

And just as suddenly, for some reason I did not know, my mouth opened of its own accord and out popped words, and this happened after my gaze locked on Minnie.

"People are staring at me," I told her.

"What?" she snapped, her expression hard, the word clipped out in a way I knew she wasn't real big on speaking to me at all.

"It happens all the time," I carried on. "People recognize me. They stare. It's worse today because of my black eye. I don't like being out in public, so I usually don't go. But Buck wanted me to have fun, so I'm here."

"Who cares if people stare at you?" Minnie asked, voice still snappish.

"Well, I do," I answered.

"Why?" she asked.

"Because I know they know who I am, and they think I'm a loser."

Pinky and Lorie exchanged another glance, and I felt Driver's body move beside me, but I didn't take my attention from Minnie.

"So? Who cares if they think you're a loser?"

"I do," I told her.

"Why?" she pushed, her voice *still* snappish.

"I don't know. I just do," I replied.

"That's whacked," she informed me.

"Sorry?" I asked.

"It's *whacked*," she repeated.

"It isn't," I said, then continued, "You don't know. They aren't doing it to you."

"Oh yeah they are, and I don't give a shit. They can look all they want and think what they want, and I don't give that first fuck."

I stared at her, finding this concept intriguing.

It was true. She was out in a halter top baring loads of flesh. She had big hair, hair that was platinum blonde and by no means a color found in nature. She had on loads of makeup. She attracted attention.

"That concept is intriguing," I stated, her head jerked.

I heard Driver chuckle as Pinky let out a giggle, and I felt Lorie's hand under the table giving my leg a squeeze.

"That concept is intriguing?" Minnie repeated after me.

"Well, yes, I hadn't thought of that," I said.

Minnie stared at me.

Then she stated, "Fuck me, in a million years I would never guess Buck would hook up with a bitch like you."

I nodded.

"I agree," I told her. "I don't know him very well, but I would guess

I'm not his type. I even asked him why, and although I believed his answer, I still find it odd he's into me."

"Are you into him?" Pinky put in quietly, and I looked at her.

"Um...yes."

"Um, yes," Minnie muttered, "I bet."

"Sorry?" I asked Minnie.

"Ain't no secret your shit's messed up, babe, not a little, a-fuckin'-lot. Now, I don't judge, a girl's gotta do what a girl's gotta do. What I do *not* like is you doin' it with Buck."

I was confused. "Doing what?"

"Takin' advantage of him to get your shit sorted out."

Oh God.

She thought I was using Buck.

"Minnie, Jesus," Driver growled, sounding mad.

"You lie," I stated, ignoring Driver, my eyes holding Minnie's.

"Come again?"

"You lie," I repeated. "You judge. You judge just like those people looking at me judge. You think you know me, but you don't."

Minnie's back went straight, and her face got hard again just as the waitress put down our drinks. We stayed silent and tense through this (though Pinky muttered, "Thank you") and then Minnie leaned in when the waitress was gone.

"Not big on a bitch talkin' trash to me like that, Clara," she warned.

"Min, honey," Lorie murmured. "Cool down."

"And this," I whispered, tears suddenly filling my eyes, "is when it gets bad. People judge and sometimes I feel it with looks and sometimes they say stuff to me. Not like what you just said, but why you said it. You don't like me, and you don't even know me. You made up your mind before you even met me. And for some reason, some reason I don't get, you feel well within your rights to lay it out for me even though I didn't do that first thing to harm you."

"Clara, honey," Lorie said beside me, her hand coming back to my leg to give it another squeeze.

But I shook my head and didn't take my focus from Minnie.

"And you know, the thing that gets me, it always gets me, is that I care. Even about what you think, regardless that you haven't been nice to me even for a second. I care that you think I am what you think I am even though I'm not. That matters to me." I sucked in breath and finished, "And it hurts."

That's when I looked down at the table, grabbed my Diet Coke and put the straw to my lips, avoiding everyone's eyes, sucking back soda and trying to fight back the tears stinging the backs of my eyes.

"There you go," Minnie said, and my gaze hesitantly went to her face.

"Sorry?"

"People say shit to you, you call 'em on it. There you go," she replied, and I noticed her face, nor her voice was hard anymore.

"Sorry?" I repeated.

"Babe, I was bein' a bitch." Minnie sat back. "You're right. And you were right to call me on it. They look at you, you feel like givin' 'em 'tude, give it to them. Say, 'What the fuck's up your ass?' Bet you say that, they won't be starin' at you no more and they'll think twice before they do it to anyone else. They say somethin' to you, you don't feel like turnin' the other cheek, you give it right back to them. Say, 'And this is your business because...?' Fuck off, asshole.' Fuck 'em. What do you care? You ain't ever gonna see them again."

"That's good advice," Pinky whispered.

"I'm not sure I can do that," I told Minnie, and she shrugged.

"Then don't," she returned. "But don't let it get under your skin. Like I said, fuck 'em. They don't mean shit to you. You walk away and you'll never see 'em again. You let them control your life, invade your headspace, that ain't right. It's so not right it's whacked."

At that point, Lorie started talking, and I turned my head to her.

"Your old man, hon, let's just say, he's a dick. He fucked you over, *big time*. But *you* are doin' this to you now. He's gone and been gone awhile. But you're still lettin' him fuck you. Stop doin' that."

"That's good advice too," Pinky added her endorsement.

I hadn't thought of it like that.

I hadn't thought of any of this like that.

I looked at Minnie and explained, "I'm not taking advantage of Buck. He offered to help. I tried to leave town, then I got beat up so that became difficult. I didn't even want to take his help, but he convinced me."

"Sucks, babe," Lorie muttered her understatement.

"I bet Buck can be pretty convincing," Pinky muttered hers.

I kept talking to Minnie.

"And I don't look down my nose at you. I'm not sure I could pull off that halter top, but I admire the fact that you can. You've got a lovely body and I think it's cool you have no problems showing it off. I'm not cool. I'm a librarian. I've always wanted to be cool, maybe not by wearing halter tops, but I don't know, in *some* way. I just don't have it in me. I think I was born an awkward, geeky, brainy librarian. I could probably wear a halter top and *still* look like an awkward, geeky, brainy librarian."

"Babe, you aren't gonna know if that's true shoppin' in Fashion Square," Minnie replied. "Ain't no cool clothes here. Except maybe at Lucky."

It was then the day took a drastic turn and this turn was perpetrated by Lorie.

And she did this by leaning in excitedly and suggesting, "Let's eat and *really* take Clary shopping."

"Oh yeah," Pinky agreed, leaning in too, her eyes bright.

I felt a thrill race up my spine and I wasn't sure it was a good one.

"Oh fuck," Driver muttered, and I turned to him.

This was not one of his favorite chores and I had the distinct feeling it was going to get worse for him *and* for me.

"We'll kit you *out*, Clary," Lorie said, grabbing my hand and giving it a squeeze. "You'll be cool like *that*," she continued, letting me go and snapping her fingers, nearly bouncing in the booth with excitement.

Oh dear.

"I'm not cool," I told her. "I tried. Trust me. The results were disastrous."

And this was true.

My junior year in high school, I tried to be cool and the results were disastrous. In fact, it was a lucky thing social media was not big then or those results would probably still be available to the population at large, it was so disastrous.

Lorie just smiled big and announced to the table, "We are *so totally* Professor Higgins to Clary's Eliza Whatever."

"This is gonna be *the bomb*." Pinky was smiling big too.

Oh.

Dear.

"Um...I'm not sure—" I started.

"Babe, get sure," Minnie ordered. "You don't have to be what you are. You can be anything you fuckin' wanna be."

Hmm.

This was a point to ponder.

But, perhaps, later.

A lot later.

"I might look ridiculous," I whispered.

"You'll only look ridiculous if you *feel* ridiculous," Minnie stated. "You feel hot, you'll *be* hot, and trust me, babe, we'll make you *hot*."

Oh God.

"I've never been hot," I told her.

Minnie stared at me.

Pinky stared at me.

And I felt Lorie and Driver staring at me.

Then Lorie burst out laughing, Pinky joined in, and even Minnie smiled.

Through it, Minnie declared, "I'm all over this Professor Higgins shit."

Oh no.

"Me too," Pinky threw in.

"Totally," Lorie added.

"Fuckin' A," Driver muttered.

Oh dear.

10

AS GOOD AS I COULD GET

My new posse and I barreled into Ace in the Hole Home Improvement laden with bags.

Not all of them were mine, but the vast majority were.

I had enough biker babe apparel to kit out the old ladies of three MCs.

I also had a new cell phone. We bought this after Yard House and before my biker babe mentors took me on a tour of Phoenix's biker babe shops.

Not surprisingly, the cell phone people weren't big fans of contracting with me due to my seriously sketchy credit history.

That was, they weren't big fans of it until Minnie got in their faces.

There was the possibility that they broke every rule in their policy book by allowing me to sign the contract, but they did it in order to shut Minnie up.

This was because Minnie was not only being loud, but also using a fair amount of foul language.

Some customers just stared.

Most of them left.

I got my phone and contract.

We were at Ace because that was the plan. Shopping and then they were going to drop me off at Ace. Buck was going to drive us home.

His kids were due between five and six, depending, Buck said, on how fast and loose Gear played the speed limit.

He told me we should plan on them being home at five.

I guessed this meant Gear normally played the speed limit very fast and loose, and this wasn't surprising, considering the loins from whence he came.

Not that Buck drove like a maniac (at least not with me in the car).

But he didn't dillydally.

I surveyed the cavernous space that was Ace as we walked in, Minnie, Lorie and Driver hanging close to me. Pinky forged ahead and threw her arms around a tall man with a full beard that needed a trim, starting this habitual grooming about two years ago. He had long brown hair that he'd bunched up at the back of his head in a messy man-bun that by no means took him twenty minutes to fashion. He also had a hint of a beer gut.

He wrapped his arms around Pinky and bent her backwards, laying a big, wet one on her for all to see.

This was when I stopped watching Pinky and who I assumed was Cruise and started to look at the store.

It was spacious with very tall ceilings and lots of rows displaying lots of stuff. It smelled like a woodworking shop and fresh paint.

Metallica was playing over the sound system.

No Muzak, not at Ace.

Metal.

I wasn't surprised, and as with pretty much everything I'd experienced that was the Aces High MC, it was cool.

We stopped close to Pinky and Cruise and I realized, after the mall drama, I'd had a good day.

I eventually relaxed, Pinky eventually spoke up, Lorie kept gabbing a mile a minute, Driver offered light relief through frequently muttering stuff that was funny and Minnie lost the attitude and was quite nice, in a hard-as-nails kind of way.

It might not have started great, but it got tons better, and the girls had a blast making me try stuff on and then hooting and hollering when I modeled it.

When Tia and I, or any of my old friends and I, went shopping, we didn't hoot and holler.

In fact, I wasn't certain I ever hooted and hollered or had been around anyone who did it.

I didn't hoot and holler with the biker babe posse either, but it made me giggle when they did.

It wasn't lost on me that I hadn't had a day like this in a long time. So long, I actually couldn't recall the last time I had one.

In fact, so long, I wondered if I ever did.

And, with that, it wasn't lost on me that I owed more to Buck than a debt of safety, protection, a roof over my head, food in my belly and a fistful of "cake."

Cruise released Pinky, though he didn't let her go. He hooked her around the neck and tucked her against his side. Then his eyes came to me.

"Shit, babe, fuck, heard they nailed you, but Jesus," he said, his gaze on my black eye.

"Yes," I replied for want of anything else to say.

However, it was the truth.

They nailed me.

"We're Professor Higgins to Clary," Pinky told him, pressing into his side, wrapping her arm around his slightly protruding belly and looking up at him with a smile. "We're making her Eliza Biker Babe."

Cruise grinned down at Pinky with a warmth to his face that I liked for Pinky, a great deal, then he looked at Driver.

"Feel your pain, brother," he muttered.

Driver grunted.

I smiled at Lorie then I looked at my watch.

It was ten to five.

Oh dear.

I'd learned today that Buck lived thirty minutes outside of the northernmost boundary of the Valley. And although Ace was situated in North Phoenix, it was a ten-minute drive to that boundary.

We were going to be late for his kids.

Not good.

I looked at Cruise and asked, "Where's Buck?"

"Dive," Cruise replied, jerking his head to the back of the store. "Go down aisle one, use the back door there." He looked at Minnie. "Gash is there too."

"Thanks," I said. "Nice to meet you," I continued even though I hadn't really met him.

He grinned.

Minnie muttered, "I'll come with."

Awkwardly, because I was carrying a bunch of bags, but also because I wasn't really practiced with it, I gave out hugs to Lorie and Pinky. I left out Driver because he'd wandered behind the long counter that ran most of the front of the store and held six registers. Also because I didn't think he wanted a girlie, post-shopping hug. He'd done enough to prove his loyalty to the Club for one day.

Then I called out good-byes and Minnie and I wandered to the back of the store.

I felt it necessary to speak, even though Minnie didn't seem to feel the same need.

"Thanks for, um..." I hesitated, "giving me a chance."

She let out a short laugh before she bumped her shoulder to mine while we were walking, banging my bags against my leg as she did it.

"Babe, seriously, we need more lessons," she noted.

I looked at her. "What? Why?"

"'Cause you don't thank people for givin' you a chance. They just should. They don't, fuck 'em."

"Do you think 'fuck 'em' about everyone?" I asked, then added, "And, well, everything?"

"Uh...yeah," she answered.

I smiled at her, looked forward, saw the back door, and when we made it there, I put my bag-laden hand to the bar and shoved it open.

I'd barely left the store, not even the doorway, but as I started to do this, I turned my head to the right and stopped so dead, Minnie ran into my back.

I didn't move.

I stared.

Outside the warehouse across the way, there were three picnic tables, where, I guessed, staff could take their breaks.

Buck was sitting on the end of one, his legs spread wide, a tall, ultra-curvy biker babe with long, lush, wavy dark hair standing between his legs. His hand was at her waist, his head tilted back. Her hands were resting on his shoulders, her head tilted down.

Her back was to me.

I also had a partial view of their sides, and it wasn't a clear view, but it looked like they were kissing.

I felt my insides begin to burn as I retreated, running into Minnie again. I pushed her back into Ace and carefully closed the door.

I put my hand on it and deep-breathed to put out the fire burning deep.

"Babe," Minnie whispered, and I looked at her.

Her gaze took in my face and she winced.

She'd seen it.

She'd seen what I had.

"Shit, already you're in deep." She kept whispering.

I shook my head, but this was meaningless denial.

I knew.

I knew with the intensity my insides were burning that she was right.

I was already in deep.

I liked him.

I liked Buck.

I liked him more than as my protector, a good guy, the guy who was taking care of me, the guy who was good in bed, who made me smile. The guy who had my back.

I *liked* him.

He kissed my nose.

I *that* kind of liked him.

While I was coming to this realization, Minnie shouted, "*Lorie!*"

I kept shaking my head.

"No, no. See, we haven't known each other for even a week." As mentioned, this was true. We hadn't. "We haven't made vows of love and fidelity to the end of time." This was true too. We hadn't. "I'm staying with him because I have to. I'm not safe. He said when I'm safe I can find my own space. I don't have any hold on him. He can kiss who he wants."

That was true too.

It was true, but it stunk.

Minnie kept staring at me as I heard the clickety-clack of Lorie and Pinky hurrying up to us. I turned to see Driver close behind.

"Driver, hon, girl shit," Minnie told him and then looked at Lorie. "Buck's out there and Nails has got her tongue down his throat."

Pinky gasped.

Lorie tensed.

Driver turned swiftly around and walked the other way.

Lorie's arm slid around my waist while she started, "Clary, hon—"

I pulled away from her, still shaking my head.

"No, I'm okay. Seriously. This isn't a big deal. It really isn't."

This was not true.

It was a big deal.

It shouldn't be.

I spoke no lies. I had no claim on him. We hadn't sworn fidelity. We hadn't even known each other for a week.

But this hurt.

It hurt on so many levels, I couldn't categorize them all.

It hurt because he knew I'd be there any minute and he obviously didn't intend to hide the fact that he had others, not only me.

It hurt because Rogan and I had it good, we had it *great*, and still, he couldn't keep his hands off other women knowing the promise of me was waiting at home.

Buck hadn't been able to have his hit off me, but obviously the promise of me for Buck, too, wasn't worth the wait.

Lorie, Pinky, and Minnie studied me, and I got the impression they knew I was lying.

I found this was true when Minnie muttered, "Look at her. She's in deep. We gotta give it to her straight."

Oh no.

I didn't want it straight.

And from the looks on their faces, I *really* didn't want it straight.

"No, I'm okay," I stated. "Just, maybe, one of you can go out there first. Tell him I'm here. While you do that, I'll browse Ace."

And I could browse Ace.

I was an experienced shopper, though not at home improvement stores.

However, there had to be thirty aisles in there. I could find something to feign interest in.

Lorie shook her head.

"You need to know now, honey. Later..." She paused then said softly, "Finding out later won't be too good."

I didn't want to know now, and I opened my mouth to say something when Pinky spoke.

"Nails, I get. Buck, totally uncool."

I turned my attention to her to see she was staring at the door and quiet, maybe-shy Pinky looked kind of mad.

"Our men are not like other men," Lorie went on, ignoring Pinky, and my attention shifted to her. "They are what they are. They are where they are because they are what they are. And they're with others who are like they are."

I wasn't keeping up with her because I could still feel the burn inside and my heart had begun to hurt.

But I decided to focus on Lorie because focusing on her could take my focus off the pain.

"They don't like rules, so much they don't live by them," she continued. "Not the ones out there in the other world. They got a different set of rules, one they can live with. Out there," she swung out her arm, "the rulebook's got a lot of pages. Here," she pointed to the floor, "it's only a few lines."

"Okay," I whispered, even though I didn't really understand.

"What she's sayin' is..." Minnie got closer. "They do what they wanna do when they wanna do it with *who* they wanna do it. You're his woman, babe, you gotta know that's the way and you gotta keep your mouth shut and put up with it. You do not give him shit, even if he comes home smellin' of her. You just keep your mouth shut."

Oh God.

This could not be.

And further, it could not be *for me*.

This had happened to me before, repeatedly, even if I didn't know it until later.

I couldn't go through life knowing it was happening *while it was happening*.

"Yeah, that's true, but they don't do it *in your face*," Pinky hissed, and I looked at her again.

"This is Nails," Minnie said to Pinky.

"I don't care," Pinky shot back. "It is *not* cool."

If I wasn't in such a state, I would have been surprised Pinky had such a strong backbone.

Or, nothing against Pinky, she was sweetness personified and I really liked her, but a backbone at all.

"Actually, it isn't. I'm surprised Buck would do it," Lorie put in.

"Jesus, it's fuckin' Nails," Minnie said to Lorie.

"Who's Nails?" I asked, even though I didn't want to know, just like any woman, I also did just for the opportunity to torture myself.

"Nails is Nails," Minnie said to me, in other words, telling me nothing.

"Sorry?"

"She's Buck's," Lorie explained. "Not like *you're* Buck's, but," she shrugged, "she's Buck's."

"He needs to get off, he makes a call, she traipses in," Pinky explained.

Oh God.

I'd been shopping all day, learning how to look like a biker babe, and Buck had been spending the day, or part of it, screwing curvy, lush, dark-haired *Nails*.

Truly, at this juncture, the questions needed to be asked.

All of them.

Why?

Why did my life stink so much?

Why, whenever things seemed to be looking up for me, did they start stink, stink, *stinking*?

Putrid.

Foul.

Unbearable.

I closed my eyes and looked away but opened them again when I felt fingers wrap around my upper arm.

I looked at Minnie who was close and had a hold of me.

"Babe, you gotta know you can do this. I know it sucks, and it does. It sucks. But it is the way it is. You ask no questions, they tell no lies. They need to be free and you gotta let them be that way. Normally..."

She glanced over her shoulder at the door. Her expression grew troubled, but she cleared it when she looked back at me.

"Normally, they won't ever throw it in your face. Not ever, babe. But you'll know. You just ignore it and know he'll come back to you. And he chooses you, Clara."

She got closer and her hand gave my arm a reassuring squeeze that didn't reassure me and kept going.

"If this goes the distance, and he decides to make you his old lady and do that official, he'll always come back to you. And that's something. I promise you, babe. Not blowing sunshine up your ass. Especially with a man like Buck, that's definitely something."

I looked into her hazel eyes, hearing her heartfelt words, and I knew.

I knew and I'd always known.

I'd known from the minute a mother who didn't want me expelled me from her body.

In my life, I had to settle for as good as I could get.

So West "Buck" Hardy wanted me for...whatever...and he might not always want me. And in the meantime, he was going to have more than just me.

But, for now, it was as good as I could get.

And since I had no choice....

No choice because I simply had no choice, no money, no car, nowhere to go.

But also no choice because I needed him to find Tia for me.

Further, I liked Driver. I liked Lorie, Minnie and Pinky. As well as Ink. And I had a feeling I'd also like Cruise.

Last, I had no choice, I had to admit, because I liked Buck.

A whole lot.

Too much.

So much, I knew, to have those kisses on my nose and falling asleep with my head on his thigh and his fingers in my hair and the care and concern he demonstrated nearly all the time he was around me, I was going to put up with it.

I was going to do what I always did.

I was going to take as good as I could get.

I mean, it was becoming clear that was the way of my life, so I had to get used to it.

Once, I'd reached for more.

I'd fallen in love with Rogan.

And he'd turned out to be like all the rest.

As good as I could get.

Until he was gone.

So I'd take it, and once Buck got rid of me, I'd take whatever came next.

And like I'd always done, I'd survive on as good as I could get.

And I'd keep doing it until I died.

"I can do this," I whispered to Minnie, and this was *so very* true.

It was the one thing I was super good at.

So I could do this.

I could and I would.

Because I liked him, I liked his friends, and I wanted him for me.

He wasn't perfect.

With what I'd just seen outside, he was far from a dream.

But he was as good as I was going to get.

11

WHAT WOULD A BIKER BABE DO?

"You all right?"

Buck was driving.

I was staring out the side window at the passing landscape.

Earlier, Pinky had recruited Cruise to go tell Buck I was there. She'd semi-explained things and Cruise had run interference. Pinky had promised Cruise would be discreet, and she knew this because she'd lied to him and told him I didn't see Nails, Minnie did.

In order to cover for Buck, Cruise, who seemed alarmingly practiced with this, had launched straight into action to avoid an unpleasant incident.

Buck found me studying hammers like they were my one life's desire. When he found me, he'd swept me into his body with an arm hooked around my neck, then bent his head and touched his mouth to mine.

I didn't feel it starting like I normally did, and thus I didn't open my mouth to invite him to deepen his kiss into a *kiss*.

The minute his lips left mine (lips, I might add, that not ten minutes before I was pretty certain had been locked to another woman's), I turned my head and pulled away.

Lorie, Minnie, and Pinky were close, and Lorie instantly moved in for another hug good-bye in what I would realize, while sitting silent in Buck's huge, black SUV (which, by the by, considering I hadn't been recently beaten up or pumped full of painkillers, I had since seen was a GMC Yukon), was an effort to cover my withdrawal. Minnie and Pinky did the same.

Buck, sensing nothing amiss (then again, he didn't really know me as, I reminded myself, I didn't really know him) took my bags and led me out to his truck.

Then we were away.

"Unh-hunh," I muttered to the window in answer to his question.

"Clara," he called.

I didn't move my gaze from the streaming landscape. "Yes?"

"Baby, did something happen today?" he asked in a gentle voice.

I closed my eyes because his gentle voice hurt.

What once was so gorgeous, in fact, it was so *everything* that I could convince myself it was the meaning of life...*hurt*.

Why couldn't one thing in my life—*one thing*—be good?

It didn't have to be perfect, but why couldn't it be good?

Like the promise of Buck had been, but the reality was *not*.

I opened my eyes but kept staring out the window.

"No, we had fun. The girls are great. I'm just tired."

"Too much, too soon," he surmised on a murmur.

"Unh-hunh," I agreed on a lie.

"I'll cook tonight," he decided. "Gear called. They got some party they're goin' to, meetin' their friends before for food. I was gonna take you to the Valley Inn, but we'll camp out at home."

"Great," I replied, relieved his kids were going to be off at a party.

An hour ago, I would have loved going out and having a meal with Buck like a normal couple.

We'd never done that. We'd never done stuff a normal couple would do—a normal couple dating or a normal couple living together and deciding on the fly to go out and share a meal.

Either way, I would have loved that.

I really would have.

And I might have even donned some of my new biker babe apparel, taken it for a test drive, assessed Buck's reaction.

Now I was glad we were going to camp out "at home."

Home.

It hit me then, my thoughts having descended into black, that I had never actually had a home. Not really. Not even with Rogan.

My home with Rogan was owned by the hundreds of pensioners who paid for it when Rogan sucked away their lifeblood (though, he didn't actually do this, he just sucked away the lifeblood of their retirement, but that was the same thing, or would be eventually).

God, I was a mess.

A pitiful mess.

I pulled in a deep quiet breath asking myself, *What would a biker babe do?*

I knew one thing from Minnie's lessons that day.

She wouldn't think of herself as a pitiful mess.

She'd either stick Buck with a knife or grin and bear it.

I wasn't the knife-wielding kind, so I was going to have to get myself together, grin and bear it.

"You get a cell?" Buck asked.

"Yes," I answered the window.

"You have a problem with the contract?" Buck asked.

"Yes, then Minnie shouted 'fuck' seven hundred times at the top of her lungs and on the tips of her toes with her face an inch away from the cell phone shop guy's face and they decided they didn't have a problem with my contract anymore."

Buck chuckled.

It was funny, but I didn't laugh.

"Seems you got on with them," he observed.

"We bonded," I replied.

"That's good, Toots," he muttered.

I didn't reply.

Grin and bear it, grin and bear it, grin and bear it.

"Clara?"

"Unh-hunh."

"Babe, you wanna tell me why you aren't looking at me?"

I looked at him.

Golly, he was handsome.

I looked out the windshield.

"It's just pretty up here. Lived in Phoenix my whole life, and probably have been up in the mountains less than a dozen times."

This was true, but as a reason for not looking at him, it was a big, fat lie.

"You have something on your mind," he stated.

He was right about that.

"I spent all your money," I told him to throw him off the scent.

"Babe," he replied.

"Actually, I spent eleven hundred and sixty-two dollars of your money. I have thirty-eight of your dollars left."

"I didn't give it to you for safekeeping, Toots. I gave it to you for you to spend it."

"Well, I did," I announced.

"Good," he muttered then asked, "You nervous about meeting Gear and Tatie?"

"Yes," I answered truthfully.

"It'll be okay," he assured.

Right.

"Mm-hmm," I mumbled.

He fell silent.

Then, for some bizarre reason, likely because the universe hated me, he asked out of the blue, "You were with your ex for ten years?"

"Yes," I answered.

"Why didn't you have kids?"

My stomach clutched.

My mouth spoke.

"Rogan said we had time."

He did say that.

We married young and Rogan had our lives planned.

According to Rogan's plan, I'd be pregnant right now or already have a wee one at home. He said when I was thirty, we were going to start our family. We'd have two kids. Then we'd stop.

And I was so happy with him, I was happy to do whatever he said.

I would never know how fortunate I was that he wanted to wait when I did not. I wanted to start a family right away. I wanted to have babies and give them everything I never had.

But I fell in with Rogan's plans which meant, when his life collapsed, taking mine with it, it didn't drag down our children.

All that had happened with Rogan was bad.

This was good.

"And you?" Buck pressed.

"Me what?"

"Did you want to wait?"

"No."

"But you waited."

"Yes," I pointed out the obvious.

"Do you want kids now?"

"No."

I felt rather than saw his eyes on me before he looked back to the road and asked, "No?"

"No, Buck. I have no home, no job and my car got repoed," I reminded him. "I need to depend on a man I barely know to keep me fed, housed and in a cell phone. I'm a mess. I've got no business bringing children into this world."

Suddenly, Buck changed lanes, going from the far left, straight to the shoulder. Then he stopped, put the SUV into neutral and set the parking brake while I blinked at the pavement ahead of us.

After all of this craziness, I felt his attention on me again.

"Babe, eyes," he growled, and hesitantly, my heart skipping rather than beating, I turned to face him. "What the fuck is up your ass?"

I stared at him.

He was angry and he was using his quiet, venom voice.

"Nothing," I whispered, feeling infected by his tone.

"Bullshit," he shot back.

"I'm just tired," I told him.

"You get tired, you get cuddly and sweet. You do not turn into a bitch."

I blinked again.

When I got tired, I got cuddly and sweet?

"I'm not being a bitch," I denied.

"You won't look at me. Your voice is flat. And what you just said was fucked," he returned.

"What did I just say?"

"You need to depend on a man you barely know to keep you fed, housed and in a fuckin' cell phone."

"This is true," I told him.

And I couldn't believe he was ticked about it, because it was!

"Toots, I've had my mouth between your legs, you've sucked me off, and I've had my dick in you."

"That isn't knowing you, Buck."

"You liked it and I liked it," he went on like I didn't speak. "You want more, and I want more. You can be uptight because you've been taught to be that way, caution equals survival for you. But when you relax, your smile comes easy and you're easy to be with. Now, you are not relaxed. Now, something is up your fuckin' ass. And I'm not takin' you home to my kids, who I want to like you, when somethin's up your fuckin' ass."

"I told you." I was beginning to get angry so my words were short and terse, not as short and terse as his, but they were still short and terse. "I'm tired. It's been a long day. We went to, like, I don't know, a hundred stores. I tried on so many clothes it isn't funny. Shopping is exhausting, Buck."

"Right," he clipped, obviously, and unsurprisingly, not an experienced shopper.

"It is!" I snapped. "And you want your kids to like me, how do you think I feel? You told me straight out Tatiana isn't going to like me. I've got a black eye, I'm dressed like a librarian with a shoe fetish, and I'm barreling in an SUV toward a sixteen-year-old Daddy's Little Girl who is not going to like me until I win her over. I don't know how to win her over! I don't know anything about sixteen-year-old girls! Even when I was sixteen, I wasn't sixteen. Do I offer to give her a manicure and ask her about the boys she likes? Do I read teenage vampire novels in hopes of finding common ground? I don't know how to give a manicure and we both know I'm not dexterous. What if I wound her while filing her nails?"

"Babe—"

"And Minnie and I got into it at lunch. It ended up okay, but she didn't like me at first. We had words and everyone was tense. We worked it out and they all decided to be Professor Higgins to my Eliza Biker Babe. They think it's fun and I don't want to disappoint them, I like them. Even Minnie, who's kind of hard to like. So I have to try to be a biker babe when all I know how to be is a geeky, brainy librarian."

"Darlin'—"

I started to sum up.

"So, Tia is smoke, your word, but when it's used to refer to my best friend in the entire world, it's not a fun word to hear. No one knows where she is, but as hard as I try to visualize her enjoying copious lattes, I'm guessing she isn't in Seattle serving coffee drinks. Instead, she's holed up somewhere, scared out of her brain, not only for herself, but wondering what became of me. I'm meeting your kids looking like Rocky Balboa's sparring partner. And I've got three Professor Higginses who are dedicated to the cause of turning me into the Premier Biker Princess, good enough for the president of the Aces High MC."

"Toots—"

I leaned in and cut him off yet again.

"So, to end, I have things on my *mind*, Buck. Weighty things. Important things. So, if my voice is flat and my mind is elsewhere, you are just going to have to *deal*."

"Clara—"

Apparently, that wasn't the end.

Because I kept going.

"And I won't take it out on your kids. Even though we've had sex, a lot of it, we had it all in one night. This does not mean I know you and you know me. But I'll educate you about me. I'm not the kind of person to take my mood out on kids. You, you're an adult. I would hope you'd eventually be able to wrap your mind around all the stuff drifting through mine and get it. Kids won't be able to do that. So, I'll walk into your house and I'll do what I can to make your kids like me. In other words, you don't have to worry."

"Baby, shut...*up*."

I shut up.

Buck studied my face.

Then his lips twitched.

Then he asked, "A librarian with a shoe fetish?"

Argh!

I turned to stare out the windshield and crossed my arms on my chest.

"Babe," Buck called, and I ignored him. "Toots," he called again, and I ignored him. "Clara," he called yet again, and I spoke to the windshield.

"I'm hungry and I want to get this over with. Are we going to stay on the shoulder all night? Because, if so, I have thirty-eight dollars in my purse and I'm walking to the nearest fast food place on the nearest off ramp and getting myself dinner."

Suddenly, my seatbelt was released. It zipped back, and I jumped, uncrossing my arms to avoid seatbelt injury. Just as suddenly, I was pulled across the cab and found my torso pressed to Buck's, both his arms were wound around me, and his face was in mine.

"The nearest turnoff is three miles away. You couldn't make it in those shoes," he informed me.

"She's hungry enough, a woman can do a lot in her quest for food," I replied.

He grinned.

It was close up and his grins close up were the best.

My heart skipped just as I felt pain slice through my belly, and I realized the despair was back. It had disappeared while my life shifted, but it was back.

I was going to have to learn to live with it *again*.

"I'll get you home, you'll meet my kids and I'll feed you as soon as you kiss me."

My heart skipped again.

"I'm not in the mood to kiss you," I stated firmly, because I definitely wasn't.

"Then we'll sit just like this as long as it takes for you to get in the mood."

I glared into his eyes.

Eyes, incidentally, whose laugh lines had deepened.

"I'm learning something about you," I told him.

"Yeah? What's that?"

"You're annoying."

His arms spasmed around me as he laughed.

I did not laugh.

I kept glaring.

His laughter died to a chuckle and then he said, "Somethin' else you should know about me, Toots."

"And that is?"

"I'm stubborn."

Oh, for goodness sake.

I lifted up and touched my mouth to his then pulled back.

"There, happy?"

His brows went up. "Are you shitting me?"

I tried to push my hands between our bodies, but failed, gave up and answered, "No."

"Babe, kiss me."

"I did, and we need to get a move on. I don't think it's illegal to hang out on the side of the road embracing, but it *is* likely something the Arizona Highway Patrol frowns on."

"Don't give a shit."

"Buck—"

"Kiss me."

"No, I'm—"

"Babe, kiss me."

"No! I think—"

His arms squeezed. "Clara, stop fuckin' around."

"Oh, all right," I snapped, lifted again, tilted my head to the side and put my lips to his.

I knew that wouldn't be enough, so I touched the tip of my tongue to his lips, those lips opened, and I slid my tongue inside.

God, I hated that I loved the way he tasted.

And I loved it.

Enough for my body to melt against his, my hands, which were on his shoulders, slid around to his back, and I pressed in, drinking my fill.

He forced my tongue out of his mouth, his tongue invaded mine, his arms tightened, and he took over the kiss.

It was amazing, beautiful, wet, deep, wild and all of those enough to make me forget he'd given the same thing to another woman not very long ago.

In fact, I forgot everything but Buck, his body, his mouth, his tongue, and the fact that I was happy that in that moment they were all mine.

After a while (a long while), he lifted his head, and I opened my eyes to stare into his.

His were dark and hungry.

Delicious.

"*Now*, I'll take you home," he murmured, his rough voice thick.

"Okay," I whispered.

He gave me another squeeze then he did something wrong.

He angled his head and kissed my nose before depositing me back in my seat.

That slid next to the despair, souring my stomach.

Buck put the truck into gear, released the parking brake, flipped on the turn signal and pulled into traffic.

I drifted my fingers through my hair then touched the tips of them to my lips.

I loved the taste of him, and I loved that he kissed my nose. And I loved that he ended a fight kissing me. And I loved that he took my diatribe and ended that by teasing me.

I loved it all and I hated it all, and I wondered if he did the same with Nails and whoever else was in his life.

But this was as good as I could get and I'd been so low, I reminded myself where I was now was a lot better than where I used to be.

And anyway, I was Clara Nobody.

What did I think I deserved?

Grin and bear it, my mind reminded me.

"Babe," Buck called.

One could say I had learned my lesson.

So I looked at him.

"Yes?"

His tattooed arm came out and his fingers wrapped around my wrist, pulling my arm to him, sliding down. His big hand enveloping mine, he gave it a squeeze.

"I gave you all that and you didn't even wince. Your ribs good?"

And there it was.

Thoughtful.

Worried.

Protective.

All of that awesome.

None of it really real.

"They're fine," I told him the truth.

"Healin'," he muttered. "Good."

At least that was right.

"We'll find your girl," he said gently, resting my hand on his thigh.

God, I hated that I loved it when he was sweet and protective.

Grin and bear it, my mind repeated to me.

Yes, I was now a biker babe and that was what a biker babe would do.

And I would be a biker babe until I needed to be the next thing I needed to be.

One thing I knew.

When I was whatever that next thing was, I'd have to grin and bear that too.

12

GEAR

I stood outside on Buck's deck, drinking a margarita and trying to find calm.

Buck had been right.

The minute Gear met me, he started flirting.

The minute Tatiana met me, however, she decided she hated me.

Actively.

Twenty minutes ago, we'd walked into his house and the kids were already there.

After Buck gave his daughter a hug and a kiss on the top of her head and slapped his son on the shoulder, he performed the introductions.

I saw that the kids were different than their pictures in his bedroom.

In the pictures, they were more kid than adult.

Now they were definitely more adult than kid.

They both looked like him and this was more than a hint.

Gear was Buck's height, which meant, I guessed, he was six-foot, six-foot-one. His body had the same build, but it was different. His shoulders not yet as broad. His frame not as filled out.

Gear also didn't have the command of his body like his dad had. Gear held himself loose, and although not boyish, it was cocky.

He had dark hair just like his father's, those gorgeous brown eyes, but he also had an easy smile.

Tatiana, on the other hand, was petite.

I was five-foot-seven, but in my high heels, a lot taller.

She was wearing flip-flops and had to be five-four, at most.

She had her dad's dark hair too, except long, cut in chunky layers— this more noticeable at the sides that fell in textured wisps from jaw to ends— and it flowed in waves down her back.

She also had Buck's dark brown eyes.

But she had beautiful skin, peaches and cream and sheer perfection, not her father's and brother's olive tone.

Upon meeting me, Gear looked me up and down, gave me a lazy smile and a handshake that lasted too long.

Tatiana looked me up and down as well, her lip curled slightly, and after giving me a dagger glare, she avoided my eyes.

Buck took my shopping bags to his bedroom while announcing he was making chicken enchiladas.

This was met with a fair and surprising amount of excitement, and Gear and Tatiana instantly decided they'd bag on meeting their friends for food prior to the party and stick around for enchiladas.

This sent me straight to the tequila and margarita mix.

Both kids got out their cell phones and their fingers flew over the screens as they texted their change in plans to their friends.

Buck came back from the bedroom and went direct to the fridge.

I asked the kids if they wanted a drink, got Gear a Coke, pretended to ignore the fact that Tatiana ignored my question, and instead asked Buck if he wanted a margarita.

His way of saying no was giving me a grin and getting himself a beer.

Buck then started moving around the kitchen, doing things to prepare to cook while I made my margarita.

The problem with this was, both his kids were on stools on the outside of the counter, facing the kitchen. I was in the kitchen, and it became apparent very quickly that Buck didn't intend to let them in on the nature of our relationship gently.

I knew this because, if he needed something around where I was working, his arm would curve around me, hand at my belly, front pressed to my back, and he'd lean into me to get it.

Or, if he needed me to vacate the space, his fingers would span my hips, and he'd pull me away, grab what he needed, then those fingers would go back to my hips and he'd return me to where I used to be.

This had two unfortunate results.

It delayed my margarita and made my face feel hot.

Finally, margarita done, my mind whirling to find some escape so I could regroup and come up with a plan, Buck sent Gear on the errand of getting tortillas and cheese for the enchiladas.

I braved a glance at the two on the stools.

Gear was smirking at me.

Tatiana looked like she'd sucked a lemon.

"Right, Dad," Gear agreed, eyes on me. "You wanna come, Clara? You'll get to experience my ride and my ride is *dope*."

I smiled a genuine smile because I had the feeling I would like Gear, and I lifted my glass.

"No, but thanks for the offer. Today I endured a Biker Babe Ritual. It was grueling, so now I need to put my feet up and drink tequila. Maybe you'll let me experience your ride another time."

Gear's smile got bigger. Tatiana's lip curled again. Buck's hand came out of nowhere, swept my hair off my neck then his lips were there for a quick kiss.

I froze and my eyes shot to Tatiana who looked about ready to vomit.

"It's a nice evening," I proclaimed, side-stepping Buck after his lips left my neck. "I'm going to go sit on the deck." I sucked in breath and offered to Tatiana, "Do you want me to get you a drink and you can join me?"

"No, when Dad cooks, I help," Tatiana replied, saying this like it was the eleventh commandment and I was a heathen that didn't know this was set in stone by the divine hand of God. "And anyway, this is my house so I can get my own drink."

This caught Buck's attention and his eyes narrowed on her.

Though, fortunately, because I didn't think it'd make me more popular with her, he didn't call her on it.

She slid off her stool, and ignoring her father's narrowed eyes, she smiled a dazzling smile at him and offered, "I'll cut up the chicken."

"Great, babe, thanks," Buck muttered, his gaze on his daughter now no longer narrow but watchful.

"I'm outta here," Gear stated, grabbing a set of keys from the counter and heading toward the door. "We need anything else?"

"Diet Coke," Tatiana replied.

"Clara?" Gear prompted.

"No, thanks," I replied, moving with him to the front door because it led to the deck.

"Dad?" Gear went on.

"A sixer of Coors and a carton of Marlboro Reds," Buck answered.

At this response, I stopped dead, turned my attention to Buck and was pretty sure my eyes bugged out.

He was asking his son to buy beer and cigarettes?

His *seventeen-year-old* son, who, in order to do this had to have a fake ID, and Buck not only knew about it, but encouraged him to use it?

And...

Buck smoked?

I'd seen the ashtrays littering the MC's hangout, but I'd never seen Buck smoke.

Though, I'd smelled it on him, but the smell was not like he did it. It was like he was around others who did.

"Gotcha, on it," Gear replied easily. "And while I'm out, want me to hit up our boy for a dime bag of weed?"

"Sure," Buck agreed.

Oh my God!

Then, when I glanced between them and processed the identical bad boy smiles they were giving me, I realized both Hardy men were teasing me.

To which I rolled my eyes.

This made Buck's lips quirk and he finally gave his son a real answer.

"No, Gear, I think we're good."

Gear nodded, opened the front door, and muttered, "I'm gone."

Then he was.

"I'll be right out here," I announced, followed him out, and as such, escaped.

I stayed escaped while I stood out on the deck, gazed unseeing at the landscape, sipped my margarita, tried to find calm, and failed because I was also trying to think of ways to break through Tatiana's dislike of me.

I knew it was early days (or actually, early minutes).

But even with Buck's warning, I was unprepared for just how much she visibly, not-making-that-first-attempt-to-hide-it disliked me.

In truth, what I wanted was to take off my shoes, my feet were killing me.

But my shoes were the only thing that made my outfit even a modicum of cool.

And by appearances, both of Buck's kids had inherited his coolness.

Gear even had his mysteriously cool styled-but-not-really hair.

Thus, I decided, I needed to keep my shoes on.

After I made that decision, I figured I was going to need more margaritas and wished I'd made a pitcher.

I looked into the house and saw Tatiana standing, doing something at the counter, her back to me, her head turned and tilted back. She was smiling up at her dad, who was close and grinning down at her.

She was very pretty when she smiled.

Gorgeous.

She said something, and he threw his head back and laughed, which made her smile bigger, and she leaned into him, bumping his chest with her shoulder.

My heart skipped at the sight.

It was cute.

It was sweet.

I liked that Buck could be like that with his girl. I liked that Tatiana had that because every girl should have that.

At the same time, I was jealous because I never did.

And the emotion wasn't jealousy that I felt at knowing I'd never see a daughter of mine do that with her father. A father that was my husband, my man, my lover, someone I trusted and loved who I intended to spend the rest of my life with.

No, that feeling wasn't jealousy.

It was something else altogether and that something caused not a small amount of pain.

I decided against going in and making a pitcher of margaritas in favor of giving father and daughter more time.

I walked to a teak deck chair that had thick maroon pads, dragged it toward the railing, sat and lifted my feet to rest the soles of my shoes on a lower rung.

That was better.

I sipped my margarita until there was nothing but ice and stayed outside, wondering if I was beginning to appear rude.

On that thought, I saw a shiny, black car that wasn't anywhere near new but was definitely cool growling loudly up the lane. I didn't know the make or model, but I did know, whatever it was, it was awesome.

Gear was home.

Five minutes later, Gear with his can of Coke was out on the deck with me.

I turned my head and smiled at him as he pulled a chair beside mine, sat in it and put his feet up on the same rung as mine.

"Dad says grub'll be up in twenty," he told me.

"Great," I replied, my stomach roiling, suddenly not in the mood for grub because eating it meant being around Tatiana, and I still hadn't come up with a plan.

I felt his eyes on me, so I looked at him.

"What's with the shiner?" he asked, a grin playing at his mouth in an effort to take the nosiness out of his question.

Though the grin didn't hide the concern in his eyes.

Really, so like his dad.

"Long story," I answered, saying it softly so he wouldn't feel rebuffed.

"That's cool," he muttered, letting it go and obviously not feeling rebuffed, which was a relief.

"Was the drive down okay?" I asked, looking for something to talk about.

"Could drive it blindfolded, done it so often."

"Right," I whispered.

He studied me only a moment before he announced on another grin, "You're nervous."

My head jerked at this straightforward comment, then I couldn't help it, I emitted a short laugh.

"Um...yes," I replied when I stopped laughing and I did it on a smile. "Is it that obvious?"

"Totally." He smiled back.

"Bummer," I muttered.

"No, it's cool that you're nervous and all," he stated. "But don't get wound up about Tatie. She and Dad are tight, but she's cool."

Again, straightforward.

So like his dad.

"Okay," I said quietly.

"She's not good with women," he informed me, and his open sharing surprised me, so I couldn't quite stop myself from staring at him. "She and Ma..." He shook his head. "They butt heads. When Dad and Mom were together, it was all good. When we first moved up to Flag, it was okay. Then something gave, and now Mom's a total bitch to her. They're always fightin'. Tatie hates bein' home, she wants to live here. We both like it here better than there. Me, because I hate Ma's old man, he's a dick. And sometimes Ma can be not-so-great with me either. Tatie, because Ma's in her face all the time and because she thinks Knuckles is a dick."

"Knuckles?"

"Ma's old man."

"I'm sorry, that doesn't sound good," I noted carefully.

"It isn't, it sucks. So when Dad told us he got himself a woman, Tatie got pissed. She wants it to be just the three of us. She likes it like that. Reckon she doesn't want to face the possibility of a female Knuckles here while she's dealin' with that dick back home. But, like I said, she's cool. She gets wound up, like Ma, but in the end, that isn't really her. It's just what Ma and Knuckles make her, or maybe it's that plus teenage girl stuff. Whatever. She'll come around."

"That's what your dad says."

He grinned. "That's 'cause that's the way it is."

I studied him. His face was expressive. He was honest and straight-forward, and it was clear he was a good kid.

Maybe he could help me out.

"Do you..." I hesitated, "have any advice?"

His brows went up. "On dealin' with Tat?"

I nodded.

He grinned big. "Just don't be a bitch to her."

I smiled back. "I think I can do that."

His grin faded and he leaned into me to share, "She doesn't have a lot of friends, Clara. She does here, the girls here like her, but the girls at home..." He shook his head again. "No. Don't get that, she can be sweet when she's not wound up. I think it's 'cause girls, well...girls can be bitches. They're jealous 'cause, she's my sister and all, but there's no denyin' she's hot."

I nodded again. "Yes, Gear, your sister is definitely very pretty, and you're right, girls can be mean, especially to girls who are pretty."

He nodded back and went on, "So she's got a ma who's up in her face all the time, and the girls at school treat her like garbage. Fuck with her head, play with her. It's freakin' whacked. I try to shield her from it, but I can't be everywhere all the time. No matter how hard I try to be that for her."

Trying to protect his sister.

Truly...

So like his father.

"And girls," he continued, "they don't let much deter them when they're set on bein' bitches."

"No," I agreed ruefully. "They don't."

"So, you know, I reckon, a woman's nice to her, eventually that'd break through."

I was a little surprised at the F-bomb dropping so easily from the lips of a seventeen-year-old, like it was nothing which was how his father used that word.

But I didn't mention that.

I'd ask Minnie about it later.

Though I suspected this was part of the biker life, what with them having a rulebook only with a couple of lines. I doubted they wasted one of them on teaching your children not to curse.

But my take from all of that was good and even hopeful.

Because I could be nice to Tatie.

And maybe, if I found a way in, I could be a woman in her life that she liked and trusted.

"Well, I can be nice," I told Gear.

"Then I reckon you'll break through."

I smiled at him again. "Sounds like a plan."

He smiled back.

I decided to change the subject. "Your car is very cool."

His smile grew huge. "Yeah, freakin' *awesome*. Chevy Nova, 1972. Classic. Dad and I worked on it for a year. It was a wreck. We worked on it out back, in his old barn."

I had seen this "old barn." I'd also wondered at its uses, since Buck, and now Gear, parked in the wide area by the side of the house where the steps up to the deck and front door were.

Now I knew.

"He never let on it was for me," Gear kept speaking. "I thought he was fixin' it up to sell it or use it himself. Then, on my sixteenth birthday, he drove up in it, Ink came with in Ink's truck, and he gave it to me. Ma went nuts, but she couldn't do shit. Not only is that car the freakin' bomb, Dad and I worked on it together and it means freedom. For me and Tat. Best frickin' present I ever got."

"You're tight with your dad too," I surmised.

"He's the shit," Gear agreed on a mutter, looking out at the landscape.

Yes, I thought, in many ways he was.

Something to contemplate.

Like Gear, I studied the landscape.

We were comfortably silent for a while.

Gear broke the silence.

"What's a Biker Babe Ritual?"

I turned to him to see he had his eyes on me and they were dancing.

"Um...did you see all those bags your dad had when we walked in?"

"Yeah."

"Lorie, Minnie and Pinky took me shopping at biker babe shops today. We went to approximately three hundred of them, I tried on biker babe apparel and they talked me into buying the vast majority of it. That's a Biker Babe Ritual."

"Doesn't sound fun," Gear noted.

"Well, you're not a girl. For a girl, something like that is fun, but that doesn't mean it wasn't exhausting."

"You goin' for the biker babe look?" he asked, eyes still dancing.

"They assure me I can pull it off, but I must admit, I'm not very assured."

"You'd probably look good in anything, Clara."

I felt my belly get warm.

"That's sweet, Gear."

"But you look good now, as you are," he continued. "You don't need to be a biker babe. Take it from me, I'm a guy, you definitely work what you already are."

I stared at him, stunned.

Something else to contemplate.

His lips twitched before he asked, "But, uh...what are you?"

"I'm a librarian."

He returned my stare a second.

Then, just like his dad, he threw his head back and laughed, loud and deep.

It wasn't rough, like his father's laughter, but it was just as beautiful.

When he stopped laughing, he wiped his hand over his mouth and muttered to the view, "Freakin' hilarious. Dad's hooked up with a librarian."

"Yes, I figure I'm not his type," I, too, spoke to the view.

"Don't know his type, Clara," Gear stated, and I returned my attention to him to see he was still gazing at the scenery. "Dad don't bring women home. Seen him with women down at the Dive, but he doesn't bring 'em home. You're the first since he and Ma split three years ago."

I blinked at him in shock as he turned his head to me.

"But if Ma's anything to go by, you are definitely not his type. You haven't once shouted or thrown anything or stomped out of the room. Seems to me he's aimin' higher than his first go."

That was such a nice thing to say, my belly warmed again.

"I'm thinking you're a good man, Gear," I said softly, and he grinned a cocky grin.

"Yeah, but don't get fooled, Clara. I'll let you in on a secret. That's how I reel 'em in," he replied brazenly, and it was my turn to stare for a moment before it was my turn to throw my head back and laugh, something I did.

It felt nice when I heard Gear's chuckle join my laughter.

When we were done, Gear sucked back soda and I chewed on margarita-flavored ice.

Then Gear muttered, "Gotta hand it to Dad, only he'd find the only librarian in Phoenix who was hot."

I couldn't help it, I laughed again.

Gear joined me.

13

TATIANA

My body was moved, and my eyes fluttered open.

Time for bed.

I blinked at the clock on the DVD player.

It was flashing twelve, like normal.

But I sensed it was early.

This was because of the program that was on mute on the TV. It had to be before eleven.

Weird, Buck never went to bed this early.

It was after Buck's enchiladas, which were by far and away the best enchiladas I'd ever tasted *in my life*.

They were so the best, they could easily be placed in the top five of the best of *any* food I'd ever tasted, thus explaining Gear's and Tatiana's excitement when Buck announced he was making them. I'd set aside plans for just about anything to eat Buck's enchiladas.

It was also after Tatiana pointedly ignored me throughout dinner as we all sat on stools at the kitchen counter, Buck and I at the counter in the kitchen, Tatiana and Gear on the stools on the other side.

This was a mistake I made innocently, assuming a seat by Buck.

It was clearly Tatiana's and I knew this when her eyes flashed fire the second I put my behind there.

I immediately slid off and offered it to her, but she refused, mouth tight, eyes angry and she didn't even try to be polite. Indeed, for some time, she milked this for the insult that resulted in a deep wound she made clear would never heal. A wound she was intent to make absolutely certain I knew I'd delivered.

Gear attempted to inject humor into the situation, and Buck tried to catch Tatiana's eyes, his holding a warning that he was beginning to get impatient with her behavior, but both deflected off her.

She then began a campaign of chatting about things that were familiar among the three of them. Things I could have no comment on, pointedly keeping me out of the conversation.

Buck and Gear just as pointedly drew me back in.

To this, Tatiana moved on to other subjects that would keep me out.

And Buck and Gear again drew me back in.

Finally, Tatiana fell silent and started pouting.

I could get her being close to her dad, and I definitely understood her wanting him all to herself, especially if things weren't good at home with her mother and the girls at school. This was her safe place. I could see that. Her father was her safe person, I could see that too.

But the pouting, at sixteen, I thought was taking it too far. It made her look juvenile because it *was* juvenile.

Though, obviously, I didn't share this opinion.

Buck did.

When the time had come for them to get ready to go, he followed her to her room, closed the door and didn't come out for a full fifteen minutes.

Although I had to agree that maybe a word (or fifteen minutes of them) was now due, I made myself scarce through this by fixing myself another margarita and taking it to Buck's room where I put away my new biker babe apparel and set my phone to charge.

I came out to find Buck drinking a beer and talking to Gear in the kitchen.

Not two seconds later, Tatiana came out wearing a skirt that was way too short, heels that were way too high, and at least a five-day supply of makeup slathered on her face.

In other words, my guess, an outfit that would make any father's head explode, even a badass biker's.

I guessed correctly.

On sight of her, Buck's body got tight, and I stepped away from him in case his head was about to explode.

Tatiana ignored it and threw him a challenging look, which, personally, I didn't think was wise.

I was pretty certain he wasn't going to let her go out looking like that, but to my shock, he did.

Although he did this at the same time warning Gear to, "Keep an eye on your fuckin' sister."

Perhaps that was the answer to one of my questions about this family.

Buck also showed no hesitation dropping the F-bomb around his kids, even doing it while speaking to them.

I didn't ask why he allowed his sixteen-year-old daughter to walk out of the house looking one step up from streetwalker because it was none of my business.

However, I suspected he did this because he didn't want to get into it with her in front of me. That would not make him or me popular, and he liked being the former and he wanted the latter.

After the kids were gone, we didn't debrief about the night.

We did what we always did: camped out in front of the TV, my cheek to Buck's thigh, his feet on the coffee table, his fingers in my hair and a beer in his other hand.

I was not wrong. After days of being careful with myself, a day of activity tuckered me out. I was asleep within an hour.

Now I was awake, and apparently it was bedtime.

Surprisingly, Buck didn't shift out from under me in order to lift me up and carry me to bed.

Instead, he pulled me into his lap.

Automatically, still half in a doze, I wrapped my arms around his shoulders in preparation for him carrying me to the bedroom.

He didn't do this either.

He touched his mouth to mine.

My eyes opened as his lips slid down my cheek to my jaw to my neck. Through this, his hands worked their way under my blouse so they were skin against skin.

Oh my.

"Buck?" I called.

"I'll go gentle, baby," he whispered in my ear. I got what he was saying instantly, and a shiver slid through me. His hands on me, his lips at my ear, all thoughts of Nails or, say, *anything*, nowhere near my head. "You seem good, but I hurt you, you let me know and we'll get creative."

Creative.

Oh.

My.

"Buck—" I breathed.

It was already starting, and it revved up when his hands moved over my ribcage and I felt one thumb slide along the underside of my breast.

That breast swelled, and to keep it company, the other one did too.

"Buck," I repeated on a breath.

His head came up, his mouth taking mine in a full-on, tongues-tangled *kiss*.

Wow.

I moved my arms from his shoulders so I could get my hands to his skin. When I pulled his T-shirt free of his jeans and slid my fingers over the sleek, hard muscle, I liked it so much I moaned into his mouth.

Buck liked that so much, he shifted so his back was to the seat of the couch, I was on top, and his fingers plunged into my hair, cupping my scalp, tilting my head and holding me to him so his mouth could plunder mine.

I let him plunder. He could plunder all night. I *loved* the way Buck plundered and I showed him this by pressing into him.

His other hand moved between us, undoing my jeans then sliding around and down, his fingers clenching my behind.

I pushed my hips into his.

"Fuck, baby, missed this ass," Buck growled against my lips, his fingers digging in, and I agreed, partially.

I missed his *hand* on my ass.

I cupped his bearded jaw and slid my lips through his thick whiskers down the other side, to his neck and onward, to the collar of his tee. I ran my tongue along the edge of the material.

He tasted good everywhere.

He flexed his fingers into my flesh again then I felt his body go still under mine.

My head came up and I looked down at him.

His head was turned, and his brows were drawn.

I turned to see what he was looking at, just caught the lights on the drive, and then I was moving. Before I knew it, I was on my feet and Buck was doing up my jeans.

"Fuck, they're early," he muttered.

"What? Who?" I asked, confused and trying to adjust from making out with Buck on his couch with his hand in my jeans to standing beside it with his hands doing up my zipper.

"Tatie and Gear," he answered, and I looked from his hands to his face as he finished with the button and his fingers moved to curve around my hips and pull me to him. "Their curfew is one. It's barely eleven. They're early."

Oh.

Big-time bummer.

"Oh," I whispered as I laid my hands flat on his chest.

His hands stayed where they were, keeping me where I was, but his head turned toward the front door.

"Not thinkin' this is good," he murmured.

"Why?"

He looked down at me.

"They both like a good time. They're never home early."

"Do they usually get in by curfew?" I asked.

"They've pushed it once or twice, but yeah, usually. Just never early."

The door opened and both Buck and I looked that way.

It took approximately three quarters of a second to see why Gear and Tatiana were home early.

Gear was angry, *very* angry, spitting-venom-like-his-dad angry.

Tatiana was one hundred percent hammered.

"Do not give me shit," Gear warned, his eyes on his father, his hand curled around his sister's biceps, propelling her drunk-and-loose-like-a-ragdoll body into the house and slamming the door.

Buck had let me go and he was on the move, making a beeline toward his kids.

"What the fuck?" he clipped, not heeding Gear's warning. "Didn't I say look out for her?"

"Yeah, you said it. She just didn't listen to a freakin' word *I* said. I dumped three beers, she just got more and did shots of everything anyone would offer her. She was on a frickin' *mission* to get totally and completely *shitfaced*."

Oh dear.

I had a not-so-vague feeling this was my fault.

Buck commandeered Tatiana by taking hold of her other biceps and pulling her from Gear, who seemed happy to be rid of her.

Her head bobbing on her shoulders, she stumbled. Her feet shifting to right herself, she slipped off her heel, and then by what would seem from her state was a small miracle, she recovered. The whole time she looked up and didn't exactly focus on her father.

"Hey, Daddy."

She grinned at her dad, then gulped, and suddenly, Buck and Gear both moved quickly, each taking a huge step away from her as she bent over and vomited on the wood floor of the entry.

Ick!

"Fuck me," Buck growled, his angry eyes aimed to the floor.

I moved while ordering, "Get her to the bathroom."

"No shit, Toots?" Buck replied as I headed to his bedroom, but I looked over my shoulder to see that he had his daughter in his arms, and he was walking swiftly my way as Tatiana's body heaved.

She was going to blow again.

I started running.

I hit his bedroom, went to the vanity in the bathroom where, in a drawer, I'd put my hair stuff, and grabbed a huge clip (one bonus of Buck not primping, I had plenty of space to move in, not only in the bathroom, but also in his closet *and* chest of drawers).

Procuring this, I ran to the bathroom that separated Buck's office from Tatiana's bedroom and saw Gear standing outside looking in, arms crossed on his chest, an expression on his face that said both, "Gross," and, "My sister's an idiot."

I scooted by him and saw Buck standing *in* the bathroom in the same exact stance with the same exact expression on his face.

I passed Buck and got to my knees beside Tatiana, trying to ignore the sound and smell. She had a hand clenched in her hair, but she hadn't captured it all and her head was over the toilet.

I gathered her hair, and she let me, her body heaving, her back bowing and contracting violently. I secured her hair in the clip and reached out to flush the toilet.

I looked up at Buck. "Can you get me a big glass of cold water?"

"She drinks it, she'll puke it," was Buck's reply.

"She's got alcohol poisoning. We need to rehydrate her at the same time counteracting the alcohol. Please, get me a glass of cold water."

"Babe, it's gonna come right back up and she won't thank you," Buck warned.

"I don't want her to thank me. I want her to get that garbage out of her system so she'll feel well enough to sleep without her foot on the floor because the room's spinning," I shot back. "Now, can you *please* get me a glass of *water?*"

Buck stared at me, scowling, but Gear offered, "I'll get it."

"Thanks, Gear," I called because he disappeared.

I got up and walked to the bathroom closet. Opening it, I grabbed a washcloth and took it to the sink to wet it with cold water. As I did this, Tatiana spit into the toilet while alternately moaning.

"I got this, Toots," Buck declared, even though he hadn't moved a muscle and was still standing there, arms crossed on his chest, face like thunder.

I guessed him "having this" was him letting his daughter live the nightmare of over-imbibing in order to teach her a lesson.

I wet the washcloth and wrung it out.

"Why don't you clean up the floor by the door?" I suggested.

"Oh no, babe." He shook his head. "Only one's cleanin' the floor by the door is on her knees in front of the toilet."

This caused another hollow, echoing moan from the toilet area and then the sound of more vomit hitting water.

I decided that Tatiana Hardy was likely not going to be excited at the prospect of enchiladas for a while.

I swallowed down the bile that rose up my own throat then moved back to Tatiana, going down on my knees. I folded the washcloth and leaned in to press it against her forehead while I reached out with the other hand to flush again.

I looked up at Buck and said quietly, "She's sixteen, West. She's going to do stuff like this."

"Yeah, and she's gonna learn she shouldn't do it too."

"I thought your motto was to live more," I threw at him.

"It is, but that don't mean you live stupid, Clara. She's sixteen, she's dressed like a whore and she's shitfaced. She didn't have her brother with her, right now she could be in a world a' hurt. I was sixteen once, and I had ears then like I do now. I heard the talk. So I know there are fuckwad boys who live for the opportunity she presented tonight. So, she learns the hard way, she doesn't give them that fuckin' opportunity."

Even as I could argue, at length, and correctly, that Tatiana should feel she could drink what she wanted and wear what she wanted whenever she wanted without any boy on this planet, any other one, in alternate dimensions or on parallel universes thinking it was their right to take such an "opportunity," I didn't have the time.

But sadly, in this universe on this planet at this moment, I had to admit, he was right.

"You're right," I whispered, and Buck just stared at me. Then I said, "But if you don't clean up that mess out there, I will."

He opened his mouth to speak, and I stopped rubbing Tatiana's back to lift my hand, palm out, in his direction.

"I get it. Again, you're right. Definitely right. Though only about the underage drinking and not being particularly smart in just how much she partook of that. But the shape she's in, that punishment doesn't fit the crime and she won't be much better tomorrow. You leave it until then with that mess out there all night, tomorrow morning, we'll *all* be punished."

His mouth got tight. Gear came in with a glass of ice water. Then Buck stormed out of the bathroom, I hoped to clean up the mess because I sure didn't want to.

Gear gave me a curious glance I couldn't quite decipher before he followed his father as Tatiana spit into the toilet bowl.

"Can you sit up, honey?" I asked, and she surprisingly did.

I took the cloth from her head and reached out to flush the toilet again. With her latest offering swirling away, I wiped her face and mouth. I tossed the cloth into the sink and reached up to get the glass from the counter and handed it to her.

"Drink slow. Sips, yes?"

She nodded, her mascara running down her face, her eyes going anywhere but me. She sipped then again gagged. I grabbed the glass and her face was back over the toilet bowl.

Tatiana and I did this routine for a while with me wringing out the cloth repeatedly and finally leaving her to run to Buck's bathroom to grab my facewash. When she settled enough, she moved with me to the sink and I helped her wash off her makeup. We accomplished this feat, but seconds after, she was on her knees again at the toilet.

Though now it was only dry heaves.

Not fun for Tatiana, but the worst had passed.

I stayed with her until she finally curled up beside the toilet and closed her eyes, apparently happy to sleep on the bathroom floor.

"You want me to help you to bed?"

"No," she whispered and started to shiver.

"You want me to get you a blanket?" I asked.

"No," she whispered again, still shivering.

She didn't want me to get a blanket, so I didn't. I went to the closet and got a clean bath towel and threw it over her. She didn't shrug it off, but instead clutched at the edge with her fingertips and pulled it up under her chin.

"When you think you might be able to hold it down, I'll get you some ibuprofen," I offered.

Tatiana moaned.

"Okay," I said quickly. "Not now."

I sat on the floor beside her and rested my back against the tub.

We were both silent until she whispered, "Go away."

"I'm happy to stay."

"Go away," she repeated.

"You can't sleep on the floor in the bathroom, honey."

"Go...*away.*"

I sighed.

I also decided, if she didn't want me around, I wasn't making her feel better. Therefore, there was no reason to hang around.

She was over the worst of it. Now she had to count on her youth and time to get her to the other side.

I stood, got another towel and threw it over her lower body.

"Water's by the sink," I told her. "Try to get it down."

"Go away," she replied.

I went away, heading to my next chore of cleaning up sick.

I hit the kitchen area to see Gear sitting on the counter, Buck standing by him, arms crossed on his chest. I saw the sick was gone, and I bit my lip, grateful.

"She feels like sleeping in the bathroom," I announced when I hit their semi-huddle.

"Bet she does," Gear muttered.

Buck didn't speak.

Both Hardy men were unhappy.

"Maybe I'll go to bed," I suggested, not knowing what else to do.

"'Night," Gear replied.

Buck just stared at me.

Hmm.

I didn't think that was good.

"Goodnight," I whispered and moved from the kitchen.

I went to Buck's room, changed into a nightie and got into his bed.

He didn't join me for a while, though I heard Gear go upstairs, and I didn't find sleep.

Finally, I heard Buck moving around the house, and what I heard was him carrying his daughter to bed.

After that, he was in his room. Rustling noises commenced as he took off his clothes and then the bed moved when he joined me. But once there, he settled and didn't curl into me or curl me into him.

Oh dear.

"You're mad at me," I whispered into the dark.

"Nope, mad at Tatie. Knew she'd make a play for my attention, thinkin' she had to battle you for it, even though, during our conversation before she went out, I took pains to share with her that was not the case. Didn't think my girl would make such a stupid play. Thought I taught her better."

"She's only sixteen, Buck."

"No age is too early to get smart, Clara."

He was right about that.

I stared into the dark.

Eventually I sucked in a breath.

And using it, I said, "You know, earlier, I saw you two through the window. She said something to make you laugh and leaned into you. Most girls who have that, what she has with you, they don't know it's precious. Gear told me she doesn't get on with her mom or that Knuckles guy, so I figure, she has it rough at home, she knows what she has with you is precious. I never had that."

I paused when I felt something strange that was coming from him fill the room, then I continued.

"So, I know, like Tatiana knows, that's precious. She's sixteen. She sees me as a threat. You might not get it, but I do. If I had something like that, I'd do anything to keep it. Anything to hold my dad's attention, even if I had to make him mad at me to do it. She's not old enough to know how to play it smart, West. But if things are bad at home, she's desperate enough to do whatever she has to do. I get that too."

I stopped talking and Buck didn't move.

I closed my eyes tight.

And he moved, curling his big body into mine, his arm around my waist, pulling me into his heat.

I felt his face in the back of my hair, and finally, I relaxed.

When I did, I heard him whisper, "Thanks for takin' care of my girl, baby."

I pressed my lips together and swallowed the lump in my throat.

"You're welcome," I whispered back.

He gave me a squeeze. "Go to sleep, darlin'."

"Okay, Buck."

He pulled me deeper into him and then his body settled into mine.

Faster than I would have expected after the day I'd had—getting into it with Minnie, Biker Babe Rituals, seeing Buck with Nails, meeting the kids, Tatiana hating me—I fell asleep.

If I wasn't unconscious, and could think on it, this would not have come as a surprise.

And as such, thinking on it later, it was no surprise when it came to me why that happened.

It was because I was in Buck's bed, in the curve of his arm, against the warmth of his body.

I was beginning to suspect (and fear) that the world could be ending, and I'd fall asleep against Buck like that.

And that was entirely the problem.

Because with West "Buck" Hardy, as good as I could get was beginning to feel like the best I ever had.

And whenever something like that happened, you held on for dear life.

The thing I didn't think about or I'd never sleep again, was one of the many things I'd learned.

That in my life...

The best I ever had never lasted.

14

MOODY

The next morning, I woke up pressed against Buck's side, my cheek to his shoulder.

The sun was shining, unmuted, through the windows.

The house was quiet, and I knew by Buck's steady breathing that he was still asleep.

I always woke before him and this was likely because he stayed up late, and I didn't.

I carefully slid away so as not to disturb him and walked to the hall bathroom.

The towels were on the floor, so I folded them and put them on the counter. Then I grabbed my facewash and went back to Buck's bathroom. I did my morning bathroom thing and grabbed my robe off the hook on the back of the door.

My robe was short, lilac and a light, soft, knit cotton-flannel. It had once been not-so-light, but I'd owned it for so long and worn and washed it so much (at one point, post-Rogan-debacle, I'd worn it for days), it was now thinner, but more comfortable and soft as a baby's skin.

I shrugged this on over my little pink nightie and tied the belt. Then I went to the kitchen, made coffee, toasted Pop-Tarts, and once the coffee was done, I took it and my breakfast out to the deck.

I set my mug on the railing and sat down, eating my tarts, leaning forward to grab my mug and take a sip when I needed it, my gaze to the view and the calming sound of a not very rapidly flowing creek serenading me.

All you could see, left, right and center, was tranquility.

It was just trees, and a creek, and the gravel lane that led up to Buck's house.

But there were also hummingbirds. And squirrels dashing about.

I wondered one day if I'd see deer.

Yesterday, I'd discovered that the roads leading up to his place had houses like Buck's, tucked in the trees.

Still, whoever planned the lots and built the homes did it for maximum solitude. They were there but you had to search to find them, a hint of roof, the sun gleaming off a window, a chimney.

If you didn't make that effort, you could feel comfortably alone.

Once done with my tarts, I took the plate inside, put it in the dishwasher, refreshed my mug, went back out and settled again in my chair.

The minute I rested my feet on the railing, Minnie's words hit my brain.

And he chooses you, Clara. If he decides to make you his old lady and do that official, he'll always come back to you. And that's something. I promise you, babe. Not blowing sunshine up your ass. Especially with a man like Buck, that's definitely something.

She would know. She knew him better than me.

Then I thought of how Ink was with Lorie, how Cruise greeted Pinky and held her close, and all the many ways that Buck could be gentle, sweet, funny and protective.

From what they said, Lorie and Pinky put up with what they had to put up with to get what they got from their men.

And what they got, I noticed, was good.

Other men, I knew, were not so good.

Like my adoptive father, who left my clearly mentally ill mother to try it alone...and fail. And he never came back, not even when the child he'd assumed responsibility for had no one else to turn to.

Then there was Rogan.

Also Esposito.

I stared at a view I knew, down deep in my heart, I would never fail to find beauty in, to gain peace from.

I did this knowing I was right to go the way of the biker babe.

This was not what Rogan did. This was not hiding it and breaking trust.

First, Buck and I hadn't been together a week. We hadn't had the exclusive conversation.

Though I knew what we had was something.

I also knew it was something for him.

It wasn't that I was living with him, all moved in and everything.

That was necessity.

It was that I'd met his kids, and according to Gear, they'd never had another of Buck's women in their lives.

Not even Nails.

So this was most assuredly something, for both of us.

But he'd done what he'd done practically under my nose, and although this did not seem *de rigueur* in the biker world with the way the girls had reacted to it, it was still part of the life they led. And maybe Buck thought I understood that.

I knew, though, bottom-lining this, that in the end, if Buck chose me, I'd have something.

Something was always better than nothing.

That said, the important part was that the something I'd have with Buck, I knew from what he'd given me already, would be better than other men had to offer.

A lot better.

On that thought, I heard the door open and I twisted to see Buck walking out wearing nothing but jeans, displaying skin, muscle and tattoos. His hair was a mess and his eyes could only be described as "bedroom" since he looked like he'd woken up only a second before.

It was a very good look.

And there it was.

Proof that with Buck, something was a whole lot better than nothing.

"Hi," I said softly.

His good morning was to walk up to me, cup the back of my head, bend at the waist and kiss me hard and with lots of tongue.

It was the best good morning I'd ever had.

Oh yes, with Buck, that something would be a *whole lot better*.

His mouth released mine, but when I opened my eyes, I was surprised to see his were displeased.

"You wake up early, babe, when the kids are sleepin' or whenever, you fuckin' wake me, yeah?"

I felt my brows hitch up.

They did this because, yes.

He was angry.

"Okay," I agreed quietly.

"And you do it with your mouth and I don't mean talkin'."

"Okay," I repeated, my mind struggling with surprise, my body fighting a happy shiver.

He kept issuing orders.

"And you can do it by suckin' my tongue in that mouth or you can suck somethin' else into it."

"Oh..." I breathed, feeling my nipples getting hard, "'kay."

Once done issuing orders, he took my coffee cup right out of my hand, straightened and raised it to his lips, taking a sip.

After that intimate gesture, he sat in the chair Gear had set beside mine the night before and lifted his legs high, setting the heels of his bare feet on the top railing and crossing his ankles.

And he didn't give me back my coffee.

"Do you, um...want me to get you some coffee?" I offered.

He lifted my mug slightly, scowling at the landscape.

"Already got some."

Okeydokey.

"Do you want me to make you some Pop-Tarts?" I asked, and his head turned to me.

Oh dear.

I'd done something else to make him unhappy.

"Saturday and Sunday, babe, I make breakfast."

This sounded like the twelfth commandment, therefore I made a note of it.

"I already had Pop-Tarts," I admitted.

His eyes narrowed.

Then he looked back at the scenery and took another sip of my coffee.

Hmm.

He wasn't normally a bear in the mornings.

Apparently, someone woke up moody.

"I'm going to go get myself a cup and let you have your mood," I muttered.

I felt his eyes on me, the feeling of them was venomous, and I froze before I took my feet from the railing and looked at him.

"Not in a mood, Toots."

"You seem like it to me."

"Woman," he started, and I braced. He'd never called me "woman" before and I didn't think that was a good sign. "Been sleepin' next to you for days, finally got my hand on your ass and your tongue in my mouth and my daughter comes home and pukes on the floor. Commence fuckin' teenage-kid, drunk drama, and I reckon you're in no mood after dealin' with that shit. Then I wake up to an empty bed. So I'm not in a fuckin' mood," he leaned into me, "I'm fuckin' *frustrated*."

This was interesting.

Although I knew he could go all night with the energy of a teenager, and he was definitely all man as in *all man*, thus I knew he had a very healthy sex drive, still, he'd had Nails just the day before.

But he was acting like he hadn't had sex since the dawn of time.

Maybe he and Nails just made out and didn't do the deed.

This would be a relief.

A fleeting one, considering I didn't spend every hour of every day with him, and he'd not only had, but would continue to have ample opportunity to carry on in that manner.

But perhaps he didn't do that yesterday, then kiss me and later start something with me.

And yes.

That was a relief.

I didn't question this verbally, for obvious reasons, the primary one being my own peace of mind.

Instead, I thought the prudent way to play it was to whisper, "Point taken."

He twisted his neck, and I did too, to see Gear wandering out onto the deck wearing a pair of drawstring gray sweats cut off at the knees and nothing else.

Good golly, I hoped he kept his clothes on around girls. With his hair a mess like his dad's, sleep in his eyes like his dad's, and a six-pack that was as defined as his dad's, except leaner, if they got one look at him, they'd tear him limb from limb.

He dragged a chair to my other side, sat in it, lifted his heels to the railing just as his father's were and sipped from his own coffee.

"Mornin'," he muttered to the view.

"You sleep okay, Gear?" I asked.

"Yep," he answered.

"Good," I whispered.

Then, for some reason, Gear said on a question, "Eggs, pancakes, waffles or French toast?"

"Your choice today, Gear," Buck replied.

"Totally French toast," Gear stated then took another sip of coffee.

I looked at Buck and saw him sip at mine.

"I'm getting coffee," I mumbled, taking my feet from the railing and putting my hands to the arms of the chair, pushing myself up.

I was attempting to squeeze through the small space between Buck's and my chairs when Buck's fingers wrapped around my wrist.

I looked down at him to see he was looking up at me.

"Get it and get your ass back out here."

Still moody.

And domineering.

I nodded.

He let me go, and I only braved my muttered, "Moody," when I was at the door to the house.

I got my coffee and then took my ass back out there.

After I settled in my chair and put my feet on the railing, Buck did an ab curl, wrapped his arm around my thighs and pulled my bent legs to rest against his elevated ones. Then he left his arm wrapped around my thighs, though in sitting back, it slid so it was wrapped at my upper thighs at the same time my chair with me in it scooted the scant inches that were present to close the distance that separated it from Buck's.

I decided not to protest.

Firstly, because Buck still seemed in a mood, and secondly, because it felt comfortable and nice. It was weird and I couldn't imagine the position was comfortable for Buck, though he didn't seem to mind.

It was also extremely proprietary in a way I liked.

There was no one there to see him stake his claim so the claim he staked seemed less possessive and more protective with not a small amount of him simply wanting to be close to me.

As with all things I was discovering about Buck, except an albeit important few (that "few" being only one), I liked this.

A lot.

I silently let the Hardy men have their own thoughts, and as I did this my belly began to feel warm.

And this was because, a week ago, if you told me I'd be sitting on the deck of a secluded house set in a beautiful hill outside Phoenix, sipping coffee with a handsome biker and his equally handsome son, I would have told you that you were insane.

But here I was.

And I'd had Pop-Tarts.

I stifled a giggle at the same exact time Buck suddenly and inexplicably roared, *"Get your ass out here!"*

I jumped and looked at him to see he was twisted to look into the house.

I looked too, and when I did, I saw Tatiana, wearing a girlie set of drawstring pajama shorts and a little camisole opening the door.

I watched her wince at the sun and saw she looked both pale and a little green at the gills.

She closed the door and made the decision to approach our congregation on Gear's side. She leaned heavily on her arms on the railing like she couldn't quite hold herself up and stared at the view with squinty eyes.

I was happy to note she had a big tumbler of water in one hand.

"Can we do this shit later, Dad? I feel like crap," she muttered.

Gear moved in his chair and I looked at him to see he looked like he didn't know whether to smile or bolt.

"Say again?" Buck asked in his spitting-venom voice, and I instantly understood Gear's reaction.

He knew Tatiana's question would not be met favorably and he was torn between watching his sister get it and getting the heck out of Dodge.

I was feeling the same dilemma.

I braced as Tatiana let out a heavy sigh before repeating, "I feel like crap."

"Yeah, could guess that, Tatie, seein' as me and your brother mopped up your puke last night," Buck remarked.

"Dad—"

"And smelled it after you hurled into the toilet, Clara rubbin' your back," Buck added.

She sighed again, straightened and turned toward us, but leaned against the railing and took a sip of her water.

Thus positioned, she invited on a resigned yet annoyed, "Just get it over with."

Oh dear.

"You got one warning," Buck stated, his voice low and sweltering, "put away that fuckin' attitude."

I made a move, whispering, "Maybe I should—"

I stopped when Buck's arm around my thighs got tight and he ordered, "Do not fuckin' move, Toots."

"She can go," Tatiana put in.

Oh...*dear*.

Gear went solid on my one side while, from the other, I felt the heat coming off Buck sear through me and Gear on a direct path to Tatiana.

"You forget last night, girl?" Buck asked quietly.

"No," she snapped.

"So you're sayin' you didn't forget Clara pulling your hair outta your face so you didn't puke in it?"

I bit my lip and watched Tatiana turn her head to look at the view, taking another sip.

"Girl, eyes...on...*me*," Buck demanded, and Tatiana looked back at him and raised her brows.

I wasn't sure, I was never sixteen and in trouble with my dad for over-imbibing, but I was thinking she wasn't playing this right.

"Answer me," Buck ordered.

"I didn't forget," Tatiana snapped.

"How 'bout rubbin' your back, givin' you water, coverin' you with towels? You forget any a' that?" Buck asked.

"No," she clipped.

"I get Clara bein' here is new to you. It's new to me. It's new to your brother. And heads up, girl, it's also fuckin' new to Clara. I'm guessin' your brother sees the upshot to this and has noticed that I got someone in my house I like bein' with and he digs that."

At these words, surprising ones, lovely ones (in a biker-lovely way), I held my breath and felt my belly get warm again.

Buck kept talking.

"I also get that it may take you longer to see your old man has found himself a good thing. That said, I did not raise a fuckin' kid who gets sick in the toilet because she acted like a fuckin' moron, and my woman took care of her, only to have that kid be a fuckin' brat the next morning. You work out your issues with your brother, with me, and you ask, I bet Clara would talk to you, you'd get to know her and even she might help you work them out. You wanna be a pain in the ass, you do it so Clara doesn't feel it and Gear doesn't have to pour you, shitfaced, in his car and leave his friends because you've decided to be a pain in the ass. I talked to you about this nice last night. You didn't listen. Now, I gotta know if you've heard me. So, Tatie, tell me, have you heard me?"

I felt that was pretty intense, and maybe a smidge too intense.

Then again, I'd never had a dad, much less a biker dad, so I didn't know.

Though, I'd had foster fathers, but I'd always put every foot right and didn't taste my first sip of beer until I was nineteen, so this was completely foreign to me.

At the end of the day, however, this lecture had been delivered in this manner because Buck had tried it a different way, Tatiana hadn't listened, and the heart of it was that Buck cared, Buck worried, and Buck wanted all of us to get along.

And Tatiana was not with that program in any way, and she didn't seem to be swinging in that direction.

So perhaps intense was appropriate in this situation.

Not to mention, it explained Buck's Saturday morning bad mood.

"I've heard you," Tatiana gritted between her teeth, her eyes glittering, her face still pale, and I had the distinct feeling she blamed this on me, and I had that feeling because her glittering eyes shifted to me frequently while her father was telling her off.

Fantastic.

"Now, say thank you to Clara for bein' cool with you last night and then you can do whatever the fuck you need to do."

Okay, according to me, that was taking it too far.

"I...that isn't necessary," I put in quickly, and said to Tatiana, "You don't have to thank me."

Buck's arm gave my thighs a squeeze. "I said she did, Toots, that means she does."

"Okay," I whispered.

"Whatever," Tatiana muttered. "Thanks..." She hesitated then sneered, "*Toots*."

"Tat, sis, be cool," Gear advised.

"Whatever," Tatiana repeated and looked at her father. "Can I go now?"

"Oh yeah, you can go. But fair warning, girl, I see you and you're still throwin' attitude, I'm not gonna like it."

I watched her clench her teeth. She looked to the scenery again, took a sip of water then pushed away from the railing and walked to the door.

Before she made it, I heard her murmur, "Who woulda thought I'd ever prefer it in Flag with Mom and fuckin' *Knuckles*?"

I felt Buck's arm tense around my legs, and I sucked in breath.

Then I heard the door close.

I let out my breath, thinking, *oh dear*.

I WAITED UNTIL AFTERNOON, after Buck made the best French toast I'd ever tasted, and after I'd made grilled cheese for him and Gear for lunch, probably *not* the best they'd ever tasted.

I wasn't a bad cook, especially considering I'd never had anyone teach me, so I was entirely self-taught, and whenever that happened, it was bound to be hit or miss.

But Buck had natural talent, and I couldn't say I had that with cooking.

Or with anything.

As they had between breakfast and lunch, after lunch, the Hardy men disappeared back under the hood of the Nova outside and I made another grilled cheese sandwich, put it on a plate, grabbed a Diet Coke and walked to Tatiana's closed door.

I knocked and walked in when I heard her impatient, "What?"

"It's me," I announced, closing the door behind me and walking in to see her sitting cross-legged in the middle of the bed, her phone on the mattress, the vampire novel opened and facedown next to her phone, what looked like a journal balanced on her knee, a pen in her hand.

She narrowed her eyes at me, flipped the journal facedown and set it on the bed too.

"Can I help you?" she asked snottily.

I walked to the nightstand, put the plate and diet on it and then walked back to the corner of the bed.

"Thought you might want something to eat," I told her.

"Thanks, Toots," she mocked, tossed the pen to the bed and picked up her phone.

Bending her head to it, her thumbs started flying over the screen.

"I get you," I told her, and she ignored me, so I pulled in a huge breath and carried on, "I grew up in foster care."

"Poor you," she muttered, obviously hit send, then tossed her phone to the bed again and grabbed her vampire novel before lying back on the pillows and lifting the novel in front of her face.

I persevered.

"I never really had a dad, so I can see you being territorial when you've got a good one."

"It's so *cool* you *understand*," she lied to her book.

"A few days ago," I pressed on, "my best friend's husband, who is *not* a good guy, but who I had to work with so he wouldn't hurt my friend, which he was doing in bad ways I won't share, picked me up, beat the heck out of me and tossed me out of a moving vehicle. Your dad arranged for me to receive medical help and then he arranged for my protection."

She moved the book an inch aside and her eyes came to me.

"So you're here because he's protecting you?" she asked, perfectly arched brows up.

"Yes," I answered.

"And you're payin' him back by fuckin' him?"

I sucked in breath.

Clearly, even the female Hardys didn't shy away from that word.

I didn't get into that.

I said quietly, "No."

"You sleep on the couch?"

"No."

"You sleep with him."

"Yes."

"What, you only do blowjobs as payback for protection?" she asked snidely.

I held her eyes.

I pulled breath in through my nostrils.

Then I said softly, "Never, in my life, have I met a good man. Not in my life. You're lucky, Tatiana, you were born to one, so you'll keep being lucky because you know what to look for. I wasn't that lucky. Not until now. I get you, honey. I get what it feels like to wake up every day and be in a place you don't want to be. I totally get that. What *you* need to get is that, as terrible as that is, you know, right to your soul, that there's someone out there who you mean the world to, who cares about you, who worries about you and who likes you close, even though he can't have that and he can't give it to you. You know that you can't wake every day feeling safe, knowing that person is in the house, but you *can* get to him. I'm sorry things aren't good at home, but you'll one day rest in the knowledge that you had *something* good and you'll be grateful for it. You don't have to be nice to me, but you and me, we can keep that between us. For your dad's sake, though, I'm asking you to pretend. He deserves that, and I'm just guessing here, but I think you know it."

I didn't give her the chance to respond.

I stopped talking, turned and walked right out of her room, closing the door quietly behind me.

I went to the living room, stretched out on the couch and clicked through programs, looking for reruns of *Dynasty*.

The time wasn't right, so I had to make do with *CHiPs*.

I preferred *Dynasty* because Alexis Carrington Colby Dexter had a great wardrobe and was good with a catty one-liner.

But it had to be said, Officer Poncherello was not hard on the eyes.

So I was back with as good as I could get.

And again...

It didn't stink.

15

DO YOU NEED CPR?

Tatiana emerged in time for Buck to take us to the Valley Inn for dinner.

I had never had occasion to frequent the area where Buck lived (in other words, until I found myself living there, I'd never been).

Thus, I found the Valley Inn was a no-nonsense but comfortable place that catered directly to the local clientele.

This being, as far as I could see, bikers, cowboys and mountain people, all who maybe worked in the city, but they didn't want to live there.

In other words, they served two things at the Valley Inn: Mexican food and steaks.

And I would find, on the Mexican food side of things, they did it really well.

I had chili rellenos and topped up my body's supply of margaritas.

Tatiana didn't throw attitude and was mostly silent.

Buck matched her silence, and I suspected he did it to concentrate on his Badass Biker Dad Attitude-o-Meter. I suspected this because he kept a close eye on his daughter and seemed prepared to take her down a notch should she mouth off or act in any other way like a brat.

This left me and Gear carrying on the conversation, which, as it had in the beginning, came easy, mainly because Gear was easygoing, easily likeable and easy to talk to.

I learned that Gear was playing the field, never had a steady girlfriend, and after he graduated from high school, he wanted to join his dad's MC and work with the guys in some capacity at Ace in the Hole.

Though, not in the store.

On the contracting side of things.

"Thinkin' electrician," he said between huge bites of prime rib. "Though might do it all, 'cept plumbing, 'cause...gross."

On my side of things, Gear (and Tatie, if she was listening) learned I'd divorced a jerk, was between jobs, and my best friends were a woman on the run and a Mexican American woman old enough to be my grandmother.

Gear suggested that Mrs. Jimenez be invited up to Buck's house the next weekend they were there so she could give her cultural stamp of approval to his dad's enchiladas. Though I sensed he did this only partly because he was a friendly, sociable guy and wanted to meet Mrs. Jimenez, but mostly he did it as an excuse for his dad to make enchiladas again.

That said, I was uncertain enchiladas were genuinely Mexican, seeing as Mrs. Jimenez definitely was, and she'd never made them. Therefore, I made a mental note to check on that (I *was* a librarian, albeit not a practicing one, we did research like no other—in fact, the only people who beat us in research were attorneys and thriller writers, of which many of the latter were both).

I also decided I liked this idea.

Both kids took off to their rooms when we got back, and not long after, we heard metal music drifting down from upstairs.

Buck opened a beer, and without asking me, made me another margarita.

He then guided me out onto the deck instead of to the TV.

I found this an interesting choice and I liked it.

August was quickly heading into September, but the weather was still warm and mild, and any deck should be utilized to its fullest when the opportunities arose.

Still, this caused me concern as Buck had never done it before.

We sat in our chairs of the morning. I put my feet up to the lower railing and sipped my margarita. Buck shoved his legs under mine and stretched them out on my rung at the railing so my legs were draped over his.

Then he spoke, and I would come to understand why we were outside.

"Did a recon of the bathroom, Toots," he stated, then sipped his beer.

I thought this was an interesting opener but had no clue why he was imparting this information on me, though I was hoping he wasn't going to take issue with me commandeering so much of his vanity space for my girlie stuff.

Therefore, I replied with a noncommittal, "Yes?"

"Babe, you aren't on birth control."

My body went rock solid.

Oh God.

This was true.

I wasn't.

I wasn't on birth control.

And a week before, we'd had sex six times.

Six.

All unprotected.

He hadn't even pulled out.

So much had happened, it hadn't even occurred to me.

And during the act(s), so much was happening, good and bad, it didn't occur to me.

Oh.

God.

I tried to calculate my period mentally and couldn't. I'd lost track. Life was too insane. I used to mark it in my day planner religiously. I even had specific little stickers (tiny little presents) I could stick in on the day it began...and the happy day it ended.

But I no longer had a day planner. I didn't even have an alarm clock (Buck did, but it was flashing twelve and I couldn't figure out how to set it, so to stop it from flashing, something that was annoying, I'd just unplugged it).

It was a wonder I knew what day it was!

Oh God!

"Toots," he called.

"Give me a minute, I'm trying not to hyperventilate," I whispered, and he chuckled.

Chuckled!

I came unlocked and woodenly turned my head to look at him.

"This isn't funny, West," I informed him of the obvious.

"Babe," was his reply.

I shot bolt upright in the chair, my legs jostling his, and Buck's arm swung around my shoulders and curled me into him so our faces were close.

"Calm down, Clara, it's cool."

I knew a lot of things it was, but the one thing I knew it was not was *cool*.

Therefore, I cried, "It isn't!"

"I'll take you to Lefty, get you some pills," he offered.

I closed my eyes.

God, humiliating.

I couldn't even afford birth control.

"Clara, honey, look at me."

I opened my eyes. "What if I'm pregnant?"

"Gotta say, Kristy and I tried for about a week before she got knocked up both times."

Oh no.

Of course.

Of course!

Of course he had superior, take-no-prisoners swimmers.

God!

I felt my eyes get wide and my heart start to pound.

Buck grinned. "We only had one night so maybe you're golden."

"How far is the drop off the deck and what do you think my chances will be that it will kill me, straight out, rather than put me in a coma after which I'll wake up and have to endure a year of painful physical therapy before I can move a thumb?"

Buck's grin became a smile and then he pulled me closer.

"If you're knocked up, we'll deal. Until we know, we'll use other precautions. You're not, Lefty'll get you on the pill. Is that a plan?"

Yes, it was a plan.

Of course, it was a plan.

I stared at him.

How could he be so calm about this?

"How can you be so calm about this?"

"Because we don't know if there's anything to get wound up about. Until we do, there's no point getting wound up."

Was he serious?

We weren't talking about an error in calculating the balance of a checkbook for an account that started with a balance that was healthy so it could take the hit of not carrying a one or even a five.

We were talking about possible *pregnancy*.

This occurring between two people who, sure, were living together.

But we barely knew each other.

Heavens, we'd only had one night of intimacy!

So we actually barely even knew each other *biblically*.

"Are you serious?" I demanded.

He ignored my question and stated, "In the meantime, we just gotta play it smart."

Oh God.

I closed my eyes again and this was a mistake. I knew it when I felt his bristly lips on mine.

I opened them to see his eyes were *very* close.

"Sucks, babe, love the feel of you. Don't want anything between you and me. We gotta get you on the pill."

It was then my brain made the unfortunate decision to wonder if he loved the feel of Nails and he didn't want anything between him and her.

Which would mean whoever she shared a bed with would be sharing a bed with me.

Oh God!

"Maybe we shouldn't have sex," I suggested, and his face moved back an inch.

"Come again?"

"Maybe we shouldn't have sex," I repeated.

"Now, babe, *that* isn't funny," he said in a very firm, *very* unamused way.

Okay, I needed to try something else.

"Or use condoms all the time, for added protection, even when I'm on the pill."

"Still not funny," he returned.

I bent my neck and looked down at my margarita.

I could be pregnant. I shouldn't be drinking.

Oh God.

I pushed back against his arm and sat in my chair muttering, "Like I need one more thing to worry about."

His arm was still around my shoulders, but it became a hand massaging the back of my neck.

"Clara, honey, listen to me." I looked at him and he carried on, "There's nothin' to worry about until there's somethin' to worry about. Drink your drink. Relax. And remember, I promised to have your back."

"Right," I whispered.

"Right," he repeated, again in that very firm way.

I sighed.

I needed to call Lorie. Or Minnie. Or Pinky. I needed biker babe advice.

"I need to call one of the girls," I blurted.

"You need to loosen up, drink your marg and sit out here with me. Tomorrow, you can call one of the girls."

It was then I realized he was very dictatorial. He issued a lot of orders and told me what to do often.

Then again, he was also usually right and now was no different.

I didn't need to mess up Lorie, Pinky, or Minnie's Saturday nights with this (possibly) dire news.

And anyway, he was right about something else.

I had enough to worry about. I didn't need to worry about stuff that might not happen.

I sighed again, did what I was told and sipped my margarita.

Then something occurred to me.

I turned my head to see he was surveying the landscape and asked, "When did you do this recon?"

"The other night."

"What other night?" I pushed.

"Don't know," he replied. "Thursday, maybe."

Thursday?

He'd waited since *Thursday* to bring this up?

"Is that why you asked me if I wanted children yesterday?"

"Yep," he told the view.

My heart started beating fast again. "So you were attempting to ascertain if I'd want to keep a child we may have created?"

He turned his head to me. "Babe, do you *listen* to me?"

"Why would you ask if I wanted children if you weren't trying to find out if I wanted children?"

My voice was rising.

"You need to let it go," he ordered.

"You need to answer my question," I fired back.

His fingers massaging my neck stopped massaging and just squeezed.

"Then, yeah, Toots, I wanted to know if you wanted kids because I wanted to know, if I knocked you up, which way you'd lean. And, even though you look about ready to have a coronary, I'll tell you where I stand on that. You got my kid inside you, it wouldn't make me happy if you wanted to get rid of him. You and me, we'd make a gorgeous kid."

That's when I actually started hyperventilating.

Buck either didn't notice or didn't care because he kept talking.

"And, gotta say, Toots, last night, the way you took care of Tatie, means today I would be even *less* happy if you got rid of my kid. You're gonna make a great mom."

Gonna?

I didn't speak because I was experiencing the odd sensation of choking on nothing.

It didn't seem like Buck could shut up, and I liked listening to him. He had a beautiful voice. And most of the time he used it to say good things.

But right now, I needed him to shut up.

"Also gotta say, seein' you take care of Tat, how you are with Gear, how he is with you, and my son is friendly, but he's not stupid. He goes cautious, especially when shit is important. But he blatantly likes you. After the shit went down with Kristy and the shit she's pullin' now with the kids, wouldn't suck havin' a kid and raisin' him...with you."

When shit is important.

Wouldn't suck, havin' a kid and raisin' him...with you.

Right.

I needed lots and lots of oxygen because I was going to pass out.

Buck watched me breathe.

Then he asked, "Do you need CPR?"

"No," I panted.

He grinned.

Then his hand went away from my neck but only so his arm could go around my shoulders and pull me close, tucking me under his arm. His eyes went back to the scenery and he sipped his beer.

Okay, it couldn't be avoided.

I had to get into it.

So I deliberated quickly about *how* to get into it, and then I got into it.

"Considering your two children are right now in the house behind us, I know you weren't a virgin before you and I..." I paused to find the right words, "enjoyed each other."

Buck looked from the view to me, and his lips were tipped up as he said, "Correct."

Right.

I was out of words.

Therefore, to get to the point, I asked leadingly, "Sooooo...?"

Even if we were not far apart, he still managed to lean toward me.

"You and me, baby, unexpected. Out of hand. Off the charts. I don't fuck around with that shit. Ever. Even with you, if I'd thought you'd been getting around, that would have dawned on me and I would have worked in a glove. But you told me you'd sworn off men. So in that department, you got nothin' to worry about. I take pains to keep clean."

Well then.

If that was the case (and I had no reason not to believe him), then if we were non-exclusive, our little snafu might not have even more calamitous ramifications.

It was thin, but at least it was one good thing to hold on to.

I nodded to him.

Buck touched my nose with his lips and returned his attention to the view.

I followed his gaze and stared at the landscape thinking I'd managed to survive foster care, Rogan and Esposito, but I was still making all the wrong moves.

Alternatively, maybe they were the right ones.

I mean, Tatiana's (somewhat understandable) attitude aside, it was without a doubt West Hardy made beautiful children.

Then I sipped my margarita and prayed, for the very first time, I got my period...and soon.

Another boy, a little one, with Buck's thick hair and his beautiful eyes hit my mind's eye and an entirely unhinged thought about the return of my monthly friend entered my head.

Because maybe I should pray for...

Not.

"WE CAN WATCH SOMETHIN' else," I heard Gear say quietly.

"I wanna watch this," I heard Tatiana put in, not as quietly.

"Clara isn't into it, Tat, it's put her to sleep," Gear returned, again quietly.

Earlier, Buck and I had come in and both the kids were in armchairs watching television.

I put my empty margarita glass in the dishwasher (possible Hardy Tot inside me had had enough tequila for one night), Buck got another beer and we headed to the couch.

I tucked myself on the opposite side of him and stayed tucked there for point-two-five seconds after Buck sat in his normal place.

Then his arm shot out.

Fingers wrapping around my wrist, he yanked me to him and settled me in my usual position with my cheek to his thigh. About point-one-five seconds later, I felt his fingers in my hair.

I avoided both Gear's and Tatiana's eyes and glued mine to the TV.

A little over an hour later (I knew it was an hour because I'd managed to watch an entire program), I fell asleep.

Now, my eyes were closed, my fingers curled around Buck's thigh, I was still mostly sleeping, but their conversation had penetrated my doze.

"She does this," I heard Buck rumble behind me.

"What?" Gear asked.

"Every night, she crashes in front of the TV. Watch what you wanna watch. Toots don't give a shit. Television is a tranquilizer. She's good," Buck answered.

"All right, cool," Gear muttered.

After that I heard nothing but the TV.

And after that, I slipped from my semi-conscious doze back into sleep.

I woke up again when Buck lifted me from the couch.

I slid my arms around his shoulders and dazedly looked around.

Moonlight was glowing through the windows, there were no lights on, and both Gear and Tatiana were gone.

I pressed my forehead into West's neck.

"See," Buck's voice rumbled all around me in a way I liked, "you get tired, baby...cuddly and sweet."

"Mm," I mumbled and then his chuckle rumbled all around me in a way I also liked.

He set me on my feet on my side of the bed, and I immediately started to disrobe. Jeans down and off. Librarian blouse (this one fuchsia pink with little ruffles on the cap sleeves) unbuttoned and thrown aside.

I turned to the bed wearing a bra and undies in order to reach under the pillow to get my nightie.

I didn't make my destination.

Buck's hands were at my hips. They turned me then slid over my behind and down to my upper thighs where he lifted me up, his hands sliding more, spreading my legs.

Automatically, I clamped them around his still-jeans-clad hips and my hands went to his bared shoulders.

My eyes also went to his.

"Buck, the kids."

"Asleep and they sleep deep."

"But, Buck—"

His mouth hit mine. "Baby, not waitin' any longer. Fuckin' you."

With that, I was on my back in bed, my head on the pillows, Buck's tongue in my mouth.

And I wasn't sleepy anymore.

Buck did not lie, he wasn't waiting. He was kissing me, deep and wet, and his hands were all over me. It didn't even have the chance to start. It went from nothing to all revved up and ready to go in seconds.

To prove that point, suddenly, my bra was gone, and Buck's mouth was at my breast, his fingers toying with my other nipple, rolling and gently pulling as he sucked it deep in his mouth.

My back arched and my hands slid into his hair.

God.

Unbelievably fantastic.

He did this for a long time, alternating back and forth, fingers and mouth, mouth and fingers, until I was squirming under him, my hands going anywhere I could touch, feeding my own need by feeling the power of him under my fingertips.

His hand left my nipple and went to my panties. He didn't push them down. He grabbed my panties and yanked them up, rough and tight, causing friction and surprising but delicious pressure exactly where I wanted it.

My neck arched, a quiet moan slid from my throat and I lost my mind.

I planted a foot in the bed and rolled him to his back.

Then I went after him.

Hands, mouth and tongue on his neck, his collarbone, down...his nipples...I traced the GEAR on his pectoral with my tongue and I did it slow, savoring the taste of him. Down...fingers gliding along his sides, tongue exploring his abs...

Down...

He unbuttoned his jeans and I slid off him, pulling them down his legs. He opened and cocked his legs and I rolled between. I took his cock in my hand then I took it in my mouth. My eyes went to him to see him on his elbows watching me, his gaze dark, hungry. He liked what he was seeing, what he was feeling, what I was doing, and he didn't mind me knowing it.

God, beautiful.

I gave him all I had to give, sucking, licking, stroking with my hand, sometimes all at once, most of the time watching him watching me, and I was really, *really* getting off on it.

"Jesus, fuck, Toots, your fuckin' mouth," he growled low, and I dropped my gaze and sucked him deep. And when I did, I sucked him hard.

"Fuck," he growled again then I felt him move, his hands under my arms.

My mouth released his cock and he tossed me to the side, yanking my panties down my legs.

He moved again, reaching to the nightstand, but I straddled him. I was ready, I needed him and *I* wasn't going to wait. I had to have him.

One hand at his chest, I pushed him down, the other between us, wrapping around.

"Clara, baby, hang on—"

I guided him inside and ground down.

Amazing.

My head shot back, and I moved, riding him fast, taking him deep.

His hand went between my legs, thumb pressing in, rolling.

Oh God.

I clamped down on my moan, head falling back, going faster.

Buck curled up, and his hand wrapped around my neck, tipping it bent.

"Eyes on me when you're ridin' me." His voice was thick as it rumbled.

"Yes," I whispered, trying to focus, feeling it coming.

His thumb rolled.

"God, Buck," I breathed.

"Let go, baby," he ordered, his thumb rolling again as I slid him all the way inside.

My hand curled around the side of his neck, my other hand was on his chest, my eyes focused on his.

"I love the feel of you. Love it," I whispered. "You deep inside me."

I got these words out right before my head shot back, and it overwhelmed me, strong, overpowering, long-lasting and *outstanding*.

But I'd barely started climaxing when he flipped me to my back, wrapped my legs around his hips, took my mouth so my whimpers filled his, and pounded hard, his cock driving into me, his grunts mingling with my mews, powering down my throat.

I wrapped my arms around him and tightened all four limbs.

"That's it, baby," I muttered against his bristly lips. "Fuck me."

He fucked me, he did it hard, then he did it harder, and then his lips ground down on mine as he thrust deep, once, twice, three times, four, five groaning into my mouth.

He stopped, planted to the root, and his tongue slid inside. I suckled it and slipped my fingers into his hair, showing him he could have my mouth, it was all his.

He took what I gave and then took more.

Eventually, he ended our kiss, lips sliding down to my jaw, my neck, his tongue touched my earlobe then he lifted his head and looked down at me.

"Gotta do somethin' about you lettin' go," he whispered, and my head twitched on the pillow.

"Sorry?"

"Babe, you hold on. Your pussy's ready way before you give it what it wants."

I stared up at him.

Then I repeated, "Sorry?"

He grinned down at me then dipped his head and ran his lips along my jaw to my ear.

"I can feel you, when you're ready to come, but you don't let go. You hold back." He nipped my earlobe before he surprised me by admitting, "Wrecks a man's control."

"Pardon?" I asked the ceiling.

His head came up and he was smiling.

"Every time I've fucked you, babe, it's taken all I got not to come before you. You gotta learn to let go."

"But," I blurted, "I don't want to. If I do, then I lose you being inside me and I like you inside me. I like it when we're connected. I like it *a lot*."

After I said that, his face changed, his body went still, and he stared at me in a way that made my face get hot, my belly get warm, and my heart start to pound.

After what felt breathtakingly like years (but was, sadly, merely seconds), he dropped his head and kissed my nose before he pulled back half an inch.

"Then you hold on, gorgeous, long's you like," he whispered. "And I'll roll with you."

"Buck—" I whispered back, thinking somehow this was a profound moment and wanting to ask why, but he pulled out and rolled to his back so I was on top.

"Go get cleaned up," he ordered, his fingers digging into my hips.

"What?"

One of his hands left my hip and cupped the back of my head, pulling my face close.

"Clara, honey," he said softly, "you attacked me before I got to eat you. And I been waitin' to eat you for fuckin' days. Now you need to go get cleaned up and come back so I can eat you."

God, we'd just finished.

And it was good.

Really good.

And he was ready to go again.

After what he just said, so was I.

"Okay," I whispered, touched my mouth to his, climbed off him, and one could say I did not take my time (at all) on my way to (and from) the bathroom.

I WAS in a sex haze that was quickly segueing into unconsciousness.

Both of us had made the effort, that was evidently taxing, to muffle each other's noises so the kids wouldn't hear should they be awake.

Still, I'd had three orgasms, two from Buck's cock, one from his mouth.

So that was mostly why I was out of it and drifting to sleep.

"Apparently," his voice rumbled from his lips and his chest, the last of which I heard beneath my ear where it was resting, "wouldn't suck for you either, I knocked you up, the way you go at my dick when it's ungloved."

My eyes popped open.

Oh God.

We'd done it again!

Or...

I'd done it again because he'd definitely (both times) tried to work that in, and I hadn't let him.

Was this subconscious?

Now that I'd seen that cute little baby boy with Buck's brown eyes in my head, was I *trying* to get pregnant?

Oh God!

I needed to get smart.

And fast.

"Condoms from now on," I told his muscled flesh.

"Right," he said, his voice shaking (and other bits of him shaking too) with humor.

I lifted my head. "Buck—"

He cupped the side of my face.

"Worry about it when there's somethin' to worry about," he reminded me.

"Condoms or no sex at all from now on," I threatened.

"Whatever you say, Toots," he murmured, still sounding amused.

Hells bells.

Well, one thing he was right about, there was nothing I could do about it now.

I settled back in, thinking possible pregnancy, when Buck and I were so new and my life was still a shambles, was for certain going to mess with my perfect track record of great sleep at Buck's house.

I was wrong.

16

HAPPINESS IS POP-TARTS

"Ace in the Hole Home Improvement and Contracting, this is Clara, how can I help you?" I said into the phone, holding it to my ear with a shoulder hitched, my fingers sifting through files in the filing cabinet.

"*Hola, querida,*" Mrs. Jimenez replied, and I smiled just as I tensed.

I'd been working in the office at Ace for three weeks.

I started the Monday after my first weekend with Gear and Tatiana.

That day, I rode down on the back of Buck's bike (and learned why biker babes wore bandanas on their hair—blowout disaster—so, while Buck searched for the "perfect helmet" (his words) for me, I'd unearthed some scarves and used those, one was Hermès, the others were Alexander McQueen and Prada, all I'd save for the new jobs I never got —these didn't scream "Biker Babe!" but they kept my hair under control, and by the by, riding on the back of Buck's bike *with* Buck was *everything*).

He took me into the office—the extremely *messy* office—and let me loose.

By letting me loose, I meant he didn't give me a hint of instruction.

This was because, in his words, he didn't know "shit" about the office.

The only clue he gave me was to find a man named Chap who'd show me around.

Though, he did not share where I might find said Chap.

What he did say was, "Chap's always around somewhere...except when he's not."

Obviously, not at all helpful.

Chap was short for, I would learn later (from Chap, after I eventually found him), "Chaplain" which was his role in the Club.

Something else I'd learn later was that this meant, mostly, he was the resident sage who all the men took their "shit" (Buck's *and* Chap's word) to, or he was the voice of reason when there was dissension among the men.

And I found Chap *was* sage.

Though I figured, for the most part, this was his role simply because he was the oldest member of the MC.

Once Buck let me loose, sharing I needed to find Chap, he disappeared.

Me, in my jeans, librarian blouse (this particular one iris purple with pintucks up the front) and strappy, high-heeled, dark purple snakeskin sandals, searched for Chap.

But at that time, Chap was nowhere to be found.

This was, I would find out later, because Chap was on a not-unusual bender.

Therefore, Chap wouldn't be found until I saw him stagger out of the Dive four days later while I was in the side lot where the warehouse was, beyond which the Dive sat. All of this, incidentally, was adjacent to their store in a one-through-four hit: their massive store, a small admin building where I worked that had my office and a well-kitted-out, air-conditioned break room, their big warehouse, and the Dive.

When I saw Chap, I'd been dealing with a delivery of home improvement stuff.

Or, more to the point, *struggling* to deal with a delivery since I had no idea what I was doing.

Since I'd started in the office, I approached every man I didn't know, hoping they were Chap.

Therefore, I met most of the MC as well as the employees who worked at Ace, either in the shop as sales associates and resident advice-givers to customers, or those who went out on jobs—electricians, plumbers, painters, drywallers and the like.

Not all of them were members. Though all of them were rough and tumble. Even the women.

So, I approached Chap as he stumbled out of the Dive and found my man.

I could proudly say I hadn't done badly in those four days.

In fact, in the end, I found it a blast.

I was hesitant at first, sorting through what appeared to be a mountain of paper debris and noting there didn't seem to be a system. Instead, it seemed like whoever had taken care of the office made an art out of *not* having a system.

Then, on day three, I figured the system was going to be mine anyway, so I dug in and organized stuff how I wanted it.

And one could say I'd learned along this journey that a research librarian liked to dig into anything that involved paper, and those papers didn't have to be contained in books or pages from Galileo's diary.

It might make me crazy but setting that office to rights was the most fun outside of being in bed with Buck I'd had for over a year.

Chap, who had a straggly gray beard that nearly touched his chest, a shock of steel-gray, long, wiry hair that he didn't bother pulling into a ponytail and a long, thin, almost gaunt body (which made me fight asking him to dinner), was, as mentioned, the most veteran member of the MC.

He also knew the office work.

He was gruff, and the first time I met him, seriously hungover. Thus, he made it clear he wasn't a big fan of giving me time to explain the office work.

But he also realized if he didn't, he might be pressed into *doing* the office work (he realized this when I explained it to him), so he gave me time.

By week two, I had it down.

I still didn't know what half the inventory the shop stocked was. Ditto with what the men told me to order for the jobs.

But I just had to check the delivery notes against the orders, match up words and numbers, decipher what was stock for the store, and what was coming in for contracting jobs, direct it to where it was supposed to go and sign off.

Easy.

Ordering, easier.

The boys just told me what they needed, I wrote it down, found out who to order it from by asking Chap (who now was on speed dial), and I ordered it.

Invoices, even easier.

Bill paying, even *easier*.

Payroll, not so easy.

But I got the gist of it after I talked to Buck, who okayed me paying for an online tutorial. I took that, it made sense and was far from rocket science, so I got relatively up to speed, ran my first with only one guy reporting an error, and I suspected the next go would be a breeze.

Gabbing on the phone with current and prospective clients, the easiest.

I found, oddly, they kind of liked the fact I had no clue.

They thought it was very "Ace" for some clueless chatty chick to gab with them and promise a callback from someone who did have a clue (this callback, incidentally, usually came from Buck, or Ink, or sometimes Chap).

In fact, some of them had become phone friends.

Not much had changed in those three weeks, except the fact that I had a job and it could be the best job I ever had (yes, even better than the Hunter Institute, where I'd actually seen pages of Galileo's diary when it floated through to be on display for a traveling exhibition).

I loved getting up and having somewhere to go and something to do and none of it was fretting or hiding from repo men or bill collectors.

Not to mention, I had complete control of the office and no one got in my business.

In fact, they let me have at it and seemed relieved paperwork no longer threatened their day-to-day existence. So the job had a built-in popularity quotient, which didn't stink.

Further, the guys and gals who worked there might be rough and tumble, but I was sharing Buck's bed, his home and coming to work on the back of his bike. I learned fast that this afforded me more than a modicum of respect.

It was like I was Queen Biker Babe.

They were nice, they were courteous, and they deferred to me instantly.

In the beginning, I found this slightly bizarre, but I had to admit, it was pretty awesome.

Moreover, the office had no hours.

When I began my job there, Buck had not plugged his alarm clock back in, and hadn't set it before I'd unplugged it, because, he explained, "I go where I go when I go, and if you're with me, and until we get you your ride, you'll be with me, so that's where you'll be."

(Interesting side note: Buck was a journeyman cabinetmaker, so for the most part, he worked in the workshop in the warehouse building cabinets that they then took to jobs to be fitted. I'd seen his work, and like everything else about him, it was amazing. Bonus to this, unless he was off doing MC things, he was around a lot and made a point to have lunch with me every day. Which I thought was really sweet.).

Thus, I showed at the office when Buck was ready to come into Phoenix. I left when Buck was ready to go home.

Sometimes, Driver or Cruise would take me back up to his place, but that was rare.

Mostly, even if Buck was off doing non-store/non-contracting, president of the Aces High MC things, he'd come back and get me.

I found this an immense relief, and after giving it thought, I understood why.

And the why was because I had been responsible for every move I made for so long, doing all the right things, being where I was supposed to be, taking care of me, it was nice to have someone else making the decisions for a change. It was nice to be wherever I was whenever I got there.

It was nice to be able to just *be*.

As the days slid by, the guys got used to me and the deference became friendliness. I always had a fresh pot of coffee going, sometimes they'd hang in the office as I'd work, and they'd joke or tease or whatever.

I liked this so much, I facilitated it by bringing in baked goods. I made boxed brownies first. Then I graduated to store-bought cookie dough cookies. Those were so well received, I made from-scratch cupcakes.

And I found that the way to badass bikers' hearts (as well as the other guys and gals) was through their stomachs.

I had not yet tried out my biker babe apparel, but I was gearing up for it. I needed my librarian blouses and high heels as familiar armor as I got used to my new life.

But since the biker life was embracing me, and it felt good, I was preparing to embrace the biker life. Which meant donning my biker babe gear.

Just...eventually.

In other news, Mrs. Jimenez was on the move (thankfully).

Raymundo had found her a first-floor apartment in a secure building in a better part of town. The rent was more than she could afford, so her kids were all kicking in to cover it each month.

Without Mrs. Jimenez knowing it, and with my very first paycheck coming my way soon (as in, the very next day, Friday), I called Raymundo and told him I wanted to kick in my share.

He tried to argue with me, but I wouldn't hear of it. Since he had five kids and nine nieces and nephews, he eventually gave in.

Making all this good even better, Minnie, Pinky, and Lorie often showed and hung with me in the office.

This was because Minnie and Pinky both worked as waitresses in the same biker bar and they did the nightshift, so they had the after-noons to hang with me.

Lorie was a hairdresser, and if she had a quiet morning, afternoon or day off, she hung with me too, and a couple of times, on my breaks, we went out and got coffee.

I'd never had a girl posse, and it felt good.

Okay, no.

It didn't feel good.

It...felt...*great*.

And it felt better because they were looking out for me. I could ask them anything and they'd slip right into their Professor Higgins role and offer advice and guidance into the biker babe world (and yes, F-words were not verboten for biker kids, but only those in their teens).

When we weren't hanging in the office we texted, and once I went out for drinks with them while Buck was busy, and he picked me up when he was ready to go home.

The good got even better in the sense that I was bonding with Gear.

He was a good kid and he didn't make any bones about liking me and liking me with his dad.

The second weekend he showed without Tatiana, which was a bummer and something I knew Buck felt, though he didn't say a word.

Then, when her weekend alone with her mother and Knuckles didn't go well, Tatiana decided she'd put up with me and came down the next weekend.

It was clear she took my advice and she didn't throw attitude like she did that first weekend, at least not around Buck.

It was also clear she didn't intend to extend the olive branch of best-friend-dom anytime soon.

For my part, I didn't push, but I was unwaveringly nice and made it clear I was open to the olive branch whenever she felt like pointing it my way. Even when she and I were alone and she let it show she didn't like me by slipping into her pouty, juvenile brat mode, I kept it up. I kept it up for Buck and for Tatiana. She didn't have it good at home, and I wanted to make it as safe as it always had been for her at Buck's.

I made this clear, left the rest up to her and hoped.

My start with Buck didn't change, except after he broke the seal on sex, that was a frequent and extremely welcome addition to our lives.

Being with him was easy.

If we were home in time, he always cooked dinner, I always cleaned up. In the morning (after sex), I always made coffee and toasted the Pop-Tarts (unless it was Saturday or Sunday). And I nearly always fell asleep with my head on his thigh in front of the TV.

Sometimes he'd shake things up by having sex with me on the couch before he carried me to bed, and once I'd kissed him on the way to bed and we had sex the landing (that was *awesome*).

But we settled into an us quickly and easily.

He fit me into his life like I'd always been there, and it was a life where I liked to be.

Last, and the only bad (outside Tatiana), Tia had not been found.

This was causing me distress, but I was trying to take a page from Buck's book and not stress out when I didn't know if there was anything to stress out about.

She could be lying low someplace safe.

And this was a possibility because Buck reported they'd learned she'd sold her wedding rings and some other jewelry as well as hocked some stuff of Esposito's. She'd done this the day after we made our plans to go on the run. She'd also braved going to the bank and withdrawing five thousand dollars as well as done the maximum cash withdrawals at an ATM for three days, the day we planned to leave and for two days after.

But no one had heard from her or seen her after that second day.

So she had her car and a good amount of cash.

That fact made me feel better.

What did not make me feel better was, the longer it took to find Tia, the more wired Buck became about it. I noticed this every time I asked (so I'd taken, of late, to letting it lie—if he had something to tell me, he would, it was just, there was no news).

He didn't even know her, and he told me himself not to worry until there was something to worry about.

But as the days slid by, his calm faded to impatience, his impatience ratcheted to extreme impatience and now he seemed pissed. Which made me think he was worried (this because anger came out when he was worried about Tatiana), and I didn't think Buck worried was a good thing.

But he promised to have my back, he'd promised to find Tia and have hers, and he'd done everything else he'd promised, so I clung to that knowledge and trusted him to find her for me.

I turned my attention back to the phone call from Mrs. Jimenez.

"Have you—?"

Mrs. Jimenez cut me off, but she did it gently. "No, *mi amor*, no word."

She called every afternoon to gab like we used to be able to do whenever we wanted, seeing as I had no job and lived next door.

She also called to report whether she'd heard, or hadn't, from Tia.

And she hadn't heard.

Dang.

"How's the packing going?" I asked.

"Now I know why I haven't moved. I got a lot of stuff, Clarita."

I smiled at the phone, knowing she was right. She had enough stuff packed into her little apartment to fill three.

I pulled out the file I needed, shifting back to the desk.

"Are we still on for tomorrow night?" I asked.

She was coming up to Buck's for enchiladas and to meet Gear and Tatiana, who acted like she'd rather have open heart surgery without anesthetic than meet Mrs. Jimenez, which I hoped wouldn't make dinner interesting.

In other words, torture for Mrs. Jimenez *and* for me.

"*Sí*, I can't wait to meet *tu novio*. A man who cooks...*aiy*. Looking forward to that, *querida*."

I sat down at the desk.

"He doesn't cook, Mrs. Jimenez, he *cooks*. He makes hamburgers taste gourmet. Not kidding. When I first bit into his burger, my toes curled, and I almost passed out with delight. He's so good, he could open a restaurant."

I was telling her this as the door opened, and my head came up to smile at whoever walked in, Aces member, delivery man or employee.

But the second my eyes hit the tall, suited man walking through the door, the smile on my face froze as did the rest of my body.

Except my heart.

As with every time I saw that man, my heart squeezed, and it did this painfully.

I stayed frozen until I heard Mrs. Jimenez call, "Clarita? Are you there?"

"I..." I swallowed and closed my eyes tight.

I opened them, and unfortunately, the fevered wish I sent to the universe when I closed my eyes went unanswered.

He was still there.

What now, and maybe more importantly, why me?

"I have to go, Mrs. Jimenez, someone just walked into the office. I need to deal with it."

"*Por supuesto,*" Mrs. Jimenez replied, sounding happy, and she sounded happy because she was happy for me.

She worried about Tia.

But me with Buck, Buck's home and the job Buck gave me, she no longer had to worry about me.

And this made her happy.

So my Mexican American Grandma.

"We'll talk tomorrow," she finished.

"Thanks, yes, tomorrow. Take care, honey."

"*Hasta mañana, cariña.*"

I put the phone in the receiver.

"How did you find me?" I asked Nolan Armitage, Rogan's slimy, arrogant attorney.

Rogan's slimy, arrogant attorney who tried to block my divorce because, firstly, he asserted it would hurt Rogan's defense, me defecting, and secondly, if I was legally untied from Rogan, Nolan couldn't come after me to pay Rogan's bills when Rogan ran out of money.

Therefore, he made the process of the divorce longer, more painful and a lot more expensive, shoving me deeper in a hole which was already pretty darned deep.

"You opened a cell phone account using West Hardy's address then you were reported as being employed with Ace in the Hole, Limited," he answered, looking around, his upper lip curled with disdain then his eyes came back to me. "I see you landed on your feet."

I wished I could be surprised he was acting like a cretin.

But considering he'd never acted anything else, I was not surprised.

"Are you here to discuss work you'd like done on your house? Because if you are, I need to tell you our clientele is exclusive, and our waiting list is long. It could be years and it's highly likely you'll need to accumulate extensive billable hours defending criminal creeps in order to afford it."

The lip curl didn't go away when he stated, "I'm here to talk to you."

I stood and turned to face him. "There's absolutely nothing I want to hear you say."

"Actually, I think you're wrong."

"No, I know I'm right."

He leaned in.

"No, Clara, you're wrong," he said quietly.

I shook my head. "Please leave, and unless you wish to talk to one of the boys about a home improvement job, don't come back."

"Rogan's got cancer."

My hand flew out and my fingertips pressed into the desk as my body rocked with this news.

"I knew you'd want to hear that." He was still speaking quietly.

"Cancer?" I whispered.

"He's been moved to a prison hospital. It's not looking good. They're giving him months, at most."

Oh my God.

I closed my eyes and dropped my head.

"You're his life insurance beneficiary," Nolan went on.

I opened my eyes and lifted my head.

"*What?*" I breathed.

"Upon his death, you'll receive five million dollars."

I took a step back.

Then I shouted, "*What?*"

"I told you, *he* told you, *both of us* told you time and again while you pushed that divorce that he was going to take care of you. You wouldn't listen. He didn't listen to me and kept you as beneficiary. Now, as soon as he wastes away, you're going to be rich."

"How could he...how could he...?" I took in a breath, leaned forward and screamed, "*How could he have a life insurance policy?*"

"Clara—"

I threw up my hands.

"That's *insane!*" I yelled.

"Clara, listen to me," Nolan demanded, walking to me.

But I retreated until I hit the file cabinets and had to stop. Though he kept at me until he was less than a foot away.

I tipped my head back to look at him and shouted, "You have to *pay* on life insurance policies! How does he have money to pay on a life insurance policy?"

The side door to the garage opened and Raul, one of our electricians, and one of the biggest fans of my baked goods, was there.

It was breaktime and he'd come all the way from a job to have his cupcake.

Totally one of the biggest fans.

"Is everything okay?" Raul asked, seeing me pressed to the file cabinets and Nolan close to me.

"No!" I shouted. "No! Everything is *not* okay!" I looked up at Nolan. "Tell me," I demanded, "exactly *how* he could pay on a life insurance policy when he has *no money?*"

Nolan was looking at Raul. "We need to talk alone."

"We're not going to talk alone," I shot back and looked at Raul. "Please, Raul, don't leave." Raul nodded, his eyes alert, and I turned back to Nolan. "Now, answer me."

Nolan's attention returned to me. "Clara, you need to ask him to go away."

"*No!*" I screeched. "*Answer me!* What's going on?"

I heard Raul say, "Find Buck," but I kept my eyes on Nolan.

Nolan spoke to me.

"He knew about the cancer before the trial started. Before he even got arrested." He paused, a significant pause I didn't entirely understand because my mind was reeling, before he finished, "From the very beginning."

I closed my eyes and looked to the side.

"Oh God," I whispered. "I can't believe this."

"He was worried things were getting..." I opened my eyes and looked at him, "*hot*, so he contacted me and made arrangements. We..." he looked at Raul who hadn't moved, then back at me, "made arrangements with some of the money. Put it in a place they couldn't find it and they couldn't claim it. When Rogan dies, you'll get that money too."

I shook my head. "I don't believe this."

"It's true, Clara. I told you to stick by him, and I told him, when you didn't, to scrape you off, but he flatly refused. Now he's dying, and it's all coming to you. The five million insurance and a million and a half that's sitting in an account in what I will share only is an undisclosed location."

Six and a half million dollars.

Six and a half million dollars!

Six and a half million dollars, and a month ago I was in ecstasy just to eat a Pop-Tart.

I kept shaking my head, whispering, "Why didn't you mention any of this during the trial?"

"Because he told me not to."

Why would he do that?

Why?

I had no idea if it would help, to reduce his sentence at least.

But even if it wouldn't, he should have *tried*.

"All that money is free and clear," Nolan told me. "The cops can't touch it. The Feds can't touch it. It's yours. At least the divorce made that part easier."

I stopped shaking my head and glared at him, feeling more bodies entering the room and ignoring them.

"First, that money is not his. It is not mine. It belongs to hundreds of people who are scrambling to make up their pensions before they retire. Second, did you, or Rogan, ever *once* think of letting me in on the knowledge there were funds available before my life unraveled because *Rogan* is a *toad* and a *criminal* and a *cheat*? And before I found myself in a place where I could have *died* because I was desperate? I mean, my car got repoed, and I got beat up by a sociopath!"

I ended my diatribe shouting.

"What the fuck's goin' on?"

I turned my head to see Buck had shoved his way to the front of the bunch of rough and tumble electricians, drywall guys and bikers who were filling the small room.

"Guess what, honey. My ex is about to die and he's going to leave me six and a half million dollars. Now we can buy that island we always wanted," I stated with saccharine sweetness, and Buck's eyes narrowed on me then they moved to Nolan.

"You wanna tell me who you are?" Buck asked.

"Not particularly," Nolan, clearly not good at reading body language nor having a keen sense of self-preservation, answered.

"All right, I'll give you that," Buck said in his quiet, venom voice. "Now I'll ask you to get outta my old lady's space, and you better have a different answer."

Nolan's brows went up. "Old lady?"

"Move the fuck away from Clara," Buck growled.

"Jesus," Nolan muttered, taking a step away, his lip curled again.

Buck crossed his arms on his chest and his eyes came to me.

"Toots, talk," he ordered.

I threw an arm out to Nolan. "Buck, this is Nolan Armitage, Rogan's slimeball attorney." I threw an arm out to Buck. "Nolan, this is West Hardy, president of the Aces High Motorcycle Club and a decent human being. You don't meet many of those, so before you go, you might want to take a picture."

Some of the men in the room chuckled.

Buck and Nolan did not.

Neither did I.

My gaze went to Buck. "Rogan has cancer. Apparently, he's had it awhile. Unbeknownst to me, he set things up to take care of me. He hid a bunch of money and has a huge life insurance policy. All of it comes to me on his death, which, Nolan reports, is imminent."

"Jesus," Buck muttered.

"That just about covers it," I agreed.

"He wants to see you," Nolan put in, and both Buck and my eyes went to him.

"Sorry?" I asked.

"Rogan. He's asked me to ask you to visit him."

I blinked.

Then I said, "Let me get this straight. He steals from people, cheats on me, completely ruins my life, sets me up for public ridicule and brings me so low, homeless people have to do me favors, and now he wants me to visit him?"

"I see you don't get this," Nolan replied. "*I* told you and *Rogan* told you...repeatedly...he has feelings for you, deep feelings. He loves you, Clara, always has. And now he's dying, and he wants to see you before that happens."

"Yes, *Nolan*," I spat, leaning into him. "You told me that and Rogan told me that, *repeatedly*. And sure, I can see that's the kind of love I'd hold dear, the love of a man who promises me happiness while he fucks everything that moves. And at the same time, while he's cheating on me, he's cheating hundreds of people out of the option of having financially-stress-free golden years." I put both hands over my heart. "I'm awash with happiness. Lead me to him straight away."

"Think it's time for you to leave," Buck rumbled.

He'd come close and was situating himself between Nolan and me.

Nolan didn't take his eyes off me. "If you don't go to see him, I'll advise him to change his beneficiary and alter his will."

"Knock yourself out," I invited, leaning around Buck. "And while you're advising, do me the favor of sharing with Rogan that he can shove that six and a half million dollars *straight up his ass*."

There were some chuckles and some indrawn breaths.

Buck made not a noise but shifted so he was almost dead in front of me.

I shifted so I could see Nolan.

"Same old Clara," Nolan muttered, eyes squinty and angry on me. "Everything that man did, he did for you."

Now that, *that* took it too far.

Without hesitation, I launched myself at him, and Buck turned swiftly and caught me around the waist, holding me back as I pressed toward Nolan.

"Babe," he said softly.

"You have got to be *joking*!" I screamed at Nolan.

"You came from nothing and Rogan wanted you to have everything," Nolan retorted. "Throughout this, all he ever did, he did looking out for you. He gave you a beautiful life, a beautiful home, a beautiful car and put himself on the line to give it to you, and you never said thanks once. You just divorced him when he needed you the most. And after you turned your back on him, he *still* did everything he could to look out for you."

"Let me educate you, Nolan, and feel free to share this with Rogan," I shot back, still straining against Buck, though mostly at that point, I was doing it so I could see around him and keep eye contact with Nolan.

"The way Rogan could have looked out for me was to *not* commit *multiple* criminal acts. And I'll throw in, he might have reconsidered *before* he paid for sex with *multiple* prostitutes!"

"Gash," Buck gritted. "Get that fuckin' guy outta here before she explodes."

There was movement in the room, but I was still entirely focused on Nolan.

"You need to arrange to see him," Nolan persevered.

"Dude, *you* need to let it go and move on," Gash, who was now close to Nolan, advised.

Nolan twisted his neck to scowl at Gash. "You touch me, you'll buy yourself problems."

"Do I look like I care?" Gash returned.

Nolan turned back to me.

Buck glanced over his shoulder to Nolan but kept a handle on me. "You got three seconds to get the fuck outta here, and you gotta know, I count fast."

Nolan glared at Buck then he looked at me. "Call me when you're ready to arrange the visit. I think you can find my number."

"Three," Buck bit.

Gash moved, and Nolan was shuffled right out the front door with Gash's hands bunching his suit jacket.

"Out," Buck went on, and the bevy of bikers and employees sifted through the door.

Raul was the last one out, and he closed the door behind him. The whole time he was doing this, his gaze was on me.

"Babe," Buck called, and I looked from the door to him, my eyes hitting his brown ones, my flesh feeling his strong fingers pressed into my waist, my nose smelling his scent, fresh-cut wood (he was on a job, working on cabinets in the warehouse), my senses feeling the power of him enveloping me.

And I disintegrated.

Buck pulled me with him as he swiveled the office chair around, sat in it, taking me down on his lap. I wrapped my arms around his shoulders and shoved my wet face against his neck as the sobs wracked my body.

He gave me a squeeze.

"Darlin', you need to go see him."

I froze.

Then my head listed up, and I stared at him through watery eyes.

"Sorry?" I whispered.

"This upsets you, baby. He fucked you over, but you're fuckin' undone. This means he still means somethin' to you. You gotta go see him. You don't, you'll regret it."

"He doesn't mean anything to me." I was still whispering, and Buck gave me another squeeze while he leaned forward and kissed my nose.

When he pulled back, he said gently, "Toots, I get you're mine, so you don't have to lie to me about this."

"I'm not lying."

He moved a hand to my jaw, his thumb sweeping through the wetness on my cheek. Then he slid that wetness across my lower lip.

"Taste that, Toots. You know what that taste is. So do I. And, baby, you don't need to lie to me. No matter what it is, you never need to lie to me."

"He babied me when I was sick," I whispered, and Buck's body got tight under mine. "Even if it was a sniffle, he acted like I was an invalid. Bought the whole drugstore, waited on me hand and foot."

"Toots—"

"I used to collect spa products. Face masks. Shampoo. Conditioner. Pumice scrub. Exfoliant. I used to spend hours in the bathroom relaxing and primping. He told me I didn't need that stuff. I didn't need to spend that time, that nothing could make me more beautiful than I already was."

"Clara, I get it. I don't wanna hear—"

"We met young. He dazzled me. Then he wound me up. Wound me up in *him*. Except for Tia, he was my whole world."

"Baby," Buck pressed his thumb to my mouth, "quiet."

I wasn't quiet.

I pulled away from his thumb and kept talking.

"But the only thing he gave me, really, was an education on what love was *not*. To this day, I'm not certain what love is, but I know what it's not. Rogan taught me that." I wrapped my fingers around the side of his neck. "And Buck, after yearning all my life for someone to love me, just love me, that isn't a fun lesson to learn."

"Fuckin' hell, Toots," he whispered.

"I'm not crying because I have feelings for him. I'm crying because I'm so sick and so, so *very* tired of finding something good and feeling the world solid under my feet and having someone come in and rock it...*again*." I dropped my head to his shoulder and muttered, "I'm just tired. Why can't everyone just let me *be*?"

Buck slid his arms around me again and he gathered me close, but he didn't have an answer to my question.

Likely because there wasn't one.

"I was talking to Mrs. Jimenez. Talking about enchiladas at your house and how good you could cook. Normal stuff. Food. Friends. That's all I want my life to be. That isn't asking much. Why is that so hard?" I asked.

"It'll pass, Toots."

I shook my head then pressed my cheek to his shoulder. "I'm thirty-two, West. It hasn't yet and I'm beginning to think it never will."

"Babe," he muttered.

"Six and a half million dollars," I whispered. "He thinks *that's* taking care of me." I shook my head against his shoulder. "As Gear would say, that...is...*whacked*." I sighed and proclaimed, "Happiness is Pop-Tarts. I wish he got that."

I felt Buck's body move against mine, and I lifted my head and looked down at him to see he was what I thought he was.

Laughing.

"What's funny?" I asked.

"Happiness is Pop-Tarts?"

"Absolutely."

He stared at me a second and then threw his head back and roared with laughter, his arms convulsing around me.

My body got stiff.

"I'm being very serious, West Hardy," I informed him.

"Yeah, babe," he said through his hilarity, his eyes focusing on me, "I know."

"I just endured a drama," I reminded him.

"Yeah, babe, I saw."

"There is nothing to laugh at," I snapped.

"Gorgeous, you just told that asshole to tell your ex to shove six and a half million dollars up his ass."

"I know, but that is not funny."

"*I'm awash with happiness. Lead me to him straight away,*" he quoted, shaking his head, still laughing. "Some a' the shit that comes outta your mouth, babe. Fuckin' priceless."

"Buck, I'm not finding this amusing."

"Do you want an island in the Pacific or are you thinkin' Caribbean?" he inquired.

"Stop joking!" I snapped and slapped his shoulder.

"It can't be too expensive. We gotta leave you at least a million to buy bikinis and pumice scrub, whatever the fuck that is," he remarked.

With a frustrated noise, I tried to shove out of his lap, but his arms only got tighter.

"You leave my lap, babe, you do it to lock the doors and close the blinds."

"It's normal operating hours, Buck," I told him haughtily. "The doors and blinds are open during normal operating hours so I can see what's going on and the boys can get to me if they need me, even if I've just endured another drama."

"They don't need you for the next half hour."

"Deliveries don't come on *my* schedule. They come when they come. And Jimbo takes his break at three o'clock sharp. I've been saving him a cupcake and he knows it."

"Jimbo's gonna have to delay breaktime, babe. Go lock the doors and pull the blinds."

I tilted my head as I looked at him and asked, "Why are you being weird?"

"Because I don't give a fuck if someone sees or walks in on me fuckin' you on the desk, but I reckon you will, so you need to lock the doors and pull the blinds."

I sucked in breath and my eyes grew wide, even as I felt my nipples get hard.

Then I whispered, "You aren't fucking me on the desk."

But I kind of hoped he was.

"Yeah, I definitely am."

Oh my.

Then I remembered where we were.

"You can't," I hissed. "They already call me Redhot. You do that, they'll hear, and I'll never live that nickname down."

"You're never gonna live it down anyway, Toots, so you might as well live it up."

He had a point there.

"I have things to do," I informed him.

"And you can do 'em. You let go instead of holdin' on, I might be able to make you come in twenty minutes rather than half an hour, then you can get to doin' the things you gotta do."

I tried a different tack.

"I can't have sex in the workplace. People don't have sex in their workplace."

"Babe, quit fuckin' around."

"But—"

"You keep fuckin' around, I do you on the desk with the blinds open and doors unlocked. You want that?"

I narrowed my eyes on him. "Why are you so annoying?"

"You can tell me I'm annoying when I got my dick inside you and you're moanin' at me to fuck you harder. Now, go lock the doors and close...the fuckin'...*blinds*."

I glared at him.

He absorbed my glare and lifted his brows.

Then I pushed off his lap, locked the doors and closed the blinds.

I did this because I was protesting, but it was only for show.

What I really wanted was Buck to fuck me on the desk.

Lucky for me, I got what I wanted and Buck "did" me on the desk, right on top of my papers, files and everything.

I was pretty certain anyone outside heard it.

I was also pretty certain Buck didn't care, not even a little bit.

What was surprising was...

I didn't either.

17

THERE'S NO WAY OUT

It was afternoon in the office the next day.
Friday.
Payday.

The first thing I did when I got to the office was log into my account online.

Promptly after, I did my first-ever, very loud whoop and holler of sheer glee when I saw I had a positive bank balance and that positive was more than a dollar and fifty-seven cents.

In concern after the big drama the day before, Raul came running.

I just gave him a homemade oatmeal and chocolate chip cookie and sent him back to the warehouse so he could load up for his job that day, assuring him all was well.

After that, I paid on all three of my credit cards and sent a check off to Raymundo for my part of Mrs. Jimenez's rent.

I didn't pay a lot on the credit cards because I liked the feel of having a positive bank balance, the next payday was two weeks away and my cards needed about six months of full-on payments to get under control, but at least it was something and maybe they'd call off their collectors.

With this start, I knew that day was going to be better than the day before.

This was thinking positively, of course, considering my life and the fact that anything could happen in it. But I was holding on to that with all I had.

And anyway, tonight was Buck's enchiladas with Mrs. Jimenez, Gear, and Tatiana.

Sure, Tatiana wasn't a bonus in that mix, but the enchiladas would make up for her not liking me.

It was now the afternoon, and there had fortunately been no dramas.

So, of course, the day took a turn.

Chap, Jimbo, and Raul were sitting on the couch in my office. Jimbo and Raul were taking a break and enjoying a fresh mug of coffee and the last of the cookies (they'd made it that long because I'd tripled the recipe, I'd learned that early). Chap was taking sips from a flask. Minnie was sitting on my desk gabbing. I was printing off invoices.

Then the door opened.

I looked up, and the room went instantly wired.

This was because Detective Rayne Scott, looking gorgeous, wearing a Henley, a sports jacket, jeans and boots, and sporting a badge and gun on his belt, walked in.

I forgot to mention.

Also that morning, I'd placed a call to the police station leaving a message for Rayne Scott.

I stared at him looking gorgeous (worth a repeat) and standing in my office.

Fantastic.

He couldn't just phone?

"Cop," Chap growled in a weirdly unhappy way as I felt Minnie, equally weirdly, get tense on my desk.

I kept staring at Scott and ignored their responses.

Many of the biker and biker babe responses were still a mystery to me. Though it didn't take years living in the biker world to know bikers and cops weren't the best of friends.

Still, Scott had just walked into a room. He didn't do it with a SWAT team at his back, gun drawn, shouting, "Freeze!"

I pointed out the obvious, "You got my call."

"Your call?" Minnie whispered.

"Yep," Scott stated, walking into the room like there was nothing amiss when there was a lot amiss.

Attitude rolled off Chap in waves, and Minnie was so tense, I felt it across my desk.

Raul and Jimbo stood and immediately shuffled out the door (but Jimbo grabbed the last cookie before he went).

I'd tipped my head back to look at Scott. "You could have called back. I left a number."

"Babe," Minnie said low, "I gotta go Professor Higgins on your ass. You called *a cop?*"

I looked at her and then swung my head to Chap when he repeated, a lot less friendly, "Yeah, you called *a cop?*"

"It isn't a big deal," I told Chap.

Chap ignored me and looked at Scott. "Think you know this territory is off-limits."

"Chap, I think *you* know *no* territory is off-limits," Scott returned.

Chap's attitude ratcheted up to tsunami level, and I stood.

"It's okay, Chap. I called him and it's not a big deal," I assured, hoping to hold back the tidal wave.

Chap's eyes sliced to me. "Cops at Ace, woman, *always* a big deal."

"This isn't," I returned.

Chap's thick, gray, needing-a-trim-due-to-wayward-hairs brows went up. "Buck know about this shit?"

"Um...no," I answered.

"Oh shit," Minnie muttered, and I looked at her.

"It isn't a big deal!" I stated, somewhat loudly, throwing my hands up, not knowing why they were acting so weird.

"Clara, why don't you just tell me why you called," Scott put in, and Chap moved closer to my desk.

I looked at Scott.

"Rogan's sick," I told him, and Scott went from alert to something else, something soft, and it made all that was gorgeous about him beautiful.

I kind of wished he was ugly and a creep. It would make dealing with him and not liking him easier.

Instead, it was becoming clear he wasn't just a good guy, he was maybe a really good guy.

"You found out," he muttered.

So he knew.

I wondered how he knew.

Considering the atmosphere in the room, I didn't ask that.

"Nolan came visiting yesterday," I shared.

"Bet he delivered the news gentle." Scott was still muttering now while also being sarcastic.

"Not exactly," I replied.

"Dick." He kept muttering.

Clearly, Detective Rayne Scott knew Nolan Armitage too.

"Anyway," I sallied forth, "apparently, there's a five-million-dollar life insurance policy and a million and a half in an offshore account," I informed Scott.

His body went alert, his eyes grew sharp, but Chap exploded.

"Fuckin' A, woman, what the fuck?"

"Oh shit," Minnie mumbled, coming off the desk, "I seriously gotta go PH on your ass."

"What?" I asked Minnie, but Minnie was looking at Scott.

"Can you go?"

"No," Scott answered.

"This won't take long," I told Minnie.

"You're givin' info to a cop," Minnie retorted, her eyes swinging to me.

"No, I'm not, I mean...I am," I replied. "But Rogan's already in jail. It isn't like he can be *more* in jail."

"You never give info to a cop," Minnie returned.

"Damn straight," Chap growled.

"Jesus," Scott muttered.

"I can't rat on someone who's already doing time for the crime," I pointed out what I thought was logically.

"Don't matter," Minnie replied.

"Can I just do what I have to do?" I asked Minnie, then swung my head to Chap. "It isn't what you think."

"Just do what you have to do, Clara," Scott urged.

I nodded, ignored Minnie, Chap and their stubbornness and launched in.

"Right. Well, anyway, what I wanted to know is...you seized the house, Rogan's car, the accounts, the portfolios and you liquidated them, giving it to the people who Rogan stole from, right?"

"Right," Scott answered on a nod.

"So, he dies. If I get that money, can you locate those people again and distribute it fairly?"

Scott blinked at me.

Slowly.

Minnie groaned.

Chap exploded again.

"Are you fuckin' loco?" he shouted.

"No!" I snapped at him, losing my patience with his attitude.

"Does Buck know about *this*?" he snapped back.

"No," I replied. "But what does it matter? That money isn't mine and it isn't Buck's, it's those people's."

Chap leaned in. "Woman, you do not make a move without Buck. You do not utter a word about important shit, like fuckin' givin' away fuckin' six and a half million fuckin' dollars, without Buck knowin' and givin' the go-ahead. And you don't deal with cops *ever* unless Buck is in on it."

"Like I said, it isn't his money, and it isn't mine," I replied.

"Babe, that guy fucked you over as in *fucked you over*," Minnie threw in, and I swung my head the other way to look at her. "You *earned* that money, and Buck pulled your shit outta the fryer so, Aces' rules, he gets his share. That money is *so* yours and you, you're Buck's old lady. Chap is right. Heads-up on the PH advice, sister, Eliza Biker Babe needs to learn right fuckin' now that she don't move on shit like this unless Buck is in the know."

Were they serious?

"Are you serious?" I asked.

"You got bill collectors on your ass, credit cards to pay off and you're on the back of Buck's bike or your ass is in his ride because A, you're his woman, but mostly 'cause, B," she leaned in, "*you ain't got no ride because it's been repoed.*"

"I know that," I told her softly.

She leaned back. "So, my guess is, you talked to Buck about this, he'd say take care a' you. And what I *know* is, an old lady takes care of her old man. He's swung his ass out there for you, you hit a windfall like this, you can find six and a half million ways to pay him back and you're gonna *give it away?*"

Oh dear.

I saw her point.

"Minnie—" I started.

She threw up her hands. "Even if you didn't look out for him, babe, you need to learn to start *lookin' out for you.*"

"She's right."

That came from Scott and everyone turned to him, but I suspected only I did it with my lips parted.

"Sorry?" I whispered.

"She's right, Clara," he repeated. "The million and a half, that's dirty money. Kirk stole from a lot of people. We recovered a good deal, he didn't piss it all away, but there was a major deficit. That won't cover it, but somethin' is better than nothin'. You give that back, they could use it and they'd be grateful. The five mil," he tipped his chin to me, "that's yours. You feel like bein' generous, you give a little back. But you cover yourself before you do that. Pay your bills, get yourself a car, buy a house, put some away, make certain where you were is a place you're never gonna be again."

This was met with silence until Chap grunted.

Scott's eyes never left mine and he finished, "Kirk dies, you come into that windfall, you know how to find me. But listen to your girl." Now his head tilted to Minnie. "And don't do anything until you take care of you."

After delivering that message, his eyes swept Minnie and Chap, he turned on his boot and walked out the door.

The second it closed, Chap turned to Minnie and pointed at her. "I'm leavin' and, 'cause she makes good cookies and cupcakes, I'm keepin' my mouth shut 'bout this shit. *You,*" he jabbed his finger at Minnie, "get her shit sharp. This kinda shit happens again, I ain't keepin' my mouth shut. You hear me?"

"I hear you," Minnie said softly.

Chap nodded, and without looking at me, he followed Scott out the door.

I turned to Minnie in time to see her hands go to her hips.

"Sit your ass down, babe, the rain in Spain is right now fallin' on the fuckin' plain, get me?"

I pressed my lips together.

I got her.

So I sat down.

TWO HOURS LATER, I was in search of Buck because we had to go get Mrs. Jimenez and meet his kids at the house.

As I searched, my latest Professor Higgins session was rumbling through my brain.

Apparently, biker babes deferred to their biker boys in everything, which meant *everything*.

The man made the decisions, the woman lived with them.

And also, if the man told the woman to do something, she did it. No matter what it was.

Or, if he told her *not* to do something, she didn't do it, no matter how much she may want to.

I had to admit, I was uncertain about this.

I also had to admit, the word "uncertain" was a massive under-statement.

I further had to admit that I was uncertain Buck actually lived by this philosophy.

I *was* certain he was domineering, but he was also sweet and gentle, in a rough and tumble way.

Still, he was.

I couldn't imagine if I wanted something badly enough, we couldn't discuss it and he wouldn't see my way of thinking.

I also couldn't imagine he wouldn't want me to be free and clear to make decisions about my life.

We were living together, but only out of necessity. Buck wasn't sure

I was safe yet (no word about Esposito, except from Buck, "He's got his hands full dealing with his own people," which I took as something that would have Esposito's total focus), and therefore, I was never alone. Unless I was in the office. But with the place crawling with people, that wasn't really alone.

I had also only earned one paycheck and my fat, as Minnie put it, was by no means out of the fryer.

In other words, I wasn't (yet) in a position to find my own space and live my own life beholden only to me.

That didn't change the fact that Buck and I were still new. He acted like I was his woman and his people acted like I was his woman, but I wasn't sure yet that I actually was.

So I figured I was still my own woman.

What I didn't know was how I felt about losing my freewill if I officially became Buck's.

This was what was on my mind as I searched through the shop, then the warehouse, and finally headed to the Dive.

It wasn't unusual for Buck to disappear and not tell me where he was going. But his SUV was out in the lot, he had to be somewhere.

The common area of the Dive was deserted, but I heard noises coming through the door that led to the hall where the bedrooms were.

I headed that way.

My mind was still whirling with my Biker Babe Lesson, I didn't even think as I moved.

I should have thought, and I should have processed the sounds I was hearing and stayed far, far away.

The minute I turned the final corner and hit the hall, I stopped and stared.

Nails, her upper body nude, her skirt bunched at her waist, was against the wall astride a biker.

She was riding him, her breasts bouncing, and he was thrusting, his face shoved in her neck.

My heart stopped beating, my stomach clutched, and I stared, immobilized, even though my brain was screaming, *Run!*

"Jesus," I heard growled from behind me.

I jumped and an arm clamped around my belly, locking me to a tall, solid body.

Nails' eyes shot open, her head jerked our way, and she arrested mid-bounce. The face shoved into her neck came out.

And I saw it was Gash.

Minnie's man.

Gash.

Oh God!

My body moved forward, *toward the action,* obviously not of its own volition.

It locked in protest but this didn't stop it from moving.

"Not smart." Buck was still growling, but now he was growling at Gash. "Minnie was in Toots's office not fuckin' fifteen minutes ago, brother."

"Fuck," Gash muttered, his eyes on me.

Nails' eyes were on Buck.

"Get this, Gash, they're tight. Minnie's gonna be hangin' here a lot. You take that shit somewhere else or at least get behind a fuckin' door," Buck ordered as he pulled us deeper *into the hall.*

He let go of my belly, grabbed my hand and dragged me toward them, also toward where Buck's room was, the opposite way from the exit, where I really, *really* wanted to be heading.

We then moved past them in a way I could not avoid seeing Gash pull Nails off his member and set her to her feet.

We got to Buck's room. He pulled me in and shut the door.

Then he stared at me, one hand at his hip, the other lifting so he could run it through his perfect greasy-wet-looking, thick awesome hair.

"Jesus, fuck, I don't even know where to begin," he muttered, dropping his hand and putting it to his other hip.

I knew where to begin.

"Who was that woman?" I asked, even though I knew.

I knew and I couldn't believe I saw what I saw. I also couldn't believe *he* saw it. I further couldn't believe he didn't seem angry Gash was having sex with his other woman.

Did Buck share?

Would he eventually share me?

Oh God.

I knew how *that* went.

"Gash," he stated.

"No," I whispered. "I know Gash. The woman."

"She's gash, Toots," he replied.

"Sorry?"

"Cunt," he went on, and that awful word hit me like a punch to the stomach and the blow was more powerful because it came through Buck's lips.

"Sorry?" I whispered.

"She's gash, pussy. She's fucked practically everyone in the Club, in other clubs, men who aren't in clubs. You ride a bike, she's down to open her legs."

Oh God.

Minnie, Pinky, and Lorie didn't tell me *that*.

But maybe they didn't know.

"Ink?" I asked.

Buck didn't answer.

This meant yes.

I couldn't believe this.

Ink seemed utterly *devoted* to Lorie.

God.

"Cruise?" I continued.

Buck's jaw got tight.

Another yes.

God!

"You?" I whispered, even though I knew the answer to that one.

"She's nothin', babe. Like I said. Pussy. That's it."

"She's a woman, Buck," I told him.

"Nope, she's pussy," he replied.

I stared at him.

Then I closed my eyes tight.

I also turned my face away.

"Eyes to me, Toots."

I clenched my teeth, looked at him, and he kept talking.

"That is not what we made her. That is what she made herself. This

Club sees a lotta different kinds a' women who have a lotta different kinds a' uses. Hers is one she chose for herself. You, Lorie, Minnie, yours is different. And you all chose yours too."

What did he mean *uses*?

"I don't know what to say," I whispered.

"It's our way of life, babe, there's nothing *to* say."

I felt my back go straight. "How many other uses does the Club have for women?"

He shook his head.

"We're not doin' that shit, Toots. You know what you need to know, and you don't know anything more. Not now. You shouldn't've been back here. You can come into the Dive, back here, no fuckin' way. Not unless you're with me or not until I make you mine by puttin' a ring on your finger. Wives, they got free rein, but then they know what they might see, and they know to avoid it. You. No."

Oh God.

Every scrap of advice Minnie, Pinky, and Lorie had shared, even the stuff I really didn't believe, or maybe didn't *want* to believe, Buck proved true in that one statement.

"I don't know how I feel about that," I told him quietly.

"Toots, doesn't matter how you feel about it. You took me on, you take my cock, you accepted my protection and you put your ass on the back of my bike. That's the decision *you* made, no one forced you to make it. This is your life. And part a' that is keepin' your mouth shut about what you just saw. Minnie doesn't need to know that shit."

She knew.

She already knew.

She didn't know about Nails, but she knew.

"I think I'm changing my mind," I whispered and then took an immediate step back because his face changed, his body changed, the air in the room changed.

The snake was preparing to strike.

"Too late," he said in a lethal voice. "You're in, and once you're in, there's no way out."

"Buck—"

He cut me off. "Get your shit and get your ass in the truck."

Was he serious?

"But—"

He leaned forward at the waist and whispered a poisonous, "*Now.*"

I stared at him.

He was serious.

Dear God, he was serious.

Then, clearly with no other choice (as usual, and if I wasn't already sick of that, which I was, I'd be sick to death of it in that moment), I walked past him, opened the door, walked down the now thankfully vacant hall, through the common area, out the front door...

And I did as I was told.

I got my "shit" and got in his truck.

18

THAT'S HOW FAMILIES ARE

We turned up Buck's drive, Mrs. Jimenez in the back.

Me, luckily saved from my thoughts because I had to pretend everything was all right.

No.

Everything was *just great*.

Instead of everything being wrong, wrong, *wrong* with quite a bit of clashing, right, right, *right*.

I had jumped from the frying pan straight into a fire.

Sure, this time, I had a roof over my head (that Buck was providing), food in my belly (ditto from Buck), a job (given to me by Buck), friends (also Buck's) and safety (provided by Buck and his boys).

All of this was good.

All of it I liked.

But all of it made me more indebted to him.

This, however, was not in the normal way partners became indebted to each other.

Like, he took care of me, and later on down the line, I listened when he had problems or I made his favorite birthday cake or I bought a set of underwear he really, really liked and let him unveil it as a surprise, giving a little back.

This was a debt that was paid by the loss of my freedom, and maybe, my choice.

Apparently, according to Buck, I couldn't leave.

And I *couldn't* leave, not realistically.

But also, according to Buck, I just *couldn't.*

The drive to Mrs. Jimenez's had been tense.

Buck, in true Buck form, tried to dispel it.

He did this by taking my hand and saying gently, "I wasn't pissed at you, baby. And I'm not now. I'm pissed at Gash. Then...and now."

"Why?" I'd asked.

"Why?" he asked back, like that was a crazy question.

"Yes, why are you pissed at him, West?"

"Because he was stupid, babe," he stated, like that was obvious.

The good of that was, it sounded genuine. He genuinely sounded pissed that Gash had been "stupid." Stupid, I assumed, because he was doing something somewhere where he could get caught.

Not pissed that he saw Gash screwing his side piece.

So that was good.

Sort of.

The bad about that was, his answer was not, "Because Minnie's a good woman and no man should do that ever, but definitely not to a good woman."

Upon which, maybe, I could open discussions about what I saw weeks ago with Buck and Nails at the picnic table.

So at that point, I'd become the woman no woman should ever become.

I tested my man.

"I called Rayne Scott today," I announced.

"Come again?" he'd replied.

"I called him. He came into the office," I shared, and it even sounded like a dare. "I told him about the money. Rogan's money that's not really his money as well as the life insurance payout."

Buck had no immediate reply.

But when I said no more, he drawled out a leading, "Okay."

"I told him he could have it when I got it. To put it back in the pension fund."

At that, Master of the Contradiction, West Hardy, who came with so much good, but also some significant bad, lifted my hand to his mouth, brushed my knuckles with his lips, dropped it to his thigh and said, "That's cool."

"That's cool?" I pressed. "Minnie and Chap didn't think it was cool."

"They didn't?" he asked, sounding perplexed.

"They didn't think it was cool I give that money away and they *really* didn't think it was cool I called Scott."

"Gotta say, wished you'd told me that, so when he showed, I could have had your back, darlin'. He tweaks you. Not a fan of not bein' there for you when you had your chat. Glad Minnie was there. But the money, it's not Minnie's. Or Chap's. It's not mine. It's yours. Though, you're right, some of it should go back to that pension fund. The money he stole. The life insurance, honey..." He let that trail.

"What about the life insurance?"

Yes.

Still testing.

"You haven't had a lot in your life, Clara," he said softly. "And that guy fucked your life and your future. He owes you that. He owes you more than that, but at least that's something. It'll be a nest egg for you. And if you're careful with it, you'll never be back where you were ever again. And I can't say I don't like that for you."

I could read from that I had been correct in my earlier thoughts.

Perhaps Minnie (and Lorie and Pinky) had to put up with a man calling the shots.

But it would seem Buck was not like that.

So...

Yes.

Pure Buck.

After some significant bad, he gave good answers, reminding me about all there was to Buck, how much of it there was, and the fact that most of it was pretty awesome.

Hmm.

Fortunately, these answers were good enough, at least by the time we got to Mrs. Jimenez's and picked her up, I wasn't in a dither.

I could do the introductions and even laugh when she stared at Buck when she first saw him like she didn't know if she wanted to flee or throw herself into his arms and lament time, wishing she was thirty again and she could make a play for him.

It was cute.

What wasn't cute was the look she gave me after.

Filled with such relief, such warmth, such happiness all that was West Hardy was at my side, I nearly cried.

Mercifully, I got a handle on it and didn't.

And now, I could bury my thoughts in Buck's enchiladas, Gear's winning personality and Mrs. Jimenez's love.

So at least, I figured, I'd be able to get through the night.

"Aiy," Mrs. Jimenez said from the backseat, "you have a beautiful home, West."

I twisted in my seat to see she had her eyes glued to Buck's house.

So I looked at his house on the short ridge, nestled in the trees, above the pretty, twinkling-in-the-waning-rays-of-sunlight creek flowing in front of it. A house with all its windows, gleaming wood, fantastic deck, the red rock foothills rising steep from beyond the valley.

She was right. I'd thought it before. It was a cool house in a beautiful location.

But it was far out of town. Hard on the gas budget, which was hard on the environment. And living there meant, if you needed anything outside groceries, or had a desire for food outside what you could get at the Valley Inn or the single Italian place that also delivered pizza, you had a long slog to get there, that same slog back.

As such, it weirdly defined Buck.

That house was awesome, the locale amazing, you had everything you needed there and then some.

But it came with drawbacks.

They didn't seem significant.

But over time, they could wear on you.

"Wait until you see the view from the inside," I told her, trying to sound excited and thinking I'd failed when I felt Buck's eyes on me.

I looked to the windshield to avoid his gaze only to see four things.

One was Gear standing outside looking strangely troubled.

Another was Gear's sweet ride, as ever, shiny clean and clearly taken care of.

The third was another sweet ride, this one an interesting shade of blue/green and definitely awesome.

The last was a hugely smiling Tatiana who was bouncing on her toes and not looking troubled, angry, pouty, blank or any way she normally looked while around me.

The last made me stare.

"Shit," Buck muttered under his breath, and I turned my stare to him to see his gaze locked on his daughter.

Buck stopped the SUV, but before he'd done it, Tatiana launched herself toward us and she was in Buck's door nearly before he got it fully open.

"Daddy! A Charger! I *knew* it!" And she threw her arms around him when he jumped down.

"Babe," he murmured as I got out, closed my door and went to help Mrs. Jimenez.

"A 1969 Dodge Charger. *Turquoise!*" she screeched.

I looked her way as I helped Mrs. Jimenez get out and saw Tatiana was jumping up and down.

"It's *perfect!*" she declared. "It's better than the last one! It's even cooler than Gear's ride! It's *the bomb.*"

"Tatie," Buck said as I closed Mrs. Jimenez's door and we moved to the hood of the truck, all this while Tatiana ran toward the turquoise car, which she was right, was quite something.

"I knew you didn't mean what you said!" Tatiana yelled, still jumping up and down, but every once in a while, stopping to touch the car reverently with both hands. "I knew you wouldn't make me wait."

We all moved toward her, Buck stopping a few feet away, Gear, for some reason, keeping his distance.

I took Gear's distance as a warning and stopped Mrs. Jimenez at a safe location not close to the exuberant Tatiana.

"Gear says it's just somethin' you're workin' on. But I know. *I know!*" she continued.

"Tatie, honey, what'd I say?" Buck asked gently, and she grinned at him.

"Yeah, you *said* that, but this isn't here just to be here." She threw her arm out to the vehicle. "I know what this is." Then she launched herself at her father, jumping up, throwing her arms around his shoulders and giving him a big hug. "I *soooooo knew* you wouldn't make me wait!" she shouted and then giggled.

She was cute when she was excited, smiling and giggling. Although I had a feeling this wasn't what it seemed to be, not for Tatiana, I thought vaguely she should be that way more often.

Buck set her away from him and repeated, again gently, "Tatiana, what'd I say?"

Her head tilted to the side, and it took a minute, but slowly the smile faded away.

Buck went on, "You smashed up the ride I gave you for your birthday within three days, and since, you got two tickets joyridin' in Gear's."

Really?

He hadn't shared any of this with me.

"I told you," Buck continued. "You weren't gettin' another car until you could control your shit. And, honey," he put his hand on the side of her neck, "sorry, but I meant it." His voice gentled even further when he shared, "That ride's Clara's."

Uh-oh.

Gear's eyes came to me.

I felt Mrs. Jimenez's eyes on me.

Buck's eyes stayed on his daughter.

But Tatiana's eyes also turned to me.

"Clara's?" she whispered.

Oh dear.

She jumped back a step, her arms curled up, tight at her sides, her hands clenched into fists under her shoulders. She leaned into her father, face going red, and screeched, "*Clara's?*"

"Tatie," Buck said softly.

"Fuck you!" she shrieked.

Buck's body went solid, and Gear was on the move toward his sister.

"Aiy, *Dios mio,*" Mrs. Jimenez whispered.

"Tat, stay cool," Gear urged, putting a hand on her arm.

But she shook it free and jumped back again, her eyes coming to me.

"And fuck you! Fuck you, *Clara*! Fuck you, fuck you, *fuck...you*!"

Then she raced into the house, Buck and Gear following her.

I licked my lips, pulled them between my teeth and bit them.

I then looked down at Mrs. Jimenez, who still had a hand on my arm, and let my lips go to say, "As you know, Tatiana isn't my biggest fan yet."

Yes, I'd shared about Tatie.

We talked every day, but also, I did it to prepare her for what she might face if Tatiana wasn't in the mood to be cool that night.

"This I can see," Mrs. Jimenez muttered, her eyes going to the house in time to see Tatiana racing out again.

"Tat! Jesus!" Gear raced after her. "Give me my fuckin' keys!"

My body jolted.

So did Mrs. Jimenez's.

Oh no!

Buck came out last.

"Tatiana, swear to Christ, you get behind the wheel of your brother's car pissed—" Buck started.

But he didn't finish because Tatiana got behind the wheel of her brother's car pissed. She locked the door. Gear banged on the roof, shouting expletives, but she fired up the engine, and with gravel spewing from the back tires, she sped down the drive.

"Take the Charger," Buck gritted. Reaching into his jeans' pocket, he pulled out some keys and tossed them to Gear, who caught them. "Track her, calm her ass down and bring her back. You leave one of the cars. She's not drivin'. We'll go pick it up wherever you leave it tomorrow."

"She fucks up my car, I'll break her fuckin' neck," Gear threatened, stalking to the turquoise car.

"Cool it. Track her, get her ass home," Buck returned.

Gear nodded, folded into the Charger and took off.

Mrs. Jimenez and I stared after Gear.

Then, in unison, our heads swung to Buck.

"Enchiladas are off," he bit out.

"*Sí*," Mrs. Jimenez agreed, and she didn't shrink back like I did when Buck prowled to us.

He pulled his wallet out, flipped it open, yanked out some bills, lifted my hand using my wrist and slapped them in my palm.

"Take her out to eat, take her home," he ordered, replacing his wallet but slapping the keyfob to the SUV on the money in my palm then curling my fingers around it all.

"What...?" I swallowed. "What are you going to do?"

"Have a fuckin' beer, a shot of tequila, and keep on havin' 'em so I won't hop on my bike, hunt down my daughter and rip her a new asshole," Buck snarled.

Oh dear.

Though, I figured the translation of that was: I'm going to stay home so I'll be here when my daughter gets back so we can talk this out, Biker Dad and Biker Babe Daughter style. In the meantime, just be home should the police call or come around because my daughter was arrested for excessive speeding, or erratic driving, or something worse happening.

My stomach clutched at that last thought.

"That sounds like a good plan," I whispered, thinking it did for Buck, but when she got home (hopefully safe), it wouldn't be fun for Tatie.

Buck scowled at me, his scowl sliced through Mrs. Jimenez, he pulled it together enough to dip his chin at her and say, "I apologize for my daughter. We're havin' some issues. Have a nice meal with Clara." And with that, he stalked into the house.

I took in a deep breath and looked down at Mrs. Jimenez.

"It isn't always like this," I assured her.

I'd told her about Tatiana and how she felt about me.

I hadn't shared as much about Buck.

Well, not the uncertain stuff, just the good stuff.

"It's usually a lot lower-key," I concluded lamely.

Mrs. Jimenez shrugged, gave my arm a squeeze and said back, "Family. The more love there is, the more friction there can be. I know. My family has a lotta love. My husband Pablo, he frowned on bad language, but I have three sons and one daughter. They fought since they came out of the womb, with each other, Pablo and me. That's how families are." She patted my arm just above her hand and finished, "You'll learn this, *cariña*."

I was learning a lot of things this day, but it had to be said, they were a lot of things I didn't really want to learn.

Just a typical day for Clara Delaney.

"Let's go eat," I suggested.

Mrs. Jimenez nodded, and I helped her back to the SUV. Then I helped her into it.

After that, I rounded the hood, and it took everything I had, but I didn't look at the house.

We went out to eat.

I TURNED in bed so I was on my back, and my gaze hit the dark ceiling.

Buck was with me, but he wasn't touching me.

This, I thought, was good.

I thought this because, even though I had been gone a long time, Buck was in no better mood when I got back.

I had dinner with Mrs. Jimenez at The Outlook (Buck gave me a lot of money, so I decided to treat Mrs. Jimenez with it, and even though we didn't have a reservation, which was usually necessary at posh restaurants like The Outlook, we only had to wait half an hour for a table. Bonus, even posh, The Outlook was in Arizona, so jeans were appropriate attire, though I was glad I had on fancy shoes, and I suspected Mrs. Jimenez was glad she dressed up to meet Buck and his family).

We enjoyed that dinner, though my mind was on other things.

She, with her keen Mother and Grandmother Senses, discerned that.

We started talking about it (some of it, I didn't share about my Biker Babe Lessons, *any* of them).

She didn't make me feel much better, but she did try, and best of all, she listened and that always felt nice.

I took her home and then went back to Buck's.

When I arrived at Buck's, the Charger was in the drive, the Nova was not, Gear was brooding in front of the TV, and Buck, surrounded by a plethora of empty beer bottles and a near-empty tequila bottle, was brooding on the deck.

Gear greeted me.

Buck, as I walked to the front door, didn't bother.

And I decided I should leave him to his thoughts because they didn't appear pleasant and I didn't want an unpleasant mood turned on me. I'd learned with Buck unpleasant meant worried, and worried meant angry.

I did not fall asleep with my head on Buck's thigh.

I watched TV with a silent Gear.

Silent, that was, after he told me what I'd already guessed.

He hadn't found Tatiana.

He also shared that she "did this."

As in, took off when she got angry and didn't come back until she'd burned it out.

She'd done it when she was a kid. She'd run away. And she did it now that she wasn't so much of a kid and unfortunately had access and legal privileges to take off in a car.

Lastly, Gear shared that Buck wasn't a big fan of Tatiana's "scenes."

I gathered that myself.

What Gear didn't share, but what I also gathered, was that he didn't like them much more. Especially when she did them in his beloved car.

When I started to nod off, I went to bed alone.

Buck woke me when he stretched out beside me. Without a functioning alarm clock, I couldn't know what time it was, though I sensed it was very late.

I did know he didn't turn into me. He didn't turn me into him, and he didn't fall asleep for a while.

I didn't know if he knew he'd woken me.

I did know, if he knew, he didn't care, had nothing to say or was simply too angry to speak.

I eventually heard his breaths even out, but my thoughts didn't even out. So for the first time since being at Buck's house, my mind didn't allow me to get good sleep.

Truth be told, I was worried about Tatiana.

I mean, I was a newbie to her scenes, but it was late.

Where was she?

And...

The last time she'd gone out in order to act out, she'd come home smashed.

And the thought of her smashed, in a car, made my stomach ache.

Badly.

Which was why I was staring at the ceiling.

And it was also why I heard it.

My body got tight as I listened.

Barely a sound, but somehow, I could tell it was someone in the house trying to be quiet.

Then I heard the low hum of the pipes, meaning the water was running in Tatiana's bathroom.

Needing to see if it was her, and not Gear down from the loft to use the bathroom, I slid carefully out of bed and headed to the door.

I did this being sure not to wake Buck. I was worried, if it was Tatie, and she was drunk, she'd driven Gear's car drunk, and Buck *and* Gear were already angry enough at her. If she did something that stupid, they'd lose their minds.

So I wanted to get to her first.

Okay, this was so I could make an effort to cover for her. And maybe that wasn't the right choice for her, her father, or her brother.

It also wasn't a way for me to ingratiate myself to her.

I just felt for her.

I had not been in a place where I felt safe to act out as a teen.

But I remembered how confusing and stressful it was to be a girl at sixteen. Things happened with your body and boys and peers and mood swings you didn't get were because your hormones were controlling your life. There was also pressure to start thinking about your future.

Add in a mom who doesn't treat you all that well, a stepdad you don't like, a dad you loved who lived too far away, and a new woman in your beloved father's life...

Times were tough for Tatiana Hardy.

So yes.

I felt for her.

She needed an ally, and even if she didn't want that to be me, she was going to get it.

When I got to the hall, I saw the bathroom door was closed, but a light was coming from under it.

Quietly, I knocked, and just as quietly, I whispered, "Tatiana, it's Clara. You don't have to talk with me or open the door. Just let me know you're okay. Are you okay?"

There was nothing except the water running.

"Tatiana," I called softly, "just tell me if you're okay."

More nothing except water.

I slowly twisted the knob and just as slowly opened the door, poking my head around.

Then my body froze.

Stock-still.

And my heart shattered into little pieces.

I saw her in the mirror, her back to me. Her lip was already fat, her cheekbone red and swollen, blood was dripping from her nose, and looking down, I saw her T-shirt was torn so badly I could see her bra. She had a jeans skirt on, it was mini, just not micro-mini, and the seat of it was filthy, pine needles still clinging to the material like they'd been ground in, the same with the back of her T-shirt.

Like she'd been lying in dirt.

No, like she'd been wrestling in dirt.

The pieces of my heart flew back together in order to start pumping blood so madly, I could feel the muscle move just as I felt the blood sing through my veins.

I slid in, closed the door behind me, my eyes never leaving hers in the mirror.

Then I whispered, "Tatie, talk to me."

And I watched, my throat closing, as she dissolved.

Dissolved.

Her face into tears and her body started folding to the floor.

I caught her halfway down and went down with her. I sat on my behind, and she burrowed in, a sixteen-year-old girl pushing into my lap, her arms coming around me, her body pressing close, her face shoved into my neck, her frame wracked with sobs.

Oh God, no.

No.

I dropped my head and whispered in her ear, "Tatie, baby, who hurt you?"

She just held on tighter and cried harder.

I held tighter too, with one arm, and used my other hand to stroke her hair.

It had dirt in it too.

And it was matted.

Badly.

No.

"Honey, who hurt you?"

She shook her head violently and kept holding on.

"How badly are you hurt, baby?" I asked. "Do we need to get you to the hospital?"

"I need a shower," she whispered.

"Okay, I get that, but you have to talk to me first. What happened? Who hurt you? How did they hurt you?"

"I need a shower," she repeated.

"Baby, listen to me, you need to talk to me right now. Tell me what happened."

"I need a shower."

I stopped stroking her hair and put my hand under her chin. Pulling away a smidge, I lifted her face so I could see her.

"Honey, please. Tell me what happened."

"I don't have any underwear on," she whispered.

I closed my eyes briefly as those words cut through me like a blade, opening me up, bleeding.

I reopened my eyes.

"Did you leave that way?"

She stared at me.

Then she said so low I could barely hear her, "No."

Oh God, no.

Please, God, no.

"Did someone touch you like you didn't want?" I asked.

"Yes," she whispered. "No," she went on. "Yes, but they didn't... they..." She shook her head. "I got away."

"So you haven't been raped?"

Her face crumpled, and I wrapped my hand around the back of her head and pushed it in my neck, my heart pumping again, the blood singing, thick and hot.

"No, but they...*hurt me*," she said softly.

I held her tighter.

"I have to tell your father."

Her body jerked and she pulled away. "No!"

"Tatie, honey, listen to me." I framed her face with my hands. "I have to tell your dad."

"No! He'll be mad at me."

Her voice was rising, and I pulled her face closer to mine.

"Honey, listen, shh, just listen, okay? Okay?" She nodded so I went on, "He has to know. We have to call the police. We need to get you to the hospital."

She shook her head in my hands fervently.

"Listen to me." I held her tighter, trying to do it gently. "They aren't allowed to touch you like you don't want. Baby, they're not. Something has to be done."

"No," she whispered.

"Tatie—"

The door opened.

"Fuck me, this again? My girl drove fuckin' drunk?" Buck growled, and both Tatiana and I looked up at him.

Tatiana's body froze against mine but mine froze right along with hers.

This was because Buck was staring at his daughter, and I knew, looking at him, that I'd never seen the snake.

Now, I was seeing the snake.

"*Gear!*" he roared and disappeared from the doorway.

Oh no!

I forced Tatiana to face me. "Hang tight for me, sweetie. Okay? Hang tight. I'll be right back."

Then I let her go, got up and raced from the room.

"*Locke! Get your ass down here!*" Buck thundered from the foot of the stairs, so I headed to him.

I dashed around him when he started stalking back to his bedroom.

I put my hands to his chest and pushed, but he kept moving, forcing me backwards, his face tight, his muscles under my hands like steel.

He didn't look at me, just kept moving.

"Buck, honey, listen to me. We have to call the police," I told him.

"Fuck that," he snarled.

I pushed harder at him, trying and failing to plant my feet.

"Buck, we need to take her to the hospital. We need to take care of Tatie."

"Get your hands off me, babe."

"Buck! Please! We have to—"

I didn't finish.

He stopped, wrapped his hands around my upper arms, picked me up and *threw* me aside.

I hit the wall of the hall with such force, the blow to my shoulder caused pain to radiate out, up and down.

Everywhere.

It hurt so much and was such a shock, I stood there, leaning against the wall, my other hand to it for added support as I stared after Buck, who didn't break another stride and disappeared into his room.

I blinked my shock away and this took a while.

So long, Buck was out of the room wearing a long-sleeved T-shirt over the jeans he already had on as well as socks. He was carrying his boots. Gear was down the stairs and standing in the hall in his cutoff sweats.

"*Dressed. Now,*" Buck barked.

Gear stared at him half a beat, then raced back up the stairs.

Buck stopped in the door to the bathroom.

"*Who?*" He continued to bark.

"Dad—" Tatiana whimpered.

Buck leaned forward and bellowed, "*Who?*"

"Those guys who go to ASU," she whispered.

"Gear know 'em?" Buck asked.

"Yes, but, Dad—"

Buck moved from the doorway, came to me, lifted a finger to point it in my face and his body followed so his face was behind his hand and his furious eyes were locked on mine.

"You call the cops, Toots, I break your fuckin' neck."

I stared at the space he used to be in, but he was gone, disappeared right before my eyes.

It wasn't five minutes before I heard the roar of a Harley and I looked out the front windows to watch Buck, followed by Gear in his Nova, tearing down the drive.

I pulled in a deep breath.

Then I pulled in another one.

After letting go of the third, I hurried to the bathroom.

I JERKED awake when Tatiana was gently pulled out of my arms.

It was light, just dawn, and I shifted to see Buck settling his daughter against his big frame. He was on top of the covers. He still had his boots on. There was blood on his shirt and on his hands, especially around the knuckles.

I knew what that meant.

Earlier, after I soothingly talked her into letting me take pictures of her with my phone, I'd cleaned up Tatiana and got ice for her eye and her lip. I held her as she held the ice to her face and slowly, stiltedly told me about the three boys who attacked her.

Three.

There had been *three*.

God, it was a miracle she'd been able to get away.

Then, my stomach burning with a despair so deep I wondered how I could move, fury so great I wondered how I didn't combust, all of it I felt for a pretty, spirited, sixteen-year-old girl who didn't really like me, I helped her to the shower. While she was showering, I shoved her clothes in a plastic grocery bag and hid them in Buck's closet.

Once she got out, I helped her into her pjs, sat her on the toilet and combed her hair for her.

I then followed her to bed, got in it with her and rocked her, speaking softly to her until she fell asleep.

Now Buck was home.

"Get your ass to bed," he ordered quietly to me, but it wasn't a gentle order, it was a command.

Tatiana's head came back, and she looked up at her dad.

"Can she stay?" Tatiana whispered, and Buck looked down at her.

"No," he answered his daughter then his eyes came up to pierce me.

I bit my lip and gathered enough courage to slide Tatiana's hair off her neck and give her a squeeze.

After I did that, I slid out of her bed and went to Buck's.

I pulled the covers up high and stared at the pillow.

It didn't take long before I twisted so my face was in the pillow, and forcing myself to be silent, I burst into tears.

19

YOU WERE STANDING IN MY WAY

I never got to sleep.

And when the sun was high enough in the sky, I got up, went to the bathroom and did my bathroom business.

That done, I pulled up the courage to lift my arms, and I stared at them in the mirror.

Four, livid purple bruises had formed on my inner biceps.

On each arm.

Four imprints of the pads of an angry man's fingers.

Slowly, I turned and looked over my shoulder.

A deep purple bruise had risen in stark relief against the white of my skin on my shoulder blade.

I closed my eyes.

He'd marked me.

Buck.

My protector.

He'd *marked me*.

I forced the bruises from my mind, put my robe on over my nightgown and went to the kitchen.

I made coffee and avoided the Pop-Tarts.

I wasn't certain Buck would be in the mood to cook breakfast, but first, if he was, I wasn't fired up to upset him in *any* way, and second, I was far from hungry.

When the coffee was brewed, I poured myself a cup, and was standing at the window, looking out and considering putting on socks and a pair of sweatpants and going out there. We were in the foothills and it was late September. The heat was still on in the Valley. Up here, the days were warm, the nights and mornings chill.

Even so, if any time was deck time, *that* time was deck time.

Since I was staring out the window, I saw the sleek, shiny, British racing green Jaguar gliding up the drive.

Two questions sprang immediately to mind.

Who on earth?

And...

What now?

The house was silent, and the clock over the microwave (one of only two in the house, the other one on the DVD player, both had been flashing twelve until I set them a week ago), said it was going seven thirty. I figured the house would be quiet for a while and I figured its inhabitants needed their rest.

So my coffee cup and I went to the door.

I pulled it open and stood in it, watching a man of average height, built like a golfer, wearing a long-sleeved polo neck shirt and chinos, with black hair shot with silver, stomping to the door.

Oh dear.

I stood with a shoulder against the doorframe, pulling the door to closing me on the inside, but I could see him.

And he could see me.

"Can I help you?" I asked when he got close.

"This West Hardy's place?" he asked back, coming to a halt outside the door, eyes narrowed, the entire line of his body communicating fury.

"May I ask who you are?"

"I'm the man who's going to be pressing charges in about ten minutes when the sheriff gets here."

Oh *dear*.

"Sorry?" I asked, buying time.

"If West Hardy and that hoodlum he calls a son are in there, you better wake their asses up. They'll probably want to be dressed when they're cuffed and taken to the station."

My back went straight, and it did this because he'd called Gear a hoodlum.

Gear was *not* a hoodlum.

"Sorry?" I whispered, but it was so I wouldn't shout and wake anyone.

"I'm telling you, you better get their asses up," he advised, leaning in, nasty sliding in to keep the angry company on his face.

"Why would the police arrest West and Locke?"

"Interesting," he muttered, crossing his arms and leaning back. "He doesn't come home and brag to his bitch when he goes out and beats the shit out of a bunch of kids."

Oh no.

He did *not* just call me a bitch.

This man, who was clearly the parent of a goddamned *monster*, did not just call Gear a hoodlum and *me* a *bitch*.

"Did you just call me a bitch?" I was still whispering.

"Isn't that your lingo?" he asked sarcastically.

I pulled in breath.

Then I wrapped one hand tight around the edge of the door in an effort to force some of my anger into my fingers rather than releasing it by tossing my hot coffee in his face.

Once I'd done that, I spoke.

"I advise you to call the sheriff and tell him you were mistaken," I said quietly.

He stared at me.

That was, he did before he grinned an unattractive grin.

"And why would I do that?"

"Because the bunch of kids you're fired up to protect attempted to rape my sixteen-year-old girl. She came home with a swollen cheek, a fat lip, a bloody nose, her clothes and hair filled with dirt. And no underwear."

I watched his face pale.

"Yes," I whispered. "She did. I still have the clothes. I also have pictures. But I remember *exactly* what she looked like. I remember *exactly* how she felt when she was weeping in my arms on the bathroom floor. So now *I* see something interesting. I see your bunch of kids didn't share *that*, did they?"

"I—" he started.

He'd said enough.

So I didn't let him say any more.

I kept going.

"She said they're at ASU. If they're at ASU, then they're hoping for a bright future. That future won't be so bright, the sheriff gets here, finds out they tried to rape her. Three boys, *three*, beat her up and *tried to rape her*. The sheriff finds out about that, he sees the pictures I took, takes one look at her face, sees how small she is...*dainty*...I give him my girl's clothes, that future gets a *lot* dimmer."

He was now not pale.

He was ashen.

"So, you have a choice," I informed him. "You can call the sheriff, call him off and accept the painful but swift and quiet punishment that West and Locke dealt last night. Or you can push this, and your boys will be behind bars right alongside West and Locke, but attempted rape with assault is worse than just assault. Especially when there's no purpose behind it, no motivation a jury would understand, like a father seeing his daughter bleeding and dirty on a bathroom floor. And then their punishment will be far more painful, but it won't be quiet, it won't be swift." I leaned in. "It'll be *very* public, and it'll be very, very *long*. Because, you see, after they get out once they serve their time, for the rest of their lives, they won't only have a record, they'll also be on a certain registry. And they will not *ever* escape that."

He stared at me and didn't move or speak.

When this lasted awhile, I offered, "Do you not know the number for the sheriff? I'm happy to get the Yellow Pages."

His eyes flashed behind me, he paled even further, and then suddenly the door was no longer in my grip because it was being pulled wider.

I turned my head and saw Buck's bloody t-shirt. Then they moved up, and I saw Buck's angry face.

"You got a choice, Conley," Buck growled. "And three seconds to make it. What's it gonna be?"

The man, clearly called Conley, opened his mouth, closed it, then opened it again.

"You can't run around beating up kids," he stated with more face-saving bravado than courage.

Buck stepped back, pulling me with him with his arm around my waist, and he slammed the door.

I stared at the door but couldn't do that for very long because Buck curled me into him.

I tipped my head back, and my eyes caught his. He had one arm around me, and the other hand came up so he could run the backs of his raw, bloody knuckles along my jaw.

"Thanks, baby," he whispered.

"Take your hands off me," I whispered back, and his head twitched.

"Come again?"

"I said," I pushed away from his arm and it fell, as did his hand, "take your hands off me."

His eyes narrowed. "What the—?"

He didn't finish because I shifted around him and marched to the steps to the landing.

I then marched to his bedroom.

I closed the door and kept marching to his bathroom. I closed that door too.

There, I slammed my coffee cup down on the vanity, bent over, opened the door under the sink and grabbed the cosmetics case I'd stowed down there.

The door flew open, Buck stormed in and stopped, scowling at me.

"What the fuck's the matter with you?"

I didn't pause in what I was doing. I had one of the vanity drawers open, the one with my makeup in it, such as it was. It was mostly dregs I was eking the last bits out of since I hadn't been able to afford makeup in months, and I was shoving it into the bag.

"I'm leaving," I announced, because I was.

I just didn't know where I was going or how I'd get there.

"What?" he said softly, and my head jerked back so I could glare at him.

"Leaving," I spat.

He shook his head and crossed his arms on his chest. "Clara, maybe it didn't fuckin' sink in, but I had a bad night, Gear had a bad night, and Tatie had a *really* fuckin' bad night. I don't need your shit right now."

My...

Shit?

"My shit?" I whispered.

"Your shit," he returned.

I dropped the makeup and case into the drawer and straightened.

"This isn't shit, West."

"Nope, it's bullshit, Clara."

"I don't believe you," I hissed.

"That makes two of us, babe, seein' as I don't believe you're havin' a fuckin' tantrum for reasons fuckin' unknown the morning after my daughter nearly got raped."

So, Tatie had shared it hadn't gone from calamitous to disastrous.

I was glad she'd felt free to share with her father.

But me?

"This isn't a tantrum," I whispered.

"That's bullshit too."

"You hurt me," I reminded him.

His eyebrows went up. "What?"

"You..." I pointed at him then pointed at my chest, "hurt me."

"Clara, for fuck's—"

I whipped the tie on my robe open then I turned as I yanked it down my shoulders.

I twisted my neck to look at him and saw his eyes riveted to my bruise.

What I did not do was allow the anguished expression on his face to penetrate.

"You did that," I stated, pulled my robe back up, turned to face him and tied the tie smartly, managing to do this with shaking hands. "You marked me," I went on. "*You* did that. That isn't the only bruise you gave me last night. One move, one second, *nine* bruises."

As I spoke, his eyes were still where my shoulder used to be.

When I was done, they moved to mine.

Then he dropped his arms, but his hand came up as he got in my space, muttering, "Baby."

He nearly touched my face, but I yanked it away and took a quick step back.

"Don't touch me," I hissed.

His hand dropped, and his gaze locked with mine.

"Clara, honey, come here," he said softly.

"No, I'm packing and I'm leaving," I replied.

"Toots, baby, come here," he repeated.

"No. I'd like you to leave. I'd like to be gone before the kids wake up."

That wasn't true.

I wanted to see Tatie was all right and the same with Gear.

But I thought, for them...clean break.

They had their dad; they didn't need me.

"You got a step to take, I'm tellin' you to take it before I take it," he told me.

I leaned forward and snapped, "I said no!"

Before I knew what he was about, he took that step and my head was between his big hands, tipped up to look at him.

He bent so his face was in mine. "They hurt my girl."

Yes, they did.

And I hated that for all of them.

Then *he* hurt *me*.

I tried to yank my head from his hands, his fingers tightened, so I stopped trying, but my hands came up and my fingers curled around his wrists.

"I understand that and I'm sorry. I'm sorry for you and Locke and Tatiana. That doesn't forgive what you did."

"I wasn't thinkin' straight."

"No, I agree. You probably weren't. That doesn't forgive what you did."

"No one hurts my girl."

"Unfortunately, last night, that wasn't true. And, again, I'm sorry.

Truly, *truly* I am. For you. For Locke. And especially for Tatie." I tried again to pull at his hands, though I failed, I kept trying. "But you marked me, and *I* wasn't the one who hurt her."

"You were standin' in my way."

"Take your hands off me."

His face got closer. "Baby, I woke up when I heard she got home, felt you get out of bed, decided to let you have a shot with her before I got in there because I was still angry at the way she took off. Heard you two in the bathroom, and you weren't leaving it. So I had to take a beat because I thought she'd come home drunk again, but this time she'd been driving drunk and I needed that beat because I was getting angrier. Then I got a look at my little girl, and I was beyond pissed. And you were standin' in my way."

"West. Take...your hands...*off* me."

"When I get like that, which, I promise you, darlin', isn't often, but it happens, you cannot stand in my way."

"Thanks for the advice, but I won't be around the next time you get like that. Now, I asked you to take your hands off me."

He didn't take his hands off me.

In fact, he put them on me *more*.

He did this by stepping fully into my space, one of his arms locking around my upper back, the other hand sliding in my hair, fisting and tugging gently. The whole time, his face stayed a breath away from mine.

"This is not better," I informed him.

"You aren't leaving," he informed me.

"Sorry, but I am."

His arm around my back got tighter, his hand in my hair tilted my head, and he bent his head so his face was in my neck.

Against my skin, he murmured, "I'm sorry I hurt you, baby."

And he sounded sorry.

So, *so* sorry.

I closed my eyes as my heart squeezed, that despair in my belly shifted, cutting through me, reminding me how much I loved it when he was sweet and gentle, just as much as I hated it right in this moment. I forced my hands into the minimal space between us to push against his abs, but he didn't budge.

"I wasn't thinkin', I was just feelin'," he went on.

"West, let me go," I whispered.

"I'm not lettin' you go."

"West, let me *go*." I finished my words with a shove on his abs.

His middle rocked back then surged right where it was before.

He lifted his head and looked down at me. "Clara, baby, I'm not lettin' you go. We'll get past this. You just gotta learn not to stand in my way."

Against my will, I felt my eyes get wet.

"Why?" I whispered. "Why won't you just let me go?"

"You stake a claim, you stake it because you want what you're claimin'. Then you keep hold, no matter what you gotta do to keep it. I claimed you and I'm keeping hold."

"I'm not a piece of land, West," I told him, lifting a hand to swipe angrily at the weak, stupid tears sliding down my face. "I'm a person. You can't do that with a person."

"Babe, you stood in that room out there and made a decision. You gave me you when you did. I accepted. I staked my claim. You can't take that away."

"Yes, I can."

"No, you can't."

Okay, so maybe I was wrong about the whole "what your man says goes" rule in the Biker Babe Rulebook.

A book that seemed to have a lot more written in it than the biker one did.

"I'm mine to give or take as I please."

"Maybe somewhere, in some other place, a place you've never lived, and you know it. A place where I don't want to live." His face got closer. "Not in here, not where *we* live."

"I don't want to live here anymore."

And he was not wrong.

Neither was I.

I didn't want to live where I was shunted from place to place, person to person, *man to man* with no will of my own.

"Like I said yesterday, Toots, you made that decision. *You.* No one forced you. And once you make the decision, with me, there's no going back."

"That's crazy," I whispered.

"That's the choice you made."

"I didn't have all the information!" My voice was rising, and unfortunately, it was rising somewhat hysterically.

"Too late," he replied.

"That's crazy too!"

"Baby, keep your voice down. Tatie's sleepin'," he said softly.

"That's crazy too," I repeated on a whisper.

He grinned. "Yeah, it's crazy. It's fuckin' nuts to a lotta people out there. But you, you get it. You get it was bad. And you get how you found good."

Yes, I did get that.

But like he said, I also got the bad.

And in that moment, that was my focus.

So I shook my head. "Oh no, I don't."

He nodded. "Yeah, I didn't think you did either. I thought it'd take you a while before we broke you in. But, darlin', I heard what you said to Conley. I saw you open the door and position yourself in it, protecting your territory and puttin' yourself between him and your people. I heard every fuckin' word you said. And I knew when I listened, you got it. So now I know, you're hurt and pissed I marked you. What you don't know is, I'm pissed at myself for doin' it. If I could take it back, I would. Bust my balls, break my back to erase those marks from you, but more, how you got 'em. It sucks, and huge, that I can't. It also sucks, and huge, that someone touched my girl with the intent to do her even worse harm. And Clara, baby, you know that in my world, that means payback, instant, swift, painful. And you were standin' in my way. Next time, you'll know not to stand in my way."

"So that's it?" I asked.

He grinned and gave me a squeeze, his hand leaving my hair so he could wrap his arm around my waist. "Yep, that's it."

"So when you get angry about something else, I don't stand in your way but somehow get in your way, do you get to put your hands on me?"

His grin died and his eyes narrowed.

"Babe," he warned low.

"I'd like to know and think I'm entitled to that knowledge."

"Shit isn't jacked, like it was last night, you got nothin' to fear from me."

"You're sure?"

His arms gave me a different kind of squeeze.

"That isn't cool, Clara."

That isn't cool?

"I'm entitled to know, West."

His face dipped close to mine and his eyes were suddenly angry.

"What you get when you get me is what Tatie got last night. And I'll remind you, you've already had it. Someone hurt you, Clara, and I hunted his ass down and I beat the shit out of him. I beat him until he was down and I kept beating him until he was no longer moving. *Anyone* hurts you or tries to hurt you, that's what they get. When you get me, you get my protection. I'm tellin' you, and I said it so many goddamned times, it's got to be in your fuckin' brain by now, I wasn't thinkin' last night and you were standin' in the way of me exacting retribution for my...*fuckin'*... daughter. I apologized, and I explained, and you need to let it sink in, babe, and you need to do that fast. You've seen me mad and you've made me mad, and you know, Toots, you fuckin' *know* you got nothin' to fear from me. Now don't play this game. Not now. Not this mornin'. You aren't good at games, babe, and doin' it now, you're only pissin' me off."

I pulled in my lower lip and bit it.

What I didn't do was say anything more.

"You done bein' a pain in the ass?" he asked.

I didn't think I was being a pain in the ass.

I thought my reactions and my questions were perfectly justified.

Obviously, I needed to make a phone call to Minnie and ask her how I *should* have reacted.

I didn't share this with Buck.

Instead I shared I was not done being a pain in the ass.

I did this by stating, "West, you beat up some kids."

"Right, and how would you want that to go?" he bit out.

"We should have called the police," I pointed out the obvious.

"One, Clara, they are not kids. They're adults. Legally and otherwise. They're old enough to know better, and just sayin', even if they were goddamn *twelve*, anyone with a dick should be old enough to know better than to hurt a girl like that."

Oh boy.

Now he was getting in there.

Because he was so, so right.

And he wasn't done.

"Two, babe, I know how that would go down. *You* know how that would go down. You got her clothes and you got those pictures, but some asshole like Armitage gets her on the stand, he talks about her short skirt and how she was seen shitfaced drunk with her face made up too much just weeks ago, and suddenly, no matter what she says, a jury *not* of her peers thinks in their fucked-up heads she was askin' for it. So jacked, somehow, they forget she should be able to wear what she wants and cake so much makeup on her face, it's draggin' on her skin, and it's *her* choice and it don't say *dick*. And it sure as fuck doesn't say, 'come and *rape me*.'"

Yes, he was getting in there.

Because he was so, *so* right.

"Three, woman, I don't want my daughter to go through that. My estimation, she'd been through enough. She didn't need to go to the hospital and have them swabbing for DNA and taking photos and cops askin' her shit. And then the long haul after, bringin' it up day in and day out, until, by a miracle, seein' as she's the daughter of a biker, and those boys got pedigree, she might find justice, but they tear her to shreds before she gets that. So she not only has to find a way to live with what they did to her, she's gotta live with the memory of a justice system that doles that out to an innocent girl who was simply at the wrong place at the wrong time with the *way wrong* assholes."

He shook his head and kept going.

"No, I did not want that for her. So *I* got justice for her. And I got no clue how a man like that might behave, considering how they've already done it. But I can hope the beatdown me and Gear delivered will make them think twice before they ever," he put his face in mine, "*ever* do that to another girl."

"Okay, Buck," I whispered.

He pulled back a smidge, and was in such a state, one I had to admit he was absolutely entitled to, he carried on.

"Just so you got the full picture, Clara, it is my thought that if you let loose the fathers and brothers and husbands, and equal opportunity and all that shit, mothers and sisters and whoever of girls and women who face what my little girl did last night. Let them loose on the assholes who do it. I bet it'd happen a fuckuva lot less. So, if you asked me, what me and Gear did last night should happen to every fuckin' one of them."

If pressed, sometime before last night, and before what Esposito did to Tia, I might be able to come up with a suitable argument to that statement.

But only if pressed.

Buck kept going.

"So last night, what Tatie got was a good woman who looked after her and a father and brother who went out and took care of business. My baby girl faced what she faced last night and came home to safety. That's what she got. *All* she got. And now we keep takin' care of her and she gets to *move on*."

"Okay, Buck," I repeated in a whisper.

He studied me closely and did this awhile before his face relaxed and his arms gave me another squeeze, this one the good kind. At the same time, the tension ebbed out of his body.

Then he muttered, "Good." He dipped his head, his mouth brushing mine and then he lifted it again and ordered, "Now get some socks on, we're sittin' on the deck, havin' coffee and waitin' 'til the kids get up for breakfast."

And I said the only thing I could say at that juncture.

"Okay, Buck."

20

WAFFLES

I lifted my legs off Buck's, set my stocking feet on the deck and straightened out of my chair.

"Where you goin'?" Buck asked, and I looked down at him to see him looking up at me.

I lifted my mug.

"More coffee," I muttered, then to be polite, my eyes shifted to his mug, and I offered, "Do you need a refill?"

He offered his mug to me, murmuring, "Yeah."

I took it and started toward the door, but his arm wrapped around my belly, and I stopped.

I looked back down at him to see he was still looking up at me.

"Come here," he said quietly.

"I am here, West," I pointed out the obvious.

His eyes moved over my face while he muttered, "No one calls me West. Used to like it when you'd call me West. Today, the way you're sayin' my name, not so much."

I waited patiently, but I didn't reply.

His eyes moved to mine.

"Come here," he repeated.

"I'm not certain how much more *here* I can get," I told him.

"Closer," he stated.

I sighed.

Then I bent to him.

"Closer, babe," he said softly.

I bent closer, he lifted his arm, cupped the back of my head with his hand, and he brought me even closer.

So close, my mouth was nearly on his.

"West," I whispered.

"That's better," he whispered back.

I blinked. "Sorry?"

"You can whisper my name sweet like that. That's better."

Oh God.

"I need more caffeine," I informed him.

"Yeah, and you can get it after you kiss me."

Oh God.

Not this again.

"What?"

"Babe, we fight, we stop fightin', you work out the rest of your attitude by kissin' me."

"Is that an order?" I asked, and he grinned.

"Yeah."

"Whatever," I muttered, bent even closer, touched my mouth to his then touched my tongue to his lips, those lips opened, my tongue slid inside, and I allowed myself to enjoy the taste of him.

I drank my fill, and as weak as it made me, I loved every second of it.

Before he could take the kiss out of my control, which meant out of all control, I broke contact and pulled away two inches where I stopped because his fingers flexed on my head.

He studied me again then murmured, "Thinkin' that didn't work."

"*Buck*, I've had about two hours of sleep. I need *caffeine*."

"Kids weren't here, babe, I'd try a different way to work out your attitude."

Proving just how weak I was, my nipples got hard.

"Can I go get coffee?"

He grinned again, his hand left my head, and he relented on a, "Yeah."

I escaped.

We were both on our second cups (Buck had done the first refill) and I poured new ones then set them aside as I cleaned out the filter and pot to start another one going. I'd need more and both Locke and Tatiana drank it too.

And I wanted Tatie's coffee to be fresh.

I was scooping coffee into the filter, thinking that the good news was, some time had elapsed, and the sheriff hadn't come calling, when I sensed movement.

My hand froze mid-scoop, I turned and saw Tatiana wearing her cute pajama bottoms and tight little camisole standing by the counter.

I wondered what today would bring, if the drama last night meant a breakthrough that was permanent or temporary.

She stared at me. I stared at her. Her lip was less fat, but a bruise had risen on her cheekbone.

Okay.

Yes.

I was so *totally* glad Buck and Gear beat the shit out of those boys.

Finally, when I could take it no more, I whispered, "Hey, honey."

That was when she moved.

Her bare feet quickly eating the distance, she threw her arms around me, pressed her cheek against my shoulder and ground coffee went everywhere.

I dropped the scoop and wrapped my arms around her.

It took a while for me to realize she was crying.

"That's it, baby," I whispered, bending my head toward her and stroking her hair. "Get it out."

"I'm sorry," she mumbled into my chest.

"What? Why?" I asked.

She tipped her head back, her eyes caught mine, and she wailed loudly, "I was such a bitch about your car!"

Then she burrowed her face into my neck and her sobs got louder.

Golly.

I forgot about my car.

I heard the door open, and I lifted my eyes, but not my head, to see Buck walk in.

"Don't worry about that," I told Tatiana, my gaze on Buck.

"If I wasn't such a baby, if I didn't take off on a hissy fit, I wouldn't—"

Oh no.

Oh no, she was *not*.

My hand curved around her head and I dipped my lips to her ear. "Don't," I cut her off. "Don't make what happened your fault. Don't you do that, Tatie. It was *not* your fault. Not a lick of it."

"I went off, lookin' for trouble," she sobbed into my chest, tipped her head back and cried, "And I found it!"

I cupped her healthy cheek in my hand. "You went looking for a way to let off steam, honey. No woman looks for that kind of trouble."

"I...I...*liked* one of those guys!" she wailed. "He never paid attention to me! I thought he was bein' nice, me bein' angry and all, listening. But he wasn't. He was just...just..."

"Shh," I whispered, moving my thumb to her lips. "He was just a jerk. He was just a big, fat, horrible *jerk*."

She blinked.

Then she said around my thumb, "He's not a jerk, Clara, he's an *asshole*."

I smiled at her. "That too."

She stared at me.

I pulled in breath, took my thumb from her lips and decided to change the subject.

"This is our deal, okay? Weekends, you get the Charger. Weekdays, when you're with your mom, I get it. We share. I think I can talk your dad into that. Do we have a deal?"

"You'd do that?"

I shrugged. "Sure. I don't need a car much anyway."

"No, I mean talk to Dad for me."

"Well," my eyes slid over her shoulder to Buck, "I don't really have to since he's standing right there and any dad's going to see that's a perfectly sensible arrangement."

Buck's lips twitched but Tatiana jerked around.

"Dad," she whispered, her body tight.

Buck's attention went from me to Tatiana. "Come here, darlin'."

She didn't move and didn't speak, not for a while.

Finally, she asked quietly, "You aren't mad?"

"Come here, Tatie."

She hesitated then, slowly at first, she walked to him. It didn't take long, though, before she ran and threw her arms around him.

He folded her little body into his big one and held her close, bending to put his lips to her hair.

"I'm not mad, baby," he muttered there.

I turned back to the coffee, not wanting more conflicting feelings about West Hardy and our crazy relationship. I had enough of those. Too many. And seeing him being a caring and loving dad would add to them.

As I turned, out of the sides of my eyes I saw movement, and I twisted my neck to see Gear standing there.

Buck had taken the time to change his T-shirt and wash the blood from his knuckles. Gear hadn't yet taken that time.

I walked to him and grabbed his hand but kept my eyes on his, which were locked on his sister.

"You need to clean up, Locke," I said softly, and he tore his eyes from his sister and looked down at me. I squeezed his hand. "Give your sister a hug and then go clean up. I'll make you a coffee and your dad's making breakfast. Tatie's choice this morning."

"Waffles," Tatiana said instantly, and Gear and I looked at her to see that Buck had hooked her around the neck and tucked her to his side. She had both arms around his middle and was pressing in.

"Waffles," I agreed, squeezed Gear's hand again and turned back to him.

That hand twisted so I had no choice but to let it loose.

But he didn't move away, and he didn't move to his sister.

Instead, he hooked his arm around my neck and he tucked me into his side, just like his dad had Tatie.

"Waffles," Gear muttered, giving my neck a squeeze.

Hesitantly, I wrapped my arms around Gear's middle and my eyes moved to Tatiana.

Golly.

So *this* was what being part of a family felt like.

I wished I didn't know this.

I was conflicted. I was unsure. I got where Buck's head had been at, I felt for him that he opened the bathroom door and saw what he saw, but I was still angry at their father.

But I had to admit, I liked the feel of family.

A lot.

Tatiana grinned at me.

I couldn't stop it and didn't try.

I grinned back.

"JESUS, your life's pretty crazy, babe," Minnie said in my ear.

It was late evening.

I was on my back on top of the covers on Buck's bed.

It was after waffles.

It was after Buck made a call, took a shower, got dressed and took off to places unknown after he gave his daughter a hug and a kiss on the temple, grabbed me by the back of the head and laid a long, wet one on me and then gave his son a meaningful look.

He then took off, not yet to return.

It was also after I cleaned the house and did a bunch of laundry.

Tatie started helping while I was vacuuming. She disappeared to the utility room and came back with a load of freshly laundered towels, folding them on the kitchen counter.

After that, she stuck to me like glue.

If I was cleaning a bathroom, she was in it cleaning with me. She helped me strip the beds. Then she helped me make them.

I told her to rest, but she shook her head.

After that, I let her do whatever she wanted to do.

Or probably in this case, needed to do.

Gear made us a dinner of corn dogs and tater tots. As these were baked from frozen, this was not done with his father's culinary flair, but it was yummy all the same.

We camped out in front of the TV, the kids watching it, or Tatie watching it and Gear and I mostly watching Tatie.

She had dark moments, I could tell. I knew Gear could see it too. I just didn't know what to do about them. And if the glances he exchanged with me were anything to go by, Gear didn't either.

So I decided to call Minnie, which was what I did, telling her everything about yesterday and today.

That was, telling her everything except about Nails and Gash. I just told her I saw a brother with a woman, but I told her I didn't see either face. She seemed to have bought it and she also wasn't surprised.

"Yeah," I agreed. "I'm kind of getting sick of a crazy life."

"This'll pass, Clary," she said softly. "It'll all smooth out."

I didn't think it would.

What I thought was, this was my life, and until Buck was through with me, I had no choice in that matter.

I thought this because Buck had told me straight out this was the case.

I had, that day, given a moment to thinking what he'd do if I just left.

And in that moment, I had another moment.

One of understanding that I didn't want to find out.

"He scared me last night, Min, and he hurt me," I whispered.

"You shouldn't have stood in his way," she whispered back, and I closed my eyes when she confirmed Buck's assertion. "Our boys, they get pissed, especially about something like that, you step back and let 'em do what they gotta do."

I opened my eyes and stared at the ceiling.

"Seems to me, the rule is, you have to let them do what they have to do *all the time*," I observed.

"Oh no, honey, like I said yesterday, with the Club, out in the world, that's the way it is. But behind closed doors, it's just him and you, you let fly. You be you. It's just out in the world, he's the man, and that's it. And, if shit goes down, like with Tatiana, you do what you did. Though, you fucked up and tried to get him to stop and phone the cops, I'm talkin' in the end. You take care of his girl and you let him take care of business."

"Well, I hope that never happens again, so I don't have to take care of Tatie, not that way."

"Me too," Minnie agreed, her words heavy. "How's she doin'?"

I took in a breath and on the exhale, said, "Not good. She hits a dark place and she does it often. This can't be unusual. She went through hell just last night. I just don't know what to do with her. I think I should talk to Buck about a psychologist."

To my surprise, this suggestion was met with hysterical laughter.

"Min?" I called through her laughter.

"Babe, you crack me up," she replied.

I sat up in the bed, crossing my legs under me. "What's funny about that?"

"Sister, we do *not* go to psychologists. We take care a' shit in the family. Are you not gettin' that?"

Oh, I was getting that.

I just didn't agree.

"I'm not certain we have the tools to guide Tatiana out of that dark place, Minnie. Three college boys attacked her last night. They took her *underwear*. They nearly raped her."

"Yeah, and you said Buck called Kristy and told her what happened, and that Tatiana wasn't goin' home for a week."

This was true.

Buck had done this.

Though it wasn't as simple as that.

The phone call lasted a long time and had not been happy.

It had been unhappy, not because Tatiana's mother had been told the dire news her daughter had been attacked and beaten and she was upset like any mother would be. But from what I could tell (and Gear and Tatiana could tell), it seemed that Kristy was pissed just to be pissed.

I didn't know how I could tell that, I just could.

What surprised me about this was that Buck didn't absent himself to shield his children, but instead had this conversation, his side of it low and toxic, while wandering the kitchen being obviously ticked off.

And it ended, not with Kristy agreeing that Tatiana should be with her dad, who she adored and clearly felt safe with, something she didn't feel with this Knuckles guy, and have some time away from school to rest and heal.

Instead, it ended with Buck inviting Kristy to, "Do whatever the fuck you gotta do, bitch," and disconnecting the call.

Minnie's voice carried on in my ear.

"You bring her to the office and Lorie, Pinky, and me'll bring in Debbie. Debbie and us, we'll help her outta that dark place."

"Is Debbie a social worker?"

"No, Debbie's an ex-'ho who hooked up with Riot."

I blinked at Buck's, rather attractive, I had to admit, paisley comforter cover that had dense swirls and curves of rust, gray and blue with hints of cream.

An ex-'ho?

As in...

Prostitute?

Then I breathed, "Pardon?"

"Debbie's solid. Shit life. She was raped when she was fifteen. Went off the rails. Got hooked up with some bad people, bad shit. She's clean now and her and Riot are tight. They got married last Christmas, big fuckin' party. She's livin' the good life now. She saw the other side and she's there. Ain't no dark places for Debbie."

I knew Riot. He was a member of the Club. He had lots of long, curly hair, a big barrel chest, wasn't very tall and had an easy smile.

He was advancing toward middle age and not the way Buck was, looking younger than his years. Riot looked exactly as old as I figured he was, maybe older.

He didn't work much out on jobs, he mostly worked in the store, but he came in regularly for coffee, cupcakes or cookies.

Last, he seemed a good guy of the Ink and Cruise variety, funny, teasing and could be gentle.

Gash, Minnie's man, wasn't funny, teasing and could be gentle. He was rough, had an edge and an attitude, like his woman.

My eyes scanned the room and fell on Buck's photo frames.

When they did, for some reason, my legs went out from under me and I scooted off the bed, going to the dresser as I said, "So, you think she'll be okay talking to Tatie?"

"She'll be good with her. We'll all be good with her, Clary. The family'll see her through."

I stared at Buck's photos.

I'd dusted them and the dresser just that day.

Right then, I lifted my hand and made adjustments, moving photos so I could see them from behind other photos, shifting frames, my eyes running over them all.

"So," I said softly into the phone, "the Club is family?"

"Yeah, babe, the boys, a brotherhood. Tighter than blood. Unbreakable. Even when they don't get along, like now, it evens out, and it's all good. They all know that, they just gotta work through their issues. We're along for that ride. We hook up, we're in. The brotherhood is the most important. Brothers then bitches, you know it, you live with it. But I been hooked up with assholes out there in the world and I'll take my brother and his family anytime, rather than playin' those games out there."

I had to admit, being burned by Rogan and watching Tia get abused by Esposito, she had a point.

"Tighter than blood?" I asked.

"Yeah," she answered.

"What about children?" I asked.

"That's different, babe, kids are kids."

"Oh," I muttered, not actually getting it, then asked, "The brothers aren't getting along?"

There was silence then, "Buck hasn't shared?"

I adjusted a frame, not really looking at it. "No."

"Uh...maybe I should let him do that."

My hand arrested on a frame, and I whispered, "Is it bad?"

"They're a brotherhood, Clary, but that don't mean they see eye to eye on everything."

Oh dear.

That didn't sound good.

I knew the members now, and knowing them, I would guess a difference of opinion would manifest itself in far more dangerous ways than out in "the world."

I stared at the frames. The people in them, save Buck, Tatiana and Gear, I didn't know, and Buck hadn't told me.

At the same time, I thought about what Minnie said, trouble in the Club, and I had no idea. And Buck had mentioned different uses for women, but he wouldn't enlighten me, even though I'd asked. Further, there was the situation where Tatie had busted up a car and got caught joyriding, and he hadn't told me that either.

It seemed there was quite a bit Buck didn't share.

I now lived in a complicated world I didn't understand, making the decision to enter that world during a trauma and without the information I needed, and now I was stuck.

There were things I didn't like, things I didn't get and things I wanted to know, and where I was, I had no right to know until Buck deigned to tell me.

None of this was good.

And none of it I could do a thing about.

"Clara, are you there?" Minnie called.

I adjusted a frame.

"I'm here," I said, felt a presence, turned my head and saw Buck, wearing jeans, a T-shirt, boots and a very cool leather jacket with a bunch of patches on it I'd never seen him wear before, striding into the room. "Buck just got home," I told Minnie, my eyes watching him approach me.

"Cool, I'll let you go."

"That isn't necessary," I stated as Buck stopped close to me.

His eyes shifted to the frames then to me. Then he bent and kissed my nose, turned and I saw the back of the jacket was exactly like the tattoo he had on his back, something I'd noted was on the leather vests or jackets many of the members wore, but the other members wore them all the time, not including Ink, Cruise, Gash and Riot who wore theirs only occasionally.

Presently, Buck shrugged it off, tossed it on the bed, and he walked straight back out.

"Now he's gone. Beer time," I guessed.

"Right," she replied.

My eyes slid through the pictures then I walked to the bed and sat down next to his jacket. "I'll talk to Tatiana tomorrow. I'll let you know when to set up Debbie."

"She'll be okay," Minnie assured.

I sighed then said, "I hope so."

"Go be with your man," she urged.

"Right," I whispered, not sure I wanted to do that.

"Later, babe."

"Later, Min."

I disconnected, got up, walked to my nightstand and dropped the phone on top.

Then I heard, "Toots?"

I turned to see Tatiana standing in her pajamas just inside the door.

I smiled.

I liked her calling me Toots in that quiet, sweet voice.

"Hey, honey," I replied.

"I'm...gonna," she looked away and back at me, clearly hesitant, "hit the sack."

"All right, sweetie. Good night."

"Would you...?" She leaned in a bit then back and muttered, "Never mind."

She started to leave, and I quickly walked forward, calling, "Tatie."

She stopped, turned back to me, and I got close.

"What do you want, honey?" I asked softly.

"It's stupid," she whispered.

"Nothing's stupid," I assured her. "What do you want?"

She stared up at me and did this awhile.

"Baby," I said gently, lifting a hand and shifting her hair off her shoulder. "Tell me what you want."

"Would you...lie down with me? Just for a while. Just until I sleep. Talk to me like last night?"

Instantly I nodded, giving her a smile. "Let me get my nightgown on, you go lie down, and I'll be right in."

She stared up at me some more, unable to hide the surprise she felt at my easy agreement to her request, giving further evidence to the fact that her mom was seriously not much of a mom, before she whispered, "Thanks, Toots."

"Anything, honey," I whispered back.

She ducked her head and left the room.

I put on my nightie and robe, washed my face, brushed my teeth, moisturized and left the room too.

I walked to hers, closed the door behind me and crawled into her bed on top of her covers.

She curled into me, and I held her close, whispering to her, pieces of nothing, snatches of my life. The good parts, like Tia, her loyalty, her humor, her spirit (before Esposito broke it, though I didn't share that), and Mrs. Jimenez, her tamales, how cute her grandchildren were, and other things, like how much I enjoyed college.

I did this until she was asleep.

And I stayed there until I fell asleep.

21

IT'S THE WORLD AS I WANT IT TO BE

I was being lifted.

I opened my eyes and automatically my arms rounded Buck's shoulders as I looked around Tatiana's dark room.

Buck carried me out the door, dropped the arm under my knees, and my toes skimmed the floor as he closed Tatiana's door.

"Buck, she needs me," I whispered.

My feet hit the floor full, and he turned us toward his room, moving us that direction.

"She had you, now she needs to sleep."

"She needs company," I told him as he guided us into his room and closed his door.

"She needs to sleep alone, Toots, like always," he replied, stopping us by the bed.

"Okay, you're right, but she can do that tomorrow. Tonight, it's still fresh."

"Sooner's better than later," he returned, tugging on the tie to my robe.

"Buck," I protested as the robe came loose and he raised his hands to pull it off my shoulders.

"I get it, babe, you're in there for her. You're also in there to avoid me."

Hmm.

It was annoying when he figured me out.

"That's not true," I lied.

The robe was gone, his hands slid over my bottom and he pulled me to him as his head bent.

I felt his lips against mine, and he changed the subject.

"Gonna fuck you slow now, baby, remind you how much you like bein' connected to me, remind you why you chose me, and I'm gonna take my time doin' it."

Oh my.

"Buck—" I started, but his fingers flexed on my behind and his mouth captured mine.

Instantly, it began.

Buck knew it and he didn't waste time.

He lifted me, spread my legs. They clamped around his hips, and he put a knee to the bed.

Then I was on my back and Buck was on top of me, his hands drifting over me, light. Lighter than he'd ever touched me, and it made me shiver in a good way.

He did this while he kissed me, and he kissed me a long time, just his mouth on mine, his tongue in my mouth, his warm, strong hands gliding over my nightgown.

He'd never taken this much time with my mouth and I liked it.

There was something sweet about it.

Something beautiful.

His lips finally detached from mine to roam my neck, collarbone, chest, as one of his hands cupped a breast, thumb making lazy circles on my nipple. That sweet feeling intensified, and I shifted under him, my hands going under his T-shirt, pulling it up, his head and arms came with it, and I tugged it off.

Then his mouth was on mine again, our tongues dancing, his thumb doing nothing but those lazy circles, his hand hot on my breast, mine drifting across the skin of his back.

God, *sweet.*

I arched my back and moved my mouth from his, breathing, "Buck."

"Want more of me, baby?" he whispered against my neck.

I pressed my breast deeper into his hand by arching my back again.

"Yes," I whispered back unnecessarily.

His tongue glided along the length of my neck from shoulder to jaw before he shifted down my body. At the same time, he shoved my short nightie up so it bunched around my ribs. His hands left my ribs and went behind my knees, lifting and spreading them. Then his mouth was on me over my panties.

Oh *God*.

My back arched again, and with it went my neck, my fingers sliding in his hair.

I loved it when he did this to me. He liked the taste of me, and he didn't mind me knowing it.

But usually, he was hungry.

Usually, he was insatiable, taking all I could give, taking it hard, fast, draining me.

This time, he didn't.

This time, he savored, he played, he teased.

Torture.

Beautiful torture, all of it over my undies, and I liked it, but I wanted only him against me.

My fingers went from his hair to my panties and I pushed down. Buck rolled away. I lifted my legs, and he took over, tugging my undies off, tossing them aside, rolling back, his hands spreading my legs wide and his mouth returned.

There it was, the hunger, his tongue driving into me, his lips latching on and pulling deep.

"*God*," I panted, lifting my hips in encouragement and plunging my fingers back into his hair. "*Yes*."

It had already started, built up. Now, it was racing fast.

So fast, I didn't have time to hold on.

So fast, all I could do was let go.

I did that.

My back left the bed, my neck arching so much the top of my head was in the pillow, my fingers fisted in his hair, my lips opened, and my moan was long and silent.

Silent or not, Buck knew he'd made me climax and I wasn't done when his body covered mine and I felt him thrust inside me. His face went into my neck, his hand at the top of my head fisting in my hair, holding me still as he drove up, rocking my body with his thrusts. His hand went between us, his thumb hitting the spot and my body jerked as his touch and the driving power of our connection scored through me.

"Buck," I breathed.

He ground himself inside of me.

"You love that," he rumbled in my ear, his thumb rolling.

"Yes," I whispered.

Buck ground in deeper. "Tell me how much you love it, baby."

My arms had circled his shoulders, my legs the same with his hips, and I lifted mine to deepen our connection.

Buck's thumb rolled again.

"God," I breathed, my neck arching again.

"Tell me how much you love it, Clara."

I twisted my neck and pressed my lips to his. "I love it, Buck, it's the world as I want it to be."

A groan reverberated up his throat, and his mouth left my ear and took mine as he started driving into me again, rolling with his thumb, too much, all of it exquisite. I couldn't hold back, and I let go, my cries drowned by his mouth.

His thumb went away, his hand spanning my hip, yanking up as he kept his lips against mine and continued taking me, hard, deep, God, *God*...

"Buck," I gasped, "I'm going to...again..."

I came again, my mew disappearing in his mouth, the grunts of his orgasm drowning it out.

He'd thrust through his climax and only stopped for moments before he moved again, slow, a gentle glide. He kissed me, thorough, wet, sweet, then he planted himself to the root, lifted his head and his hand in my hair slid down to the side of my face.

His thumb swept my cheekbone as he murmured, "Fuck yeah, baby."

I closed my eyes and turned my head to the side.

His hand left my face and I felt his lips at my ear, "You let go, gorgeous."

I didn't respond.

"Liked it before, fuckin' loved it. But now, Toots, *fuck*. Hot."

I kept my eyes closed and my head turned away. He allowed this for long moments before I felt his teeth nip my ear.

Then he whispered, "Clara, honey, I get you're freaked. I get your strugglin' to find your way." His hips pressed into mine and I liked that so much, I had to swallow my moan. "What you gotta get, baby, is you gotta think a' *that* when you got doubts. You gotta think about how much you love what we got and how hot it can be, how intense, how deep that connection is. 'Cause, babe, people don't have this shit. This is just for you and me."

Oh no.

I liked that.

I liked it too much.

I knew I felt that for me. I knew what we had like this, like now, was something special, something beautiful.

I just didn't know he felt the same.

I closed my eyes tighter.

I felt his nose sweep my jaw before his lips went back to my ear. "And something else you gotta get, darlin', is that I'm here. I'm always here. I promised to have your back and I mean that every way you can mean that to be."

I didn't understand this, not exactly.

But Buck saying that set visions sliding along my closed eyelids, memories shifting through my brain.

Buck holding Tatiana and kissing the top of her head.

Gear talking about Buck surprising him with the car they worked on together.

Buck telling me he liked to make me smile.

Buck making me and his kids French toast, waffles, everyone getting a turn to decide what they wanted, and Buck giving it to us.

Buck making me kiss him to end a fight.

Falling asleep with my head on Buck's thigh, his fingers in my hair.

Buck handing me money for a day out with the girls, a dinner with Mrs. Jimenez.

Buck looking for Tia and getting upset because he couldn't find her.

Buck giving me a home and making me feel welcome there, my place, my space, never making me feel temporary, a nuisance, a burden.

Before I could stop myself, I turned to him, and his head lifted up when it did.

"I never thanked you for my car," I whispered.

I felt his body relax on mine and I didn't even realize it was tense.

"Babe," he muttered then touched his mouth to mine.

Once he'd done that, he pulled out, rolled to his back and lifted his hips, yanking off his jeans. He threw them aside and then tugged the covers out from under us, pulled them over us and curled me into his side.

Then he asked, "You drive it yet?"

"Tatie and I cleaned the house. Then Locke made us corn dogs and tater tots. I wasn't certain a joyride in the car that started..."

I stopped talking as I realized where I was leading.

Buck's arm around my waist gave me a squeeze.

"Toots, friend of a friend was in a jam, needed money fast, had to unload his Charger to get it. I've had that car down at the shop and been fuckin' around with it for months. Was gonna fix it up and sell it but didn't wanna. It's a sweet ride. The minute I met you, I knew your ass had to be in that ride, so I finished it, and Ink and me brought it up while you were workin' yesterday."

Oh dear.

I liked that too.

I liked that he went out of his way to surprise me.

I lifted my head and looked down at his shadowed face. "The minute you met me, you knew I had to have that car?"

His hand not around me came up and cupped my jaw then slid into my hair, pulling me closer to him.

"All right, maybe not. The minute I fucked you against the wall and knew I was gonna be fuckin' you for a while, I knew your ass had to be in that ride."

"That car is cool and I'm not cool," I told him.

"No, that car is sweet, and that car is hot and, babe, you're both a' those."

Oh *no*.

I liked that too.

I shook my head.

He was something else and the something else he was being now felt nice.

Then I dropped my head to press my face in his chest.

After I did this, two things occurred to me.

One, he was apparently settled in for the night without the need for a quick visit to the bathroom, and two, there was wetness between my legs, and it wasn't all mine.

My head shot up.

"Did you use a condom?" I breathed.

"Uh... no, babe, you coming against my mouth like that, wasn't gonna wait to get my dick in there."

"Oh God," I whispered.

His hand still in my hair tensed.

"Babe, it's no big deal."

"Buck! I still haven't started my period."

"You will."

"I won't if we keep forgetting condoms!" I snapped, something we had not done since our early days.

Oh God!

He pulled my face close to his again.

"Babe, learn now. Read me. When you start to freak out, calm down a second, take a breath, think about it and *read me*."

At first, I had no clue what he was saying.

Then, I still had no clue and I was too busy freaking out to take a breath and "read him."

Finally, I took a breath, forced myself to calm down, and it struck me that he didn't *need* to calm down.

When he said he had my back and that he had my back in every way that could be, he had my back.

He didn't care if I got pregnant, because, he might not be trying to start a family with me, but if it happened, sixteen years down the road, he'd give our child a car and I could be on his deck or I could be on the phone with him, and it was up to me if I was a bitch.

Oh...my...God, God, *God*.

"You don't care if I get pregnant," I whispered.

"Not so much," he replied instantly. "Like I said, you'll be a good mom. And just sayin', got even more proof that's the motherfuckin' truth after last night, this morning, and tonight."

"Oh my God," I breathed then my eyes narrowed in the dark. "You aren't...*trying*, are you?"

He rolled into me and both his arms went around me before he said, "Life is life, gorgeous, and you gotta let go and live more. I love the feel of you. You love our connection, and babe, I feel the same. I don't like anything between you and me. A kid comes outta that, so be it. You need to get on the pill. We had so much goin' on, we've let that slide and we need to get on it. Until then, I'm happy to take my chances if I get what I get from you. And I get what I get from you, I get it a lot and it's always fuckin' good. Tonight, better than ever. So, no, I'm not tryin', but I also don't care. If that's the price of havin' you the way I want you, I'm happy to pay it."

Oh dear.

There it was again.

I liked that too.

It wasn't romantic.

It wasn't flowery.

It all seemed to be about sex.

But he loved the family he had. His kids meant a lot to him.

And the fact he didn't mind having more, as crazy as it seemed, said a lot about him.

"You're a very unusual man, West Hardy," I blurted, because he was.

No man just shrugged at the thought of creating a child and all that meant to his future in order to get great sex.

Buck was silent then he shifted into me, shoving his face in my neck to muffle his bark of laughter.

I tried twisting my neck and pressing my head in the pillow to get him to look at me, but I failed, so I called, "Buck."

He pulled his face out of my neck and brushed his mouth against mine.

Then he whispered, "Yeah, gorgeous, I'm *unusual*," and he whispered it, still chuckling.

"Buck—"

He rolled to his back, tucking me into his side, saying, "Wiped, Toots. I had less sleep than you last night and a seriously jacked-up day. Time to crash."

A seriously jacked-up day?

Did he just mean Conley, Tatie, and dealing with me?

Or did he mean something additional to all that?

I wanted to ask. I really wanted to ask.

I didn't.

Instead, I muttered, "All right."

He gave me a squeeze, and muttered back, "Thanks, baby."

He was settling, he was ready to sleep, he told me, and I felt it as I took a second to read him.

Therefore, I slid an arm around his flat stomach. "'Night, Buck."

He didn't reply, but he also did.

His arm gave me another squeeze.

And then he replied.

But not to say goodnight.

To say, "And babe, also worth a repeat, we'd make a gorgeous kid."

Words which had me wide-awake and again wondering if he was *trying* to get me knocked up.

Buck slid right to sleep.

It took me a while, but not long, and then the crazy of the day and night before washed out of me, and I was back to my regularly scheduled program of deep, restful sleep in Buck's bed in his house.

And in his arms.

22

THE BIKER BABE INITIATION

The next morning, as usual, I was up, in my robe and in the kitchen making coffee before anyone else was the same.

Not as usual, as I was pouring my first cup, I sensed movement.

I turned as I shoved the pot in the coffeemaker to see Tatiana, looking cute and sleepy and about five years younger, shuffling toward me.

I braced when I realized she wasn't going to stop, and I took the hit as her body collided with mine and her cheek landed on my shoulder.

She also curved her arms around me.

I felt her casual, unconscious affection rush through me, warm and sweet, and it was a feeling I'd never had before.

Not in my life.

I slid an arm along her waist and looked down at her face.

Her fat lip was nearly gone, but the bruising at her cheek had darkened.

By my experience, she had another day of purpling in that bruise before it started to fade.

It was good she wasn't going to school like that.

I gave her waist a squeeze.

"Sleep okay, honey?"

"Mm," she mumbled, and I hoped that was a yes.

"You want coffee?"

"Mm," she mumbled again, this time nodding a bit in the affirmative, giving me a clue.

I moved her with me, not letting her go as I got a mug out of the cupboard and then poured her some coffee. We shuffled as one to the fridge to get the milk, shuffled back, and I sploshed in milk and spooned in two sugars, handing her the cup when I was done. She lifted her head just enough to take a sip as I reached for mine and followed suit.

"You want me to toast you some Pop-Tarts?" I asked, giving her another squeeze. I looked down at her and smiled. "We won't tell your dad. Our secret."

She grinned a sleepy grin back at me.

"Depends, Toots," she murmured. "It's your choice for breakfast today. What're we havin'?"

I stared down at her.

So far, I hadn't had my choice for breakfast.

Something about getting my turn rushed through me warm and sweet too.

"Well, you and your brother always pick waffles or French toast, so I'm going to switch it up a bit. Bacon and eggs."

"Dad makes awesome poached eggs."

I bet he did.

"And fried," she went on.

"I'm sure he does, sweetie."

"And scrambled. And eggs Benedict. He makes the sauce from scratch and everything."

I found this interesting.

Hollandaise sauce was not easy, even for experienced cooks.

Buck was a fantastic cook, but that took it to a whole new level.

I took another sip of coffee then stated, "Eggs Benedict it is. Then, we'll get showered and you and I'll take the Charger on its maiden voyage. Well, not maiden as it's a classic car, but maiden voyage for us."

She tipped her head to the side, her eyes lightly dancing.

"Maiden voyage?"

"Yes, its first journey, or its first with you and me."

"I know what it means, Toots, but who talks like that?"

I grinned at her, lifted my mug and said, "Me."

She grinned back and I kept talking.

"I have to go to the grocery store. I take goodies into the folks at Ace. They like the homemade ones best. I'm thinking a cake. Some kind of sheet cake. One that goes far. Like chocolate with cream cheese frosting and maybe we'll sprinkle mini-chocolate chips on top. What do you think? You want to go to the store with me and then help me bake a cake?"

"Sure, that'd be cool," she whispered, that hint of surprise on her face again.

I guessed she and Kristy didn't often bake together.

That was awful, and the sweet warmth washed out of me as I realized that I'd always yearned for a mom who would put me on a stool and wrap a kitchen towel around me and teach me how to bake even as I made a mess. And then later guide the way as I made treats for my boyfriends.

Tatie actually had a mom, and she didn't have that.

It was high time, for both of us, and thinking that, I gave her a squeeze.

"Then our plans are set for the day," I decided, at the same time deciding more.

She had a dad who seemed to be able to kit out his room pretty well, but Tatie's was like a guest room.

That week, we were going to fix up her room.

And get her more vampire novels.

And journals.

Makeup and jewelry and clothes too. She had to get right back in the saddle of being at one with who she was and caring how she looked, something she'd done pre-incident, and I was going to see to it that she continued to do so now.

Her father was okay with handing off hundreds of dollars to me to "have fun," I had no doubt he'd be okay with my plans.

These were my happy thoughts as Tatie tensed and her head turned to look out the windows.

I followed her gaze and saw a car heading fast up the graveled drive.

It, too, was a classic car, like the Nova and Charger.

What it was not was a cool classic car that was restored and well taken care of.

It was a junker.

"Holy shit, that's Mom," Tatie breathed, and I sucked in my own breath.

"Sorry?" I whispered.

She pulled woodenly away, and I saw her face was panicked when she looked up at me.

"Clara, God, that's Mom!"

Oh dear.

"Go," I ordered, putting down my coffee mug. "Go now. Wake up your dad."

She didn't move.

"Tatie, honey, go," I repeated, taking her mug away and setting it beside mine. "*Now*, baby."

She nodded and dashed away.

I hurried to the door, pulling my robe further closed and tying the belt tighter as I felt my heart start to race.

"Why?" I muttered under my breath as I unlocked the door. "Why couldn't we have a day of eggs Benedict and making blinkety blank *cake?*"

I threw open the door and pinned a smile on my face.

That smile faltered, but I just managed to hold it when I saw the two angry people stomping toward me.

Buck had a type.

And that type was not me.

Nails was dark, and Kristy was the same with brown eyes.

Kristy was shorter though, than both Nails and me, and she carried extra weight. She did this well, it looked good on her.

What didn't look good on her was her still-pretty face twisted in fury.

And Kristy had a type too.

Knuckles was with her and he was big and dark like Buck. He, too, had a good many tattoos on display on his arms and up his neck. And he, too, had been handsome.

At one time.

Now, he was not.

Now, lines scored deep in his face. His gray eyes looked mean. And the once muscle of his big body had turned to flab, evidencing the fact that he didn't live a busy life working on homes, or cabinets and taking care of an MC. He lived a sedentary life, likely drinking beer, eating a good deal of food, not much, if any healthy if the sallowness of his skin was anything to go by, and smoking way too much.

Which he was doing now, except he was done, and he flicked the butt in Buck's drive.

A goodly number of the MC brothers smoked, and there were over-flowing ashtrays outside every door that was connected to any building at Ace.

Buck didn't smoke and neither did either of his children. His driveway was a driveway made of gravel, but it was a drive situated next to a fabulous house that was next to a meandering creek in Arizona, for God's sake. Flicking out a cigarette butt so casually not only was a massive fire hazard, it seemed strangely like giving God the finger.

I shoved this thought aside and my feelings about it, beat back my urge to run out and grab that butt and put it out, because I had a feeling another fire was imminently going to start, and I needed to douse those flames early.

And to do so, I kept my smile steady.

"You must be Kristy and Knuckles," I greeted in as friendly of a manner as I could muster as they got close.

"Outta my way, bitch," Kristy non-greeted back, and she made her demand so by shoving me out of the way and pushing into the house.

I hit the very solid doorjamb, unfortunately doing this on my bruised shoulder, which made me flinch at the same time blink in shock as Knuckles walked right by me, his eyes sliding over me from head to toe, making me shiver, and this was in a *bad* way.

"Fuck, tell me I did not just see you do that," I heard growled, turned and looked into the house to see Buck in jeans, the top button undone. He was pulling a navy, long-sleeved tee down his cut abs as he stalked down the steps of the landing.

I stepped in the house and closed the door behind me as Kristy spoke.

Or, more to the point, shrieked.

"Gear, Tat, get your asses packed and out to the car!"

Uh-oh.

"Clara, ass over here," Buck clipped, and I didn't hesitate.

I moved swiftly.

Giving Kristy and Knuckles a wide berth, I walked to Buck who was now standing a few feet away from the steps to the landing, feet planted, hands on his hips.

I moved to stand behind and beside him, wrapping my arms around my middle.

"Get outta my house," Buck ordered, but Kristy's eyes went from him to the landing where Tatie was standing, and her face got red.

Or, redder.

"Fuckin' hell, fuck...in'...*hell*," she snapped. "Girl! What am I always tellin' you? Fuckin' hell. Look at your fuckin' face." Her eyes cut to Buck. "And I'm always tellin' *you*, you gotta get a handle on her. You don't, she'll find trouble, and fuckin' look at her, out findin' fuckin' *trouble* under *your* watch!"

I turned my head and saw Tatiana looking no less panicked, in fact shrunk into herself.

Um.

No.

Wait.

That would be, um...

Hell to the fuck no.

I looked at Kristy and opened my mouth to speak but Buck got there before me.

"I said it once, I'll say it one more time, then I'll do somethin' about it. Get...the fuck...outta my...*fuckin' house*."

"Eat me, asshole," Kristy shot back.

Oh dear.

Buck looked at Knuckles. "She had her warning, now you got yours. Get me?"

Knuckles crossed his arms on his chest and scowled at Buck.

Hells bells.

It was going to be me, even though I really didn't want it to be, who had to be the voice of reason.

In order to do this, I stepped forward and spoke.

"Okay, this is a tense situation and emotional. Understandable that tempers would get frayed. Why don't we take a second, calm down, and I'll get everyone coffee?"

Kristy leaned my way and snapped, "Fuck you, bitch, and you can shove your fuckin' coffee right up your fuckin' ass."

"That's it," Buck bit out and was instantly on the move, and I knew enough not to stop him, but suddenly, we all heard, "Dad, don't."

Gear was there on the landing at the top of the stairs, wearing nothing but his cutoff sweatpants.

Buck stopped and turned his head to his son.

"You get her out or I do it," Buck stated.

"I'm not leavin' until my kids' asses are in the Nova and I'm followin' them down your drive," Kristy stated.

I stepped forward again and spoke to Kristy.

"Listen, please. I can see you're angry, but we've had a rough weekend, and this isn't making it any better. Especially for Tatie. Now, I'm asking you, please—"

"*Especially for Tatie*," Kristy mimicked me, her voice pitched high, her face twisted even uglier. "She done a number on you or what? *Especially for Tatie.* Jesus, that girl is trouble. She was trouble the minute she pushed her way out, squawlin' the whole fuckin' time. She acts like she acts, shit is gonna happen. It happened. Practically every teenaged asshole with a dick has hit my daughter here *and* at home. Now she cries rape? Bullshit."

I stood in stunned, shocked, furious...no, *enraged* silence.

Gear moved forward, and I noticed vaguely his movements were quick and angry as he said, "That's not fuckin' true and you know it!"

I also noticed vaguely that the snake beside me had awoken, and I could sense enough poison emanating from Buck, it was a wonder we all didn't drop where we stood just inhaling it.

But me?

Me?

I lost my *ever-loving* mind.

I lunged forward, and with every ounce of strength I had, I smacked Kristy Hardy Whatever-Her-Name-Was-Now hard across the face.

Her head jerked to the side and immediately jerked back to straight, her hand to her cheek, her eyes huge and incensed, and she stared at me as I stepped even closer and got in her face.

"Take that back!" I shouted at the top of my lungs.

Kristy did not take it back.

She pounced.

She might have been a biker babe of a lot longer standing than me.

But I grew up in foster care.

Sometimes, it could get rough.

And sometimes at school, kids could be cruel.

You didn't last long unless you learned how to defend yourself.

It had been a long time, and I was in a robe and nightie, but I knew my way around a catfight.

And she'd underestimated me, so I had surprise on my side.

In no time at all, I got her on her back, straddled her chest, my knees in her biceps, incapacitating her arms (and her nails), and I bent into her face.

"Now, *take it back!*" I screamed.

"Fuck you!" she screamed back.

I wrapped my fingers around her throat and screeched, "*Take it back!*"

Suddenly, I was in the air, a strong arm around my middle, and then I was set on my feet. Buck got in front of me and shoved me back farther with a hand in my chest.

"Jesus, Toots, calm the fuck down," he ordered.

I pushed against his hand at my chest and yelled at Kristy, "Take it back!"

"Kiss my ass!" she yelled in return, getting to her feet at the same time pushing off Knuckles who was trying to help her up.

Buck gave me a shove, and then he turned.

I started to move but stilled and stared in complete and utter awe as Buck entered the fray and dealt with Knuckles *and* Kristy.

Without delay.

Kristy was first.

He grabbed her wrist, dragged her, fighting, to the door, and hurled her out with such force she went flying. She flew into a chair, bounced off it, and landed on the wood on her behind.

Knuckles went after her, or more accurately, Buck and he met head-on with a low roar.

Buck was ready and he threw one punch. It connected with a hideous thud against Knuckles' jaw and Knuckles flew back, stumbled and nearly dropped to the ground. He didn't because Buck caught him by the throat, lifted and twisted him around and shoved him out the door.

Knuckles came back at Buck swinging.

His movements were lumbered, and Buck easily ducked. Knuckles missed.

Buck came up, grabbed Knuckles' head in both hands, then, with wondrous eyes, I watched as Buck *headbutted him.*

Headbutted him!

It was glorious!

Before Knuckles could stagger back, Buck's torso dipped low, his movements powerful, and he savagely connected with a fist between Knuckles' legs.

Knuckles fell to the deck on his knees with a heavy noise, his hands covering his crotch, his low groan painful to hear.

After that, Buck straightened and pointed at Kristy.

"He recovers his junk, you get his ass in your car and get the fuck off my land. I don't see you until Gear graduates. You don't see Gear until tonight. That is, if my boy feels like goin' home. You don't see Tatie until next Sunday. That is, if *she* feels like goin' home."

"*The judge'll hear about this,*" she shrieked.

"Do your worst," Buck fired back, walked in, slammed the door, locked it and then turned to face me.

Buck and I stood staring at each other, both of us frozen, but only me breathing heavily.

I felt Gear's and Tatiana's presence, but my eyes were glued to Buck.

Eventually, we heard the cough and roar of a tired, ill-kept engine, and then we heard gravel spew. Finally, we heard Kristy and Knuckles' car careen down the drive.

It was, I decided, time to move on to eggs Benedict and cake baking.

"My turn to pick breakfast," I announced into the noise void left behind when we could no longer hear the car. "Tatie told me so, and I pick eggs Benedict."

Buck's head jerked slightly back.

Then he asked, "Toots, are you shittin' me?"

I shook my head and crossed my arms.

"No. Your waffles are awesome. Your French toast is ambrosia. But it's time to branch out."

"Babe, you just wrestled on the floor with my kids' mother," he reminded me.

"Yes," I stated, my eyes slid to a gaping, still-astonished Gear, who was staring at me. "Sorry about that." I looked behind me at Tatie, who was also gaping, clearly astonished as well and still slightly pale. "Tatie, honey, you too. Sorry." I turned back to Buck. "But now, I'm hungry."

Buck studied me.

Then he moved, sudden and swift.

One second, he was standing just inside the door.

The next, he was at me.

Not *at* me.

He had his arms around me just below my bottom, he hefted me up and swung me around, my calves flying, my torso listing drunkenly.

He stopped, slid me down his body, and one arm stayed clamped around my waist as the other hand cupped the back of my head firmly, his head bent, and he kissed me, long, hard, and *very* wet, right in front of his kids.

When he lifted his head, I was blinking, my stomach was melting, and my fingers were curled deep, holding on to his shoulders.

"Think you just passed the biker babe initiation, Toots. You're a full member now," he declared, smiling down at me huge, his eyes dancing.

I blinked again, heard Gear laugh, and Tatiana giggle.

I'd done something to please him greatly, and I didn't know if this was the fact that I went into smackdown with zero hesitation, my adversary his very-much-a-bitch ex-wife, if I did it in defense of his daughter, or both.

However, he might declare me a biker babe, but I wasn't certain I was one.

Not yet.

Catfight or not.

And the proof of that was that I had to decide what a biker babe would do right then.

I came up with saying, "Right, wonderful, but Buck, that doesn't make me any less hungry."

He shoved my cheek to his chest, his arm around my waist squeezed the breath out of me, and I heard his roar of laughter.

Both of the kids joined in.

All right.

So.

This was what family was too.

I didn't know what to make of that.

But at least this once, the side I was on came out on top.

And I was down with that.

23

PRETTY-PRETTY

I was in my super-sweet Charger on my way into town when my cell went.

I dug through my purse on the passenger seat, pulled it out and looked at the display.

It said TATIE CALLING.

Oh dear.

It had been almost two weeks since the incident.

We'd baked cake.

We'd gone shopping, hit Urban Outfitters and Cost Plus World Market, and Tatie had done up her room.

I was right. Buck had no problem (none whatsoever, in fact he'd said strangely, "It's about time," when I asked) loading me down in hundred-dollar bills to spoil his daughter the week after she was sexually assaulted.

So we'd spruced up her space, and Tatie had a couple new outfits, some new shoes, jewelry and makeup, and a lovely new handbag.

She'd come into the office with me every day, helping out or sitting on the couch doing homework assignments her teachers sent after Buck called the school.

During one of these days, we finagled a talk with her, Debbie and the biker babes that went so amazingly well, I was shocked.

Misery, however, loves company, and Tatie felt a lot less alone knowing that every woman in the room with her had had their fair share of jerks doing seriously jerky things and we all made it to the other side.

It wasn't a fun club to belong to, but she now knew she had her club, and in times like those, clubs like that were good things to have.

Later in the week, Mrs. Jimenez got in her old clunker, drove to Ace and we went out to lunch, Mrs. Jimenez making Tatie smile, Tatie charming Mrs. Jimenez—as charming, I'd learned, was something Tatiana definitely could be.

Gear had come back on Friday night, and we'd had a good weekend.

And then Tatie made the decision, because of school, that she needed to go home.

That hadn't been so good, and it stayed not good.

She called me all the time.

Before school, at school, after school. Girls being mean to her, her mother being a screaming bitch.

It was morning and that had to mean Kristy had started early.

I engaged my phone and put it to my ear.

"Hey, baby," I greeted.

"Mom's a complete, fuckin' *bitch*," was Tatiana's greeting.

Yes, Kristy had started early.

I sighed.

"Tell me," I invited, and she did, and she was right.

Kristy was definitely a bitch, and she proved it every day.

Tatiana finished with, "I'm callin' Dad. I'm done with this shit. No one likes me in school anyway. It's been years, but most of my friends are there, not here. I can switch schools, no problem. I wanna live with Dad."

"Okay, but you need to get to school now. I'll talk to him later and have him call you."

"No fuckin' way, I hate it there. I'm ditchin' today."

Right.

This was very bad.

She might have acted out, but I'd discovered that grades were important to her.

And grades were important to her because she was charming, but
she was also smart. School smart. Book smart. And smart enough to
know, if she got an education, eventually, she'd find it easier to gain inde-
pendence, and she would be able to get away from her mother.

Thus, the only reasons she went home were because she was
worried her grades would suffer and, "Gear can't be with them all by
himself. He'll get the lot of it and that's not cool."

Gear getting "the lot of it" further did not make her father happy,
or me.

It wasn't okay Tatie was facing whatever was happening up there.

The both of them?

But, for now...

"No, Tatie, don't. Go to school, tough it out. Your dad will call you
later."

"Fuck that!" she snapped.

I had learned to pick my battles with Tatie, and addressing her
cursing tended not to take priority when assessing the bigger picture.

Like now.

"Tatie, sweetie, listen to me. You know the only person you hurt is
yourself if you don't go to school. Learn. Be smart. Try to ignore the stuff
around you. I know it'll be hard, but concentrate on your teachers, your
books, your assignments. Each minute that passes is a minute closer to
getting away. When you get home, go to your room, avoid your mom,
and your dad will call you the first chance he gets. I promise. Listen to
me, okay?" She was silent so I prompted, "Tat? Okay?"

"You don't mind," she stated bizarrely.

"Mind what?"

"That I come and live with you and Dad."

I felt my brows draw together. "Of course not. It's your house, why
on earth would I mind?"

She was silent again, and when she spoke, I had to concentrate to
hear her, her voice was so quiet.

"You're the shit, Toots. I'll go to school."

On that, I heard her disconnect, and I turned off my phone, feeling that warm sweetness rushing through me.

I'd tossed the cell aside, and it barely bounced on the seat when it rang again.

I snatched it back up, keeping my eyes on the road, but I chanced another look at the display.

It said BUCK CALLING.

I took the call and put the phone to my ear.

"Hi," I greeted.

"Where the fuck are you?" he replied, sounding gruff and sleepy.

And annoyed.

I blinked at the road.

A week ago, he gave the all clear for me to move around without a bodyguard. He told me that Esposito was firmly out of the picture (and fortunately, he didn't go into detail about that, but I got the gist) and my "shit was cool."

I was relieved.

I hadn't really noticed it, but it was nice to be able to get in the car and go to the grocery store or pop out to get donuts for the boys without an escort.

Life felt normal again.

That was, normal for a biker babe.

"Didn't you see my note?" I asked.

"Yeah, Toots, saw it, can read, so I read it. But, deal is, you wake me, you go down on me, I go down on you, or both, I fuck you, and we go to work together."

This was the deal, though I hadn't exactly signed a contract, just fallen into a rather enjoyable habit.

"You got home late last night."

He had. It was poker night with the boys at the Dive.

These were not scheduled, they were haphazard. He'd had a couple of them before.

And last night was one.

"Yeah, so?" he replied.

"Very late."

"Right. So?"

"Very, *very* late."

"Clara," he growled his warning.

"I thought you'd want to sleep in."

"I got a choice between sleeping in and your mouth workin' my dick, babe, I pick door number two."

Well, you couldn't get any clearer than that.

"So noted," I replied.

"How far away are you?" he asked, and I realized he expected me to come back, and realizing this, I didn't know whether to laugh or clench my teeth.

Truth be told, I was leaning toward laughing, and if I wasn't already in Phoenix, I would have turned back.

This was not about Buck being the king of our castle.

This was because I liked having my mouth around his cock.

And his between my legs.

And...other.

"I'm nearing the 101," I told him, informing him I was in Phoenix proper and nowhere near turning back.

"Fuck," he muttered.

"I'll make it up to you tonight," I offered.

"No, you'll make it up to me when I get to work, blinds closed, doors locked, babe."

Oh my.

Adventurous.

We weren't exactly in a rut.

But it was always good to take preventative measures on that kind of thing.

"Okay," I whispered, then changed the subject. "Tatiana just called me. She's already been into it with her mom this morning."

"Fuck," he muttered again, annoyed gone, frustrated in its place.

One could say Buck felt for his children's plight.

Like, a whole lot.

And as such, he felt hemmed in that he was powerless to do much about it.

"Buck," I started, pulled in breath, gathered courage, and stated, "honey, you need to do something about that."

"Right. You got any bright ideas?"

"Hire an attorney and get custody of your kids."

"Tried that," he replied.

"Try again," I suggested.

"Puts them through the wringer, Toots. They get their hopes up, I get fucked, then they get fucked. I don't like them to experience that and I don't like bein' fucked."

"Okay, then hire an investigator and *then* hire an attorney. I'll talk to Tatie. She can start taking notes. They're old enough to talk to a judge and tell them where they want to be. She shares how Kristy is, Gear corroborates it, your investigator gets dirt on Kristy or Knuckles, maybe the result will be different."

"Two can play that game, Toots, and I ain't dirty, but the MC hasn't always been clean. We do not wanna go there."

We probably didn't.

"Try anyway, just not the investigator."

"Clara—"

"She's in a bad way, Buck. You know it, but she trusts me, she shares, and as bad as you know it is, I'm telling you, it's worse. Try anyway."

"As bad as I know it is, it's worse?" he asked, the toxin threading through his tone.

Oh boy.

"If it was that bad, honey, I'd tell you," I said soothingly. "But yes, it's worse."

He was silent for long seconds before he muttered, "I'll call the Club's attorney."

I let out a breath.

Then I said, "You need to call Tat, later, after school. She needs to rest in the knowledge that you're doing something to help out."

"I'll call her, babe."

"Thanks, Buck," I whispered.

He was silent again for long seconds, before I heard him say, "Love that you look after my girl, gorgeous."

And I loved doing it.

And I really liked him calling me "gorgeous."

"I'm glad," I said softly.

"You didn't bake last night. You swingin' by to get the staff donuts?"

"No. Cookies from Safeway. That's why I left early, it's out of my way."

"Save me some."

"I'll try, but Jimbo's been hungrier than normal."

"Jimbo eats more a' your shit, Toots, Jimbo will stop bein' useful 'cause he won't fit in the aisles of the store."

This was unfortunately true.

Jimbo was a big man when I met him, and he was growing.

"I'm uncertain of my desire to discuss diet and nutrition with Jimbo and equally uncertain of my willingness to wrest a cookie from him."

Buck's chuckle came at me from the phone.

That made me feel warm and sweet too.

"Remember, babe," he finally said, still chuckling, "your man's got your back."

Without saying good-bye or letting me do it, he disconnected.

I dropped my phone on the passenger seat and headed to Safeway.

I did this thinking of my phone calls that morning.

I also did it thinking of the post-sex conversation Buck and I had the night Tatie and Gear went back to Flag last weekend.

I was on top of him, draped down his body, where I had noted he liked me to be, especially post-sex.

I had also noted I liked to be there too, post-sex or whenever.

He had his arm around my waist, where it normally was, his other hand, though, usually wandered.

But that night, he'd cupped it to the back of my head, holding my cheek to his chest.

He'd then asked, "Do you miss it?"

I stared at his shoulder, but I felt my body tense.

"Sorry?" I asked.

Buck rolled me to my back, positioning his long, hard frame body down my side, but his chest was pressed to mine, his face close.

This position change, I felt, was important, denoting this conversation was important, and I felt my breath get funny.

"Do you miss it?" he repeated.

"No," I said quickly.

I then kept talking.

And I also did this *quickly*.

"No, Buck. Never. The house was big, and we had a nice pool and the pulls in the drawers in the bathroom had Swarovski crystals in them. Rogan did it all up just so, meticulous, top-of-the-line everything. I had a big soaking tub I could spend ages in. And I loved doing that. Unwinding with a good book and a glass of wine in the tub. But I don't miss it. I don't miss any of it. I prefer your deck. And your room, which is all warm colors and filled with Buck smells. And the quiet. And the peace. And knowing, during the week, we'll have the kids back on the weekend so the house will seem busy and full. But I also like it, just you and me for Pop-Tarts in the morning and at night in front of the TV. I've never slept as good in my life as I have in this bed. So, no. I don't miss it."

For a second, he said nothing.

For that second, I couldn't read his face.

And then he said, "Buck smells?"

It wasn't teasing.

I looked to his beard and mumbled, "You smell good."

"Baby?" he called.

I looked to him.

"I was talkin' about your job."

His tone was serious. Questioning and warm, but serious. Not playful or amused.

"Oh," I muttered, feeling like an idiot.

"I don't even know what they do there," he said. "But everyone knows the Hunter Institute. I reckon, for a librarian, that's a big score."

"It was," I said quietly. "We...a library usually has as much stuff on every subject as they can afford to have in as much room as they can get to house it. A research library has a depth of things on one or two subjects. Hunter is rare books and papers. We had things like scratch paper John Lennon and Paul McCartney wrote lyrics on. Or letters written by famous people to other famous people, like we had a letter written by Abraham Lincoln to the mother of a fallen soldier. Or letters written by non-famous people to non-famous people but about famous things. Or early or first editions of books. We had all of Hemingway. Copies of the *Pickwick Papers*. Things like that."

"The *Pickwick Papers?*"

"Serial publications by Dickens."

"That's pretty impressive," he muttered.

"I loved it," I told him. "I was training to restore when they got rid of me."

Buck had nothing to say to that.

"But they got rid of me, Buck," I reminded him.

"You should look for a job as a librarian," he murmured.

"They got rid of me, Buck," I repeated.

He again said nothing, but now he kept his silence as he studied me intently.

"I did nothing. I was never even charged. And they got rid of me," I stated. "You were right when we were fighting. I know the other world, and I don't belong there. I don't belong with the snobby, snooty women who lived in my neighborhood. Or their men who drive BMWs mean and aggressively, like where they have to go is more important than you, or anyone. The generation of the entitled whose parents gave them everything they wanted for reasons I don't understand. It seems to me the best thing a parent can give, outside of love, is good lessons. And learning you need to work for what you want, and that you are just one of many in this world, we're all living in it together and we all have to work together, are two of the most important lessons you can get."

"Yeah," he whispered.

His tone on that one word was one I couldn't read either.

Though it was heavy.

But I was on a roll, and I had a point to make, so I kept explaining.

"They know nothing of foster care or the system or living paycheck to paycheck or struggling to make ends meet. But I do. And I didn't belong there. I never felt comfortable there, even before it all happened and my place was taken away."

I took in a big breath and kept going.

"So, to answer your question, no. No, I don't miss it. There are things about it I miss, especially at the library, but they showed no loyalty to me. I was good at what I did, and I was an exceptional employee because I know how important it is to have a good job and further know to take care of it. None of that mattered. Reputation mattered. And they didn't like theirs dragged through the mud whenever I was mentioned in a paper along with where I worked. No one there had the guts to say, 'We know Clara Delaney, she's an exceptional librarian who has given years of service to our Institute. She's a good person and she had nothing to do with this. So we stand by her.'"

I shook my head.

And yes, continued explaining.

"But now, I have my own domain. My own system. Responsibilities. People count on me. Good people who get it. Who work hard, like I do, and who appreciate having a great place to work because they know that is a rare thing to find."

"Is it enough for you?" he asked.

And it was my turn to stare intently.

Then I shared, "West, the most fun I've had since my life turned inside out, besides being with you and the kids, or Lorie and Minnie and the girls, and maybe even more fun than being with the girls, is when I got to make that office my own. Do I want to work admin for Ace in the Hole for the rest of my life? I don't know. But I'm not coasting now. I love going to work. And not just because I'm glad to have work. I love *the* work. It's about detail and organization, and there is no other who's better at either of those than a librarian. Not to mention, your people are good people."

"My people are your people," he replied.

Yes.

I'd struggled with it.

But really, there was no denying it.

They were.

"Yes," I whispered.

That got me a very different intense look before it got me a kiss and Buck rolling me, so I was again on top.

And then it got me more.

The next day, Driver was my ride home, because Buck texted me to say he was busy.

I thought he was off doing president of an MC stuff.

I thought wrong.

Because when Driver dropped me off, I saw three things at Buck's house.

Ink's bike parked by Buck's.

Chap's old, faded-red Ford truck parked by Ink's bike.

And the bathtub in the master bath was outside on the deck.

I wandered into the house, my extremities tingling, and I didn't even put my purse down before I wandered straight to the master bath.

All three men were in it.

Buck and Ink were re-tiling the bathtub/shower space in a tile that was different, but complementary, to the tile around the vanity.

Chap was doing something in the floor with plumbing.

And taking up most of the rest of the room where they weren't working was a huge, oval, vessel-shaped, freestanding, gorgeous soaking tub.

"Hey, babe," Buck greeted, like I came home to him doing something so *insanely wonderful* every day.

"Hey," I forced out.

"Give me a kiss then get us all a beer, would you?" he asked.

I said nothing.

I gave him a kiss then got them a beer.

They'd had to let the tile dry. They'd had to grout it and let that dry. Then they'd had to pull out and then put in an entirely new floor (penny tile, it was going to be fabulous) because the tile Buck had before was discontinued, and the new tub would expose more floor.

So we were showering in Tatie's bathroom because it'd take another day or two to get the tub in and the new showerheads installed.

Buck did not make a big deal of this.

Any of it.

But it was a big deal to me.

Huge.

Because I had been right way back in the beginning. Buck was not the kind of guy who took baths.

But I told him I did, and I loved doing it.

And soon, I was going to have a fabulous bathtub to do it in.

These thoughts on my mind, I hit Safeway and bought enough cookies to feed the shop people, the contractor men, the Aces members, the delivery men, Lorie, Minnie, Pinky, Debbie (if they popped around) and myself.

In other words, I cleaned Safeway clear out of cookies.

I also took the opportunity to grab two big tins of coffee, fresh half and half, some flavored half and half (vanilla, which was Minnie's and my favorite) and I headed out to my super-cool car.

I did this thinking I could do this.

That "this" being, I was in a place in my life where I bought cookies (or made them, or cakes, or cupcakes or other) for people I liked. People who took care of me. People who cared about me.

Genuinely.

People who had my back.

Friends (in Minnie, Lorie, Pinky and now Debbie's case).

Real ones who'd never cut me out unless it was me, personally, who did something nasty.

Real ones who'd accept me just as I was, if I wore my biker babe clothes, or if I stayed in my librarian blouses.

I did this also thinking that I couldn't leave my house without my man phoning, irritated I left it without connecting with him in some way.

Sure, Buck talked about having sex. He was a guy, a guy just woken up, and men tended to be in a certain mood when they woke up.

He was also my man and he'd woken up without me.

So I was sensing he was more ticked about the fact I left without saying good-bye.

And I did all this and walked out to my super-cool car that I'd driven down from the nice house in the tranquil setting where I lived.

It wasn't grand.

It wasn't phony.

It was full of food and love (and on the weekends) people.

More people who cared about me.

And eventually (in fact, very soon), it would be perfection because it would have a soaking tub.

But even when it was just me and Buck, the only other person in that house cared about me.

He gave me a car, yes, and a job, that too (and if I did say so myself, after a rocky start, I did it well). He gave me money to buy a cell and clothes.

But he did not shower me with riches, a fancy home, an expensive vehicle, in order to meet some need he decided I had that he had to do awful things to assuage (and let's be real, what Rogan did was not all about me, and I wasn't going to shoulder that blame).

That said, I gave in return.

As far as I could tell (and evidence mounted daily when I discovered more stuff I had to sort, this was true), I was the best office manager Ace in the Hole ever had. There were tons of employees with employee issues. Constant deliveries. Orders that had to be submitted, and accurately. Quotes to prepare. A variety of jobs being worked all the time that had to be monitored, progressed and kept straight. Clients to communicate with and keep happy.

I got paid for this, but it was one less headache for the brothers. I didn't know if they had a lot of headaches, but everyone could use one less. And I knew for a fact at least Chap was glad I was around so he didn't have to deal with the office.

And Buck and I gave a happy home to the kids when they were there.

It wasn't like we were fake and tried too hard and forced them to do happy things all the time or took them shopping to spoil them (well, I did that with Tatie, but the time was nigh for her room and the situation prior was extreme).

It was hanging out in front of the TV, on the deck, eating breakfast together in the mornings, dinner at night if the kids weren't off doing something.

But they came home to two people who wanted above all else for them to have fun when they were gone and come home safe and sound.

And when Buck wasn't being King of the Castle *BIKER!* he was sweet and loving, affectionate, funny. All of this in a rough, no-nonsense way, but it worked for me.

He thought I was "gorgeous," but he didn't feel the need to tell me every day and make it weird or seem false.

He was just real with me. He was just himself, yes, even the bad parts, and he gave me that, and I could be myself (for the most part), and he made no bones he liked me just as I was.

And he went out of his way to give me a beautiful soaking tub.

So I bought cookies and took them to my super-cool car, thinking that maybe, all this biker babe stuff, and the biker babe's place in the biker lifestyle, really wasn't all that bad.

In fact, most of it was really super good.

I'd stowed the bags in the trunk, slammed it down, and suddenly, I felt someone in my space.

Too in my space.

I cried out because I felt something unpleasant in my side, sending something equally unpleasant zinging through every inch of my frame.

After that, I went down.

I WAS TOSSED, kicking and struggling, on a bed.

Seconds later, the bonds securing my wrists and ankles were snipped.

My hair was in my face.

I shook it out, and my body stilled.

Standing beside the bed was Imran Babić, Bosnian lunatic.

Oh no.

He sat on the bed, and I scooted up it, shoulders to the headboard, remembering to be terrified.

But I stopped scooting (but not being terrified) when he leaned across me, resting his weight into his hand at my opposite hip.

"Did you...did you...?" I swallowed, shoved more of my hair out of my face and forged ahead, "Did you kidnap me?"

"No, Clara, I'm checking up on you."

Yes.

Definitely a lunatic.

"You tased someone, bound them and took them to an unknown location to check up on them?" I asked.

He grinned a grin that I was pretty certain could be sketched and printed next to the entry for "psychopath" in dictionaries.

Through it, he answered, "I couldn't be assured you'd accept a written invitation to dine with me."

This wasn't good.

His eyes traveled my body and it didn't take a clairvoyant to note he liked what he saw.

This was worse.

His attention came back to my face. "You're looking well, Clara."

I'd gone semi-biker babe that day, and now I was regretting it.

I was wearing my own cashmere turtleneck sweater, but I'd paired it with tight, faded jeans I'd bought while out with the girls and spike-heeled boots I'd also bought out with the girls.

The jeans had some fraying and rips in them, and I was pretty certain strippers wore my boots when they were off-duty and some of them when they were on.

The boots were hot, and I knew this because, the second I walked out wearing them last weekend before Buck took me and the kids to the Valley Inn, Gear had said, "Shit, Clara, those boots are fuckin' hot."

Buck, on the other hand, had taken one look at them, his eyes running up the rest of me, and then he'd laid another big wet one on me right in front of his kids.

Clearly, Bosnian lunatics also liked off-duty stripper boots.

"Uh...thanks," I muttered.

He moved so his hip was resting against my hip, and I tensed.

"I've been worried about you," he told me.

"I'm good," I assured him quickly. "Really good. Life's good. I've got a job. A car. A man. It's all great."

He shook his head and his eyes went funny. "You miss your friend."

My heart skipped and I stared.

"My friend?" I whispered.

"Tia," he whispered back in a scary way.

Oh God.

What did he know about Tia?

"Tia?" I asked, and he nodded. "What do you...?" I swallowed again. "What do you know about Tia?"

"I know what West Hardy won't tell you because he knows you'll leave him if he does."

My heart skipped again before it slid up my throat.

"What won't Buck tell me?" I forced out.

"That, many weeks ago, Tia Esposito's car was sold to a used car salesman. She took some cash and a trade. Smart move, but too late. Ten miles from the dealership, her new car was found abandoned on the side of a road, door open, her bags in the trunk, her purse in the front, no sign of her except the blood."

Oh God.

The blood?

Oh *God*!

That could not be good.

There was no way that could be good.

I closed my eyes, put my hands over my face and dropped my head.

"No," I whispered to my hands, tears stinging my eyes.

"Yes," he whispered back.

I dropped my hands and looked at him as one tear slid down my face.

His gaze followed it, lighting as it did like he enjoyed seeing me cry. He mumbled something in Bosnian and his hand came up, finger crooked, and he traced the tear with his knuckle with creepy reverence.

I pulled my head away, and his hand dropped.

"It was a lot of blood, Clara, too much," he went on.

I felt my lips quiver as my throat blocked and he watched my lips with eyes alight.

I forced down a swallow and asked, "Buck knows this?"

"Everyone does, pretty-pretty, everyone but you. Tucker and Sylvie Creed are working this job for Aces. They went to the scene themselves, and I know for certain they reported everything to Hardy four weeks ago."

Four weeks?

Four weeks?

"Where was this?" I asked.

"Nevada."

On her way to Seattle.

On her way to safety.

My idea.

"Have they found her?"

He shook his head. "No, pretty-pretty."

It was also creepy, him calling me that.

Actually, everything about him was creepy, and I didn't need creepy when I found out bad news about my best friend.

No.

I didn't need creepy *ever*.

"Why didn't Buck tell me?" I asked him a question, the answer to which he couldn't possibly know.

But he answered anyway.

He pressed up closer and leaned in, and when he did, I shrank back against the headboard.

"You. You need men for reasons. This was your reason for needing Hardy. He knows this. You..." he lifted a hand, I shrank back farther, and he dropped it, "a man will want to keep you. He does. So he won't tell you."

"I'm not with Buck for Tia," I whispered.

He leaned closer, and I couldn't shrink back because I had nowhere to go.

"We all use each other, Clara. Now that I've told you what you need to know, I will tell you what *I* need you to know. Then you are free to leave. My men have brought your car. It's outside. Or you're free to stay. This will be your choice. But what I need you to know is that I'm happy for you to use *me* any way you like, and in return, I will use *you* any way I like. I'll take care of you. I'll buy you nice things. You'll be treasured. Now, I'll leave you to think about that. You can stay or you can come back. I will wait for you."

Then he leaned super close, my body went solid, he shoved his face in my neck and I heard him sniff as his nose traveled up my jugular.

"Pretty," he whispered.

I shivered as he lifted his head, gave me his psychopath-defining grin, got up and walked out of the room.

I stared at the door and didn't move.

It took a while for me to look around the room.

It was nice. Heavy furniture, dark wood, silk drapes.

Expensive. Almost ostentatious.

Dark.

Suffocating.

I spotted my purse on the foot of the bed lying there next to my keyring.

I twisted, scurried down the bed, snatched them up and ran the heck *out of there.*

24

YOU LIVE IN THE SUNSHINE

I was in such a state, it took me a long time to figure out where I was when I left Babić's house.

This meant I got even more lost.

By the time I found my way to something familiar, I wasn't in a state, I was a mess.

I'd been kidnapped.

Tia's car had been found, filled with lots of blood.

Buck knew, and he didn't tell me.

I drove through Ace in the Hole's big parking lot, around back to the loading area by the warehouse where I normally parked.

As luck would have it, or maybe not, Buck was coming out of my office and spotted me.

I knew this because I saw him walking out the door as I parked, his gait swift and determined.

I set the parking brake, killed the ignition, and got out on jellied legs.

"Fuck, babe, where have you been?" he called as he approached. "You go to a Safeway in Tucson to buy—?"

He stopped talking when he got close enough to get a good look at my face. Then he started jogging as I moved out of the door and slammed it, my eyes locked to him.

I turned my body his way as he rounded the trunk, and then he was there, his hand at my jaw, the other one digging into my hip, his neck bent. I could feel the heat from his body and his eyes were sharp on my face.

"Talk," he clipped.

"Imran Babić kidnapped me outside Safeway," I whispered.

His hand tensed at my jaw and his eyes fired.

The snake was stirring.

"He told me about Tia." I was still whispering.

At that, he closed his eyes, his lips thinned, and then he tipped his head back, face to the sky.

He knew.

He *knew*.

He'd known all this time.

Weeks.

And Buck knew that my best friend in the world, the *sister of my soul*, was either in danger...

Or worse.

"Buck," I whispered, my hands coming up, fisting in his T-shirt, and his head dipped down, his eyes coming to mine. "Blood," I whimpered then I pressed my face between my hands in his shirt. "They found lots of blood," I sobbed into his chest.

His hand at my jaw slid to the back of my neck, and his hand at my hip slid around, pulling me close.

I threw my head back and screamed, *"Why didn't you tell me?"*

"This, baby, *this* is why I didn't tell you." He squeezed my neck and his face got close to mine. "*She* wasn't found. Just her car. I knew if you knew, it would mess with your head."

"Was the blood hers?" I snapped, and he squeezed my neck harder as he pulled me closer.

There was my answer, but he confirmed it by whispering, "Yeah."

I closed my eyes and dropped my head, my forehead colliding with his chest.

"Doesn't mean shit, baby," he said into the hair at the top of my head. "Not shit. Listen to me. It doesn't mean shit."

I jerked back again to look at him.

"Blood. Abandoned car. Her purse and bags left behind. What *else* could that mean?" I cried.

He gave me a gentle jerk and his face got in mine again.

"It means we don't got a dead body. We don't got a dead body, we got hope. And, fuck me, baby, but you've had enough of your hopes shit on and dragged through the mud and fucked over, I wasn't all fired up to be the one who delivered another fuckin' blow."

My lips parted as I stared into his eyes as what he said washed over me.

You've had enough of your hopes shit on...

My world was collapsing, *again*, but here was Buck, tall and strong and capable and mine, here, right *here*, saying these things to me.

I wasn't all fired up to be the one who delivered another fuckin' blow.

Washing through me.

Warm.

And sweet.

One could say I wanted to know everything about my best friend, even if it was bad.

One could also say I got why Buck didn't share it.

And he didn't share, because from birth, I'd sustained blow after blow.

Thus, he was now the first human being in my life who moved to block me from one.

"Buck," I whispered.

"So I got Tucker and Sylvie on it. And Gash has contacted every MC in every state in the country that we're allied with and we got their asses on it. I got two men who rode out and stayed out, sniffin' her trail, which is cold, but they're still out there, turnin' over fuckin' rocks. I even called Scott, and he has the heads-up to feed whatever he may hear to me. And I did all that and I'll keep doin' it as long as there's hope."

As long as there's hope.

"Tucker and Sylvie?"

"They're private detectives. They're good at what they do. The best in Phoenix."

The best in Phoenix.

Which undoubtedly meant the costliest in Phoenix.

And they were trying to find Tia, likely not doing it out of the kindness of their hearts (meaning, free).

Not to mention, every MC the Aces were allied with.

Aces brothers on the road.

He'd even called Rayne Scott.

To give me hope.

Hope.

All of that just to keep me in *hope.*

Before I even knew my brain had told my hand to move, it moved, sliding up his chest, his neck, into his hair.

I then pulled his head the inch it had to go, rolling up on my toes at the same time, and my mouth collided with his.

His lips opened, my tongue slid inside, and I made every effort to communicate with my kiss just exactly how grateful I was that he protected me against the knowledge Imran Babić got off on telling me and that Buck was going all out to give me hope.

I succeeded wildly in this endeavor and we ended up making out hot and heavy in the dock area of Ace in the Hole Home Improvement and Contracting.

When our lips detached, his arms had closed tight around me and he let my head move away, but he didn't release me.

"Thank you," I whispered, feeling my lips quivering again.

"Those words are nice, gorgeous, and I appreciate them, but you got nothin' to thank me for. You take care of my girl, my house, my business, and you take care of me. Deal was, you take care of me, I take care of you, and that's all I'm doin'."

"I don't take care of you," I said quietly.

"Baby, I got clean towels I didn't have to clean. I can see the floor in my bedroom. You fall asleep with your hair all over my lap. My daughter finally has someone she can trust. My son can settle in knowin' his old man is not home by himself when they leave me, but he has someone with him he digs having around. Every person I employ and every brother who swings into Ace comes in with a smile on their face 'cause they got coffee, cupcakes and you to look forward to. And they know what they ordered will be in the warehouse and their paycheck will come on time. You give it to me regular and each time is sweet. And a good life for you revolves around Pop-Tarts. You don't get it, but that's takin' care of me, Toots."

"Oh," I whispered.

He smiled before he whispered back, "Yeah, *oh*."

I dropped my head, turned it, pressed my cheek to his chest and moved my arms from around his shoulders to lock them around his waist.

Buck let me hug him for a while before he spoke.

"Be happy to spend all day standin' in the sunshine with you pressed up to me, Toots, but a fuckwit kidnapped my woman and I gotta do something about that."

Oh dear.

I tipped my head back to look at him.

"He didn't hurt me, just, um...tasered me and tied me up, and he scared me and, um...creeped me out. He called me 'pretty-pretty,' and I think he enjoyed it when I got upset about Tia. And then he told me he wanted me to be his girlfriend, but it was my choice. I walked, or kind of *ran* out of there and no one tried to stop me."

After I finished, I wondered what on earth I was thinking, sharing all of that with West Hardy.

I knew better than that.

And because I did, I was holding a snake in my arms and I was going to have to learn how to be a charmer pretty danged quick.

"He *tased* you?"

Uh-oh.

"Um..." I mumbled.

"Fuckin' shit," he muttered, tensing his arms around me.

"Buck—" I started but stopped when his arms tensed again.

"Babe, I'll share 'cause you'll worry if I don't. An asshole like Esposito, middle management who thinks he's bigger than he is and his bullshit is pissin' off the big man, I can ride in, beat the shit out of and leave unconscious. The Bosnians, no. The Bosnians require planning. I'm not gonna ride in, backed by my boys, and beat the shit outta Babić, not if I don't want C4 blowin' up Ace and everything around it, mine and my boys' garroted bodies lying in the Dive before the explosives are triggered."

I sucked in a shocked breath, and he kept talking.

"So, I plan, and we take care a' this shit so it won't blow back. And we *will* take care of this shit so it won't blow back. But you, you got a brother at your side whenever I'm not."

Not that again.

"Buck—" I started but stopped when his arms tensed again, this time squeezing the breath out of me.

"Clara, babe, do not even *think* about tryin' to discuss this shit with me."

"Okay," I wheezed immediately, and he loosened his arms so I kept talking, normally this time. "But before you go, can we make another deal?"

"Depends on the deal."

Figured.

"I want to know what you know about Tia, and I want to know it when you find out about it. But I *don't* want to know the possible results of taking on the Bosnians."

"You can't have the first, you got the last."

My brows rose and I asked, "Pardon?"

"You like your car, you like your job, you like my kids, you like my house and you like sharin' my bed. I keep you in the know as nothin' or somethin' that makes you cry with your face planted in my chest rolls in, babe, you likin' that shit dims and you walk around under a cloud. Let me deal with the cloud. You need to know, I'll tell you. Until then, darlin', my meaning in life is, you live in the sunshine."

Oh God.

It was happening.

God!

Let me deal with the cloud.

I stared up at him, knowing it was happening.

My meaning in life...

You live in the sunshine.

I was falling in love with West Hardy.

And I knew what this feeling was, and it wasn't what Rogan led me to believe was real and then walked all over.

This actually *was* real.

This was the real thing.

This was it.

This was love.

I was in love with a biker.

I was now, truly, officially a biker babe.

Oh God!

How did I go from not knowing if I wanted this life to falling in love with the president of an MC?

He gave me another squeeze.

"Do we have a deal?" he prompted, clearly not having any clue about the turmoil of my thoughts.

I couldn't speak, so I nodded.

"Good, then lay another one on me, babe, I got shit to do."

"Buck."

"What?"

I stared at him, warmth and sweetness rushing through me, and accompanying it was fear.

I was falling in love with him.

But right then, after being kidnapped, after finding out things were very not good with Tia, I couldn't hack it if he wasn't doing the same with me.

That being falling in love.

He'd said I took care of his house, his office, his kids, his sexual needs and his towels.

He did *not* say I held a place in his heart.

So to his question, I only had one reply.

"Nothing," I whispered, got on my toes and laid another one on him.

25

A MAN WITH VISION

M y head jerked around when I heard the crash and Buck's hand slid down to cup the cheek of my behind.

"It's okay, baby," he murmured. "They're just gettin' rowdy."

I looked down and relaxed into him.

More aptly, he meant rowdi*er*, but I didn't have it in me to correct him.

We'd just had sex, good sex, *amazing* sex in his room in the Dive.

It was good being there with him, even though the room was no less filthy.

It felt nostalgic in a happy way because this was where it all began.

This room.

This bed.

This was where I started to fall in love with him.

It had been three weeks since I realized I was taking the fall, the day I'd learned about Tia.

And in those three weeks, I'd fought it, feared it.

But I fell.

It was done.

A *fait accompli.*

I was in love with West Hardy.

Nothing had happened in those three weeks except life. I did not get kidnapped. No one attacked one of his children. No angry fathers showed up on the doorstep.

Although Buck had filed custody proceedings and Kristy took her anger about this out on Tatiana, and, I was suspecting (even though he didn't say anything, keeping a stiff upper lip for his sister and his dad, and me too), Gear, she, nor Knuckles roared up the drive itching for a fight.

Tatiana and Gear were coping at home.

Tatiana because, for the first time ever, outside of her brother, she had a listening ear, and in the life stakes for Tatie, I was a double threat. I had the heretofore unknown capacity to talk sense into a sixteen-year-old girl and I had all the time she needed to listen.

But Debbie, Minnie, Lorie, and Pinky were also checking in, texting her, sending her funny gifs or hilarious TikToks.

All of this just letting her know she wasn't alone. She might be far away, but at home, she was missed and loved.

And lastly, there had been no news (that I knew) about Tia.

However, I had started my period and finished it. Lefty had told me the delay was likely due to stress. And now I was on the pill.

But that was all that had happened. The big news in life, a custody feud and the end of a pregnancy scare.

The rest was just work...food...family...friends...sex...Buck...life.

And outside of the nagging worry I tried not to feel (and failed) about Tia, life was good.

Now it was a Thursday, and for some reason the members decided to throw one of their big parties.

This was, I'd learned from the girls, something they did often.

The party could be about anything or nothing. It could have a theme, like beer and brats with the old ladies bringing side dishes and desserts, or it could be a free-for-all, like delivered pizza and brothers riding out and bringing back half a dozen kegs.

Whatever it was, the word got out, and everyone they knew (and everyone who everyone *they* knew) came, got drunk, ate what was on offer, drank from a keg (or the endless supply of booze from behind the bar), listened to music inside and outside and got rowdy.

STILL STANDING

Buck and I had been out there for hours.

This time, it was about Chap's "world-famous, double-trouble cheeseburgers," which probably weren't world famous, but I'd found they were exceptional. Meat smooshed with Worcestershire sauce, sprinkled with Lawry's seasoning salt, grilled to perfection, and you had no choice but to have the double. Because one had a slice of melted cheddar and one had a slice of melted swiss.

The result was sublime.

I also found that partying with the Aces was brilliant.

I drank beer, ate a delicious burger, shot tequila, gabbed and laughed with everyone, because I knew practically everyone, and they knew me, and I played several games of pool very badly.

Sometimes I did this (though not the playing pool part, obviously) with Buck's arm curled around my neck, my front pressed into his side, my arm around his waist, a beer in my other hand, one in his. We'd sip and chat and laugh.

Sometimes I was with the girls or the guys, but I'd find Buck, seeing him, tall, strong and handsome among his people—*our* people—looking both cool and hot, and that warmth would sweep through me.

Or I'd feel his eyes on me, usually when I was laughing. I'd turn my head to meet his gaze and I'd feel that sweet rush.

Eventually he found me, grabbed my hand and walked me into the Dive, through the common area where people were talking, laughing, drinking shots, smoking cigarettes (and other things), playing poker and pool, and even though I turned my eyes away, I saw folks making out and also *making out*, as in, two seconds away from full-on sexual relations.

In other words, Aces knew how to party, and like their namesake, everyone was flying high.

Buck had guided me to his room, closed the door and then took me to bed.

Now we were both naked, Buck on his back, me draped on top, the sheet down to our waists, our legs tangled with each other's as well as the sheet, and I was happy.

I worried about Tia.

It gnawed at me, and I understood even more why Buck didn't share.

Because it was always there, that undercurrent of fear.

Before, the hope I could hang on to was that she was in Seattle, safe and serving coffee drinks.

Now, Buck was right, there was hope, because we didn't know where she was.

But it was harder to get a handle on because where she was (and I had to believe she still *was*), she was without her purse, phone, car, money and a goodly amount of her blood.

He'd wanted to shield me from that. And when he failed, not of his own doing, I completely understood why he'd tried.

I worried about the custody battle.

Tatie needed to get out of there, and things weren't all that great for Gear either. It was so bad for Tatie, and Gear was protective, he didn't talk much about what he was facing. But apparently, Kristy took the unhappy life she was leading out on both her kids.

And Knuckles was just a straight-up dirtbag.

But I had money in the bank.

No bill collectors breathing down my neck.

And a bottle of bubble bath in Buck's bathroom (my first purchase that I made just to spoil me).

Also a soaking tub and now a new vanity. One Buck built himself. A bigger one with a double sink (no Swarovski crystal pulls, but who cared? the new vanity was *fabulous* and the addition of it made the entirety of the bathroom *stupendous*) because Buck said we couldn't have a "kickass" tub without a "kickass" vanity.

"And anyway, babe," he'd stated, "you got a lot of woman shit."

I did, but not so much there wasn't room to store it.

However, I read his meaning.

Now, I could expand.

And last but oh so not least…

I was in love.

I shifted up Buck's body and looked down at his face.

God, he was handsome.

I lifted my hand and traced the lines coming out of his eyes, then down, my fingers gliding through his beard.

"Babe," he muttered, and my attention moved from his beard to him.

"Yeah?" I asked.

"What's in your head?" he asked back quietly.

I smiled and his gaze dropped to my mouth at the same time his fingers tensed on the cheek of my behind.

"I figured out one of the MC's uses for women," I informed him, and his focus cut back to my eyes.

"Yeah?"

My smile got bigger. "You boys have groupies."

He smiled back. "You got that?"

I nodded, moved my face closer and whispered, "*Lots* of them."

"There are some bitches who just like bikers," he stated.

I tipped my head to the side, quietly laughing.

"This I can see," I told him. "They also like free beer, pot, shots, world-famous, double-trouble cheeseburgers and getting them some. And, as far as I can tell, all those in equal measure."

"Can't live the life without knowin' how to have a good time."

"I see this too."

He grinned, lifted his head, and touched his mouth to mine.

Keeping it there, he whispered, "Like you like this, Toots."

"Me too," I whispered back.

I pulled up a smidge and brushed the hair away that had fallen on his forehead, then slid my fingers into it at the side of his head. I moved more on top of him and I touched my lips to his.

Both his hands came up and pulled the sides of my hair back as he took my lip touch and turned it into a hot, heavy kiss, his knee cocking between my legs, his thigh moving up to rest against the heat of me, and I pressed my chest into his.

"Hot," he muttered when his lips detached from mine.

I slid down and rested my cheek against his shoulder. His hand moved to draw random patterns on my behind. My hand came up and I traced the GEAR on his pectoral.

"Do you have a tattoo for Tatiana?" I asked.

His answer was to lift his right arm. I shifted to look, and using his other hand, he pointed at a coil of barbed wire that started at his wrist and snaked through all the tattoos up his arm to end piercing the tail of the snake.

"That's Tatie," he stated then went back to his random patterns on my bottom.

I was surprised so I lifted my head. "Tatie is barbed wire?"

His eyes caught mine. "My girl binds me, keeps me straight, keeps me clean and keeps me loyal to the mission."

The mission?

What mission?

"Sorry?" I whispered.

He studied me a moment.

Then he asked, "You good with the groupies?"

This question confused me, so I repeated, "Sorry?"

He stopped drawing with his fingers and cupped my behind.

"The groupies, babe. You good with that?"

Something about the way he was looking at me, his hand holding me, the feel of his body under mine, made me understand this was an important question.

I just didn't understand the question.

"I don't understand what you're asking me, West," I whispered.

"Lotta women, lotta people, Toots, see what's goin' on out there and judge. My people like to have a good time and they like to spend their time with people who like to have a good time. No hang-ups. No judgments. Booze, and a lot of it. Food, and they don't count calories. Shots. Grass. Shouting. Laughin' hard. Fightin' when they get drunk and stupid. And fuckin' anything that presses up against them. You got a problem with that?"

I did if he was the one that was doing the last and it wasn't me pressed up against him, but being a full-fledged biker babe now, I knew I couldn't tell him that.

I actually couldn't even think of it, because I was still not at one with it.

So I was ignoring it.

Instead, I said, "I might have missed it, but I didn't see a van filled with bound and gagged groupies who were then forced to smoke pot and drink vodka straight from the bottle. But I was pretty into my cheeseburger, seeing as it was tasty. Did I miss that while I was eating my burger?"

He stared at me a second before his lips twitched and he said, "No."

"Then no, I don't have a problem with it."

He studied me again while his hand came up and tucked hair behind my ear, moving to my jaw where his thumb came out and swept my lower lip.

And then he said, "I don't wanna do this."

I blinked at the change in his voice.

That change didn't bode good tidings.

"Do what?" I asked.

"Hand you somethin', straight up, that might make you stop lookin' at me like you're lookin' at me right now."

I felt my body tense.

"Buck—"

"But you want it."

I wanted it?

Wanted what?

"I don't understand what you're saying," I told him.

"I see it."

"See what?"

"You lookin' at the pictures in my bedroom, Toots, I see it."

What?

I pushed up to an elbow in the bed, but kept looking down at him, and his hand dropped from my face.

"Buck, you aren't making any sense."

He ignored me.

"You're just not askin' for it, because you know, I give it to you, it might fuck what we have, you and me."

Oh God.

Somehow the evening had taken a drastic turn.

I didn't want to turn with it.

I really didn't.

But I loved this man, I wanted a future with him.

So I had to.

"What are you talking about?" I asked.

He kept talking like I didn't speak.

"But I'm gonna give it to you, Toots. Give it to you, but remind you, this is where you are, and this is where you're gonna be. No matter what."

Oh *God*.

I was not a huge fan of when he talked like that.

"Buck—"

He cut me off.

And gave it to me.

"My father's in prison. Has been, in and out, for decades. Lotsa shit, most of it no big deal, stretches were not long. But it kept happening, which meant he had a record, a long one. So, when the Club got in a situation where the other guys didn't come out of it too good, he was sent up for a stretch, and now he probably won't ever again see freedom."

My body went solid and I felt my eyes grow wide.

"What?" I whispered.

"I go visit him. Even when you've been with me. I just don't tell you where I'm goin'."

Oh God.

"Loved him," he stated. "Still do. Good man, great fuckin' dad. Taught me everything I needed to know. Led me to me. He was Aces. And that was because his dad was Aces. Granddad was one of the founding members. I grew up in the life, never knew a time when I ever questioned the life was for me. I had a dirt bike when I was twelve. Got my first Harley at seventeen. Big family, with the Club, Mom, my sisters, brother, it was good. Knew where I was goin'. Never had a time when I didn't know who I was gonna be."

"Okay," I whispered.

"Then Dad went down. War between MCs. Stupid-ass shit, but it happens. Happened more back in the day, but still happens. Dad took a hit for the Club. Not sayin' he didn't do what he had to do to protect his Club, just sayin' he didn't do what he went down for. But that's what you do. You take your hit if you need to protect the Club. The family splintered. Not the Club. My family. My brother lost it. Didn't get why Dad went down for his brothers. Took off. Lives in Utah now. Found God. Used to hear from him, he'd spew shit about Dad, Mom, my sisters, our lives, how much he thinks we suck, Dad and Mom suck forcing him to live that life. How we're sinners. Goin' to hell. Shit like that. Don't hear from him anymore and like it that way. He's a dick."

He sounded like it.

I didn't share I felt that way because Buck kept going.

"I took off. Dad and I were tight, and I couldn't be where I was when everywhere I turned, I remembered how much better it was when he was free. Went to Flag. That was when I met Kristy."

He stopped speaking.

So I said encouragingly, "Okay."

And he started again.

"Fell in love with her. We were ready to start a family right away. Knew the only way to do that was to come home. Home here, Phoenix. Also home to the Club. Came back from Flag. Tied myself to Kristy. Built my life here. Liked it. One of my sisters, she got in the life, but a different one. Has a man who's a brother in a Club up in Denver. Good Club. Called Chaos. My other sister..."

He shook his head.

I waited.

It took a bit, but he started again.

"Both of my sisters were tight with Dad too. Neither really survived the splinter. But only one of them took Mom down with them."

Oh no.

This did not sound good.

He stopped again, so I prompted, "She took your mom down with her?"

He nodded, but he only nodded once.

"I'd barely left when she went off the rails. Why I can be tough on Tatie?"

He asked this last as a question, and even if I didn't quite understand it, I said, "Yes?"

"That was how Meg was. 'Cept a lot worse. Booze. Pot. Harder shit. For Meg, life was just a good time. And for the most part, I agree. It is. But that doesn't mean you don't gotta do what you can to get by the best you can for yourself, your family."

I agreed with this, so when Buck went silent again, I nodded.

And he kept talking.

"For her, it was just finding good time after good time. Brought that shit home to Mom. Fucked it on the couch while Mom was upstairs. They fought. Mom's shit got stolen, hocked. Mom'd kick her ass out, my sister would break in, take more shit, crash in the bathroom, puke all over the kitchen. Get lit. And that was it. One time she broke in, got lit. Drunk, high, lost, whatever she was doin', caught the house on fire. She was so out of it, she went up with the flames. Smoke got Mom before she went up in them too."

"Oh my God," I whispered, horrified at what he was telling me.

Horrified and hurting for him at these terrible, awful, heartbreaking things he was sharing with me.

"Yeah," he agreed. "My brother, he said they got what they deserved. Said God had a hand in the cleansing. Told me that shit, said it right to me standin' by their fresh graves. Then I gave him what he deserved for spewin' that. That's when I quit hearing from him. Makin' matters worse, shit was gettin' fucked with the Aces. Life was changin' here. Turbulence. Then more. Aces changed focus. It wasn't about the life and livin' it the way we wanted it to be. It was about money. We didn't have the store, just the contracting business that, at the time, was all brothers and it was small. The Great Recession, no one building, no one doing improvements, a lotta guys had time on their hands and needed cash. So they got tied up with some shit, started running protection. Drugs and guns."

I tried not to gasp but didn't succeed.

Buck didn't hear me.

He was focused on his story, therefore, he kept sharing it.

"Even though they spouted a lot of shit about it bein' a big 'fuck you' to the establishment, it was about money. I get it. Times were lean. But that shit was whacked. Drugs and guns? Fuck. That wasn't the man my father taught me to be. That wasn't the Club my father was in. That wasn't the Club my grandfather and his brothers built, for it to end up with that kind of legacy."

"What kind of man did your father teach you to be, growing up in an MC?" I asked quietly.

Buck's focus shifted to me and it was piercing.

"The kinda man who's loyal to his brothers, who's willin' to fight for his way of life. And yeah, that life isn't what some think is normal. It's a big step out of suburbia and soccer moms and desk jobs and wearin' suits. But the people in it are good. Solid. Dependable."

This was definitely my experience, so I nodded again.

Buck kept going.

"And Dad taught me to be a man who's willin' to put his ass out there to defend his MC. I can't tell you everything Dad did was what's considered legal. I can tell you he wasn't playin' any part in putting drugs and guns on the streets, and he didn't crawl up the asses of shitheels that ruin lives. His MC did their business with people who made their own choices, and his MC played their own games by their own rules, and they didn't make deals for the sole fuckin' purpose of linin' their pockets with cake."

"But you didn't get out of Aces."

"No, I fuckin' did not. This is *my* Club. My father's Club. My grandfather's Club. And these are *my* brothers. You earn your patch, babe, you don't disagree, take it off and walk away. You suck it up and fight for the MC. That's the kind of man my father taught me to be. And I got kids, kids I didn't want goin' off the rails and fuckin' up their lives, growin' up with that shit around them. Growin' up with a dad who made that shit easier to find on the streets."

"So you changed things," I whispered.

"No, Toots, I didn't," he replied, and I felt my stomach twist.

"You didn't?"

"Fuck no."

"I don't get it."

"I didn't. *We* did. My brothers did. We *all* did. I was a part of that, and it was my idea. But they only did it eventually."

"Sorry?"

"That's what you gotta know. I was a part of all that shit. I didn't keep myself clean. I voted my vote, got voted down, then went the way of the vote. I did what the MC decided."

"Oh," I whispered.

"Yeah," he whispered back.

"But—"

He cut me off. "That Club up in Denver my sister's old man is in? Chaos?"

I nodded.

"Years ago, they went the same way. A bad way. Then they got a president who went balls to the wall to get them clean. It sucks, but even as it does, it doesn't make it any less true, money makes the world go 'round. I learned from what my sister told me about Chaos. We needed to cover the money. That was what Chaos did. They had a garage and sold pot. Got deeper into shit. Same time they did that, this brother, the one who wanted them clean, started an auto supply store, built that up, built up the garage's reputation, and boom. Brothers worked at something good and clean, could pay their mortgages, raise their families, live good lives. So I talked the men around. We opened the store. Built the contracting. And we covered the money."

"You?" I asked.

"Yeah, like I said, it was my idea. Brought it to the men. Ink, Cruise, Gash, Riot, Chap, Lynch, Slate worked it with me. So, when I made my play to get the gavel, I got the vote. We started the shop. Store doin' business, jobs piling up, money coming in, men having their place in all that, less time on their hands, responsibility to the others to keep things tight, we got our shit together. For Chaos, it got ugly. For us, I can't say it was easy. Those ties, they bind, and I'm not sure you ever get loose. You gotta keep your rep up. You gotta make certain no one thinks they can fuck with you. That's just the way of any MC. But when you start dealing with garbage, you got more to worry about. You sink in that, you never really get rid of the smell. It's always threatening."

The troubles in the Club.

This was what Minnie was talking about.

"So you don't run protection for drug and gun runs," I said softly.

"Nope, Aces took that hit. Unanimous decision in the Club. Unpopular out of it."

"So it's okay now?" I asked uncertainly.

"No, babe." He shook his head. "It's not. We still got heat and pressure to re-enter the game. And some think what we did was pussy. So there are constant turf wars, dickheads like Esposito leanin' on us. It's not okay. Every meet we have, we gotta vote about how to deal with some shit someone is shoveling. Sometimes it's a pain, members of another MC talkin' smack to an Ace out at some bar, thinkin' they can rile us with disrespect just because they're bored, stupid or both. Dumb shit we don't bother with because it isn't worth the effort. Other times, it's a pain in the ass because it's a situation that requires handling. Carefully. But bottom line is, the shop and the jobs have to produce. Each month's split has to be worth it. Because not a single brother has forgotten what used to be. They remember it as easy money. Some of them forget, not only was it dirty, it was also a lot of other things."

"Buck," I whispered, not believing all he was telling me, not believing he hadn't shared this with me, not believing he could deal with all my problems, his kids' problems *and* all of this swirling around him.

Constantly.

"The good life comes with money, babe, it's just the way it is."

This was true.

Rogan, in his way, did the same thing.

It was also false.

"Depends on what you consider a good life, honey," I told him, and he stared up at me.

Then he whispered, "Yeah."

"Can I ask why, you telling me that, you'd think I'd look at you differently?"

"Babe, I was a part a' that shit. It didn't last decades, but it did last a few years."

"Okay, but you aren't now."

"Yeah, but I was."

"And you aren't now. And you're keeping the Club clean."

"That shit bought me my house, Toots. The one you live in. It bought me my bed. The one you sleep in. You gotta know that."

"Okay, now I know it."

He stared at me again and kept at it.

"Clara, you're fuckin' a man like the man you used to be fuckin'."

My body grew taut, and I snapped, "I am not."

"Any day, any meet, the vote might not go my way, and we're back in that."

"The vote will always go your way," I told him.

He shook his head. "No, babe, shit can happen, and that vote can swing."

"It won't."

"Toots, it will. I swung it and it can swing right back."

"You won't let it and your boys won't go there. Not unless you lead them there and you won't do that."

"You don't understand the Club. Or maybe *any* Club."

"No, but I know those men and I know you. When I walked into this building two months ago, I knew exactly who you were before I knew who you were. There are men and there are leaders of men. Your father was a leader and he taught you to be one too. I have not met another member of Aces who has what it takes to be a leader. You were able to take over this MC because you have what it takes to take over this MC. And your boys know that even better than me."

"Toots—" he started, but I kept talking right over him.

"There might be conflict and the only thing that cuts through conflict is someone who isn't conflicted. You know who you are, and you've always known who you were meant to be. You are not conflicted about your path or where you wanted to lead your Club. And others are drawn to a man with vision. Your members sense that and they'll follow your vision."

"Clara—"

I kept right on talking over him.

"Is that why Kristy and you split up? Because she liked the life that stuff could give her, and she knew you intended to cut it off?"

"Partially. Mostly it was that I didn't used to have to work all that often, she had my attention when she wanted it, and I was around more often to take care of shit at home. And when I had to work, at the store, in the workshop, out on jobs, and I wasn't home all the time, especially when it came to lookin' after the kids so she couldn't go off and do whatever it was she wanted to do, she wasn't down with that."

My eyes narrowed as I snapped, "What a bitch!"

"Babe—"

"So she was okay with the Club running drugs?"

"Can't say I shared all the Club's business with her, but she was okay drivin' a Corvette to go meet her girls for lunch and then hitting the mall for a shopping spree. Bitch had so many clothes, I had to keep mine in Gear's closet. What she was not okay with was me makin' waves, not in the Club, not to her life. There was a spell, didn't last long, but it was there, when money didn't flow as steady as it had before. We had to tighten things up. She wasn't a fan of that. She liked her life just as it was. Maybe, if some outside force had changed it, she would have learned how to deal. The fact that I had an active hand in changing it did not make her happy."

"So she's actually a weak, risk-fearing bitch that's down with living it up on dirty money but who was *not* down with standing by her man not only as who he was, but who he wanted to be."

Buck stared at me yet again.

This time, his lips twitched while he did it.

Then he said, "Somethin' like that, yeah."

"How on earth did you hook up with her anyway?" I snapped.

"Babe, she's got a great ass," he told me then added, "Or she did."

I rolled my eyes then rolled them back to him to see he was full-on grinning. "Even so, a bitch is a bitch."

"Clara, honey, I was nineteen, I just lost my dad, a year later I lost my mom and my sister. I cut my brother out of my life. I was away from my people. She had a great ass, she gave great head, I was young, stupid and my brain was in my dick half the time. And when she's happy, gettin' what she wants, she's not a bitch. It's only when she doesn't get her way that she is."

"Still," I muttered, and he chuckled.

I looked down at him and felt the warmth from his body, sensed the power of it and realized, belatedly, that he'd been worried about what I would think about him and the life he'd led. And this was likely the reason he didn't share it with me.

I wasn't a risk taker. I made my moves cautiously, every step measured and filled with anxiety (until recently).

But I knew then—lying in Buck's bed in Buck's room in Buck's MC's hangout—that some risks were worth taking.

So I didn't measure my next step, and I didn't move cautiously.

I let go and prayed life would take me where I needed to be.

Doing this, I dropped my head and kissed his throat.

Leaving my lips there, I whispered, "Nothing you do, nothing you've done and nothing you'll ever do will make me look at you differently."

I felt his body turn to stone, but I still slid on top of it, running my lips down to his chest as his hands came up and sifted into my hair.

While this happened, I kept talking.

"I was as low as I could go with no way out, and you taught me to play pool, you gave me a hamburger, you made me laugh, and then you offered me a way out."

"Baby," he murmured, doing an ab curl, lifting us both up so I was straddling him and looking down at him.

His eyes were heated, but they closed when I pushed a hand between us and wrapped it around his cock.

"I know the kind of man you are, West Hardy," I whispered, and his eyes opened. Blazing now, they locked on mine. "Or I know who you are to me."

I stroked as I spoke and felt him harden in my hand. His hands glided along my skin and he dropped his head so his lips could do the same at my chest.

I kept stroking but slid the tip through the wetness between my legs, and I felt his growl against my skin as he cupped my breasts, the rough pads of his thumbs sliding across my nipples and that felt *nice*.

I wrapped my other arm around his shoulders and kept whispering, "And that man is *my* man, West."

He tipped his head back and looked at me.

"You about to fuck your man, baby?"

"Oh yeah," I whispered, grinning.

"Do me a favor, Toots."

"Anything."

One of his hands left my breast to cup the back of my head, bringing my lips to his.

"Do it hard," he ordered low, then his mouth opened under mine, and as his tongue thrust between my lips, my hand between us moved away, and I impaled myself on his cock.

I commenced doing the favor he asked for, doing myself a favor in return.

It was after I'd come, and he'd come. I was holding tight with my arms around him. I was still seated on him, and he was still hard and seated deep inside me. His hands were at my hips but back, his fingers pressing into the flesh of my behind. My breaths were heavy against his neck where I'd shoved my face and I could feel his against mine.

And I realized that despair I'd carried in my belly all my life was gone—gone completely—and my world was just as I wanted it to be.

There were issues. There were worries. And some of them were huge.

But life was life.

There always would be.

But *my* life. My real. My now. My world.

Was solid.

For the first time ever.

Because Buck made it that way.

Because Buck gave that to me.

I was about to tell him that, thank him for it, and lastly, and most importantly, tell him I loved him, when the door opened suddenly, crashing against the wall.

Buck's head snapped up, and my neck twisted.

And I stared in shocked disbelief mixed with no small amount of embarrassment, despair, and last, anger, at Nails standing in the door.

26

I LIKE IT LIKE THAT

"Get the fuck outta here," Buck growled as I tensed to move away. He didn't let me.

The fingers of one of his hands dug into my hip, putting pressure on, keeping me where I was, sitting astride and filled with him.

But his other hand moved out and swept the sheet up to my waist and his torso pressed against mine even as his eyes skewered Nails.

She ignored his order and listed into the room.

"Wanna party, baby?" she slurred.

Oh no.

It was even worse than it seemed, and already, it was bad.

Heart-breakingly bad.

Mortifyingly bad.

Unbelievably bad.

This bad being Buck's other woman walking in the second before I was going to confess my love for him.

And the thing making it worse, she was hammered.

"I said...get...the fuck...*out*." Buck was still growling.

She slipped to the side, her feet crossing over to right herself, and her eyes were hazy, but still, she managed to glue them to Buck.

"She's too straight, hunnnee," she mumbled. "You wanna party, I'll call Nonna. You like it like that. Nonna and me, we'll give you a pah..." she leaned forward, "*tee.*"

She stumbled with her lean, her hand flying out and touching the bed.

My eyes narrowed on her hand on the bed.

Oh no.

Hell no.

No to her touching my man's bed, not with me in it. I had to put up with knowing that stuff, I sure as hell didn't have to put up with seeing it.

I jumped off Buck, taking the sheet with me. Standing at the side of the bed, I wrapped it around me and bent, snatching up my panties.

I felt Buck come out of bed with me and saw his jeans disappear from the floor.

"Woman," he was *still* growling, "you turn your ass around and walk out, or I put you out, and you're shitfaced, but I think you get me when I say, I gotta put you out, that means you...are...*out.*" He paused before finishing, "Permanently."

I shimmied the undies up under the sheet, but my attention returned to see Buck buttoning his fly and noticing that Nails had straightened, but her torso was circling.

"You won't put me out," she whispered on a drunken, come-on smile.

"You don't move to the door, you'll see," Buck warned low.

"Baby," her lids hooded, and the word was an insinuation, one that wasn't lost on me, "we both know you don't *wanna* put me out."

Oh God.

My stomach clutched as I bent and quickly gathered the rest of my clothes.

And Buck moved.

I didn't watch to see what he did, not this time. I clasped my clothes to my chest and ran into the bathroom, slamming the door.

I was dressed and back in a now-empty room sitting on the side of the bed, my socks up, pulling on a boot when Buck stormed back in from wherever he'd taken Nails.

I glanced up at him, seeing he did whatever he did wearing only his jeans, then I looked back down at my boot and yanked up the zip.

"Babe—"

"No!" I cut him off, shaking my head and pulling on my other boot. "No, we're not talking about this. This didn't happen. You enjoy your party. Have fun. Do whatever it is you need to do. I just don't want to know. I'm going back to your house."

"She's trashed and that made her stupid and now she's no longer a problem," Buck stated.

"Whatever. I ask no questions, you tell no lies. But part of what I get is not having to discuss this," I muttered.

This was met with silence.

Then Buck asked, "What the fuck are you talking about?"

My head shot back, and I glared at him.

"Part of what I get is not having to discuss this," I repeated.

His hands went to his hips. "I heard you, babe, and I still don't know what the fuck you're talkin' about."

"I ask no questions, you tell no lies. I get it." I stood and ignored his brows snapping together. "I get it now. Lies tear people apart. If you don't have to lie, then that lie won't tear us apart. So that went down. We ignore it. I go to your house and you do what you have to do. It didn't happen. It doesn't happen. It happens for you, but it never, *never*, Buck, it *never* happens for me. That's what I get. *You* get what *you* get, but that's what you give to *me*."

I knew, but didn't care, that the snake was uncoiling when he said, low and lethal, "Clara, I'll ask you one more time and then I'll find another way to get you to tell me what in *the fuck* you're talkin' about."

"I know who she is," I announced.

"Yeah, babe, you saw her ridin' Gash. I know you know who she is."

"Right," I stated like that said it all because it gosh darned did!

"Right?" he asked like it didn't.

"Don't you stand there and lie to me, Buck."

"Babe, I'm warnin' you, this shit, it's pissin' me off, and I don't even know what this shit *is*."

That was another lie.

It wasn't pissing him off.

One look and the sound of his voice, I knew, for some insane reason, he already was.

He was pissed *at me* after his *other woman walked in when he was still inside me.*

"I can't believe you!" I shouted.

"What the fuck can't you believe?" he fired back. "Not ten minutes ago, your pussy's wrapped hot and tight around my cock and you're holdin' on like you'll never let go, and now I got a whole other woman on my hands, babe, pullin' fuckin' multiple personality bullshit on me."

"Oh no, you did not," I whispered. But it wasn't a whisper when I said, "Do not turn this on me!"

"Babe, for fuck's sake, *what the fuck are you talkin' about?*" he shouted, and he'd never shouted at me.

Not once.

Not ever.

And it snapped something in me.

I marched to him and shoved his chest then leaned into his face, in his space, up on my tiptoes.

"I was about to tell you I love you!" I yelled.

I watched his head jerk but kept right on ranting.

"Then your...whatever you call her...other woman, mistress, play-thing, *whatever*," I screeched the last word, "walks in. I know who she is *to you*, and I know I have to put up with it. I also know that *you* are supposed to hide that stuff from me. And now something beautiful has turned nasty and you're making it *worse* by standing there *lying to me.*"

"Jesus, fuckin' shit, Toots, you know this. I told you this the first goddamn night we met. I do *clean!*" he yelled.

"What?" I yelled back.

He bent, and I got off my toes or his angry face would have hit mine.

"I fuck clean. I *only* fuck clean. In any way I can get that clean. Nails is so dirty, the bitch is *polluted*. I do not fuck dirty."

At that, I whispered, "What?"

"Yeah," he clipped. "*You* are clean."

I stood still and stunned.

I pulled myself out of it and told him, "I saw you kissing her."

"The fuck you did."

"I did!" I snapped, my temper flaring again. "It was the day I went shopping with the girls that first time. I saw you sitting on a picnic table, kissing her."

"Fuckin' hell," he muttered, and then his eyes narrowed before he continued, "No, babe, you saw me sittin' on a picnic table coverin' for Gash. An old lady hits Ace at the same time a boy's hittin' a piece who's *not* his old lady, we cover."

"That's ridiculous," I hissed.

Even though I knew it wasn't. I'd seen Cruise jump into action to do that very same thing.

"And I wasn't kissin' her. Fuck, her mouth's been everywhere. I don't share that shit with my brothers. They do. I don't. Which is exactly my point."

"I saw it," I asserted.

"And I'm tellin' you, you did not," he shot back.

"I did!"

"Clara, Nails," he shook his head, "not too smart. You know the use of one kinda woman, the kind like you. You know the use of what you call groupies, women that like to have a good time, no hang-ups, they just wanna party. Then there are women like Nails. Nails, she thinks she can lead a man around by his dick. And she is not wrong. I've seen her do it. It doesn't last, but she gets off on it while it does. And she does it gettin' him addicted to her snatch. She opens it, wide and free, doin' that makin' it so she'll never *really* hook a man. And that isn't about her getting around. It's that she's stupid and she's ambitious. She aims high and her aim is me. So she fucks who she wants with an eye to me. And men will take what she offers, but they won't do it for long when she makes it obvious she's with one man and she's gagging for another one."

Well then.

That did sound stupid.

And ambitious.

Buck wasn't done.

"So she'll take what she can get, a boy lets her in, but she's been comin' after me. When you rolled in with the girls, Gash got the heads-up, he rolled Nails out, and I kept her occupied so Gash could get her washed off him and get to Minnie before Nails did something stupid if *she* got to Minnie. She had my attention, and Clara, that was the first time she had my attention, but she didn't see it for what it was. She was stupid enough to think she had a shot. She took it. She got in my space, and I let her. But she didn't kiss me. I didn't kiss her. No fuckin' way."

"You had your hand on her," I informed him.

"Yeah, so? It wasn't down her fuckin' pants. It was to keep the bitch from getting any closer to me."

This was true.

It wasn't down her pants.

"The girls told me she was yours."

"The girls would think that seein' as their *boys* told them that to save their own shit. She hangs around and she does it a lot. She's got a use, or she *did*, now she's out. But she had a use, they used it. Gash and Cruise aren't gonna say she's around so they can get a fuckin' blowjob anytime they're lookin' to get off."

Oh dear.

That made sense.

They wouldn't say that.

In fact, the rules were, they *couldn't.*

"Ink?" I asked quietly.

"Ink nailed her before Lorie. Ink finds a woman, he's like me."

"And, um..." I hesitated then went on, "what are you like?"

He scowled at me but didn't deign to answer.

Oh dear.

"But, uh...you're like that, but when we saw Gash, you were angry at him just for being what you called stupid."

"Yeah," he clipped.

"Stupid, Buck? Stupid enough to get caught?"

"Tell me, even though Minnie's a tough broad, she's good to the bone. Tell me what's more stupid than riskin' losin' her by hittin' a rank piece like Nails? Or any piece at all?"

Nothing.

Nothing was more stupid.

It was dawning on me I'd made a big mistake.

Though, since we were clearing the air...

"Who's Nonna?" I asked.

"Nonna's clean. I've hit Nonna. I've hit her more than once. She's here and she knows you are, and she knows *who* you are and what you are to me, so Nonna's smart enough to stay the fuck away from you and from me."

"I think..." I hesitated again then carried on, "I may have made an error in judgment."

His brows shot up. "You think?"

"Buck—"

"Now that your fuckin' head's straight, what I wanna know, you stood there tellin' me you love me at the same time you stood there tellin' me to do what I had to do, and I get it that you meant put my dick where I wanted to put it, and you didn't give a fuck that where I put it wasn't in you."

Uh-oh.

I had a feeling biker babe orientation and training had gone off the tracks somewhere along the line.

At least where Buck was concerned.

"Buck—"

"I gotta say, babe, I do not share. I don't know what fucked-up shit this is, but if you think you can let me be free so you can spread your legs for whoever you wanna take, I am *not* down with that."

"I wouldn't do that."

"I hope fuckin' not, because you think that, we got serious problems."

"I wouldn't do that," I repeated.

"Good, then now we gotta talk about why you wouldn't, but you got no problem lettin' me."

"Um..." I mumbled.

"You had no issue a minute ago spewin' shit, Clara, so speak the fuck up."

Okay, I was sensing he was mad. Madder than he'd ever been at me.

So I explained hurriedly, "Minnie, Lorie, and Pinky were Professor Higginsing me."

His head jerked again, then he asked, "What?"

"I told you weeks ago. They were Professor Higginsing my Eliza Biker Babe. Minnie was with me when I saw you with Nails. They gave me the lowdown about how I had to put up with certain, uh...*things*...if I wanted to keep you."

He stared at me hard a second, then he lifted a hand and ran his fingers through his hair, leaving his hand clenched around the back of his neck as he looked to the ceiling, muttering, "Fuckin' shit."

"They were trying to help," I told him quietly.

He dropped his hand and his head to look down on me.

"Yeah, they're good women. They tried to do right. It was *you* who fucked up."

"Sorry?"

"A-fuckin'-gain, you didn't read *me*. You didn't pay attention to the things I was sayin', and I'm seein' now you sure as fuck didn't pay attention to a fuckin' thing I was *doing*."

"Buck—"

"Babe, I like your tight jeans and I like your sexy boots, and you can keep wearin' 'em, if *you* like 'em. If you're tryin' to be something for me, you are *not* cluein' in, because I hooked you because of who you were, tight skirt and high heels that showed off your ass, but you had no fuckin' clue they showed off your ass and how good they did it. Thankin' me for offerin' you fuckin' refreshments when I was playin' you. Prim and fuckin' proper until I got that skirt around your waist and your ass in my hands and fucked you against the wall, then you were hot, and your mouth and pussy, babe, hot and sweet. And nothing's changed, even when you wear your tight jeans and fuck-me boots. The world and me, we get the cute librarian, but you're in my bed, it's only me that gets the wild sex kitten, and I like it like that."

I felt that familiar warm rush glide through me as I stared up at him and lamely murmured, "Oh."

"Oh," he bit back.

"Buck," I whispered.

"No, Toots, nope." He shook his head and stepped away from me. "Months, I been there. Months, we been together. You didn't ask me about those picture frames, even though, more than once, I saw you studyin' 'em. It was *me* who had to come clean about that shit. Months, not only those frames, but you never asked *dick* about me. Now I find out, months you think I've been steppin' out on you, with fuckin' Nails.

Christ," he clipped. "We were even both together when we saw her with Gash, and you didn't say a fuckin' word."

"Buck—"

"You just kept your trap shut, ready and willing to let me be an asshole and play you, but it's not me playin' you, is it, Clara? It's you who's been playin' me."

I felt my stomach drop as I whispered, "Sorry?"

"Babe, I'm seein' you'd put up with a lot and do what you gotta do, *anything* you gotta do, to keep a roof over your head, your belly full and money in your account."

I took a step back.

He didn't just say that to me.

"Did you just say that to me?" I asked.

"How long's it gonna last?" he asked back. "'Til I find Tia, or confirm she bit it, then you take what you can get and motor?"

He did.

He said that to me.

All of it.

And he thought that about me.

He thought that about me.

I was in love with him. I even told him that. It was in a rant, but he heard me.

And he thought that about me.

I stared at him and didn't say a word.

I was wrong.

Again, I was wrong.

I had no stinking *clue* what love was.

Sure, I could see, considering he didn't do what I thought he did, not only didn't do the actual act with Nails, he just didn't do that *at all*, that he'd be angry I thought he did.

And I could even see he'd be *incredibly* angry about that. He was entitled. I'd feel the same way if the tables were turned.

I'd messed up.

Huge.

What I *could not see* was Buck saying I was trying to live in his world to keep a roof over my head and food in my stomach.

I wasn't doing that.

I was doing it because I was *falling in love with him.*

I turned to the dresser where my purse was, opened it, pulled out my wallet and cell phone. I walked to the bed, flipping through the bills, keeping only what I needed, which wasn't much. Then again, I'd never needed much. I threw the rest on the bed and tossed the cell phone he bought me next to it.

"Clara—"

My head snapped around to face him but only for the briefest of moments.

Then I aimed my eyes at my boots, turned and walked his way.

But I only headed in that direction because that was where the door was.

He wrapped his fingers around my upper arm, and I stopped.

"Fuck, Clara—"

Viciously, I yanked from his hold. "Your new office girl can call Mrs. Jimenez if she has any questions about where to find anything. I'll call her back."

"Jesus, babe," he clipped, grabbing hold of me again.

It was then I looked him dead in the eyes.

"We're done, West. I'm out. And you can hold me where I want to be, but you can't force me to be where I *don't* want to be."

"Babe—"

"Take your hand off me."

"Toots—"

"Take your hand off me!" I screamed.

He didn't take his hand off me. He tried to draw me in front of him.

I didn't let him.

With a savage twist I tore free.

Then I ran, fast.

I was wearing high-heeled boots, but Buck was barefoot, bare-chested in late October and his boys were drunk, randy and having a good time, thus it was not easy to get their attention.

Therefore, I got away.

Kind of.

See, running down Bell Road in a blind search for a payphone to call a cab, a car stopped beside me.

The door was thrown open, a man got out and hooked me at the waist, pulled me into the car with him and reached across me to slam the door.

Then he ordered the driver, "Go."

The car shot forward.

In the throes of yet *another* kidnapping, thus in a panic, I looked at the driver.

It was Tia.

27

HE HAS NO PROBLEM BRANCHING OUT

I looked from my place on the couch across the open-plan living room into Detective Rayne Scott's kitchen, and I stared at Scott and the tall, handsome, dark blond man Tia called Damian.

"Clara, honey, you okay?" Tia asked me, and I turned my attention to her sitting close to me on the couch.

"No," I whispered, "but I'm glad you are."

"Honey," she whispered back.

"I thought you were dead," I told her quietly.

"I'm sorry. I tried to call, but by the time I could, I called Mrs. Jimenez and her number had been disconnected. I didn't remember her cell number, and those aren't listed. Damian sent a man to your apartment, and the man said you and Mrs. Jimenez both were gone. I didn't know how else to reach you."

"She moved, and got a new number, but she told me she arranged the service so her new one was announced," I explained.

"It wasn't."

Oh dear.

Perhaps we should have checked.

I stared at my friend. Then I hooked her behind the neck and pulled her forehead to mine and closed my eyes.

"Doesn't matter," I said softly, opened my eyes and looked into hers. "You're here now."

"Yeah, Clara, I'm here now," she replied, just as softly.

We stared into each other's eyes, and I watched her smile. Then I let her go but we both only moved back a bit.

"I'm sorry that here is here," she said to me.

"What?"

"Detective Scott's place. I know that you...that he..." She shook her head and continued, "He's Damian's friend. I told Damian you wouldn't like it, but he said it was safe for you and for me."

A police detective's apartment was probably as safe as you were going to get.

I nodded.

"And I know we both decided to actively hate him for the rest of our days, but I've found out he's kind of a nice guy," she went on.

I looked into the kitchen to see both sets of eyes, one light brown (Scott) one hazel (Damian) aimed in the direction of the couch.

They didn't look away.

I did.

"Yeah," I replied. "But let's talk about where the heck you've been for-blinkety-blank-ever."

"I want to talk about why you were running from Ace in the Hole," she said to me.

"No." I shook my head. "Your car was found filled with blood. That story takes priority. Any story that includes pools of my best friend's blood takes priority."

Her face got soft.

"You knew about that?"

I nodded.

"Oh, honey," she whispered.

"Talk to me," I urged.

She didn't make me wait, she got closer and shared.

"Well, when we made our plans, after I hung up, I kind of got excited. Of course, I was totally scared, but you sounded so confident, I was also excited. And I remembered, you and me together, we always made it through. We always survived. I also started to remember some of the stuff we went through and how I knew what was happening was worse, way worse. But together, we could take care of each other."

She paused.

I nodded because she was right.

We'd always made it through.

I wished we'd remembered that earlier.

She kept going.

"So something was going down and there was no one in the house. All Enrique's guys left with him, and I thought it was a sign, telling me we had our opportunity. But I decided to get smart. I took stuff I knew was worth money and I took stuff that I knew Enrique had. I decided we didn't just need money, we needed insurance."

Uh-oh.

"What'd you take?"

"I didn't even know. I just knew he wouldn't want me to have it. Files, papers, photos and flash drives. What I didn't know was that he *really* didn't want me to take it."

"Oh, Tia," I whispered, stunned she would do something like that, scared for her even though it was over and admiring that she had the courage.

"Anyway, when you didn't show, I worried something was wrong. But I'd stolen stuff, I couldn't go home. So I hung out in Phoenix as long as I could and laid low, hoping to connect with you. I kept going by your place, but I was worried they'd look for me there and your lights were never on and Mrs. Jimenez was never home either."

Staying with Raymundo because she'd been tied up.

Darn.

Tia kept talking.

"Then, I saw them, and they saw me cruising your house, and I had no choice but to go. They followed me, but I thought I lost them. I decided to get set up in Seattle and find a way to contact you and you could meet me there. I needed to ditch my car though, so, in Nevada, I sold it to a used car salesman and traded it in for new wheels. What I didn't know was that they'd been following me. They forced me off the road, and that's when I also found out Damian was following me."

"Um...who *is* Damian?" I whispered, leaning super close.

She smiled.

I stared, and I stared at the *way* she was smiling.

Oh my.

"You wouldn't believe me if I told you," she whispered back.

"Try me," I invited.

She shook her head.

"Later, when he can't hear. He can hear everything. He's, like, Superman or something."

She said this like it was a good thing. The absolute *best*.

I forced my eyes to stay on hers rather than look again into the kitchen at a tall, blond, hazel-eyed Superman.

"Anyway," she went on, "there was a firefight. I was caught in the middle of it. Damian won the firefight. I was injured, and I have no idea what happened to the other guys, because I was sort of bleeding a lot and not paying attention. But Damian took me, the stuff I had on Enrique, and then we holed up in a house in the mountains. He stitched me up, I recuperated while he stayed with me and now, we're back to rescue you."

I was staring at her again.

"He stitched you up?"

"Yeah."

"You were in a firefight where you were wounded by bullets, and he *stitched you up?*"

"In another life, he was a field medic."

I kept staring at her.

"Honey," I said quietly. "Field medics *patch* you up so they can stabilize you to be transported to surgeons who'll *stitch* you up."

"He's very confident. He has no problem branching out."

Oh my *God*.

"Tia—" I started.

"Now...you," she demanded.

"No, you aren't done. Are you safe? Who *is* he? What happens next?"

She smiled at me. "It's all good. Damian gave the stuff I had to Rayne. He told me Rayne is," she lifted her fingers and did air quotation marks, "*running with it*, whatever that means. We just needed to get to

Phoenix, give it to him, pick you up, and then Damian is taking us to Seattle or wherever we want to go."

"When did you get home?"

"About five hours ago. We got here and Rayne told Damian you were hooked up with the Aces High Motorcycle Club. He made some calls, found out West Hardy was at a party there, told us you were likely with him, and if we wanted to find you, we had to go to a party. But we got there, and there you were, running down the street. That was pretty surprising. Rayne said you were solid with what he called," more air quotation marks, "*the MC*, but I didn't believe that. My Clara doesn't run with a motorcycle club."

Hmm.

She smiled again. "And I was right. You were running away."

Hmm.

"I was solid with them," I admitted, and this time, *she* blinked.

Then she leaned into me. "What?"

"If Damian has Superman ears, my story is for later. *A lot* later."

Her eyebrows shot up. "Why?"

"Because it's private, personal, and when I tell you, I want it to be just between you and me."

She examined my face and I knew she read it because hers got soft again and she whispered, "Okay, honey."

That was my Tia.

My Tia.

My Tia could read me.

And she wasn't dead. She was sitting right next to me.

Not dead.

Not dead.

I moved forward, wrapped my arms around her, gave her a tight hug, and it took a lot, a whole lot, but I managed to do this without sobbing.

"I've been so worried," I said in her ear, my voice sounding clogged.

"I'm sorry," she said back, her voice clogged too.

I held on and Tia held me back, and we did this for a long time.

Finally, she gave me a squeeze and we let go.

I took in a shaky breath.

Tia spoke.

"So, tomorrow, we'll get your stuff and we'll head out."

I shook my head.

"No stuff. We'll just go."

Her brows knitted. "What?"

"Buck has my stuff and I'm leaving it. Fresh start all around. I have a little money in the bank. We'll just go visit Mrs. Jimenez so she can see you're okay and we can say good-bye, and then we'll go."

"You can't leave your stuff."

"I can."

"You can't, Clara. They took everything from you, but you held on to what you had left. You have to hold on to what you have. You *always* hold on to what you have. We both know that."

We did.

We'd learned that early, packing our little suitcases with our meagre belongings that were prized possessions and taking it from foster home to foster home.

Still, I was letting it go.

"I'll get a job making coffee and buy tie-dyed shirts and hippie jeans. I'll be good."

"Clara—"

"We're leaving it."

"Honey—"

I couldn't do this.

I *could not* do this.

Not right now.

Buck thought I'd been using him.

When I'd been falling in love with him.

I felt the tears sting my eyes, and I whispered, "Don't. Please. Don't."

She examined my face again.

Then my sweet Tia whispered, "Okay."

"This is unnecessary, I can take the couch," I told Detective Rayne Scott as I stood by his big, very comfy-looking bed in his bedroom while he opened a dresser drawer.

I was freaking out because the arrangement was, I was sleeping in his bed, and I was freaking out more because the arrangement included Damian and Tia sleeping *together* on the queen bed in his second bedroom.

"I'm good on the couch," he muttered, pulling something out of the drawer.

"No, really, I can sleep anywhere."

"Good," he stated, closing the drawer and turning to me, carrying a T-shirt. "Then I'll know you won't be tossing and turning here."

Oh dear.

"Listen, I—" I started, but he made it to me, and his hand came up and curled around the top of my shoulder.

"Clara, I'm a cop. Cops learn early to read people. On you, sweetheart, I'm readin' heartbreak. It's written all over your face. What you need to do is take my tee, put it on, climb into bed and go to sleep. What you do *not* need to do is expend the little energy you got left discussin' somethin' meaningless with me."

I didn't know what to say.

He was right.

And Tia was right.

So I also suspected he was a nice guy.

More than nice.

So I said, "Okay."

He nodded and let me go. "Okay."

Then he handed me the T-shirt, I took it and he started to the door.

"Rayne," I called, he stopped and turned back to me. "Thank you," I whispered.

He stood there and stared at me, his eyes moved to the bed and they came back to me.

He then tipped his chin up and walked out, closing the door behind him.

I took off my clothes, folded them and put them on the armchair in the corner that was also comfy-looking, perfect for curling up and reading a book. I donned his tee, climbed into his bed and turned off the bedside lamp.

What I didn't do was sleep.

Not for a while.

And I had a feeling my track record for sleep was about to take a major hit.

First, I stared into the darkness.

After that, I stared into it some more.

A while of that, I turned my face into Detective Rayne Scott's pillow, and I cried.

And cried.

I kept doing it.

Until I'd cried myself to sleep.

28

IS THIS REALLY HAPPENING?

Getting to sleep late after a crying jag, I woke late and found, when looking in Rayne's mirror in his master bathroom, that I had puffy eyes.

Fantastic.

I made his bed, folded his T-shirt, put it on his pillow and donned my clothes.

Then I went out and found Tia alone in the kitchen.

She smiled at me. "Coffee?"

"Please."

She got up and got me a mug.

I sat down at the kitchen table in a bay window and looked out at the Phoenician sunshiny day.

"Sleep okay?" Tia asked, sliding the brew on the table in front of me.

I looked down and told the mug, "No."

I picked it up and took a sip as Tia perched on a bent leg on a chair across from me.

"The boys are gone, we can talk now," she said softly.

"That's good since I'd like to know why you're sleeping with Superman Damian Field Medic in Another Life."

Her eyes got dreamy.

Oh wow.

"You like him," I whispered my observation.

"Yeah," she whispered her answer.

"Tia—"

She didn't let me start.

"He makes me feel good." She closed her eyes and did short shakes of her head before opening them again. "I don't know. I don't know how to explain it, but he makes me feel good...*about me*. I never thought I'd like to..." she pressed her lips together and released them, leaning forward and whispering, "*you know*, again, not after what Enrique let those men do to me."

I nodded to her.

I knew.

I knew something else too.

If he'd wrought this miracle, Damian was *all kinds* of Superman.

"And you like to...*you know*...with Damian?" I queried.

Her eyes got dreamy again.

She liked it.

She definitely liked it.

Wow.

And...

Yippee!

"So Superman Damian seduced a convalescing gunshot victim?" I asked on a tease.

"Oh yeah," she answered then giggled.

I couldn't help it, it had been so long since I'd heard her giggle, and I'd thought I'd never hear it again, I giggled with her.

My heart wasn't in it.

But that didn't mean I wasn't really happy for my best friend.

She wiped her eyes and then shared, "At first, he was very gentle."

"I hope so," I replied on a grin.

"Then, I got stronger, and, um...not so much."

I started laughing because I could see, plainly, she liked the *not so much*.

Carefully, I asked, "Did you share about what Enrique did to you?"

She shook her head. "I didn't have to. He knew all about it. And he doesn't care, Clara, not even a little bit."

Okay, maybe Damian *was* Superman.

I took a sip of coffee and continued my interrogation.

"So I take it he's hanging in Seattle with us?"

The happy went out of her face and she looked out the window.

That wasn't good.

"Tia?" I prompted, and she looked back at me.

Then she shrugged.

"I don't know. I don't care. His life is kind of...different. He has no roots. I don't know if he wants to be rooted with me. If he does, then I'll take it. I'll snatch it up and I'll take it. If he doesn't, if he needs to be...out there...I'll let him. But now, I just like feeling..." she shook her head and then finished, "*me* again. Or who I think I'm meant to be. And I like being with him and I'll take from him whatever he's willing to give me."

I wanted more for her, but I also knew that we two, we had to settle for as good as we could get.

And Damian made her smile, made her giggle when she talked about him and made her feel good about herself again, and that was pretty darned good.

So I reached out, grabbed her hand and squeezed it.

I let her go, took another sip of coffee and sent a wish silently to the universe that rootless Damian would want to grow roots with my Tia.

Hopefully in Phoenix.

"Now you," she stated. "We're alone, so you can tell me all about this Buck guy."

I shook my head and it was my turn to look out the window.

"Clara, honey—"

I looked back at her and interrupted, "I can't." I shook my head again. "I will, but I can't now. What happened, happened right before you and Damian found me. It's too new. It hurt too much. The wound is too raw."

I watched her face get soft. "Oh, babe."

"Yeah," I whispered.

"That bad?"

I couldn't speak, my heart had slid into my throat, so I nodded.

"Babe," she whispered.

I bit my lip and looked out the window.

"Well!" she said suddenly, and I turned back at her. "The good news is, the boys talked this morning. Rayne knows where your stuff is, so he and Damian went to get it."

Oh.

My.

God!

"Pardon?" I breathed.

She smiled at me, for once not reading me.

"Rayne knows where this Buck lives. They went up to—"

She stopped talking because I bolted from my chair, spilling coffee on the table and the floor.

"No!" I shouted, panicked. "Call them! Call them now! Tell them to come back."

She was staring up at me, her face pale.

"I can't, honey. I mean, I can. But they left well over an hour ago—"

Oh God, no.

Over an hour.

Plenty of time to get to Buck's house and make him furious, furious when he sees Rayne Scott and thinks I've moved on to my next mark not even a day after I walked away from my last one.

That last one being him.

I put my coffee cup down, muttering, "This can't be happening."

"Clara, babe, what on earth are you so upset about?" she asked, rising slowly from her seat.

"I told you I was leaving my stuff!" I yelled.

"You can't leave your stuff!" she yelled back.

I shook my head. "He's going to be mad."

"So what? It's *your* stuff."

"You don't get it!" I shouted, throwing up my hands. "He'll see Rayne and think—"

"Good," Tia snapped. "I see you. I see he hurt you. He sees good-looking Rayne and he deserves to think whatever he thinks!"

I stared at her and I knew Damian *was* Superman. She was again

Tia pre-Enrique with a hint of attitude and the protective instinct of a lioness.

I was in trouble.

The front door opened, and I looked into the living room to see Rayne and Damian coming through.

I also heard the pipes.

I knew those pipes.

People who weren't around motorcycles for weeks on end wouldn't hear the difference. But all the pipes on Harleys were different, distinctive, and those were Buck's pipes.

Oh God.

Rayne prowled directly to me, stopped toe to toe and bent his neck so his face was in mine.

"You know he's here," he stated.

"I know," I whispered.

"He was not real thrilled to open his door to me," he went on.

Oh God.

"I know," I repeated on a whisper.

"You can stay in here and I can have him removed."

My body jolted involuntarily.

"Removed?"

There came a pounding at the door.

Oh God!

"I'll call the cops, Clara," Rayne explained.

More pounding at the door.

Oh *God!*

"No," I shook my head. "No cops."

"Clara," both his hands came up and curled around either side of my neck, "make a smart choice here."

"No cops."

"Sweetheart, you wanted me to protect you when that shit went down with Kirk. I'm tellin' you now, you ask, you got my protection. I'll see that you're safe and I'll see that you're taken care of. That's a promise."

I had a feeling he meant more than just calling his buddies in, and I couldn't go there.

I needed to do this with Buck, whatever it was going to be, get my stuff and go to Seattle.

And then back to my vow of no more men...

Ever.

"I need to finish it with him," I whispered.

I whispered that, barely able to get it out, even in a whisper.

Because it had to be said, I didn't *want* to finish things with Buck.

However, with what he said to me, what he thought of me, I needed to.

And now that this was happening, I also realized that Tia was right.

I needed my things.

Like that little girl I was with her crappy stuff in her crappy little suitcase, I needed to hold on to everything I had because I had no idea what was around the corner, so I had to keep what I'd earned close.

You never knew when you'd get more.

All you knew was that you couldn't afford to lose what you had.

"Sweetheart—"

"I need to do this."

He stared into my eyes and I stared into his.

It hit me that his eyes were ones I could stare into a long time and never, never get bored.

But that was for a different woman.

Not the woman that was me.

Nope, it would seem the good stuff was never for the woman that was me.

I just hoped, whoever that woman turned out to be, she knew she was lucky.

"Then do it," he said gently.

I nodded, inhaled through my nose, he let me go, and I walked to the door.

I opened it to see the snake coiled out there, ready to strike.

Now, if you asked me to tell you the top five things I thought West Hardy would do when I opened the door to a police detective's apartment, what he did was not one of those five things.

It wouldn't have been in the top ten.

Or even twenty.

Maybe even thirty.

And this was because what he did was immediately dip a shoulder, plant it in my stomach, wrap his arm around the backs of my thighs, heft me up and stalk away.

"*Oh my God!*" I heard Tia scream.

"Buck!" I shouted.

"Jesus fuckin' Christ," I heard Rayne clip.

"Buck!" I repeated on a shout.

"Shut it, Toots," Buck growled and stalked down the stairs that led up to Rayne Scott's apartment.

"Put me down!" I yelled.

"Shut it," he clipped.

"Put her down!" Tia yelled, and I knew she was chasing after us.

Buck planted me on my feet by his bike.

I took a step away, and he hooked an arm around my waist and hauled me to his body.

With that done, he turned his head to Tia.

"Shit, babe," he said. "I got everyone I know in fifty states lookin' for your girl, you're out one night, and there she fuckin' is."

Was he for real?

I pushed against his arm. "Let me go."

His angry eyes sliced to me.

"You're on the back of my bike."

"Let me go!" I yelled.

"Hardy, let her go," Rayne stated.

He and Superman Damian were also there.

Fantastic.

"Do me a favor," Buck said to Tia, ignoring Rayne. "Get her purse."

"Are you *nuts?*" Tia screeched, the last word so high it was a wonder all the glass in Rayne Scott's very nice apartment complex didn't explode.

"Let me go!" I shouted, pulling against Buck's arm, and he looked back down at me.

"You're in love with me," he declared.

"Not anymore," I shot back.

"Darlin', you can't fall outta love in one night."

"Why not?" I returned. "I fell into it in one night."

Buck blinked slowly.

Then he grinned.

All his anger gone.

Vanished—*poof!*— in one second.

Then, because the universe hated me, his other arm closed around me, he bent his head and he kissed me.

That's right.

He *kissed* me

Long, hard, deep and open-mouthed.

And weak, stupid me, I let him.

When his mouth released mine, I was holding on to his shoulders and it was me who was blinking, and I did it so much I finally blinked sense into myself.

"Let me go," I whispered.

"I was a dick," he whispered back.

"Yes, that's why you need to let me go."

"Clara, baby, I've told you, I'm not lettin' you go."

"You were mean to me."

"You pissed me off."

"So?"

"You told me you were okay with me fuckin' other women."

"I did not!" I snapped. "I told you that's the way the biker babes told me I was supposed to be."

"Yeah, babe, and that was fucked."

"Gotta say, I like this guy's style," Superman Damian put in at this point.

"*Damian!*" Tia shrieked.

"Tia, honey, look at him. He's into her," Damian replied.

"I don't care! You don't carry a woman out of an apartment. That's crazy!"

"I've carried you places," Damian returned.

"Yes, but I was *bleeding* from multiple *gunshot wounds.*"

Multiple?

Damian looked at Buck. "Bro, you want me to shoot her? It'll help you get an in with her best friend."

"Pass," Buck replied, sounding amused.

Amused!

"Oh my God," Tia muttered, glaring at Damian.

"Is this really happening?" I asked Rayne.

Rayne shook his head, but he answered, "Yes."

God!

I looked back at Buck and yelled, "Let me go!"

"Babe," was his response.

Ugh!

"She wants you to let her go!" Tia shouted.

"Honey, look at her," Damian urged. "Your friend spent all night crying about this guy."

Oh no.

Was it that obvious?

"And?" Tia shot back.

Darn.

It was that obvious.

"Tia, beautiful," Damian said quietly, snaking an arm around her waist and pulling her close. "*Look* at her. She's right where she wants to be."

I glared at Damian.

Tia studied me.

"Do you mind?" Buck requested, then finished, "Privacy."

"Fuckin' hell," Rayne muttered.

Tia kept studying me.

I kept glaring at Damian.

Damian drew her back, murmuring, "Let's go."

Tia looked at him, then at me, then she made her decision.

"I'll be right upstairs."

I turned my glare to her.

She pulled in her lips and bit them as Damian moved her to the stairs.

Rayne didn't move.

He planted his fists on his hips and his eyes were locked on me.

"Scott, you need to find your own woman," Buck stated.

Rayne's eyes cut to him, and he clipped, "Bite me."

Then he looked at me again and his gaze dropped to Buck's arms around me. A muscle jumped in his cheek and his gaze came back to mine.

Then *he* made a decision.

"It doesn't go your way, sweetheart, all you gotta do is yell."

Fantastic.

Even the police were deserting me.

I didn't respond because I didn't get a chance. Rayne turned and jogged up the stairs.

When he disappeared from sight, I kept my attention on the stairs.

Buck's hand cupped the side of my face and forced it forward just as he tipped it back and dipped his close.

"You been cryin'?" he asked gently.

"No."

His eyes roamed my face then caught mine again before he whispered, "Liar."

"Buck, seriously, let me go."

"I was a dick."

"You already said that."

"Now you need to get over it and get your ass on the back of my bike."

He wasn't annoying.

He was *infuriating!*

"You said some mean things."

"And you already said that."

"They were *mean*, Buck, awful. Below the belt. You accused me of using you."

His arms got tighter and his face got closer.

"Clara, baby, we were havin' a good night. No," he shook his head once, "not a good night, a fuckin' *great* one."

I felt my chest get tight.

He was right. We were.

The best.

Making love. Sharing souls. Accepting each other just as we were.

The kind of night that changed lives and altered worlds.

"Then Nails crashes our party and you lose it and tell me you love me in the middle of a rant at the same time tellin' me you're okay with me fuckin' other women," Buck regrettably continued.

"I didn't actually say that, Buck. I was ranting because I didn't *want* to say it."

"Yeah, babe, but look at it this way. Last night, I gave you me. You didn't ask for it, but I gave it to you. And when I did, you didn't fuckin' hesitate with showin' me that givin' you me was as important to you as it was to me. And you said words to me, Toots, words that meant a fuckin' lot. Words that, if you were in my bed, on my bike, believin' in me the way you do, would mean I'd have had the balls to move on what Aces was doin' and I'd have done that a long time ago. Then, not an hour later, you're tellin' me you're happy to give pieces of me away. Important pieces. That pissed me off, Clara. The things you said, the way you were, that meant somethin' to me, and then you gave it away."

"I didn't," I whispered.

"I took it that way," he pointed out the obvious.

"You were wrong," I told him.

"Yeah, I was. And I got pissed and said some shit that was jacked because of it."

"Stuff comes out when you're angry, honest stuff, and that tells me somewhere in the back of your head you think I've been using you."

"Stuff comes out when you're angry, Clara, stupid, jacked-up stuff that you say just because you're angry and you don't mean a fuckin' word. You hurt and then, no matter it's wrong, you can't stop yourself. You hurt so much, you wanna strike back."

Darn, he was right.

And I'd hurt him.

I'd hurt him by accusing him of cheating on me.

Worse, saying I was okay with that. Okay with him giving away pieces of himself that belonged to me.

They belonged *to me*.

If he said that to me, if he told me, even in the beginning, he was okay with me playing the field, giving myself to someone else, that would have gutted me.

Definitely now.

Yeah.

Darn.

He was right.

I pulled in my lips, bit them, and pushed my cheek against his hand to look away as the tears stung my eyes.

"Baby, look at me," he whispered.

"No."

"Clara, honey, fuckin' look at me."

I shook my head and inhaled sharply through my nose to control the tears.

Then I felt his mouth at my ear.

"You're not reading me again," he whispered there.

I let my lips go and clenched my teeth.

He went on, "You think I'd get that pissed if I didn't love you too?"

At his words, my eyes instantly unfocused and my body went statue still.

His arm around me got even tighter and his lips moved to the skin of my neck where he said, "Clara, I love you."

I remained statue still.

His hand at my jaw tensed. "Toots, baby, please, for fuck's sake, look at me."

My head turned, his lifted, and I looked at him.

"You love me?" I whispered.

His thumb swept my cheekbone.

"Yeah," he whispered back.

"When?" I asked.

"What?"

"When did you know you loved me?"

His thumb moved to sweep my bottom lip when he replied, "When you were pullin' back Tatie's hair when she was pukin' in the toilet."

Seriously?

"That's gross," I declared.

He grinned a small grin. "Babe, you were lookin' after my girl even after she'd been a bitch to you." His head dropped, he touched his mouth to mine before lifting it again and saying quietly, "You look after everyone. Savin' Jimbo a cupcake and chattin' with Gear on the deck and doin' somethin' with Tatie's space so she feels at home when she's at home and makin' Minnie feel important by listenin' to her babble about her biker babe shit. But only *I* get to look after you."

Oh dear.

That felt nice.

It felt nicer, how much he paid attention.

I closed my eyes and whispered, "West."

"Get on the back of my bike, babe."

I opened my eyes and noted quietly, "You have a really, *really* foul temper, Buck. It comes out physically and it comes out verbally, and I get understanding a person and how they react to things, adjusting your behavior when you can and letting them be who they are. But I cannot live with the worry I'm going to do something and you're going to strike, poisoning me or us with your anger."

"Then I'll get a lock on it."

I was again blinking rapidly.

"Sorry?" I asked.

"You're right. I let loose and it isn't cool. Think you get from what you saw of her, the scar I got that's a constant reminder, that Kristy, when she blows, she's worse than me. A lot worse. Grab a knife and carve your anger into someone worse. I learned through years with her, you're backed against a wall in a relationship, a family is at stake, you fight fire with fire, babe. You are not that. You are not Kristy. I haven't had a long-term situation since her. And I've never had a long-term situation without her. And then I got one and I didn't adjust. I was asking you to adjust, and I didn't do it. Now, I'll do it."

He'd mentioned just last night that he'd been nineteen when he met her.

Still, really, a boy.

And all he knew was her.

And now...me.

I wanted to believe what he said.

I really, *really* did.

However.

"Easy as that?" I asked quietly.

"No. Figure I'll fuck up again. But you gotta know, a man gets his head straight real fuckin' fast when his woman gets the look on her face I planted on yours and she runs away from him, disappearing in the night. I gave you the worst in me, and right after I did, you told me nothin' I could do would ever make you look at me differently. And not an hour passed, and I did somethin' ugly that made you look at me differently."

Yes.

He really paid attention.

"That tat I got?" he asked.

"What?" I asked back when he said no more.

"That tat I got, Clara. The one that says, 'never again?'"

I nodded.

"That is about never letting a woman treat me like shit like Kristy did. Dragging our kids down with it. Imploding our family because she wants what she wants and nothin' else matters. Now it's also about never forgetting that look on your face, baby. Watchin' your hair fly as you ran away from me. I will never..."

Abruptly, he shook his head before he dipped his face closer to mine.

And when he spoke again, his voice was low and coarse.

"*Ever*, darlin', forget that. And I'll never make you feel that way again. Thinking about it now, feels like I got a knife in my gut, but this time, it was me that drove it there."

I didn't want him to feel that.

In fact, I wanted to take that feeling away.

All that he was feeling because he wasn't hiding any of it.

And it meant the world to have it, a precious gift, even if it was difficult watching him experience it.

But we still had something to go over.

"And if I stand in your way, will—?"

"Honey, I see somethin' else happenin' here. I keep tellin' you to read me, and straight up, you gotta learn to do that. But I also gotta use my words. I'll start now. If you did not think that day and the time after I was not runnin' scared, you need to pay a fuckuva lot more attention."

Running scared?

Buck?

"Wh-what?" I stammered.

"You were distant from me all day because I marked you, and I spent all day tryin' to figure out how I could make you trust me again. Talked to Ink about it. Chap. You're at home with my baby girl and my son, you and my boy lookin' out for Tatie after what happened to her. I was out tryin' to figure out how I could erase what I did to you. I get home, you're on the phone, you let me kiss your nose, then you don't even come out and say hey. You go right to bed with my girl."

That day...

After Tatie was hurt.

He was...

"You were out...talking to the guys...about how to—?"

His eyes got a look I'd seen in them only once before.

When he'd seen the bruise on my shoulder.

Anguish.

Oh my God.

"Clara, I *marked* you. Think about it. Think about bein' so out-of-your-brain pissed, you did something that hurt me."

I flinched.

"Yeah," he grunted.

"You talked to Ink and Chap about it?" I asked softly.

"Mistake. I told him, Ink was so pissed at me, I thought he'd throw down. And Chap was so disappointed in me, I thought he'd kick my ass out of his house. But he didn't. He sat me down and said I had to do my time. I had to sort my shit and do my time. I had to remind you why you were there, get my shit straight so it never happened again and do my time."

"Do your time?"

"However long it took to make you trust me again. And babe, we'll just say a few of the boys heard you screamin' at me then saw you run outta the Dive last night, and by the time I hit the bar, I had so many angry faces up in mine, I had no hope of followin' you."

Wow.

"*Wow*," I whispered.

"They dig you," he muttered.

They dug me.

And suddenly, I was reading Buck.

Reading and reading and reading.

Reading soaking tubs.

And reading him wanting to make sure I liked my job, felt fulfilled there, and I didn't need more.

And reading, not days into us being us, him making me go out with Lorie, Minnie, and Pinky and make friends in his world, have a girl posse who would also have my back.

Reading him shielding me from losing hope about Tia.

Reading him not caring all that much if he got me pregnant.

Reading him teasing me about buying islands and bikinis.

And how he didn't mind if I called Rayne about Rogan's money, he just wished he'd been there to have my back if Rayne upset me.

Reading how hard it was for him to share things about himself that he worried would color the way I thought of him.

Reading how he'd never let me go.

Reading.

And reading.

And reading.

Something was happening in my belly. It felt like a soda pop was fizzing there.

How I'd missed all this, I did not know.

I had been at my lowest ebb and I was in survival mode.

But I'd quit surviving the minute he carried me out of Lefty's clinic.

And from that point on, me and the man in my life had been falling in love.

"Now, Toots, you gonna get on the back of my bike?"

"Tia," I said.

"Are you gonna get on the back of my bike?"

"Yes, West. Of course I am. I love you."

He closed his eyes and his forehead landed on mine with a thud.

Oh my.

He really, *really* loved me.

"Baby," I whispered

He opened his eyes and lifted away.

"Tia," I repeated.

He shook his head. "Reunion can continue tonight over enchiladas.

Now we're goin' home and havin' make-up sex." I stared at him and he concluded, "All day."

My eyes got big. "All day make-up sex?"

His hand slid from my jaw down to the side of my neck where he squeezed. "Okay, maybe not all day, since the kids'll be here tonight, but we're stayin' in bed all day. Eventually I'll need to crash, or enchiladas will be shit."

"You need to crash?"

"Babe, sat up all night waitin' for you to come home. You raced outta Ace and disappeared into thin air. Then fuckin' Scott shows at my door sayin' you're with him and he wants your shit. So I've been up all night and spent the mornin' pissed as hell and scared as fuck and on the back of my bike comin' into the Valley to deal with my woman. Now I'm not pissed, I've dealt with my woman and we're goin' home, we're fuckin' then we're crashin'."

That soda pop feeling was getting stronger and it was *effervescent*.

"You sat up all night waiting for me to come home?"

"No, I got on my bike, left Ace and went to Mrs. Jimenez's place and waited for you to show there. When you didn't, I figured you'd cooled down and went home. So I went home and you weren't there. Then I stayed up and waited for you to cool down and come home 'cause you tossed out your money, Toots, and someone'd have to pay the taxi."

"Pay the taxi?" I parroted.

"You went to Ace on the back of my bike so, after you tossed most of your bills on the bed, and a taxi home would cost a whack, with no way home and no cake...yeah, pay the taxi."

We'd had our fight. He'd said what he'd said, then he'd gone to the only places I could go, Mrs. Jimenez's and his house. And in the end, after we had our fight and he said what he said, he was waiting up to pay my taxi.

Oh my God.

He *so totally loved me.*

And I'd been right. I'd finally been right.

I'd found the real thing.

I knew what that feeling was in my stomach.

That lightness.

The froth.

It was joy.

I was feeling *actual joy*.

I'd never had that in my life.

But I knew precisely what it was.

Buck clearly didn't feel the joy.

I knew this when he ordered, "Babe, quit starin' at me and get on the back of my bike."

I didn't quit staring at him.

I kept staring at him, and I did this awhile.

Firstly, he was so incredibly handsome, I could look at him forever.

And secondly, obviously, I liked everything I could see, and the best part about it was that everything I could see was mine.

All *mine*.

"Babe—" he started, sounding impatient.

He stopped talking when I slid my hands down to rest on his chest.

"I need to go get my purse, then we can go home," I whispered.

It was his turn to stare, but he didn't do it as long as I had.

His hand at my neck shifted, going back and up, his fingers in my hair. He put pressure on, pulling me up as his head came down. His mouth hit mine and he kissed me.

Then he ended it.

"Buck?" I called.

"Right here, Toots," he answered, and he was.

We were no longer kissing, but we were still plastered together, and his face wasn't even an inch away.

"Consider it erased."

His head ticked.

His eyes flared.

Then we were making out again.

This time, it lasted longer before he ended it.

He let me go but took my hand.

We walked up the stairs.

I got my purse, invited Tia and Damian to enchiladas (Rayne declined, not surprisingly), we walked back out...

And I got on the back of Buck's bike.

29

NEVER EASY

I saw the car coming up the drive after Buck was done with me, he'd passed out, I'd passed out, but I'd had some sleep, he had not.

So he was still passed out, and I was in the kitchen, making a sandwich.

I didn't know whose car that was, I just knew it was fancy.

And seeing a fancy car, I got worried and sifted through my mental database in an attempt to decipher if I held the knowledge as to what the statute of limitations was on assault.

I did not hold this knowledge.

That said, I suspected it was longer than a few weeks.

So this could mean Buck and Gear were not in the clear with those ASU boys.

Or more to the point, their angry parents.

Girding for battle, even if I only was wearing a pair of panties and Buck's tee, and since I couldn't risk going back to the bedroom to dress because that might wake Buck, I headed to the door.

And even if it was a little chilly outside, I stood out on the deck in front of the door and glared angrily at the man getting out of his fancy car.

The good news, evidence was suggesting that Buck and Gear were still in the clear.

The bad news, Nolan Armitage, Rogan's attorney, was back.

"I'm uncertain how to make myself any clearer, Nolan," I called as he made his way to me. "However, I do know I had witnesses to your last visit, which was unwelcome, so now we may be bordering on harassment."

He stopped at the foot of the steps and declared, "Rogan's dying."

"You told me that before."

"Yes, and when I did, Rogan was dying. Now, they're making him as comfortable as they can, waiting for him to die."

It came out of nowhere.

I didn't expect it.

Not after what I went through. Not after what Rogan had put me through. Not after what came next for me and for Tia.

But even so, it came.

Pain.

"He wants to see you, Clara," Nolan declared.

I hadn't noticed, my mind had shifted to what I was feeling, but when I refocused, I saw he was speaking to me, but he was looking behind me.

I sensed why even before Buck said, "Tell us where and I'll get her there."

"You should go today," Nolan advised.

Today.

We should go *today*.

Oh God.

Rogan was *dying*.

Nolan moved up the steps, reaching into the breast pocket of his suit. I saw Buck's arm come out and take the slip of paper Nolan offered him.

Nolan stepped immediately back as if being in close proximity to me might mean he'd catch something nasty. He then turned and walked down the steps.

But he turned back and looked up at me.

"He won't tell you this, but you should know, the stealing began when he got his diagnosis and the prognosis was what's happening right now."

I didn't move, didn't speak.

"He had to make sure you were covered," Nolan stated. "He had to know, when he was gone, you never had to worry about anything."

My husband had to embezzle forty million dollars to make certain I never had anything to worry about?

"This isn't on her," Buck said, low and angry. "Quit fuckin' with her head because it isn't on her."

"It's partly on her, weak women who lean too much on men," Nolan retorted.

Buck made a growly noise.

I jerked out of the vacuum I'd fallen into at the understanding the first man I'd ever loved was imminently dying and came back to the conversation.

"I have a master's degree and worked at a world-renowned research library," I reminded him.

"Which would not put you in a five-thousand-square-foot, six-million-dollar home in Arcadia," Nolan shot back.

I studied him.

Closely.

What I saw was bitter.

Planted in him by someone else.

Now aimed at me.

"You know," I said softly, "I don't know what women you've had in your life, but they are not me."

His face went hard.

Yes.

Bitter.

"I loved my husband," I told him. "I did not need the house in Arcadia. And I survived a number of things since I was seven years old. Sure, none of that was as bad as what Rogan left me with after what he did, though some of it was close. Nevertheless, I would have survived with him gone. What would have been the struggle that would have stuck with me until the day I left this Earth, was watching the husband I loved die of cancer."

"You say that, Clara, but you are even now not standing on your own two feet. You're standing in nothing but another man's shirt, which leaves little to the imagination of what you've been doing, and it isn't even two o'clock in the afternoon. And you're doing this at his home, not working the job, incidentally, that he gave you, but definitely living a life he allows you to lead."

Another growly noise came from Buck, I felt him move, but I stepped in front of him, even as I didn't take my eyes from Nolan.

I also spoke through this.

"I'm standing here because I have cute taste in shoes and good manners. You see what you want to see, whether that's been sadly distorted by women who have used you in your life is not on me. Like what Rogan decided to do in his desperation at getting a hopeless diagnosis is not on me. What my husband should have done was come home and trusted in me. He did not do that. He underestimated me."

"And whored around on her," Buck added.

Yes, there was also that.

Nolan's head ticked.

"Yeah, don't got an excuse for that, do you?" Buck bit.

Buck was wrong.

He did.

"There are appetites a man has he doesn't take to his wife. He takes them somewhere else. Especially when he only has a short time left to live."

"Then he chose wrong again, asshole," Buck declared. "'Cause the wife he had has her own appetites, and they're the kind, a man gets them in his bed, he'll never go wanting."

Wow.

That was sweet.

I turned my head and looked up at Buck.

"Really?" I asked.

He looked down at me, and I had confirmation as to his tone and vibe.

He was far from happy.

Now at *me*.

"Are we goin' over this again?" he asked.

"No," I muttered.

"Good." He did not mutter.

"I'll take my leave," Nolan said.

"Take it for the last time, man," Buck warned.

Nolan lifted a hand and walked to his BMW.

I watched him do this.

Buck, I suspected, did not.

"Babe, you need to get dressed."

Needless to say, the soda pop feeling was gone.

"Never easy," I mumbled as Nolan closed himself into his car.

"Baby?" Buck called, his arm curling around my waist.

I looked up at him again.

"I guess that's life, right?" I asked. "A woman who does not want a child gets pregnant with one, she gives it up. A woman who wants a family gets one, her husband leaves. She can't cope, and even though that child has nobody, *nobody*, she takes her own life, leaving that child very alone and entirely defenseless."

"Clara, darlin'," Buck moved closer to me, sliding his hand up my jaw and into my hair, "you need to get in. Get dressed. It's cold and you got somethin' you gotta get outta the way."

"And then," I went on like he didn't speak, "that child gets shunted from home to home. Careful, always, to do the right thing. Because maybe the people in one of the homes, they'd like her. Maybe, if she makes all the right moves, someone might want her."

"Christ, baby," he whispered.

I saw the pain in his eyes, so deep, it could be described as agony.

That, for me.

That, because he loved me.

I didn't like that for him.

I didn't want that for him.

But I couldn't control it.

My first love was dying.

He was thirty-six years old and he was *dying*.

So I kept going.

"But they don't. And she struggles through. Gets an education. Makes something of herself. Falls in love."

"Please come inside with me, Toots," he begged quietly.

"And it wouldn't have mattered either way, Buck," I carried on. "Either Rogan got the news he got, and he did what he did, which left me out there, alone, without resources and desperate. Or Rogan got that news and he came home and told me, and I'd have to prepare to watch the man I loved die. For me, there was no win. For me, it wasn't ever going to be easy."

Buck rested his forehead to mine and whispered, "Baby, *please.*"

"Then I find you," I whispered back. "And I can live on hope Tia's okay. Because I've got you. And I can step up for Tatie. Because she's sweet and because I've got you. I can fall in love again. And I can make you fall in love with me. And you're mine. All of you is all mine. And we don't even get an entire day to enjoy that, and now...this."

Buck stopped trying to get me to go inside.

Instead, his fingers curled in my hair and he pressed his knuckles tight to my scalp and didn't move away.

"I should get dressed and see Rogan," I muttered.

"Yeah," he muttered back.

Neither of us moved.

We stood out in the cold, the thin Arizona creek meandering by us, and stared in each other eyes.

Eventually, it occurred to me that I was wearing his tee.

Buck was out in nothing but jeans and bare feet.

I needed to get my man inside.

"Let's just go do this," I said.

"Babe?" he said.

"Right here."

"My sister burned herself and my mother to death, and I'm still standing."

I sucked in breath.

Buck kept speaking.

"My dad's incarcerated. Probably the only way you'll ever know him is sittin' across a table from him in a visitation hall in a prison. You'll never taste how good he can make a meatloaf or hear how loud his laugh booms or be able to hand our kid off to him and watch him get down on the ground and play like he's good to do that for weeks. I hate that like fuck, but I'm still standing."

Our kid?

Buck went on, "The woman I loved turned into a bitch I couldn't stand the sight of and took my kids away from me, and I'm still standing."

"We'll get them back," I promised.

"We might. We might not. But whatever happens, Gear will be standing. Tat will be standing. You'll be standing. And I'll be standing. That's my only goal. That's what I live for. And that's life, Toots. You're right. It's never, not ever, easy. The key, gorgeous, is to stay standing."

This was very wise.

Sad.

But wise.

I nodded, the movement of my head moving his.

"Now, let's go do this," he murmured.

He also made to shift, but I stopped him by catching his beltloops on either side.

"I feel pain about this, Buck," I admitted.

"You loved him. That's not a surprise. It'd be a surprise if you didn't."

I nodded, but said, "I just want you to know, it's not about still having feelings for him. It's about *having had* feelings for him."

"I know that, Clara."

I studied him closely.

"You sure?"

"Babe, if I thought you were holding a torch for this guy, you would not be in my bed. Remember? I don't share."

"Oh, right," I mumbled.

His lips twitched and he replied, "Right. Can we get out of the cold now?"

I yet again nodded.

But this time, he didn't move.

"Are we going inside?" I asked when we both kept standing there for a good while.

"From the minute I learned all of it, I wanted the power to erase your life, write it new."

My eyelids fluttered rapidly, shock and something else, and that something else was something beautiful, pulsing through me.

"I didn't have that power, Clara, so I did what I could do."

Oh my God.

He did what he could do.

And there I was.

I had, indeed, leaned on a man.

Because I needed to.

And he gave me a home, a family, a job, a car.

And his love.

"West," I whispered.

"I lied," he declared.

Again with the eyelids fluttering.

"Sorry?" I asked.

"I knew just how deep I was in it with you when you were holdin' Tatie's hair back when she was pukin'. But I fell in love with you over a game of pool."

Oh.

My.

God.

I melted into him and didn't have it in me to do anything but breathe, "*West.*"

"We can't do anything about those pages that were already written, baby. But we're past those. Now we're writing it new. You with me?"

I was so with him, I could become him.

If I did that, however, I couldn't kiss him.

Which was what I did to share I was with him.

We made out for a spell on his deck in what Arizonians considered cold (when it was probably around seventy degrees).

Buck ended it.

And took me inside.

30

STILL STANDING

"You've got to be fuckin' *shitting* me."

Buck spoke words I was thinking when we saw Kristy's junker sitting outside his house on our way back from visiting Rogan.

I went in to see him alone.

I went in prepared.

I found, upon seeing my emaciated ex-husband, who'd once been so handsome I could barely look at him and breathe at the same time, now had aged thirty years in six months, and I was not prepared.

What I was, was forgiving.

He needed that.

He was dying.

I gave it to him.

I wasn't sure I meant it, not totally.

What I was sure of was that I no longer had the time to find my way to the place of forgiveness.

I also knew I wouldn't have been able to live with myself knowing I didn't offer it even if I wasn't there yet.

And last, I knew that now he could die having it.

I also assured him I was fine. I had a good job I liked doing and I was moving on.

I did not tell him about Buck.

That was something he didn't need to know before he was lost to this world.

"It was stupid," he'd rasped before I left.

"We don't need to talk about it, Rogan," I told him.

"I wanted it, when I was gone, to take the place of me," he explained.

He was talking about the money.

"Nothing could have taken the place of you," I replied.

It took visible effort, and was hard to watch him make that effort, but he nodded.

"You're going to think I'm an ass, sweetheart," he warned. "But I don't regret doing something stupid to look out for you. I regret that doing something stupid took you away from me so I didn't have you. Not when I needed you. That I just didn't have the time I had left with you."

I didn't know how to respond.

I went with honest.

"I regret you did that too."

"You loved me, right?" he asked.

My throat closing, I took his hand in mine and kept being honest.

"I loved you, Rogan. So, so much. You were the best thing in my life up to that point. I'll always have that. And I'll have it because you gave it to me."

And I could tell by the expression on his face that was what he needed to know before he was gone.

Needless to say, I was in a quiet, reflective mood.

And Buck was giving me that, but doing it holding my hand tight in his, resting on his thigh.

Now it was even tighter as we drove up his lane to see Kristy get out from her car.

It was still early. The kids wouldn't be home for at least an hour or two.

And she was alone.

No Knuckles.

Buck parked, but before he got out, angry eyes on Kristy, he was Buck.

So he issued orders to me.

"Right. In the house, baby, make yourself a margarita. I'll be in soon's I can."

"No way."

That made his attention shift to me.

"You've had enough today," he declared.

"And I'm still standing," I replied.

He stared at me.

Then he scowled at me.

Then he stated, "Next time, I'm gettin' a weak woman who leans on me and does what she's told."

"Seeing as I've got my hooks in you and I'm never letting go, good luck with that, baby," I returned, throwing open my door and pulling myself out of his SUV.

Kristy's eyes were going back and forth between us, and I barely got a few steps in before I had Buck's arm around my neck, curling me to his side and halting us a good ten feet away from her.

This was probably a good call.

I was in no mood.

"We haven't had a good day, so whatever shit you got planned to lay on us, pick another time," Buck demanded.

"I just want to talk," Kristy said.

I felt Buck's body move in surprise, which was the same thing mine did.

Not just her words.

But her whipped tone.

"What do you wanna talk about?" Buck asked cautiously.

"Can we go inside?" Kristy asked back.

"No," Buck denied.

Her jaw got tight.

Buck said nothing.

I didn't either.

This lasted what felt like a *long* time.

"Okay, listen, things aren't good with Knuckles," she finally said, each word sounding like it took the gravest of efforts to force it out.

"And I care about this because...?" Buck let that trail.

More self-forced confessions from Kristy. "I'm not proud of it, but maybe I've been takin' that out on Tatie and Gear."

Buck again said nothing, and neither did I, but our bodies did the surprised sway again.

"Tatiana mostly," she muttered.

"I'll repeat, I care about this because...?" Buck pushed.

She narrowed her eyes at him. "Because I don't want you to take my kids from me, asshole."

"Well, callin' me names makes me feel all kinds a' good about makin' your life easier when you got it shit and you take that shit out on my kids," Buck replied.

"My kids too," she fired back.

"Woman..."

Uh-oh.

His tone had changed and was such, I slid both my arms around his middle in case I had to hold *him* back.

"...your daughter was assaulted. She was nearly raped. And you're not gettin' on with your old man, you show the fuckin' *day after that shit happens*, and lay my baby girl *out*, and now you're layin' claim to those kids like you're saving your place in line for mother of the year?"

"She's a handful," Kristy hissed.

"I know that," Buck bit back. "She's also a teenage girl. You been one, you didn't see this coming?"

"You don't know how it is day to day," she returned. "It's tough day to day, puttin' up with her shit."

"Okay then, it's so tough, I'll take that chore off your hands," Buck stated instantly.

"Buck, listen to me—" she began, leaning forward.

"No, *you* listen to *me*, bitch. I have not been a teenage girl. But I had two sisters. And growin' up with them, I got the drift. Shit happens for girls. It's worse, the kids at school are fuckwads. What my sisters had was a mom and dad who gave a shit. What my daughter has is a dad who gives a shit who's two hours away and a mom who's so up her own ass, most a' the goddamn time, my baby girl is blowin' in the wind."

"I'm gonna get it together, Buck," she bit out.

"It's too late," he returned. "I sense you're concerned about the custody battle, but you comin' here hat in hand is not gonna stop that."

"I'm gonna get it together!" Her voice was rising.

And at that, I lost hold on Buck as he broke loose and advanced on her, so the only choice I had was to follow, and fast, since he was moving like a bullet.

He was going so quickly, Kristy almost tripped in her retreat.

She hit her car.

And Buck got close, bent right into her face and thundered, "*She was nearly raped!*"

I put my hand on his back and whispered, "West. Honey."

But my eyes darted to Kristy when I heard her broken words.

"I know."

Okay, maybe not mother of the year and maybe late, as in *too* late.

But knock me over with a feather...

She cared.

From his next words, Buck clearly did not see this.

"You think she had a mom at home who gave more of a shit about her daughter than her own problems, she might not act out and maybe wouldn't have been in a position to get herself nearly... motherfucking...*raped?*"

Okay, that might have a kernel of truth.

It was still below the belt.

"West," I whispered again.

"You think I haven't thought that?" Kristy demanded.

"No, I think you haven't thought that. 'Cause, see, since that happened, my girl isn't callin' home tellin' us about the joys of livin' with her mom and her stepdad and how understanding and supportive they are and how she can't come down for the weekend 'cause all her friends got all sorts of plans, she can't tear herself away. She calls Clara and bitches about what a bitch her mom is and how she needs to get the fuck outta there 'cause she's goddamned *miserable.*"

Kristy's attention came to me when he mentioned me, but it went back to Buck on the word *miserable.*

"I'm gonna try harder, Buck," she reiterated.

"Too late."

"I think I'm gonna leave Knuckles."

"I think I don't care."

"He doesn't get on with the kids."

"No shit?" Buck asked sarcastically.

I knew Kristy had had it just by the expression on her face, even before she spat, "You know, you're not perfect."

"Yeah, I do know that. I also know that house," he swung his arm out behind him to point at the house, but he didn't take his face out of Kristy's, "is a safe place for my kids. *Safe* from their *mother*. And I'm gonna do what I can to give them more of that. I might lose. I might also win. We'll see. But I don't *think* dick. I'm gonna fight to give my kids some happy. And whatever happens, they're gonna know their dad went to the mat for them. That's what I know."

They stared at each other, Kristy was near tears, Buck was not backing down.

"Go inside, West," I said.

He turned his heat to me.

"No fuckin' way."

"Go inside, honey," I whispered.

He didn't go inside.

He took a step back from Kristy and crossed his arms on his chest.

I turned to her and said, "I think you should let the kids come live with us."

Her face twisted, she opened her mouth, but I got there quicker.

"For a spell. If things aren't good with your partner, sort that out. Tell them you need to handle it, and you need to protect them from it while you do. Tell them you want to see them and keep the path clear should they want to see you. Or come down here and see them. Buck won't stand in your way."

Buck grunted his indication he was not at one with the last part.

I persevered.

"Kristy, you have this shot to take care of your kids. I know it seems like losing them, but in the end, it might be winning them back."

"So *you* get my kids," she said snidely.

"No, *all three of us* get to look after them while you deal with your life issues and start on the road to repairing your relationship with them," I replied.

Now she and I were in a staring contest.

Ours didn't last as long as hers did with Buck since Buck wasn't feeling it.

"We're done. Go home," he said to Kristy, catching my hand and beginning to drag me to the house.

"If I have to move out on my own, I won't have the money to fight for custody," she called after us.

Buck made no response, he just kept dragging me.

"For fuck's sake, Buck, Gear is nearly eighteen!" she shouted. "I'm not stupid. I know he's gonna bail as soon as he's legal to do it. He's gone come May, and then I only have a couple of years with Tatie."

Buck turned at that. "You know, I have not one single fuckin' issue with you feelin' my pain. You took my kids from me, not across town, two goddamn hours away, and then you made their lives a misery and I could do *dick*. So no, Kristy, I do not have one single *fuckin'* issue with you feelin' my pain."

It was yet another shock, but at that, Kristy looked ashamed.

"You've made your point, baby, let it go," I whispered.

A muscle jumped through Buck's beard, he jerked up his chin, then he finished tugging me to and in the house.

He slammed the door.

And locked it.

He stalked into the house and immediately went to the cupboard where the liquor was kept.

I went to the end of the counter.

"Uh..." I didn't really begin.

"No, babe, unh-unh." He shook his head, pulling down the ingredients for margaritas. "Do not fight that bitch's battle."

"I think she's genuinely remorseful."

With the tequila and margarita mix down, his hands still around the bottles, he turned his gaze to me.

"And I think she's done with puttin' up with Knuckles' shit, she senses some serious alone time is in her near future, her kids fuckin' hate her, or at least Tatie does, and she needs them now. She needed them before to shit all over them when her life wasn't goin' as she'd planned. And she'll need them then when she wants a shoulder to cry on. Your ex's attorney, babe, he's an asshole. But he's got one thing right. There are women out there who are weak, but they don't just latch on to men. They latch on to whoever they have in order to see them through because they don't got the balls to do it themselves. Kristy is that kind of woman."

"Well, you know her better than I do," I said softly.

"Yeah, I do. Don't be taken in by her shit. She'll do whatever she has to do to get what she wants. And if that fails, she'll crumble. It is not a kid's job to take care of a parent who cannot cope with their own fuckin' life. It's a *parent's* job to look after their goddamn *kids*."

"Right," I whispered.

He moved to the cupboard and got out a pitcher.

Since Buck didn't drink them, apparently, I was going to enjoy a fair amount of margaritas that night.

"Worst part about that is," he mumbled, "you just did what you had to do, and it sucked, and we come home and we gotta deal with her shit."

"It's okay, West."

That brought me his attention again.

"It is not, Clara."

"Okay," I murmured.

Buck got down to the business of making margaritas.

He had a heavy hand with the tequila.

Then again, he always did.

"Um...since we're kind of on the subject, though perhaps you're not in the appropriate mood to discuss this at this juncture, so I'm fine to defer it until later...but after Nolan left, you mentioned our kid," I noted.

"Yeah," he said.

"Our kid?"

He looked to me. "Yeah, our kid."

"Um..."

I had no more to say.

Buck, on the other hand, did.

"I didn't knock you up, babe. But I'm gonna."

What?

"You are?" I breathed.

"Yeah," he replied casually.

"Um..."

Again, I had no more to say.

"You don't wanna get married because the first one didn't go too good, I understand," he stated, standing at the freezer, filling a tumbler with ice.

Yes, a *tumbler*.

He came back to the pitcher he'd filled and started pouring while still talking.

"But I wanna get married. Want my ring on your finger. That doesn't just mean shit to women, it means shit to guys. You're gorgeous, I want you wearing my claim on you."

I was having trouble breathing.

He walked to me, set the tumbler of margarita in front of me, then moved back toward the fridge, *still speaking*.

"So all I ask is you think on that. Again, you're not down, I'll find a way to be good with it. But I'll say now, I'd prefer you find your way to being down."

He got out a beer and twisted off the cap.

It sounded strangled when I queried, "Are you asking me to marry you?"

He was taking a drag from his beer.

He stopped doing that, swallowed, and said, "No. Not gonna do that shit after you sat down with your dying ex who fucked you over huge then we had a scene with my ex, who's been fucking me over huge for years. But I'm gonna."

"Oh...okay," I muttered, unable to do more than that.

"I see you're not down," he said quietly.

And he looked disappointed.

Oh God.

I really, *really* loved this man.

"When you ask me, I'll try very hard not to scream 'yes!' and then do cartwheels all the way down to Phoenix."

His head ticked.

Then his lips twitched.

And finally, his eyes lit.

"But you're right. Now isn't the time," I finished.

"Good we agree, babe," he said, his voice filled with humor.

"Mm..." I hummed, my heart filled with warmth.

His humor fled and he asked gently, "You okay?"

Was I okay?

Buck was going to ask me to marry him (someday) and we were going to have a baby (or perhaps two, with him, I'd want two, but he already had two—we'd discuss that later as well).

So, yes.

I was okay.

I was very, *very* okay.

"Yes, I'm okay."

"Clara, darlin', *are you okay?*"

I got it then.

"He was not in a good way," I whispered.

"I see that, considering," he whispered back.

"It was hard, seeing him that way," I told him.

"I see that too."

"But I'm okay."

He studied me and he took his time doing that.

When he saw what he wanted to see, he spoke.

"Great, then how 'bout you be okay over here where you can be okay in my arms."

That gave me a delightful tingle.

However.

"You could come over here and take me in your arms," I suggested.

"Babe," he replied.

Yes.

Buck was Buck.

Me and my margarita went over there.

He took my drink from me, set it and his beer aside, and pulled me in his arms.

And I was even more okay.

"Think you should call your girl and cancel enchiladas," he declared.

"I can't, she's going to want to know I'm all right after our *first* scene this morning. And when she finds out about Rogan and that I had to go see him, she's going to want to know I'm all right after that. And she'd be angry if I didn't tell her that happened and let her be around to be there for me after it did."

"Clara, she was vapor for two months and you worried those two months. She can wait a day for you and enchiladas."

"She had reason to be vapor."

"Not enough reason."

Was he serious?

"West, she was shot," I reminded him.

"You think I'd get shot, knowin' you knew my vehicle filled with my blood was abandoned on the side of the road states away and leave you hangin' on that?"

No, I did not think that.

I thought, if that happened—and Lord forbid it did, and please God, don't let it—he'd move Heaven and Earth to make sure I didn't worry.

Therefore, I abandoned that line of argument.

"She tried to find me."

Buck was over this conversation and he shared that by ordering, "Cancel enchiladas."

"West—"

"Just family tonight," he declared.

I liked that.

Just family.

With me being a part of that family.

And that family being a wonderful one.

However.

"Tia is family."

"Fuck," he gave in.

I beat back my grin.

Though I didn't beat back melting into him.

"And Mrs. Jimenez is family," I added. "We should ask her too. She'll want to see Tia is okay."

"Baby, love you and want you to have what you need always, definitely right now, but don't push it."

Since he loved me and had demonstrated repeatedly he would do everything he could to give me what I needed, I gave in.

"Okay," I mumbled.

"Right, the kids are gonna be here in about an hour. And your girl is gonna be here about an hour after that. You wanna fuck again real quick, or you wanna sit out on the deck and drink your margarita?"

Like he had to ask that question.

I shot him a look.

He grinned.

Then he let me go but only to take my hand and lead me to the bedroom.

We fucked "real quick."

It was real awesome.

After that, we cleaned up, got dressed, rescued our drinks and Buck got started on the enchiladas.

31

ALL GOOD

"Okay, I wasn't sure about him, with the whole carry-you-down-the-stairs thing, but...*babe*."

It was after enchiladas, copious margaritas (the girls, Buck even allowed Tatie to sip at one, and not a virgin one), beers for the boys (even Gear) and getting-to-know-you chitchat.

And it was the end of the night.

We were standing outside by Damian's truck.

I was with Tia.

Buck and Damian were giving us space, talking a few feet away.

And I knew what her *babe* meant.

She approved of Buck.

"I'll share the whole story one day, when it's just us," I told her. "It started crazy and I wasn't paying attention. He loves me, though, Tia. And this time, it's the real thing."

"It's not just the real thing. It's that house. It's those kids who think you walk on water. It's the way his face changes every time you laugh. No." She shook her head as that sparkle started again in my belly. "It's *everything*."

"Yes," I whispered.

And it *so* was.

"I'm so glad you have that," she decreed.

I glanced at Damian.

"And I have what I have too. We've both scored," she stated. "Who woulda thunk?"

I smiled at her, even if I wasn't sure about Damian.

Yes, his face changed when she laughed too.

Yes, he seemed super into her.

But no, I remembered her words about his rootless life and that they'd made no promises to each other.

I had future marriage and babies and all things Buck, Gear and Tatiana to look forward to.

Tia?

Not so much.

"Ready, honey?" Damian called.

"Ready!" she chirped on a cute jump.

Then again, at least she had what she had now.

And her future...

Well, I'd be around whatever that might bring.

We said our good-byes and Buck and I watched them drive away, Tia waving, me waving back, Buck not waving, but holding me against his side with his arm around my neck.

When their brake lights could no longer be seen, Buck turned me to the steps and led me into the house.

Gear was in the den, playing some computer game.

Tatie was in her room, light on, door open.

I went to the kitchen to tidy up margarita glasses while Buck headed to the living room to grab spent bottles of beer.

"Was a good night," he said.

"The best," I replied happily.

I felt his eyes on me, but I didn't look at him.

I had to get used to happy.

He had to get used to making me happy.

Because life was going to get hard again somewhere along the way.

But we'd always have this.

Cleaning margarita glasses and picking up beer bottles with the kids doing their thing.

Happy.

His phone rang, and I looked at him when I heard it.

He was dumping bottles in the recycling at the same time checking his screen.

His gaze lifted to mine.

"Kristy," he murmured.

Hells bells.

I nodded.

"Takin' it in the office," he said.

I nodded again, glad, whatever that would bring (although I wished he didn't have to shoulder it, at least, after the night we had with my friend and his kids), the kids didn't have to hear it.

He took off.

I finished with the margarita stuff and wandered to Tatie's room.

I knocked on the doorframe, seeing she was in bed with her journal.

I also saw that, with just a little, we'd made a lot.

She had new tassel-trimmed sheets that were cute. A pretty tapestry tacked up behind her bed. Funky trays and stands on her dresser where she could put her jewelry. Some framed graphic art on her wall. One that was white and said No Bad Days in black. One that said Stay Rad in multi-colors. A smattering of throw rugs on the floor. Pretty square baskets she'd set on their sides to build a kind of shelving unit, in which she'd put her books and some knickknacks.

It was finally a teenage girl's room. Eclectic, but lived-in and warm with lots of style.

I loved it for her.

I also loved she spent time there but did it with the door open. Not closing us out. But liking to be in her space, with the way open to her family.

"Hey," she said. "I like Tia. She rocks."

I smiled at her and took that as an invitation to walk in.

"Maybe we can talk her into going shopping with us tomorrow," I suggested. "It's never too early to think of Christmas."

"So Clara," she muttered as I sat on the side of her bed, her gaze on me and it was glittering. "All organized and shit."

I shrugged.

"I'm not gonna say no to shopping," she said. "But we should buy pumpkins and carve them."

That sounded much better.

"I'm down with that."

She grinned at me.

"You feel like talking?" I asked.

Her head tipped to the side, her lustrous hair tipping with it.

"About what?"

"Whatever you want," I offered.

She looked at me, long and hard, before she patted the bed at her side.

I shifted and got in bed with her, both of us up against the headboard, legs out straight.

She looked at my hand.

Then she took my hand and fiddled with my fingers.

I didn't know what to make of this, but I kept my silence and let Tatiana take her time in telling me.

Eventually, she whispered, "Don't be mad."

Oh boy.

I forced my tone to be light when I asked, "Mad about what?"

Her gaze came to mine and she kept whispering when she said, "I talk to Debbie."

This was not what I expected.

"Sorry?"

"I mean, it's never happened to you," she said like it was a confession.

But I understood.

"Honey, I'm not mad you talk to Debbie."

"You're not?" Now she sounded surprised.

"Of course not, Tatie. I arranged it so you could meet so you'd have someone who got it to talk to. But beyond that, you're free to do what you want, spend time with who you want, make friends with who you want, live your life how you want." I paused and added, "Within your father's rules, that is."

She seemed bemused.

"So you're not mad that I lean on Debbie and not you?"

All right, maybe I wished I'd got another smack in with her mother that afternoon.

Tatiana totally didn't know how to do this.

I'd never even had a mother and I knew more than she did.

"No, I'm not mad. Not even a little bit. I'm glad. I'm glad you have someone to talk to about what happened to you. I'm glad you have people who care about you and you know it. I'm glad you have anything that makes you happy or makes you feel protected or looked after and loved."

"Okay," she said softly.

"Can I ask you a question?" I requested.

"Shoot," she invited.

"Why didn't you do up your room before we did it together?"

After I asked this, her eyes moved around the room.

And when she spoke, she spoke to the room.

"We moved up here, way before they broke up. Dad wanted to make the move before Gear and me got deep in school so we didn't move when we were in the middle of making friends. But I think mostly," she turned her head to me, "he did it to give Mom a cool house. She was never happy with, like, *anything*. Dad liked to be around his brothers. He didn't wanna be on the road goin' back and forth to home when he could be with his family. But Mom was always talkin' about havin' land. Dad getting us a cabin somewhere so we could 'escape.' So he found this and got it. For her."

"All right," I said when she stopped and said no more.

But she was watching me closely again.

And she explained why when she asked, "That doesn't upset you? That he bought this place for Mom?"

"No. It's his now. So, no," I answered.

"I did up his room, after they split," she said like this was gravely important. "The whole thing. The bed isn't even the same."

I took control of her hand, which was still holding mine, and gave it a squeeze.

"Your mother doesn't factor in our lives in that way, Tatie," I promised, then grinned. "Though, you have good taste. I always wondered why your dad's bedroom was so fantastic."

She grinned back.

"That said, honey," I went on, "it doesn't explain why you didn't claim your room. You'd been living here—"

"They broke up when I stopped being a little girl."

I closed my mouth.

She carried on.

"It was Dad. He has sisters. He said my little girl room had to go. And it was pink, Toots, pink with lots of purple and some glittery stars and other shit Dad thought a little girl would like. And I did like it when I was a little girl. He moved it all out, repainted, got new furniture and they split up and...and..." she drew in a visible breath, "and I guess I didn't have anybody to help me fix it back up."

Her fingers twisted so they were threaded through mine.

And she finished on a whisper, "Now, I do."

"Now, you do," I whispered back.

And now, I did.

I had a girl to help fix up her room and sit on her bed and talk about stuff.

And to love.

I didn't have that myself, when I was a little girl, or a teenage one.

But I got to give it to Tatie.

And for me, that worked.

In a *big* way.

"My room sucks at Mom and Knuckles' place," she told me.

Hopefully, soon, that would be a memory.

"Well, you have your space here," I unnecessarily reminded her, since we were lounging in it.

"Yeah, I got a lot here," she said.

Uh-oh.

I was going to cry.

"Toots, don't," she begged. "'Cause I'll start bawlin' with you and your friend is sweet and I'm glad she's back, safe and sound, and her man is *hot* and they look happy and it's all good." Her hand shook mine. "Yeah?"

I nodded, but said, "I'm supposed to reassure you."

"Well, I get to do it sometimes too," she retorted.

"Hate to break this up, my two girls," Buck said low from the doorway.

We both turned our attention that way.

And yes.

Buck standing there looking like someone handed the world to him on a platter just seeing his woman and daughter talking together.

It was *all good.*

"Talk to you a second, Toots?" he asked. "Then you can come back."

"I'm gonna hit the sack," Tatiana announced. She then leaned into me, kissed my cheek, and said in my ear, "Love you and love you worry about me, but I'm okay. I get in a bad place, I call Debbie. She's, like, my after-assholes-fuck-with-you sponsor."

I pulled back, stared in her eyes, and tried really hard not to take her in my arms because I figured I might crush her to death with what I was feeling after she told me she loved me.

"Good, baby," I whispered. "Sleep tight, yes?"

She nodded.

I kept whispering.

"Love you too."

Her eyes got bright with tears, we both squeezed our fingers, held tight for the second it took her to get a lock on it, let go, and I got out of her bed.

I walked to Buck, saw he had some papers in his hand, but with his other, he grabbed mine and called to his girl, "Sleep good, honey."

"Thanks, Dad. 'Night."

We both bid our goodnights as she swung her legs to the side of the bed, probably to get up and change into pjs.

Buck led me to our room.

He closed the door behind us.

He then took me to the end of the bed.

"Was she a bitch?" I asked after Kristy and did it quietly.

"First, this," he said, lifting the papers up and shaking them.

I turned my attention to them and saw, even with the shaking, they were my credit card bills.

I'd left them in the office.

Oh dear.

I shifted my gaze back to Buck.

"Buck—"

"I can pay these off in fifteen minutes online," he declared.

Yes, I was right.

Oh dear.

"West...no," I refused carefully.

He dropped his hand with the bills in it.

"I have to do it," I told him.

"Babe, I figure with all that happened today, you get what's goin' on here."

"I do, honey, but I have to pay those."

"We're partners in this, and by 'this,' I mean everything."

Yeesh.

Was I going to fall in love with him more every day?

Every hour?

Every minute?

"Will you listen to me?' I asked.

"Fuck yeah, I'll listen to you, and you don't have to ask."

Yes.

I was going to fall in love with him more every minute.

"I need to pay those," I asserted.

"Clara—"

"West, *I need to pay those.*"

He stopped talking.

His gaze moved over my face.

Then he tossed the credit card statements on the bed, watched them fall, and turned back to me.

"Right, then, choose the one with the lowest balance. Focus on it. Pay monthly on the others, five, ten dollars more than the minimum payment so you're doin' something to draw down the balance. Sock everything else you got at the one with the lowest balance. Once that's paid off, sock everything you got to the next lowest one. You're payin' as much as you can, spreadin' that out along four of 'em. That's going to draw this out for-fuckin'-ever. You get one outta the way, you got more to throw at the next. And then again. And again. And it's done. Yeah?"

That was very smart.

So I said, "Yes."

"Then you cancel two of 'em. No one needs four credit cards."

I nodded.

He was definitely right about that.

"Since we're...you know, this is happening, I'd like to contribute to the house."

His face shut down and he said, "Babe."

"West, I love that you want to take care of me, but you need to get that I don't need it. What I need is to be a partner in our lives. I also need you to let me."

"Okay, Toots, and what *I* need is to take care of you. You won't let me pay those." He jerked his head to the statements. "You don't do dick for yourself because you pay those, and you buy treats for the office, and you send money to help cover Mrs. Jimenez. You deal with those." He jerked his head to the statements again. "You do it on my plan, you'll be down to two in four months. You get down to those two, and start doin' shit for yourself, buyin' pumice scrub or whatever the fuck, we'll talk about how you can contribute to our lives."

That sounded...

Like a plan.

"That's a plan."

"Thank fuck," he muttered, clearly thinking he'd get backtalk.

I didn't comment on that.

I prompted, "Kristy."

He'd gone unfocused, such was his relief I didn't argue with his plan.

But he focused then.

And his focus was a deep, intent, gleaming, *magnificent* focus.

Instantly, I read my man.

"Oh my God," I whispered.

"I do not know the woman I just talked to," he confirmed what I'd read. "But she wants me to call the school to start the transfer, and she says, once that's sorted, we can move 'em down."

"*Oh my God,*" I breathed.

"Yeah," he said.

Suddenly, he caught my head in both hands and put his face in mine.

"I do not trust this shit, so I don't wanna say anything to them. I told her I want that in writing. I want an emailed letter, I want it by tomorrow morning, with her printing it out, putting her goddamned signature on it and sending it to me. I'm still callin' the school first thing Monday. But we don't tell the kids until I got that email. You with me?"

I nodded mutely.

"Tatie good?" he asked.

I nodded again mutely.

"You gonna pass out, seein' as you're not breathing?"

"We're getting the kids," I whispered.

"Yeah," he whispered back, that intent, gleaming *magnificent* look back in his eyes.

I caught his head like he had mine. I yanked his mouth down on mine. I kissed him hard.

Then I broke away, turning from him.

I bent over, pumped my arms rapidly at my sides, jerked up, then clapped silently, jumping up and down.

"Jesus, fuck, Toots, you *are* a dorky librarian," he noted, smiling broadly.

"We get the kids, we get the kids, wegetthekids," I chanted quietly.

He kept smiling.

"We get the kids, we get the kids, wegetthekids," I repeated my chant quietly.

"Baby, don't make me wanna fuck you. Both of 'em are still awake. You know we don't fuck until they're out."

"We get the kids, we get the kids, wegeththekids," I said yet again.

He burst out laughing, doing it hooking me by my neck, and I face planted in his chest because he made me.

I wound my arms around him.

He pulled me closer, smooshing my face in his chest.

I turned so I had my cheek to it instead.

Then, in the top of my hair, he whispered, his voice guttural.

"We get the kids."

"Yeah," I replied.

He held tight.

I did too.

And it was all good.

32

THE LIFE AND TIMES OF WEST HARDY

L ater that night, I was in my nightie, sitting cross-legged in the middle of the bed, my gaze on the frames on the dresser across the room, when the light went out in the bathroom.

I swung my head that way, seeing Buck walk in wearing cutoff, flannel pajama bottoms.

He rarely wore pajamas. If he had to don something, he put on jeans.

But sometimes, for reasons known only to West Hardy, he put on one of the three pairs (all cutoff, all frequently washed) of pajama bottoms he owned.

I didn't question this.

First, because he looked good in them.

Second, because I got to take them off.

I watched as he turned his head to glance at the picture frames while he walked to the bed.

But he didn't come to the side.

He went to the foot.

And then, stunned immobile, I watched as his big body teetered and then he fell to the bed.

After he bounced (and I did as well), this ended with his muscles and back tats on display, his head in my lap and he added winding his arms around my hips.

He had his bristly cheek to my inner thigh, he didn't make a move to take anything further, and it came to me that I had a different West Hardy on my hands.

No.

That wasn't right.

For the first time, I had *all* of West Hardy on my hands.

Really *all of him*.

And having it all, I immediately learned there was more to like.

Because he now felt free to be like this with me.

Having a good night.

Getting great news.

And giving me a biker cuddle.

By the way, it was the best...cuddle...*ever*.

I slid my fingers in his dark hair, seeing occasional threads of silver catch the light, watching the thick strands embrace my fingers, feeling the smooth silkiness, and again marveling at the perfection.

He didn't purr at my touch.

But he rubbed his beard against my thigh.

And that was better.

"Tell me," I urged quietly.

"Tell you what?" he asked my thigh.

"About it."

He tipped his head well back to catch my eyes but didn't lose hold on my hips.

My God.

God.

This was my man.

And I had all of him.

"About what?" he asked.

"Your mom. Your dad. Your sisters and brother. How you fell in love with Kristy."

A teasing light hit his eyes. "All that right now?"

I wasn't teasing.

"Yes."

He studied me a moment before, regrettably, he took his arms from around me and did a one-armed plank.

Not regrettably, he wrapped the fingers of his free hand around my ankle and tugged.

I bit back a cry as I slid down the bed, having no choice but to fall to my back, head hitting the pillows. He pushed up a bit.

And then he settled his weight on me.

I liked him with his head in my lap.

But this was nice too.

Very nice.

"Dad's name is Locke. We named Gear after him," he told me.

Instantly, I felt a wash of relief.

Of gratitude.

Contentment.

Happiness.

Just knowing his father's name.

Just knowing the name of the man I'd seen in those pictures time and time again.

Just knowing more about my man.

"Another reason we call my boy Gear. To avoid confusion," Buck went on.

"Right," I whispered.

"Mom was called Lenora. Sisters, Sheila and Megan. My brother was called Bruce 'cause Dad's a big Bruce Lee fan."

I nodded, my head moving against the pillows.

"And you're West because...?" I prompted.

"We live in the Wild West, darlin'."

I smiled up at him.

"And how did Buck come about?" I asked.

His expression grew cautious.

Uh-oh.

"You can tell me," I said softly.

"Right, so I lost my virginity at age fifteen and I got caught doin' it."

My mouth dropped open.

"From then on, I was Buck."

I started to laugh.

He smiled down at me.

"And why am I Toots?" I pressed on.

"Baby, you are a Toots. From the tips of those spiked heels you wore to the Dive the first time I saw you, to your round ass in that tight skirt, nice tits, prim and proper blouse, big eyes, lotsa hair. You're Toots top to toe."

I liked that.

And to share that with him, I slid a hand up his back.

I then got us back to business.

"So, let's start with your sisters," I suggested.

Buck nodded.

"Sheila is sweet and quiet. Like Lorie and Pinky. Just a good woman through and through. Her man's called Dog. He's solid. Decent. Good guy. Loves my sister a lot."

"I'm glad."

"They been together for a while, through a lot of tough times. Stayed solid. Those times were about his Club. They were also them tryin' for a kid. Both wanted one real bad. It just didn't happen."

"Oh no," I whispered.

He nodded, his nod communicating the gloom in my words.

"They decided against adoption 'cause they thought there were too many kids who needed love who were already around, and those weren't the babies. So they became foster parents."

I stilled under him.

"Yeah," he said. "First kid they got, though, it was love all around. They adopted. So they did it again. And again."

I closed my eyes, pieces falling into place, all that made West Hardy.

"Great kids, great family. They still foster. They're happy," he said quietly.

I opened my eyes.

"That's good."

He stared down at me, his face gentle.

Then he said, "Meg, Meg was like Mom."

Oh boy.

This was the rough stuff.

"Yes?" I asked softly.

"Yeah. Dad was funny and open and had a booming voice and an even bigger laugh. Mom was edgy. Opinionated. Tough. But she did a lot of mom things, like she taught me how to cook."

That explained that.

And when it did, more of that relief washed through me.

Gratitude.

Contentment.

This from receiving the gift of knowing more about him.

What made him.

And what made him amazing.

"So she was an exceptional cook," I remarked.

A grin quirked his mouth. "Yeah. Mostly, though, she was a mom. She was an old lady. She didn't put up with any shit. Not from her kids. Not from Dad. She held her own. That didn't mean she wasn't affectionate. She was. But Dad was the good-time guy, she was the tough nut. They worked it, because, for the most part, we kept our shit sharp. But if we jacked around too much, she washed her hands of us, went to Dad, and he'd lower the hammer. And since that wasn't him, if he did that, we knew shit was serious. So we got ourselves in line."

"Sounds like they had a good system."

"They were great together."

God, his voice when he said that.

"I love it that you had that, Buck."

He bent to brush his lips on mine, moved away and replied, "I do too."

I sighed under him, loving that he had that, sad for him it was gone.

He kept sharing.

"Mom wanted a good life for her babies. She's the one who pushed me to learn a trade. And sayin' 'push,' there was pretty much no other road I could take."

He paused.

It was a weighty pause.

Then he said, "Dad worked hard. Mom did too. We didn't want for much. And we had all we needed. But she told me no one was gonna hand me shit. I'd have to work for it. I had to learn that. I couldn't go through life expectin' the world to look after me. I had to look after myself."

Perhaps not the same words, but the same message I'd shared with him I thought was important to teach children.

And his reaction to that of weeks ago was also explained.

I dug my fingers into his beard at his jaw and stroked when I hit bone.

"She sounds pretty awesome," I noted.

"She was. And she and Dad were..." He trailed off.

"They were what?" I prompted when he didn't go on.

"Lookin' back, especially recently, I think the reason I was so fucked up about what happened with Kristy and me was because I wanted that. I wanted what they had. I wanted it for me. And knowin' how it felt, havin' it growin' up, I wanted to give that to my kids."

I sensed there was something there I needed to tease out.

"Was there more to what they had and what they gave you kids that you haven't told me?" I asked.

"They were into each other." He tipped his head to the side. "The reason I don't stray? The reason I *won't* stray?"

I nodded for him to go on, keen to hear this.

Not that I wasn't keen on it all.

But I definitely wanted to know this.

"Dad would never do that. He got it and I get it that there are some bikers who are in the life so they can live theirs a certain way, without the strictures of traditional society fencing them in. And that's part of it. Bein' free to do with your dick what you want. But Dad would never turn to another woman, and not only because Ma would lose her shit, turn him out and not look back. He was just into her. She was into him. They made out all the time. They touched a lot. They disappeared in their room for long stretches of time. They were partners. But they were also lovers. And it wasn't unhealthy or inappropriate how they did it, but they didn't hide it."

More explanation of why, from the start, Buck did not hide what he and I were from his kids.

"And they talked," he continued. "Dad had a bad day, he'd take it to Ma, and she'd listen. Mom, she could hold on to things. But he could

read her. And he'd pin her into a corner in the kitchen or somewhere
and pull it out of her. He couldn't stand it. Not her being in a mood.
Something bothering her and him not doing something about it."

I was falling in love with his parents already.

"And I didn't have that with Kristy," Buck continued. "My folks had
all the time in the world for their kids. We had family times. Family
dinners. They took us on family vacations. They loved us and let that
show too. Kristy was about Kristy. I'm not sayin' she doesn't love Gear
and Tatie. I'm sayin' they were like accessories. Like a handbag you were
happy to show off, but then you'd set it aside when you weren't usin' it
and get on with other shit that took your attention."

Buck was now reading me, I knew, when both his hands came up to
frame my head.

"That makes it sound worse than what it was," he muttered. "She
does love them. But when you love yourself most of all, you can't really
love a kid the way that kid needs to be loved."

"Or a husband."

"Yeah," he whispered. Then he said, "Baby, relax. She's gone."

"I'm allowed to be mad about this, West."

"All right," he murmured. "But so you can get over it, I'll give it all to
you."

I already knew there was more to give.

I just no longer wanted to have it.

Though I needed to have it, for Buck, me and the kids.

However, I didn't have to pretend to like it.

So I didn't.

"Fantastic," I said sarcastically.

He grinned.

Then he kept talking.

"We fought. Even in the early days, we fought. We fought more
later. Then more. Back then, I didn't get it. I had on my hands this pretty
girl who was sweet as sugar then could turn on a dime. I was too young
to know she was sweet as sugar when she was getting her way, and she
made that turn when she was not. I had no clue what I'd gotten myself
into. I just knew what my folks had. I wanted what they had. I was all in
to start a family because I loved the one they made. And that family had

fallen apart. I wanted it back. I was too young to know Kristy was not the right woman and I made a family with her and then it was too late."

"Oh, Buck," I said quietly.

He shook his head.

"I do not regret havin' my kids. I regret that was what they grew up with. And it scared the fuck out of me. Because, seein' us, their mom up in their dad's shit all the time. Screaming at him. Him shoutin' back at her. Her sticking him with a knife. They wouldn't know what they should look for. What they should expect. Some version of what my mom and dad had. I'm not sayin' Mom and Dad didn't fight. They did. But the bottom line always was that they loved each other. They were into each other. They listened to each other. They liked spending time with each other. And I did not give that to my kids."

He shook his head again.

I didn't say anything and waited.

He kept going.

"Took Kristy to see Dad. A few visits in, he asked her if he could have some time alone with his boy. She took off and left me with him. And he said, 'Son, get shot of her. She's not the one.' By then, Kristy was pregnant, but we didn't know it yet. It didn't matter. I thought I was in love and I told him he didn't know what he was talking about. But he's my dad. He knew what he was talking about."

"Sometimes we have to make our own mistakes."

"That one, my kids paid for."

"Buck," I whispered, feeling that for him because he wasn't hiding how deeply he felt it.

"Mom had only been around her a couple of times before she died. She never said, but I don't think she thought much of her either."

"West, you were a very young man," I reminded him. "Nobody ever has all the answers or makes all the right decisions. Even adults. But you were nineteen. Twenty. That's two, three years older than Gear. Think about that."

"Yeah," he grunted.

"And they have you and I'm not sure you realize what a steadying force you are in their lives."

"They also now have you."

At that, I engaged my other hand to use his beard to pull him down to me for a quick kiss.

I then pushed him back and reiterated, "But they've always had you and what you and Kristy had might not have been great for them, but I can assure you not ever having it, that having one parent who knocks himself out to show them love and teach them good lessons and give them a safe space really works."

"I hate you didn't have that, darlin'," he said in a voice that shared eloquently how much he meant it.

"I know you do," I replied. "But that's over, West. And it's on the other side, but I have it now. And the kids will soon be here full-time, so I'll *really* have it. It's all good."

He took his time examining my face as if to ascertain if what I said was true.

When he got that from me, he moved on.

"Thinkin' on things, again recently, been wonderin' if I didn't do right by Kristy."

That surprised me.

"Sorry?"

"I expected you to just snap to and get with the program. That program bein', I just expected us to fight. That's what I had with her, and we were together for fifteen years. I just expected there were times it was gonna get ugly and you'd not only roll with that, you'd meet that ugly time after time. It didn't hit me, again until recently, that I had a different kind of woman on my hands. And now I'm wonderin' if I expected too much of Kristy."

"Expected too much in the sense you expected her to look after her children and not stab you with a knife?"

"Babe—"

"I know she was young too," I said curtly. "But you make adult decisions, you learn very fast to become an adult. You have no choice. And it seems to me, you stepped up. You wanted a family. You made a family. You learned a trade and provided for that family. You joined your Club and offered more family to your family. And you love your children and show it. You could be tough on Tat, but never when she didn't deserve it. I'm sorry, Buck, but Kristy doesn't get an out on this. I'm glad you came to the realization that I'm not her and we're not going to have what you had with her. And the kids are not going to have to endure what you two had. But she doesn't get a pass on being a shitty mom."

"All right, baby, cool it," he whispered.

But his eyes were glinting humor.

"I'm not finding anything funny," I warned.

"I know. And I love you for it. 'Cause you're pissed for the kids. You're pissed for me. It's cute. Sweet. Hot. And I cannot even begin to tell you what it makes me feel, seein' you tonight, sittin' in bed with my little girl, talkin' about whatever you were talkin' about. Just a girl who needs the example of a good woman, and that good woman bein' right there. And me bein' the dad who found that for my girl."

Oh no.

I pushed my hands between us and gave his chest an ineffectual shove, snapping, "Don't make me cry."

"You said not five minutes ago I didn't know the steady I give my kids. Just pointin' out the good you bring to that equation."

"This isn't helping me not to cry," I warned.

"Right, then, we done with you learnin' about my family and Kristy so we can fuck?"

"No, I have thirty-eight years of the life and times of West Hardy to learn."

His brows shot up. "Tonight?"

"No. Though, I will warn you, I also want to know your hopes, dreams and deepest desires."

"My deepest desire right now is to get blown before I fuck you."

I rolled my eyes before I said, "We can talk about sexual desires too, but maybe we can round that out with other stuff."

"Like what other stuff?"

"Like, you clearly want a future with me."

"Yeah," he stated firmly. "I clearly want that."

"And you want to eventually get married."

"Told you this already."

"And you want a child with me."

"Told you that already too."

"Do you want two?"

His head cocked to the side. "Do *you* want two?"

"Yes," I whispered carefully.

"Then I'll knock you up twice. Do you want three?"

Three?

"Five children are a lot of children, Buck."

"So you don't want three."

"Well, do you? Want three more, that is?"

He sighed before he stated, "Okay, let's cut to the chase. I want what you want. I like kids. Too bad you didn't come into my life earlier, 'cause first, I got a load of you, I'da dropped Kristy like she was a pan left on the heat too long."

A surprised giggle escaped me.

Buck continued speaking.

"And second, Gear and Tatie, when they were little kids, were cute as fuck. Tatie pullin' some a' her shit notwithstanding, kids are awesome. You want three, I'll give you three. You want two, we'll just have two. You want four, we gotta have a discussion because I'd like to enjoy my retirement, not be attending graduations when I'm eighty, those bein' graduations of my own fuckin' kids. That sound like a plan?"

It sounded like *the best...plan...ever.*

"Yes."

"You up to blow me now?"

"Yes."

His head dropped, I thought he was going to start it, but he only gave me a brief kiss before he pulled away.

"Love you wanna know about me, baby," he said softly.

God, he was *amazing.*

"Sorry I didn't ask before."

"Doesn't matter, you're askin' now."

"It kind of messed us up a little bit," I admitted.

"Yeah, maybe it did, but you're right. Kristy doesn't get a pass on being a shitty mom. But you get a pass when your life's fucked right the hell up, you find yourself a man who knows right off the bat he wants to go the distance with you, and you're so up in your head, it takes you a while and a huge fuckin' drama to clue in. I'll give you that pass and learn, you don't seem to be cluein' in, I best get on helpin' you with that."

I could even feel my gaze was heated when I informed him, "It's time for me to suck you off now, Buck."

He smiled, all white teeth in dark beard.

And it was *totally* time for me to suck him off.

Right now.

He kissed me again and this time it wasn't brief.

He rolled us while doing it.

Eventually, I got down to business.

Then Buck took over.

33

FAMILY

I was dead asleep when Buck shook my hip.

I opened my eyes to see it was still dark.

I did this also to a sleepy feeling of surprise that Buck was ready to go again.

Needless to say, the kids imminently going to be living with us, me asking Buck to share about his life, us knowing what we were to each other, we'd celebrated.

Energetically.

And this was on top of an emotional day where we'd celebrated (energetically) on and off all day.

I turned to him and he whispered, "Baby, I'm sorry. But it's happening."

I didn't like his tone.

And I didn't understand his words.

"What's happening?"

"He's slippin' away."

It was then, I understood.

Oh God.

"You were in with him," he kept speaking. "Talked to 'em, told 'em to call when it came time. They called. You wanna be with him?"

"Yes," I whispered.

"Get dressed." He paused then his voice was weighty when he said, "Hurry."

I got out one side, Buck got out the other, and I hurried.

Even if I hurried, Buck was dressed and out of the room before me.

And by the time I followed him, I saw the lamp by the couch lit, Buck at the door, and Gear was with him.

Dressed and ready to go.

I looked to Gear then to Buck.

"West—"

"Gotta wait for Tat. She's hurryin'," he said.

I made it to him and whispered. "I don't—"

"Family," he grunted a grunt that said I need not reply.

I gave up on him and turned to Gear.

"You don't have—"

"No way, Clara. No way you're doin' this without Dad and me and Tat," he declared.

I shut up.

Tatie dashed out of her room hopping, still pulling on a boot.

"Ready, ready...I'm ready," she said.

Buck had planned all this.

He'd told them.

Prepared them.

And when it was time, they were ready.

We walked to Buck's SUV.

But for my part, I did it with difficulty because Buck's arm was so tight around my neck, Tatie had a death grip with both hands on my biceps, and Gear was crowding Tatie.

We got in the car, Buck started us on our way, and then he tossed his phone in the back seat to the kids.

"Don't care which one of you do it but get on the line with Tia and then call Mrs. Jimenez," he ordered.

I turned my head to him.

"Buck—"

I again got no more out.

"You think those two women will ever forgive me if I let you do this without them?"

Well, putting it that way.

I didn't answer.

"Right," he muttered.

"Yeah, hi, is this Tia?" Gear asked from the back seat.

I stared out the windshield.

"We'll get there, babe," Buck assured.

"Yes," I whispered.

He took my hand and held it.

He drove.

Gear's voice came from the back seat.

And Buck got us there.

"I di-didn't think, you...you'd—"

"Quiet," I whispered to Rogan.

His parents were across the bed from me, as well as his sister.

They all looked immensely sad,

I'd liked them. They'd liked me. I'd missed them. And from the looks on their faces when they saw me, they'd missed me.

There had been no bad blood, they understood.

But I'd left them when I left him because I'd had to leave it all behind me.

"I'm sorry," Rogan said.

"Stop it," I said.

His eyes went to his mom. "I'm sorry."

"Stop it, honey," she whispered, her voice catching.

He looked to his dad.

His father made a noise I never wanted to hear again in my whole life.

Before he carried on with this, I leaned over and touched Rogan's face.

He turned his gaze to me.

"That's not how Rogan Kirk goes out," I told him. "The man who was so handsome, I found it hard to breathe, just looking at him."

"Clara."

His voice was so weak.

So weak.

"My first love," I went on.

He closed his eyes.

"You asked me if I loved you, but you didn't notice I didn't have to ask if you loved me."

He opened his eyes.

"I always knew, Rogan. You never let me doubt it."

"The women—"

"Stop it," I hissed.

He shut up.

"Our wedding day, do you remember?" I asked.

"Yes."

God.

His voice was getting weaker.

"You trying to get to me, and Tia was barring the door, shouting about how a groom isn't supposed to see the bride," I continued.

His eyes closed.

His lips curved.

"But you got in, didn't you? Nothing could keep you from me."

"So beautiful," he whispered.

"Yes, that's what I thought about you. And then I tripped during our first dance."

His lips stayed curved.

"You caught me and laughed so hard and held me close through the rest of the song, just swaying."

His lips stayed curved.

"Whispering in my ear what a klutz I was and how cute you thought it was."

His lips stayed curved.

"I loved you, Rogan."

"Loved...me."

The words drifted.

"I loved you so much, Rogan."

His lips were still curved.

"I loved that you loved me."

His lips remained curved.

"I loved how much you loved me."

His lips stayed curved.

"Sorry, sorry, I'm so sorry," a woman said quietly. "He's gone."

His mother's sob tore through the room.

I dropped my head to his hand I was still holding.

And I remembered him holding me so close, laughing as he swayed me on the dance floor the day we got married.

It took me some time, but I lifted my head and I didn't look at him.

I didn't want to remember him that way.

I just kissed his hand and straightened away.

My eyes caught on his family.

His dad was holding his wife and daughter in his arms, both crying in his chest.

His father was looking at me.

"Thank you," he mouthed.

I nodded.

Turned.

Walked out of the room on legs that felt strange.

Down the hall.

Buck got to me first, wrapping both his arms around my head and shoving it against his chest.

Tatie wrapped herself around me next.

Gear, after that.

Tia pushed in.

Mrs. Jimenez rubbed my back.

I let the love of my family instill some strength back into me.

Then I put some pressure on my head and Buck loosened his hold.

I tipped it back.

"Can we go home?" I asked.

He stared into my eyes.

And answered.

"Absolutely."

34

VOODOO

"Jesus, you need to chill out, darlin'."

"Yeah, Toots, it's only Granddad. You need to chill out."

"I think Clara's bein' kinda cute."

This was coming from Buck (the first), Tatie (the second) and Gear (the last).

We were standing by a round picnic table that was bolted to the floor in a big room that was a sea of round tables that people were standing by or sitting at.

All of this in a prison.

I was in high-heeled booties, dark-wash, bootleg jeans, a long-sleeved white tee and a spruce blue, open front, high-low, waterfall cardie.

This outfit had taken three days, five phone calls to Minnie, two to Lorie, and one to get validation from Pinky before I decided on it.

It had a minimal edge (the booties), so it did not scream *BIKER BABE!*

I should have worn my high-heeled boots and a jeans miniskirt (an item of apparel I did not own).

Then again, we had a dress code we had to adhere to, and miniskirts were prohibited.

A door at the far end opened and a bunch of men in orange jump-suits started strolling in.

Too late now.

"Oh dear," I whispered.

"Babe," the arm Buck had around my neck gave me a squeeze, "he's gonna love you."

"Right," I muttered.

"He's totally gonna love you," Tatie added.

"Right," I repeated.

"Clary, fuck, you love us, we love you, he's not gonna have to get with the program," Gear said, sounding like he was laughing. "He's just gonna *be* with the program."

I was about to look at Gear.

But then a tall, handsome man with a good deal of silver in his still-dark hair came sauntering through the door. A man I'd seen younger in pictures. A man who exuded magnetism and charisma, even in an orange jumpsuit with a white T-shirt under it.

And I just barely curbed my desire to bolt.

He caught sight of us, and a big smile lit his face, widening the silver-and-dark goatee around his lips.

"Granddad!" Tatie called.

He put his arms out before he got to us, so when he made it to us, they were in position for Tatie to fall into them.

And she did.

We were allowed physical contact.

Hugs. Cheek kisses. Handshakes.

At the beginning and end of the visit.

Tatie got her hug and cheek kiss.

Gear got his hug with several stout pounds on the back.

Buck got his hug, no pounding on the back, it was tight, and it lasted longer.

Oh God, yes,

Locke Hardy loved his son.

A lot.

Buck broke from his dad and turned to me.

"Here she is. Clara," he introduced.

"Honey," Locke Hardy said softly in his gravelly voice that reminded me of Buck's.

My eyes instantly started stinging, but gamely, I shoved out my hand.

He was shifting my way, but he stopped when I did that and stared at it.

"She's nervous, Granddad," Tatie announced.

"And she's being a total dork," Gear added.

Locke looked to his namesake.

"Son," he said with soft reproach.

"Well, she is," Gear replied.

"It's nice to meet you, Mr. Hardy," I declared.

He looked at me with his warm, brown eyes.

"All right, darlin', I'll give you that one, but then we're not doin' that anymore. Yeah?"

"Sorry?"

He moved right past my hand and hugged me.

Okay.

Yes.

I was totally going to cry.

"Thanks for lookin' after my granddaughter," he whispered in my ear.

Oh God!

Totally going to cry!

"And makin' m'boy happy."

"My, uh...it's my pleasure."

"And I'm Locke, or you can call me Dad. Though you can wait on that 'til we get to know each other better. Your call."

He wasn't helping!

"Okay," I said shakily.

He lifted his head but didn't take his arms from around me and shared, "You can hug me back. I don't bite."

"Oh no!" I cried. "It wasn't that. I just—"

"Buck talks to his daddy," he said softly. "I know you don't got a lot of practice with this, Clara. We'll get used to it, though."

I nodded.

Then I slid my arms around him.

He pressed his jaw against the side of my head, gave me a squeeze and let me go.

Buck claimed me, smiling down at me with a smile that shared he thought I was a dork.

We moved to the table, all of us sat, and Tatie started babbling about...well, about everything.

I'd never seen her so animated.

Then again, Locke could not have a lot of interest in half the things she said, but he looked like all of it was pearls of wisdom he could scoop up and be the wisest man in the world.

Gear got his turn.

And finally, Buck shared, mostly news about the brothers, the Club and the business.

Locke did not share.

They didn't press.

I figured he didn't have much to say about the life he led, and furthermore, if he told them, they wouldn't want to know.

So they didn't ask.

But his eyes did eventually move between Buck and me before he asked, "So, when you two gonna get hitched?"

"Soon's possible," Buck said.

At the same time, I said, "After Christmas."

Buck looked down at me. "After Christmas?"

I looked up at him. "Is that too soon?"

"Did you not hear me say 'soon's possible?'" he asked.

"I did. But you haven't even asked me officially yet. Therefore, 'soon's possible' is indefinite."

"But you know I'm gonna ask."

"I do, and Christmas is a good time to ask."

"Christmas is over a month away."

Oh my God.

My voice was pitched higher when I queried, "Were you going to ask earlier?"

"Tatie helped me pick out the ring. You want it, I'll give it to you tonight."

"Oh my God," I whispered.

"I think she wants it, Dad," Gear put in.

"I want a baby sister," Tatie added.

"No way, a baby brother," Gear contradicted.

"Okay, no. Dad's got all his brothers in Aces. We're outnumbered. We need a girl," Tatie returned.

"I gotta have a chance to show a baby bro the ropes," Gear shot back.

"Think we don't got a problem sharin' with the kids we got plans to expand the family," Buck drawled.

"*Awesome*," Tatie breathed excitedly.

"Clary, baby bro, get on that," Gear ordered.

I tore my gaze from Buck's amused, happy one and looked to his son.

"I can't pick the gender, Locke," I replied.

"We'll do some voodoo or somethin'," he said, grinning.

"Yes, voodoo to get a baby sister," Tatie demanded.

"I'm down to attempt voodoo, but I'll warn you, if it worked, voodoo practices to guarantee the gender of a child would be far more widespread," I informed them.

"Doesn't hurt tryin'," Gear said.

"Just as long as we don't have to kill a chicken or something," Tatie laid out her boundaries.

"You always have to kill a chicken," Gear, the new voice of voodoo authority, educated her.

"We won't be killing any chickens," Buck laid down the law. "And you'll get what you get, however it pops out."

Tatiana looked to me and said, "Pops out. As if. *Men*," before she giggled.

I rolled my eyes, shook my head, and smiled at her.

"Son," Locke called.

We all looked to him.

But I felt what he had to say but did not verbalize as he stared at his boy.

I felt it from the kids.

I felt it from Locke.

Mostly, I felt it in the way Buck was suddenly holding his body very still.

And it felt beautiful.

I suspected they could spend the rest of the visit staring at each other that way.

But we only had two hours.

So I sallied forth.

"What do you want, Locke? A boy or a girl."

His brown eyes came to me.

And I was again awash.

Joy.

"Whatever grandbaby you give me, girl. Just keep yourself safe and healthy givin' it to me."

"That I'll do," I promised.

He reached a hand across the table, turning it, palm up.

I took it.

We squeezed.

He let go fast, probably because physical contact wasn't prohibited entirely during the visit.

But we had to be careful.

And I hurt for all of them because they were a touchy family and I knew they needed it.

I also now hurt for me.

Tatie forged in to cover that loss. "Dad topped up your commissary for you, Granddad. And we brought some things. We left them at reception."

"You always do, baby, and I always love whatever you bring," Locke replied.

The rest of the visit went well, considering.

But at the end of it, Locke asked to talk to Buck for a second alone.

The kids and I walked out to the SUV.

Fifteen minutes later, Buck walked out.

I wasn't going to ask.

It was theirs.

I didn't have to ask.

Before Buck started the car, he reached out, wrapped his fingers around my knee and held on.

I looked into his eyes.
I read him.
And then I smiled.

35

PROBLEMS

Buck

The atmosphere in the Aces High meet room was intense.

Some of the brothers did not like certain company they were keeping.

Some of the brothers didn't like any company in the meet room of the Aces High MC that wasn't Aces.

Not surprisingly, it was Sylvie Creed who had the balls to break into it.

Sylvie, five-foot-two, blonde, mother of Buck didn't know how many since that number kept growing, and a badass.

"Right, way I see it, you boys got three problems," she declared.

No one said anything.

Buck sat at the head of the table, drumming his fingers, because they'd had a good run.

From Rogan Kirk's funeral to now, five days before Christmas, it'd been trouble-free.

Kids home, happy to be back with their old friends.

Gear had his first girlfriend.

Tat was dating, and Buck might be the only father breathing who was relieved when his gorgeous daughter went on a date.

But Gear had shared the kid was solid.

And Clara had informed him, "Tatie really likes him, and I think this is turning an important corner, honey."

Since their first date, Tat had been out with the guy three times, and Buck had met him. He couldn't find fault in the kid. He was into his girl. He didn't seem like a creep or an asshole.

The rest remained to be seen.

Buck's dad dug Clara to the point he wasted no time and made no bones about the strength of his stamp of approval.

One visit, she won him over.

Then again, it was Clara.

Buck had fallen for her in about the same amount of time.

Further, the store was doing a good turnover.

And they had so much work on the contracting side, they were going to have to recruit more people, or more brothers, or they'd have to schedule far out, which might mean they'd lose business.

Clara had embraced her new tub and had a little table set up next to it filled with all sorts of shit.

She'd also paid off her credit cards early.

This was because she had a little less than three million dollars in the bank.

The government took its share.

She gave the million and a half back to the pension fund.

But now, his woman was loaded.

For him, that manifested itself in sexy underwear, something she was on a mission to one-up her own damned self in getting a rise out of her man with each new set.

She achieved that feat.

She got a rise out of him.

Every time.

But she didn't need the underwear.

That said, Buck didn't share that with her.

Life was steady.

Good.

And then what started happening, happened.

Ending in what happened yesterday.

Which was why Buck was drumming his fingers.

Because he was pissed that run was over.

"First one," Sylvie continued. "As we all know, Enrique Esposito was found, relieved of his head, yesterday."

Yeah.

They all knew that.

Rayne Scott was staring at the table so hard it was a wonder his gaze didn't burn through it.

He probably wasn't a big fan of Esposito's.

He was less a fan of murder.

But beheading took that *way* to the highest level.

Sylvie kept going

"We also know this wasn't a loss to humanity. Onward from that, this happened because he let Tia Esposito get her hands on some pretty damning shit, and that was part of what led to the arrests Scott and his boys made last week."

Yeah.

They knew that too.

Didn't take long for the higher-ups to link who went down with those arrests to what Esposito had knowledge about, and corroborating evidence for, and for them to take care of Esposito.

The issue with that was, they didn't gut him or shoot him.

They beheaded the motherfucker.

Everyone was wired just because of that.

That said some serious shit.

"So," Sylvie went on, her gaze locked to Damian, "you wanna share with the class why Tia Esposito is still in Phoenix?"

"She wants to have Christmas with her girl," Damian replied, his tone openly unhappy.

Because he was.

It didn't take a psychologist to see the guy was twitchy.

And he was that way because he wanted himself and Tia in Bali or someplace like that about two weeks ago.

"We got players spreadin' the word that it was what they thought it was. Esposito was pissed they took him down a notch, so he laid those boys out by handing shit to the cops," Lynch put in, and Buck looked to him.

Lynch and Slate were back after spending months trying to find Tia.

And of course, Clara had met them.

After which, she'd felt the need to inform him they were "exceptionally good-looking, almost as handsome as you!"

Buck studied Lynch.

He didn't see it.

"Tia's back, Damian is tight with Scott, you don't think they'll put those together?" Tucker Creed, a good friend of Buck's and Sylvie's husband, asked.

"I think we're runnin' the best interference we can on that until Damian can haul her ass outta Phoenix," Slate responded to Tucker.

Buck looked at his other brother.

He didn't see it with him either.

He then sighed.

Tia being hauled out of Phoenix had two meanings for him.

The first, it was clear Damian was not going to do anything without Tia with him.

And as such, his woman could quit worrying that Damian was going to get shot of her girl to carry on his "rootless life."

He could have called that two months ago, something he told Clara repeatedly.

The man was gone for her girl.

Clara still worried.

The second, now he was going to have a woman on his hands who again was going to lose her best friend.

Yeah, Buck had given her Lorie, Minnie, Pinky, the rest of the old ladies, and Toots and Tatie were thicker than thieves.

Fuck, they were at the Valley Inn the other night and some woman had told Clara, "You and your daughter are so sweet together!" And Clara was the only female alive who was barely old enough to be claimed as a mom of a sixteen-year-old who would beam that bright at that comment.

But she was going to feel the hit of Tia being gone again. Even if she could talk to her.

Those two were *tight*.

He reckoned, given the lives they'd lived together, navigating the system, that happened.

So he didn't want his woman to lose her girl.

"She gonna go after Christmas?" Sylvie asked Damian.

"After Christmas, I'm not giving her a choice," Damian answered.

There were a number of approving grunts sounding in the room.

"Right, second problem," Sylvie continued counting them down. "Aces High is back on radar, times two. The Esposito shit, which, I don't need to remind you also includes a personal member of the family being tied to it, and along the line, they might remember that."

Buck felt a muscle jump in his cheek, seeing as Clara was that "personal member of the family."

"Redhot has dick to do with any a' Esposito's shit," Chap clipped.

"She's just saying, you might be in a position to remind them of that," Tucker pointed out.

No one had a response.

Sylvie kept talking.

"And Imran Babić is a very poor loser."

This was what Buck wanted to talk about.

And this was why Buck had called the meet.

Pinky had left work the night before, went to her car, and found a note under her wiper blade that said, *I don't get her, I want you.*

It had freaked her, she'd told Cruise about it, Cruise told Ink about it within earshot of Lorie, and Lorie had shared she'd had the same thing. She thought it was a mistake, or some crazy marketing thing, so she'd thrown it away.

Commence Ink tagging Buck, and Buck hauling everyone in for this meet.

They knew it was Imran because Lynch and Slate went to the bar where Pinky worked, demanded to see their security tapes, and they saw one of Babić's boys place the note.

Those boys knew those cameras were there. They weren't acting sneaky.

That meant Babić wanted them to know who was communicating.

The other old ladies were asked, none of them had received one, but now, they were on high alert.

It didn't take much to jump from I *don't get her*, the "her" being Clara, I *want you*, that Babić, like Babić could do, was going to start playing with them.

And Babić was a lunatic.

So that was a problem.

And he was already a problem, kidnapping Clara at all, much less the way he had.

So now, he was a *big* problem.

"Your last problem is that Eleanor Moynihan is one serious liability," Sylvie finished. "Because a woman who's convinced herself she was wronged is a helluva wildcard."

Buck looked to Gash.

Eleanor Moynihan was Nails.

And since Buck had turned her out in a way she would never get back in, she'd been fucking with them.

It started with a "pregnancy scare" that ended up nothing.

But that didn't mean she didn't rope Gash and Cruise into that situation, sharing it could be either of their kid.

And she did this by telling both Minnie and Pinky that she might be carrying one of their men's baby.

Pinky had been devastated.

Cruise had lost his mind, pissed at Nails, but even so, he'd focused since he was more concerned with the thought of losing Pinky.

Buck had given the man some time because he was a brother, a friend, and a good man who had occasion to do something seriously stupid.

Chap, however, turned him out.

Some things Chap was willing to counsel you about.

Others, he figured you should just know. And if you didn't, he wasn't going to waste his time educating you.

Cruise talked Pinky into trying to work it out.

They were trying.

From what Clara said, it wasn't really working.

But they were still trying.

Minnie had scraped Gash off.

Done.

The end.

Which put Buck in a tough position because—on threat of having access to Clara's body being denied "for an appropriate time of punishment, you've got your brother code, I've got my sister one" (her words)—he couldn't tell Gash that Minnie was in his living room with his woman, crying her eyes out about the man she loved cheating on her, losing him and her family.

But there was no turning her back.

Not that Clara had tried.

She'd just explained to Buck, "She knew, or figured it was a possibility. I think it's more about him acting like he was innocent and throwing you under the bus. Being a man like that and taking a good man down to be able to keep doing it. I also think she's embarrassed that cast aspersions on her Professor Higginsing. She was pretty proud of being my biker babe mentor."

For Buck's part, it went against the brother code, but he'd shared with Clara that Gash had not been a stranger to the liquor stock in the Dive and was making it his mission to down as much of it as he could in order to drown his guilt and loss.

An endeavor which appeared to be failing.

And after sharing this, Buck had not denied Clara the option of giving this to Minnie.

She had, and Minnie might have been affected by it, but not enough to give Gash a shot at redemption.

So now Buck had this issue both ways, Gash as a brother, Minnie as his woman's sister, and they'd had to declare boundaries.

Minnie got their house, and Gash wasn't allowed there if there was something happening where people could be invited, occasions where Minnie always showed.

Obviously, Gash got Ace.

But Nails wasn't done.

A week ago, in the store, she'd pretended to slip and fall and hit her head on a display.

Bitch didn't consider they had cameras everywhere.

And while she was moaning and threatening lawsuits, Jimbo pulled up the video on an iPad of her sitting her own self down and then starting to shout and showed it to her.

They now had pictures of her everywhere, in the store, warehouse, even in the Dive (but that was just a joke), put up by Driver, that said, IF YOU SEE THIS WOMAN, REPORT HER TO MANAGEMENT IMMEDIATELY.

Unfortunately, someone had told Nails about this.

Which meant yesterday, she'd come in, trying to tear all of them down, and so no one was in danger of having her claim shit if they laid hands on her, they'd had to call the cops.

But she wasn't done.

They knew this because, under escort of the police to her vehicle, she got in her car, shrieking, "*I'm not done with all y'all in the Aces High MC!*"

"So, to sum up," Sylvie said, "you got possible issues with a drug cartel, whatever Babić is, but all he is, is no good, and a skank bent on vengeance. Over to you, Scott."

She ended with her gaze on Scott.

"I cannot say Tia, or Aces, is not in deep shit," Scott said like he really did not want to. "We're gonna have to turn over the evidence to the defense. So they'll know how much we got, where it came from, and this could cause some uncomfortable questions to be asked. And those won't be uncomfortable for the DA. They'll be uncomfortable for Tia and maybe Aces. Tia was followed. Enrique's boys knew what she had. We don't know, but they could also know she was going to go on the run with Clara. Which is another link between them and to this shit that's not good."

No, it wasn't.

"Thought those boys were neutralized," Sylvie noted.

"I am not here for this part of the discussion," Scott said, but he didn't move.

Shit.

Buck might have to start liking this guy.

"Don't know if they reported in. Don't know if the threat of her havin' that shit was passed up the chain. Don't know if Enrique talked before they axed him," Damian put in, still unhappy. "So Tia is a ghost come December twenty-sixth."

Fuck.

Damian looked at Buck. "And the men who went down, they're middle management. Important, but not too important. Though, they know the drill. They'll keep their mouths shut. And if they do, and it ends with them, this will blow over. If they don't, and other dominoes fall, she may be a ghost forever, man."

Fuck.

Buck shook that off and asked Scott, "You got anything on Babić?"

"Keep your shit sharp with that nutjob," Scott advised.

"That doesn't help, Rayne," Buck noted.

"If you gave me the choice of taking one person off the street and incapacitating him forever, I'd pick Imran Babić," Scott declared. "The problem is, we got nothin'. We know he's fucked in the head. We know he's dirty. But he's like a criminal savant. Crazy as fuck. But genius at keeping his shit under wraps."

Buck sat back in his chair.

"You want, I'm on Eleanor," Sylvie offered. "Got a colleague named Sixx, she and I'll have all sorts of girlie fun handling her. Usual fees apply, of course."

Tucker turned his eyes to the ceiling.

Tucker's response meant, if they gave the go-ahead to that, Nails was fucked.

Buck looked through the room and tallied unanimous chin lifts.

"Do it," he said to Sylvie.

Sylvie grinned.

Oh yeah.

Nails was fucked.

He then turned his attention to Damian.

"I want a brother on you at all times."

"I got it," Damian said.

"You also got Clara's best friend in your care. She had one person her whole life who didn't fuck her over in some way before she had me, and that was Tia. So I want a brother on you at all times."

Damian didn't like it. Buck sensed he worked alone, always.

But he nodded.

"The rest, brothers only," Buck declared.

He didn't have to explain that, and it didn't take long for Sylvie, Tucker, Scott and Damian to clear out.

He waited until the door was closed and then he waited longer.

Then he said to the table, "Resurrection."

"Damn straight," Chap grunted.

"You want me on the line with Beck?" Slate asked.

"Vote," Buck said. "All in favor we contact the Resurrection MC to help us handle Babić?"

"Yea," Ink said.

"Yea," Cruise said.

"Yea," Chap unnecessarily.

"Fuckin' yea," Lynch said.

The rest of the men voted unanimous, and Buck looked to Slate.

"Call Beck."

Beck being the president of the Resurrection Motorcycle Club.

There was general talk about a variety of things, and men moved out.

In the end, it was Buck, Chap, Ink, Cruise, Gash, Riot, Lynch and Slate.

Ink, the voice of reason, spoke.

"I voted yea, but Resurrection is some serious shit, brother."

"Babić is gonna play with us and do it through our women," Buck reminded him.

"They're the angels of death, Buck." Ink did some reminding of his own.

"I give them the words 'former foster kid' and 'woman,' they'll tear Phoenix up before they let any more hurt fall on Clara," Slate remarked.

"This is what I'm saying," Ink replied.

"No more hurt is gonna fall on Clara," Buck said.

"Buck, brother—"

"No. More. Hurt. Is. Gonna. *Fall*. On. *Clara*," Buck decreed. "He picked her girls. Only her girls. He did that for a reason. He's not fuckin' with me, or you, Ink, or Cruise, or the Club. He's usin' us to fuck with her. And she's not gonna feel that. I don't give a fuck what we gotta do, she's ours. She's family. And she's not gonna feel that."

Ink sat back.

He was on board with that.

"I got a call to make," Slate said, rising while pulling out his phone and leaving the room.

It didn't take long for the rest of the room to empty.

Leaving him with Chap.

"Proud a' you, bud," Chap said.

Buck said nothing.

"Your dad would be proud of you too."

Buck looked his friend in the eye.

He felt his words in his chest.

But said nothing.

"I'll tell him that, I visit him. You takin' Clara and the kids to see him for the holidays?"

"We're goin' tomorrow."

"He thinks Clara is the shit."

"I know, that's 'cause Clara is the shit. I also know 'cause he's told me."

"He hated Kristy."

Buck fell silent again.

He knew that too.

"You done good, bud," Chap said quietly.

And he knew that too.

Fuck, yeah.

He knew that too.

EPILOGUE
HOWL AT THE MOON

An hour and a half after the meet, Buck navigated the various cars in his drive to park, exit his vehicle and climb the stairs to his front door.

Gear, Damian, Ink and Raymundo were sitting out on the deck under a space heater.

"Take my wise advice, Dad," Gear said. "Do not go in there."

Buck looked through the windows into his house.

There was the hugest-ass Christmas tree he'd ever seen in the corner covered in so many ornaments, you could only just make out there was a tree under there somewhere.

It was lit bright.

There was a fire in the fireplace.

Tia was on the floor in front of the fire with some little kids, putting together a puzzle.

He moved his eyes left.

Clara was in the kitchen with Tatie, Mrs. Jimenez, Minnie, Lorie, Raymundo's wife Griselle and some other kids, and it looked like a red and green icing bomb had exploded in it, detonating some little silver and gold balls along with it.

Though, it was mostly icing.

Icing was everywhere.

Including in Clara's hair.

"Gingerbread men decoration," Gear informed him. "She wants to make sure Mrs. J can take a tin full of 'em to all her kids."

"I have one brother and two sisters," Raymundo shared, grinning. "And a warning, *hermano*, Ma's got all the grandkids in there."

He'd already seen that.

"Correction, Clara wants to make sure they each have a *huge-ass* tin," Gear amended.

"You go in there, tell them you gotta come right back out with fresh beers," Damian suggested a way out.

Though it was more an order because Buck could see he was almost dry.

"I'm making you all hamburgers," Buck reminded them of the reason they were all there.

"You got 'em formed yet?" Ink asked.

"No," Buck answered.

"Good luck with that," Ink muttered, belting back another slug of beer.

Buck let out a deep breath and headed to the door.

"Buck," Damian called.

He stopped and looked at Damian.

"Tia and Clara, never in their lives, surrounded by people and little kids, made gingerbread men," he stated.

He didn't have to be reminded.

But the reminder still served its purpose.

This had been, from the minute Rogan Kirk bit it, a situation.

Because Buck had only wanted to make certain Clara knew she had her people and they had her back.

What he'd done in actuality was show her she had a big family, and she'd made it her meaning in life to take care of it.

Pure Clara.

This was the first icing bomb that had exploded.

But he'd formed a fuckuva lot of hamburgers since that day.

He walked into his house.

"Daddy!" Tatie cried and raced to him.

She had icing in her hair too.

She'd also never made gingerbread men in her kitchen with her family.

"Hey, Buck!" Tia greeted.

"*Hola*, West," Mrs. J called.

"Yo, bro," Minnie said.

"Hiya, Buck," Lorie called.

But Clara just looked at him, her gorgeous face soft and sweet and happy her man was home.

Tatie hit him, and he put his arms around his girl.

"We're making gingerbread men. Doesn't it smell *awesome?*"

It totally did.

"Yeah, honey," he murmured, grinning down at her and giving her a squeeze.

She glowed up at him, squeezed him back, then let him go and dashed off, grabbing a little kid and throwing him in the air, the kid squealing as she did.

And she went right back to Clara.

Jesus, not five months ago she was on the floor of the bathroom, beat to shit, having managed by a miracle to escape three assholes intent on altering her life for the extent of it in ways she'd never completely recover from.

This escape happening after they'd altered her life in a way he knew, and it tore him apart every time he thought about it, she'd never completely recover from.

Now, she didn't go out and party and get drunk. She dated that guy. Hung with her friends. Stayed home and did her homework when she had homework to do.

And worshiped at the altar of Clara.

She was getting a car for Christmas, Clara's idea, but Buck agreed completely.

Cruise had found it. A vintage, drop-top Mustang.

It was parked down at the warehouse. Driver and Gash had agreed to get it up to the house sometime late Christmas Eve, early Christmas morning.

She'd love it.

He had no idea if she had dark times. He just knew from Clara, "Debbie has that covered."

He also knew, if Clara hadn't been around, the girl he had would not be the same girl.

He would hope he'd find the means to be what she needed him to be and give her what she needed in order to push through.

But it could not be denied, he was lucky in more than the countless ways he was already that Clara was around when that shit went down.

He said hey to Griselle, got attacked by a couple of kids, and finally made it to his woman.

He got a lip touch then a sober, "Talk to you a minute?"

Oh shit.

He nodded.

She didn't delay and took him to their bedroom.

When she closed the door, he informed her, "You have icing in your hair."

Her hands flew up.

"Really?" she asked.

"Babe, do not touch your hair with those hands."

She dropped her green-and-red-stained hands that still had bits of liquid-sugar encrusted on them, and looked at them.

Then she giggled to herself.

Christ.

Christ.

She was happy.

He gave her that.

Icing in her hair and a huge-ass Christmas tree she and Tatie kept coming home from wherever they went with more and more new ornaments for, and that giggle.

He gave her all of that.

The very idea of something happening to him and his kids going into the system made him feel the need to hurl.

Her story wasn't the worst, but it was not good from the moment of birth to the moment she'd walked into the Dive.

And now he could hear Christmas music, chatter, and smell even their bedroom reeked of cookies.

And his woman was giggling.

No matter he felt that down deep in his gut, and it was the best feeling he'd had except the moment he'd learned both his kids had come safe and healthy into the world, he wanted to get this over with.

Clara's "talk to you a minutes" came often these days.

That was because the woman was loaded, and Christmas was coming.

He'd already nixed her paying for Tatie's car, but barely.

He'd nixed her renting some luxury house in Mexico for Gear and all his buds—from there *and* from Flag—for their senior spring break, but barely.

He'd nixed her footing the bill for a top-of-the-line family whale watching cruise in Alaska (of all fucking things), but barely.

It came to the point he'd had to throw her a bone, so they were going skiing in Vail after Christmas. That said, they were splitting the cost of it.

He was a biker. He didn't ski.

But the kids boarded.

So the kids could board, and he and Clara could fuck.

In other words, that worked.

"Let's get this over with," he muttered.

"Sorry?" she asked.

"Whatever you got in your head to give to one of the kids, ask me. I'll say no, since it's probably diamonds for Tatie or a world tour for Gear, then I can start forming burgers. I got mouths to feed."

"I'm done Christmas shopping," she shared.

Thank fuck for that.

They'd run out of room under the tree a week ago, so that shit had started spreading all over the floor.

"Kristy called."

He felt his body jerk.

"Come again?" he asked.

"Kristy called," she repeated.

"Tatie?"

"No."

"Gear?"

She shook her head.

He heard a hissing in his head and whispered, "You?"

"Yes. But—"

"She called you."

"Yes. And—"

"Personally. Your phone."

She nodded. "Yes, West. But, listen—"

"How'd she get your number?"

"I don't know. I didn't ask. Now—"

He pulled his phone out and engaged it.

He didn't get further because her hand was around his wrist.

"What are you doing?" she asked.

"Calling her ass and making it clear you are off fuckin' limits for her."

"Buck, she asked what the kids wanted for Christmas," she said softly.

Jesus.

"Seriously?"

"And she wanted to know, since they both dissed her for Christmas stuff, if we could do a day-after-Christmas thing. Like a lunch or something."

Buck stared at her.

"I told her we were going to Vail the day after—"

"Babe, that's a surprise and she's gonna share that shit," he growled.

"No. I told her it was their present and she promised she wouldn't."

She got closer and dropped his wrist but fitted her tits to his chest.

He could smell her.

See the bright in her eyes.

And feel her.

So he suddenly felt a whole lot better about just about everything.

"She wasn't exactly nice, but she was polite. I think she was a little embarrassed she had to ask. But she did. And she said she'd be cool to wait to do an after-New-Years thing."

"Right," he muttered, sliding his hands along her waist.

"And I told her it'd be cool for her to come down and deliver her gifts. Not tomorrow. We're visiting Locke tomorrow. So I said the day after. If you agreed. And she agreed if you agree. So...do you agree?"

"She wants the kids here when she drops them?"

"That'd be optimal."

"It's up to them, Toots."

She nodded.

"The after-New-Years thing is up to them too."

She nodded again.

"I'll tell Kristy that. I don't want her to think she has a line to you."

"It wasn't a terrible conversation, West. And it was for good reasons."

"I'll talk to Kristy. I don't want her to think she has a line to you," he mostly repeated.

Again, she nodded, but this time, she put her hands on his shoulders when she did.

"You're gonna get icing on me," he murmured, having lost interest in the conversation with her mouth that close.

"Do you care?"

"Fuck no."

"I didn't think so. Are we gonna make out?'

"Fuck yes."

"I thought so. But, West, we can't do it for ages. We have comp—"

He kissed her quiet.

He didn't do it for ages.

And when he was done, they both had to go to the bathroom and brush icing out of their hair.

She giggled through doing this.

Buck enjoyed listening to her giggle through it.

After, they rejoined their company.

He formed burgers.

He grilled them.

The women cleared away the cookie shit and got down to frying tots, slicing tomato and onion and sorting other hamburger stuff.

He fed their family.

And it was Buck's estimation they overstayed their welcome.

But seeing Clara, ass on the floor in front of the tree, leaning against Gear, who had his arms around her, both of them talking and laughing...

He couldn't find it in him to give much of a shit.

"You want an early Christmas present?"

"No."

"Are you sure?"

"Yes."

"Are you sure you're sure?"

"Yes."

"Are you *certain* you're sure you're sure?"

Buck rolled his woman off him onto her back and looked at her through the moonlight.

Everyone was gone.

The kids were out.

They'd just finished fucking.

They didn't have a long drive tomorrow to see his dad.

But it was late, he'd come hard, he'd made her do the same, and he needed sleep.

And now she was giving him this.

"Is it another set of underwear?" he asked.

"Nooooooo." She drew that out.

"Is it a trip around the world?"

"Do you want a trip around the world?"

"No."

"Then, no."

Fuck.

"*Was* it a trip around the world?" he asked.

"Buck, just let me give it to you."

She wanted to give him something?

She dug doing that (and she did)?

He'd let her do it.

"Right. Go for it."

"I'm pregnant."

Buck grew solid.

"And it's confirmed. Like, not pregnancy-test pregnant. Doctor-test pregnant. So we can tell Locke and the kids tomorrow!" she stated gleefully.

"Were we trying?" he asked.

"Well," she said, now hesitant, "only in the sense that you seemed to want to have a baby. And I'm not twenty-two anymore. You aren't either. And we have our wedding planned for the day after Valentine's Day, because Valentine's Day is too gooey, and that day falls on a Saturday. And..." She paused, a long time, and then asked, "Did you not want to, you know, uh...see, I thought it'd be a really good present."

"I'm trying not to howl at the moon."

"Pardon?"

"I am trying not...to howl...at the moon," he said slowly.

"Is that, um...a good thing?"

"You got my baby in you?"

"Yeeeessss," she drew that out too.

"And you gotta ask that shit?"

"You don't seem very...elated."

"Until I have a minute to let the news settle, I might hurt you, I'm so...elated."

"Really?"

His hands moved and her body jumped, they did it so fast.

But he caught her head and put his face in hers.

"Clara, do you have any fuckin' clue what it feels like to be a man who got it so damned wrong the first time around, he had to watch his kids pay for that, knowin' he's got something totally fuckin' right, and he gets to give a kid that?"

"I didn't, but I think I'm getting it," she whispered, her voice strange.

"You gonna cry?"

"You're being very sweet."

"Clara, darlin', you got my baby in you. That's no reason to cry."

"Happy tears."

Fuck.

Happy.

She was happy they were going to have a baby.

"Do you know what it's like to have it wrong from the start and be given the gift of being able to give a child something so completely right?" she asked.

"You didn't have it wrong."

"It was still wrong. And now it's very right."

Fuck.

"I love you, Buck," she said.

"I know you do, baby, and I love you too."

"Are you happy?"

"I'm elated."

She let out a little hiccupping giggle.

And ended it crying.

He kissed her, rolling them to their sides.

And then he kept kissing her.

He ended it reaching up to touch his lips to her nose and then tucking her tight to his front.

He thought she was going to sleep.

She wasn't going to sleep.

He knew that when she said, "You know, we had to go through it all to get here and *get* what we have...right here."

"I know."

And he did know.

But he didn't have to like it.

"So, if you had the power to erase it, I wouldn't know, after all that, how amazingly lucky I was to be *right here.*"

Amazingly lucky.

Buck closed his eyes.

And said, "I know."

"I can't wait to tell the kids."

"Yeah."

"And Locke. I think he'll be happy."

"He'll be happy. I'm happy and you're happy, baby. So yeah, he'll be really fuckin' happy."

"I love to make you happy, Buck."

"It's good you're doin' something you love."

She giggled and then she snuggled.

He gathered her closer.

"'Night, West," she murmured, all sleepy. "Merry early Christmas."

"'Night, Toots," he whispered. "Thank you for the best fuckin' present ever."

She pressed even closer.

"My pleasure."

He grinned into the dark.

Clara fell asleep.

Buck remained awake.

After a while, he tipped his head back and looked out the windows at the moon.

He didn't howl.

"You'd like her, Ma," he said quietly.

The moon had no reply.

HE'D GET the reply seven months later, when they had her, and they had a name all picked out for her. But sweaty and red-faced, hair sticking to her skin, Clara's gorgeous blue eyes came to him with their little girl curled all mucky on her chest, and she said,

"I think she's Lenora."

That wasn't the name they'd picked.

So Buck knew.

His mom approved.

But in that moment, to his wife.

He agreed.

TWO WEEKS AFTER THAT, he carried Lenora and the bag he had into their bedroom.

Clara was curled up in the chair in the corner, reading.

"Did you guys have fun running your errand?" she asked.

"Mm," he hummed his answer.

She didn't hesitate to put her book aside when he handed her their girl.

Buck then went to the bed, dumped what was in the bag on it, and got on with sorting it.

Once he took the thing out of the cardboard envelope and put it in the other, he turned to the dresser.

Making adjustments, he shifted a bit to the side the pic Tatie took with her selfie stick of the four of them wrapped around each other in front of the tree on Christmas morning that was front and center.

And he shifted back the frame that had a pic of the four of them at the foot of Vail Mountain, all in winter gear, the kids with their boards planted in the snow, Clara looking cute with a hat with a big fluffy ball at the top of it pulled down to her ears.

And he shifted the frame that was angled with the first one he'd moved, holding that center space.

A frame that had the pic of Clara standing next to him out in the area beyond the front of the deck. She was wearing a white dress with thin straps, lace with the tiny dots and big flowers stitched in overlying it, sleeves of that lace that went down to her elbows. It had a semi-wide skirt that had a slit up the front to her mid-thigh and a thin white belt tied around her waist.

A gown she'd worn with bright pink, sexy sandals.

She had her arms around his middle, her cheek to his white shirt, her foot kicked back, exposing her shoes and a shapely calf.

A massive smile was on her face.

Same as him.

That was because, beside them, Tatiana, wearing her bridesmaid dress, had just jumped up on Gear's back.

And Gear had caught her.

Both his kids were full-on, eyes closed, mouths-open laughing.

He had good-looking kids.

He set the new frame down. Eight by ten. Pride of place in the middle.

The couch in the living room.

Buck had Lenora in an arm.

He also had Clara in his lap.

Both their kids were on either side, leaning in, arms around them and each other.

Chap had snapped that shot.

Once Buck had positioned it where he wanted it, he looked to his wife and baby girl.

"Soon, we're going to have to get another dresser," she remarked.

"I got no problem with that," he replied.

Then he took them in, and while he did, he sent out word, seeing as it seemed God had been paying a fair amount of attention for about the last year.

So, since he already had a gorgeous girl with dark hair, he hoped Lenora coming out bald as the cue ball her mother was unable to successfully hit in order to win a game of pool meant his new baby girl would have her mother's honey.

"You good?" he asked.

"Always," she answered.

Buck went to her.

Bent deep.

Kissed her nose.

Bent deeper.

Kissed a tiny baby nose.

Then he walked out of the room.

The End

The Aces High MC will return...
in the Wild West MC Series

DISCUSSION & REFLECTION QUESTIONS

Book Club Discussions
Still Standing

1. Moments in your youth define your life, and things, sometimes even little ones, can mold your reactions and responses for the rest of your life. On the surface, Clara's relationship with her first husband looks like hers was a charmed life when, in fact, she had very humble beginnings that included foster care. To look at Buck's life, you'd think maybe his childhood was marred with strife. It was, however, not. He had two loving parents.

Book questions: Were you surprised at Clara's backstory? Buck's? Were you surprised to see a loving family surrounding Rogan in the end?

Reflection-Discussion questions: What is something from your upbringing that you think shaped the way you live and operate in the world today? Do you see this as something you wish to change about yourself, or it is something that makes you stronger?

2. Desmond Tutu said, "Forgiveness says you are given another chance to make a new beginning." Forgiveness is a major theme in *Still Standing*. Clara runs up against it multiple times in ways that cut deep. In fact, it seems like the men in her life often require her forgiveness.

Book questions: Do you feel Clara should have forgiven Rogan? Do you feel she should have forgiven Buck? Do you feel Buck should forgive Kristy?

Reflection-Discussion questions: How do you forgive? When do you forgive? Is it okay to never forgive?

3. Motorcycle Clubs are big on a couple of things, live free and party hard are the easy ones, loyalty and brotherhood are the core.

Book questions: How do you feel about the men's demonstration of loyalty when they're covering their brothers' cheating?

Reflection-Discussion questions: How do you define loyalty? In a marriage or relationship? In a friendship? With family? And what about blind loyalty? What do you do when being loyal requires you to make yourself small in some way?

4. With Clara coming from a foster home situation and Buck being part of a MC, found family is as vital as blood. In some instances, found family is stronger than blood.

Book questions: Were you surprised Clara fit in with the MC family? If so, why?

Reflection-Discussion questions: Who is your found family? How did you find them? What's the wildest thing you've ever done for part of your found family?

5. If you could pick one song that fits Clara and Buck's love story, what would it be?

6. Are you a sweet or savory breakfast person? What would you want Buck to cook for you? Do you have a favorite Pop Tart flavor?

7. You've read *Still Standing*. What was your favorite part? Which was your favorite scene? Who was your favorite secondary character? Where do you see the Aces High Motorcycle Club heading next?

Buckle up for more of the
Wild West MC series.

Core and Hellen's story in
Smoke and Steel.

WANT MORE WILD WEST MC SERIES
TRY SMOKE AND STEEL

Smoke and Steel
Wild West MC Series #2

She wasn't a white dress type of girl...

Hellen Moynihan didn't have dreams. She had goals. She knew who she was and what she wanted. She also knew what she didn't. So when her long-term boyfriend didn't make the grade, she moved on. And when her best friend's boyfriend showed signs of being a scam artist, Hellen was on the case.

And he wasn't a white hat type of guy...

Dustin "Hardcore" Cutler didn't have dreams or goals. A troubled past led Core to do something irredeemable. The only thing he and the men of the Resurrection MC could do was vow to live their lives making up for an unforgiveable act.

And they did.

This duty leads Core to being a part of a covert protection detail, looking after Hellen Moynihan when trouble is coming to town.

At first, Core finds this dynamo of a woman intriguing, but he's decided she's off-limits.

Then Hellen and her friend wade into a multi-state swindling scheme.

Suddenly, off-limits for Core is out the window.

He's got no choice but to get up close and personal.

Keep reading for for a tease of *Smoke and Steel*

SMOKE AND STEEL

Bree trailed off and her attention did the same, wandering slowly across Fortnum's, a used bookstore on Broadway where we hung most Sunday afternoons, gabbed and drank coffee.

Marcy, Kyra and I turned to see what caught her gaze, and for the first time in my life, it happened.

You know that lightning bolt all the books said hit a woman when she saw a man she knew in an instant she wanted to jump?

That lightning bolt just hit me.

Dear God, he was fine.

Faded jeans. Black T-shirt. Biker boots. One of those wallets that was chained to his beltloop, the chain hanging down his hip and then looping up to his ass like the dip in a roller coaster you really wanted to ride.

He had dark, messy, overlong hair that had a lot of curl in it and a face you wanted to wake up to.

Tying the bow on the package that was him: he was tall, his shoulders were broad, and his ass was awe-inspiring.

I knew this because I was awed speechless and immobile, the only thoughts in my brain being how hot getting razor burn from his stubble would feel and how full my hands could get with that tush.

He was rough and I was ready.

As if he felt us staring at him, he turned our way.

When he did, I couldn't hold back letting out a small gasp, because I could see the striking light blue of his eyes from where we were sitting in the huddle of furniture by the window.

I was so engrossed by how amazing he was, I didn't realize until too late that he might have turned our way, but he'd done it to look right at me.

Ohmigod.

"Ugh, you just broke up with Bryan, did you not give a shit about him at all?" Bree asked loudly.

I watched the guy's lips twitch (and Lord have mercy, *what lips*), and he turned back to the line.

I turned back to our group in order to give squinty eyes to Bree.

"Oh my God," Kyra said in a whisper. "You just cock-blocked a sister."

"Uh, have you heard of a rebound?" Marcy was also whispering. "And that tall drink of water practically has 'rebound' tattooed on his forehead."

"Did you care about Bryan at all?" Bree ignored them and asked me.

"I looked at a guy, I didn't ask him to marry me," I replied. "But to answer your question, yes. I did. After I packed his box and put him out, when he was gone, I curled up in bed and cried until I was useless. I not only didn't finish baking the cookies I was making, I didn't eat them. Not a one."

Kyra gasped, such was the power of this revelation.

Yes, my cookies were that good.

But I hadn't shared the worst of it.

"I miss him. I pick up my phone half a dozen times a day to text something to him. I don't want to clean my sheets because they still kind of smell like him. And he's going to get in touch in a few days after giving me space, and he's going to ask to talk, to work it out, and it's going to gut me all over again because I know he isn't right for me. He isn't good for me. He won't make me happy, which means I won't make him happy. So I might ghost him, though that's unlikely, because what we had means he doesn't deserve that. So I'll call him to set a time to sit down and share what he wants is not what I want. This will be nearly impossible to do. So then I'll probably cry myself useless again."

"I didn't know you cried like that," Marcy said quietly.

"I broke up with my boyfriend," I pointed out.

"You should have called," she returned.

I shrugged.

Marcy was still speaking quietly when she noted, "You know, you're allowed to be human and lean on people when the occasion merits it. We can be there for you like you're there for us when we need you. You don't have to be strong for everybody all the time, like you had to be when your mom left your dad."

That meant a lot, and I hoped the look on my face shared that it did.

Marcy's answering smile, which was full of sympathy, said I succeeded.

"Never go through a breakup alone is my motto," Kyra put in, her gaze kind and worried and resting on me.

"You're not a cynical loner like Hellen," Bree stated.

Everyone's eyes cut to her.

"There's a girlfriend line," Marcy snapped. "And, sister, you just jumped over it like you're Carl fucking Lewis."

Bree stood, picking up the Dior saddle bag she paid five thousand dollars for, when she just had to wait a season and she could buy it for twelve hundred dollars less.

She tossed it over her shoulder, tossed her strawberry blonde hair, then declared. "I'm in a bad mood and being bitchy. I need to go home to Ben and Jerry's." She settled her gaze on me. "I'll think about what you said. But really, Christos is very sweet. I mean a lot to him. You can't imagine how embarrassed he was to ask for my help. He's Greek. They're macho. I could see how upset it made him. But it's a temporary situation. He's cash poor. He promised me, it'll turn around. Still, it didn't feel good to watch a guy I'm falling in love with grovel like that, then you guys piling on didn't help."

We'd hardly "piled on." Not until she got bitchy.

I didn't get a chance to refute it, she kept talking.

"It'd also be good you think on what I said, not the bitchy way I said it. I got mad because you all don't really know Christos, but it also doesn't feel good you kinda think I'm an idiot."

"We don't think you're an idiot," Kyra cut in.

"It feels that way."

Well...

Shit.

"That wasn't what was intended," I said.

"And I didn't intend to be bitchy, but I was, and I'm sorry. Now I need some Phish Food."

Pure Bree, when she was done, she was done.

She did an air kiss and took off.

The bell over the door rang. When we first started coming there, Fortnum's was so popular, it rang all the time and drove me batty.

I didn't even hear it anymore.

She waved to us through the window.

We waved back.

When we lost sight of her, I asked, "Either of you know how much he's into her for?"

She'd shared she gave him another loan, she just hadn't shared how much.

"First time, she gave him five hundred," Kyra gave it up immediately. "This time, it was seventeen."

Whoa.

"Seventeen hundred dollars?" Marcy asked, her neat, black, arched brows nearly hitting her tall, soft Afro.

Kyra nodded glumly.

A short, sharp whistle rent the air.

We turned toward the door.

Tall, Dark, Rough and Ready was there, carrying a to-go coffee in his long-fingered hand.

The minute he caught my eye, he winked at me, his white teeth showing in a brash, sexy-as-hell Hollywood smile.

Then he slid his mirrored aviators on his nose, the bell over the door chimed, and he strolled out.

"I don't know whether to think that was completely gross, or a total turn on," Kyra said.

I knew.

It was door number two, thank you.

Smoke and Steel is available December 6, 2022

ABOUT THE AUTHOR

Kristen Ashley is the *New York Times* bestselling author of over seventy romance novels including the Rock Chick, Colorado Mountain, Dream Man, Chaos, Unfinished Heroes, The 'Burg, Magdalene, Fantasyland, The Three, Ghost and Reincarnation, The Rising, Dream Team and Honey series along with several standalone novels.

She's a hybrid author, publishing titles both independently and traditionally, her books have been translated in fourteen languages and she's sold over four million books.

Kristen's novel, *Law Man*, won the RT Book Reviews Reviewer's Choice Award for best Romantic Suspense, her independently published title *Hold On* was nominated for RT Book Reviews best Independent Contemporary Romance and her traditionally published title *Breathe* was nominated for best Contemporary Romance. Kristen's titles *Motorcycle Man*, *The Will*, and *Ride Steady* (which won the Reader's Choice award from Romance Reviews) all made the final rounds for Goodreads Choice Awards in the Romance category.

The Will, the first novel in Kristen's Magdalene series, was made into a motion picture with Passionflix and released on Valentine's Day, 2020.

Kristen, born in Gary and raised in Brownsburg, Indiana, was a fourth-generation graduate of Purdue University. Since, she has lived in Denver, the West Country of England, and she now resides in Phoenix. She worked as a charity executive for eighteen years prior to beginning her independent publishing career. She now writes full-time.

Although romance is her genre, the prevailing themes running through all of Kristen's novels are friendship, family and a strong sisterhood. To this end, and as a way to thank her readers for their support, Kristen has created the Rock Chick Nation, a series of programs that are designed to give back to her readers and promote a strong female community.

The mission of the Rock Chick Nation is to live your best life, be true to your true self, recognize your beauty, and last but definitely not least, take your sister's back whether they're at your side as friends and family or if they're thousands of miles away and you don't know who they are.

The programs of the RC Nation include Rock Chick Rendezvous, weekends Kristen organizes full of parties and get-togethers to bring the sisterhood together, Rock Chick Recharges, evenings Kristen arranges for women who have been nominated to receive a special night, and Rock Chick Rewards, an ongoing program that raises funds for nonprofit women's organizations Kristen's readers nominate. Kristen's Rock Chick Rewards have donated over $146,000 to charity and this number continues to rise.

You can read more about Kristen, her titles and the Rock Chick Nation at KristenAshley.net.

Connect with Kristen Ashley

facebook.com/kristenashleybooks

twitter.com/KristenAshley68

instagram.com/kristenashleybooks

pinterest.com/kashley0155

goodreads.com/kristenashleybooks

bookbub.com/authors/kristen-ashley

ALSO BY KRISTEN ASHLEY

Rock Chick Series:

Rock Chick

Rock Chick Rescue

Rock Chick Redemption

Rock Chick Renegade

Rock Chick Revenge

Rock Chick Reckoning

Rock Chick Regret

Rock Chick Revolution

Rock Chick Reawakening

Rock Chick Reborn

The 'Burg Series:

For You

At Peace

Golden Trail

Games of the Heart

The Promise

Hold On

The Chaos Series:

Own the Wind

Fire Inside

Ride Steady

Walk Through Fire

A Christmas to Remember

Rough Ride

Wild Like the Wind

Free

Wild Fire

Wild Wind

The Colorado Mountain Series:

The Gamble

Sweet Dreams

Lady Luck

Breathe

Jagged

Kaleidoscope

Bounty

Dream Man Series:

Mystery Man

Wild Man

Law Man

Motorcycle Man

Quiet Man

Dream Team Series:

Dream Maker

Dream Chaser

Dream Bites Cookbook

Dream Spinner

Dream Keeper

The Fantasyland Series:

Wildest Dreams

The Golden Dynasty

Fantastical

Broken Dove

Midnight Soul

Gossamer in the Darkness

Ghosts and Reincarnation Series:

Sommersgate House

Lacybourne Manor

Penmort Castle

Fairytale Come Alive

Lucky Stars

The Honey Series:

The Deep End

The Farthest Edge

The Greatest Risk

The Magdalene Series:

The Will

Soaring

The Time in Between

Mathilda, SuperWitch:

Mathilda's Book of Shadows

Mathilda The Rise of the Dark Lord

Misted Pines Series

The Girl in the Mist

The Girl in the Woods

Moonlight and Motor Oil Series:

The Hookup

The Slow Burn

The Rising Series:

The Beginning of Everything

The Plan Commences

The Dawn of the End

The Rising

The River Rain Series:

After the Climb

After the Climb Special Edition

Chasing Serenity

Taking the Leap

Making the Match

The Three Series:

Until the Sun Falls from the Sky

With Everything I Am

Wild and Free

The Unfinished Hero Series:

Knight

Creed

Raid

Deacon

Sebring

Wild West MC Series:

Still Standing

Smoke and Steel

Other Titles by Kristen Ashley:

Heaven and Hell

Play It Safe

Three Wishes

Complicated

Loose Ends

Fast Lane

Perfect Together (Summer 2023)

Printed in the USA
CPSIA information can be obtained
at www.ICGtesting.com
LVHW092119220724
786227LV00027B/81